THE

IN THE

ENVELOPE

BOOK 1

Kristiana ✻
You were made to shine.
Never let anyone dim your
glow. ✻ *Laura D.*

Laura Detering

ISBN: 978-1-7351404-0-7 (e-book)
ISBN: 978-1-7351404-1-4 (Paperback)
LCCN: 2020922332

Interior Formatting: Evenstar Books
Book cover Designer: Moor Books Design
Proof Editor: Camilla McCann
Copy Editor: Shawneen N. Lee-Storlie
Developmental Editor: Kim Chance

First printing edition 2020.

Visit the author's website at lauradetering.com

For Luke
who believed in me when I didn't, who loved me when I couldn't,
who reminded me that I still had divine purpose when I felt none,
who helped me walk when I couldn't, who wore my hats when I didn't,
who challenged me to find the good in my darkest hour, and who
believed, when I didn't, that MDDS and VM wouldn't forever limit me.
I love you more.

Contents

Before - The Younger Years

After

Pronunciation Guide

Nicholas Klaus: *Knee-ko-lus Clow-ss*
Arbolias: *Are-bow-lee-us*
Cristes Aventus: *Crease-tis Ah-ven-tis*
Eira: *i- Rah*
Abishai: *Ah-beh-shy*
Hellebore Niger: *Hel-le-bore Ny-jur*
Ceástaté: *C-es-tah-tay*
Fouettés: *fweh-teiz*

Before

THE YOUNGER YEARS

June 1988

Today, I was going to ride my new bike, even if I only had Mom's permission to go to the corner and back. The garage door creaked and moaned as it rolled up. I waited until the sun lit the darkness of the cluttered space before stepping into the garage. Maneuvering between my parent's projects and tools, I squeezed through the boxes and toys that my siblings and I had strewn about. I wrangled my pink Schwinn bicycle from behind some glass-bottle soda crates. I swung my leg over the flowered banana seat and peddled out.

"Car!" the second-grader in my class, Chris, called out. Like a well-rehearsed dance, the boys all grabbed the nets and their gear and hustled to the curb. As soon as the car passed, Chris screamed, "Game on!" and they all shuffled back to the exact spot in the game where they'd left off. I rode down the driveway, gaining speed on the decline, and raced in the opposite direction from the boys before they spotted me.

I cycled from one end of the sidewalk to the other. I paused at the corner and contemplated disobeying Mom. *What could happen if I continued around the block?* I turned back around and continued on. A loud, repetitive beeping blared to life, interrupting my thoughts and I skidded to a halt. A massive U-Haul truck missed the driveway and jumped the curb, its tires tearing through the pristinely manicured rose bushes. A tall woman strode out of the garage, waving to get the driver's attention. Half of his body hung out the truck's window as he tried to gauge where to put its butt. She succeeded in guiding him the rest of the way and the truck made it securely within the confines of the asphalt driveway. *Who were these people?*

I skidded to a stop directly across the street from their brown, brick house. My heart thumped in anticipation as I stood, straddling my bike, but I forced myself to stay put. Anxiety brewed in the pit of my stomach over the prospect of meeting new people, and the idea of me initiating was too much.

A moment passed, and a little blond-haired boy ran squealing from the side of the house. His laughter made me smile. Another boy, a few inches taller, chased after him.

"I'm gonna get you, Charlie!"

More squeals of delight from the cute little boy ensued. The dark-haired boy was about to grasp Charlie when he stopped and un-crouched from his tickle attack mode to stare at me. All I could do was stare back.

The urge to cross the street grew stronger, the feeling

beautifully unsettling and hauntingly familiar. I desperately wanted to meet this dark hair boy—I never cared to meet anyone before.

Little Charlie tugged at the boy's tank top.

"Will, Will! Tickle fight!" But Will didn't move. Charlie started yelling, "Mom! Will's broken!" An avalanche of metal clanged within the garage, and the woman I saw earlier rushed out.

"William, what's wrong? Are you hurt?" she asked. Her hands moved frantically across his face, then to his head and the rest of his body, checking for an injury. But he didn't answer.

The woman followed his gaze and her eyes sparkled when they met mine. She stood and seemed to float above the sidewalk as she gracefully walked towards me, her long, pleated skirt billowing in the breeze. *Her eyes are so pretty. Like lightning bugs, only greener.* When she smiled at me, I could have sworn they glowed.

"Hello there. My name is Mrs. Jamison. What's your name, sweetie?"

"Lydia! Where are you?" I twisted to face my house and found Mom searching at the end of our driveway with my little brother, Mickey, on her hip.

I pivoted away from my mom's call and looked back at Mrs. Jamison. "Um, my mom told me I'm not supposed to talk to strangers. I better get going." Instead of hopping back on my bike, I turned to look at Will again and found him still staring at me. Charlie played with a little yellow ball at his feet.

"Ah, I see," said Mrs. Jamison. "Is that her?" She gestured to Mom, who now walked toward us, Mickey bopping with each sway of her hip. I nodded. "Well, since we are going to be your new neighbors, do you mind introducing me to her? Then we won't be strangers anymore." She winked, her dark hair flowing in the breeze.

I turned my bike around and walked it toward Mom, continuously checking over my shoulder to see if Will still stood there. He did.

Mrs. Jamison stretched out her thin hand, the movement more graceful than a practiced ballerina. "Hi! I'm Lana, Lana Jamison."

"Oh, you must be the new neighbors! I'm Eve Erickson. This is my daughter, Lydia, and this little one—" she nuzzled my brother's cheek— "is Mickey. It's so great to finally meet you. The whole block has been wondering who bought the Elrick's place."

"That would be us." Lana smiled warmly. "It took us a while to make it up here. Work-related issues."

"You must tell me who is taking care of your property. It's been immaculate this entire time."

Lana paused. "My husband's company took care of that for us. Would you like to meet my Brantley? He's bringing boxes into the house."

"Of course! But I'm such a mess. This little one kept me up all night and I was hoping to make a much better first impression," Mom fretted as she raked her fingers through her hair in an effort to tame it.

"Oh, please, you look fabulous. I've been there with my youngest as well!" They both laughed.

"Anyway, I'm sure you have a to-do list a mile long. We won't keep you any longer. It was nice meeting you. Let's go, Lydia."

"Actually, Lydia seems to be about the same age as my son, William. Would you mind if they played out in my yard together?" I could see the uncertainty in Mom's eyes, but Lana continued, "It would be such a huge relief to Brantley and I to know our kids were playing with such a responsible young lady instead of watching cartoons all day or getting under our feet."

Mom beamed with pride as I was called a 'responsible young lady', but a look of concern etched her face as her eyes found mine. "To be honest, Lydia really prefers playing on her own." Mom tried her best to support me.

I tugged at Mom's shirt to get her attention. "I want to. I want to play with William."

"Are you sure you don't mind, honey? You really don't have to."

"I'm sure." I smiled.

I watched as relief washed over my mom. Her shoulders relaxed and she smiled at me as she cupped my cheek. "Well, if it's good with her, it's good with me."

"Great! That's wonderful. Brantley already ordered pizza for lunch. What time would you like me to walk her home?"

"How about I have one of Liddy's older sisters bring you guys dinner and pick her up then?"

"You mustn't feel obligated."

"Nonsense, I insist," Mom replied sincerely.

"Well then, it's a plan." Lana smiled.

Mom walked home as I followed Mrs. Jamison back to her house and into the garage. Her height, grace, and beauty mesmerized me.

"Brantley, would you come here please?"

"Just a second dear," he responded from somewhere inside

the truck.

Will joined us in the garage and stopped at my side. I turned my head to look up at him and a smile tugged at the corner of his mouth, revealing a slight dimple. He stepped closer to me and our hands touched for the briefest of moments. With anyone else, my natural reaction would be to pull away. But when Will enclosed his hand with mine, I welcomed his gesture of friendship.

"Did you need something, Lana?" Mr. Jamison asked his wife without looking down to notice me. She patiently stood behind us, placing a hand on Will's shoulder and then I felt her other hand gently rest on mine. Brantley dropped the box he held when he finally took us all in.

"Is this...? That was fast," he said eagerly, coming over to us. He got down on his knees in front of me, his bright blue eyes alight with excitement. "Hi, I'm Mr. Jamison. What's your name?"

"Lydia," I responded. *These people sure are nice.*

"It's a pleasure to meet you. I can tell you and Will are going to be great friends." Mr. Jamison stood, grabbed his wife's hand, and walked over to the corner for privacy. I couldn't hear what they said, but by the way their eyes lit up when they hugged, I could tell they were extremely happy. Will and I looked at each other, shrugged, then ran off hand in hand to play in the yard.

April 1989

"NOOO!" I shrieked.

"Lydia, what's wrong?" Mom asked, sleepily.

"Please, don't! Get away!" I wailed and thrashed, not trusting that she was really my mom. I feared her hands would turn into claws any second.

"John! A little help, please!"

"What's wrong?"

"It's Lydia again. Hold her down. She's going to snap her neck if she arches back any further! She already scratched the heck out of her chest."

Dad swooped me in his arms and cradled me against his chest. Something cold and wet pressed against my forehead and I flinched.

"Eve, dear. She's frightened to death, shaking like a leaf.

Try talking to her like you did last time. It seemed to work."

"Of course!

"Just breathe, sweetheart
It's just a dream
Just breathe...
No one is out to get you
Just breathe...
You are safe
Breathe"

It was just after eight when I came downstairs. I stopped short of the kitchen when I heard parents' hushed voices from the family room.

"John, I don't understand. They are getting worse."

"Nightmares are normal."

"She never had them before. Why now all of a sudden? And every night that intense? Poor thing is worn out and she's starting to hurt herself."

"Let's try giving her some chamomile tea before bed. If that doesn't help, we will call the pediatrician, do a sleep study or something."

"OK, but I'm only giving it a few more weeks."

I slipped into my seat at the kitchen table and shoveled toast and fruit in my mouth, pretending I hadn't overheard my parents. Besides, Will would be here any second.

"Lydia," Mom said, exasperated as she came into the kitchen. "Slow down! You two play almost every day. No sense in choking just to..." *Ding dong*! I shot out of my chair. "Nooooot so fast, young lady. You are not leaving until you clear your plate."

"I'll get it!" Dad called from the family room. I shoved the remaining pieces of food in my mouth, my cheeks puffed like a squirrel, and stood at the edge of the kitchen, chewing furiously.

"Good morning, Mr. Erickson. Can Liddy play?" I overheard Will ask as he stood on our front porch. I hastily tried to swallow the remaining pieces of breakfast as I moved to the dining room, giving me the perfect view of our entryway.

"Come on in, Will. What's it been? A whole thirteen hours since you've seen my Lydia?" Will averted his eyes and took a big gulp. "I'm just messing with ya, kid." Dad playfully tousled Will's hair.

I swallowed and whipped around. With my mouth open wide, I stuck out my tongue to show Mom I'd finished my breakfast.

"Come in, come in," Dad continued. "I'm sure she's just about done with breakfast."

"I'm ready, I'm ready!" I called out as I sped to the door. Will smiled at me.

"Where are you two off to today?" Dad asked, grinning as we mounted our bikes. He knew we were always planning an adventure.

"To the fort, Dad."

"Ah, yes. I forgot. Be home for lunch."

Will and I rode our bikes in silence. It was something I really liked about being with him—we didn't have to talk all the time.

Will approached the dead end at the back of the neighborhood first and slowed our pace to maneuver through the narrow opening between the two large signs. After a few minutes more of pedaling, we made it to the clearing in the field and dropped our bikes in the grass.

The first time we got permission to go past the dead-end barriers, we discovered the abandoned shack, wedged between two blooming cherry blossoms. The trees offered both shade and a hint of secrecy, and immediately we knew we wanted to claim it for ourselves. As it stood, it wasn't much to look at, just a sad mix of discarded plywood formed the four walls and a sheet of pleated metal lay across them as a makeshift roof. The scent of cherry blossoms breezed through the air.

"I brought paint and brushes," I said, staring at the fort. Last year, Mom painted our basement, so Dad helped me find the leftover paint samples stashed in the back of the garage.

"I brought a hammer, nails, and rope," Will replied.

We worked quickly, not saying much but also never leaving each other's side. When we finished, several shades of green covered the outside of the fort. Swirls of purple and white stars decorated the inside walls and ceiling. We found branches and roped them together to make a door. The final touch was a sign that read: L&W'S CLUB—KEEP OUT. We lay on the floor of the fort gazing at our makeshift night sky when I checked my Wonder Woman watch. One hour until I needed to be home for lunch.

I closed my eyes, exhaustion enveloping me.

Will grabbed my hand. "Liddy, why are you always so tired? Are you sick or something?"

I guess I wasn't as good at hiding it as I'd thought. "No,

I'm not sick. I...I have bad dreams."

"About what?"

Will would be the first and only one I'd open up to about my nightmares. I was too ashamed to tell my parents. In fact, I needed to get better about hiding them, and fast. "A beautiful but terrifying witch." I flinched as the image of sharp claws replacing her fingernails flashed through my mind.

Will squeezed my hand. "What makes this pretty witch so scary?"

I scooted closer to Will and yawned. "There is always so much sadness around her. The worst dreams are when there are other kids seated around this large chair she sits in, and they're all crying. She's always surrounded in black clouds. Then, she tries to grab me so she can take my heart." I swallowed, then admitted softly, "That one's the worst."

"Well, good thing they're only dreams. Try to fall asleep thinking of something that makes you happy."

"What if they aren't just dreams?"

Will propped himself up on his elbow. "What do you mean?"

"Promise me you won't laugh." I knew I could tell Will anything, but even I had a hard time believing the witch might be real.

"You know I would never laugh at you," he responded.

"Two nights ago, I woke up with a scratch on my chest, right in the very spot one of her long, red nails had grazed me as I fought to wake up." I closed my eyes as I brought the collar of my shirt down a few inches, enough to show Will the start of the scratch near my left collarbone.

When I didn't hear anything, I opened my eyes and turned

my head slightly toward Will. He stared at the ceiling and furrowed his brows, but still solidly held my hand.

He turned to look at me. "I wish I could make them disappear. I will never let anything bad happen to you and I will keep you safe."

"You already do. I feel the safest whenever I'm with you."

"Good, because I am not going anywhere. I will always be here for you." Will let go of my hand, slid his arm under my neck, and pulled me into him. "Now sleep, Liddy. I will wake you when it's time to go home."

December 1990

I JUST FINISHED ZIPPING MY ELECTRIC-BLUE COAT when I heard the knock at the door and opened it.

"Hey, Liddy, you ready?" Will asked, a large smile on his face.

"Yes, just one sec. Mom, Dad! Mr. Jamison is here to take us to Huskie Hill!"

"Have fun!" Dad called back from the living room where he untangled Christmas lights.

"It will be dark in about thirty minutes. Stick together and be safe!" Mom yelled from the kitchen.

I closed the door behind me. Will and I slowly shuffled across my yard, careful not to disrupt the plastic Nativity scene as we fought to move in our snowsuits.

"You look tired again... Another nightmare?" Will asked. I

shifted my gaze away from him. I hated to see him worry over me. I squeezed his hand gently and he squeezed mine back as we approached the Jeep's door. "I hope it's alright, but Charlie is coming along tonight."

Lifting my head, I smiled. "I don't mind at all. I love Charlie."

As if he heard his name, Charlie barreled toward me with his arms wide open, screaming, "Wiiiiidy!"

I knelt with my arms open to embrace him.

Will opened the door for me. I shoved myself in and helped Charlie who grunted into his scarf as he tried to get buckled.

Mr. Jamison spoke as he drove toward the park, "You guys are going to love the hills at Huskie Park." A hint of excitement embellished his voice. "Charlie, you need to listen to your big brother. No running off. That last hill is pretty big and I heard some kids even engineered moguls on it. You could catch some serious airtime, but if not prepared, you can wipe out pretty hard."

"Got it, Dad!" Charlie said, giving him the thumbs up.

"That's my boy. Will, I think you will love the plethora of Christmas roses that have bloomed there as well," Mr. Jamison said, pulling into the parking lot. Mr. Jamison had caught Will giving me a Christmas rose on our last sledding adventure in the neighborhood a few weeks ago. Will and I had read some fairytales at the library that spoke of their magical properties and we became fascinated with them.

"Daaaaad," Will groaned, hiding his face in his hand. Mr. Jamison smiled wide at his son and put the car in park.

"Bye, Dad!" Charlie called out as he climbed out of the car. When we were all out, we waved at the black Jeep driving away.

Mr. Jamison honked in response.

The field, a blank canvas of glistening snow, sat nestled in a valley surrounded by towering Sycamore trees that seemed to touch the night sky. As we walked toward the first set of hills, my excitement grew, the only sound the swishing of our snow pants. We had the entire park to ourselves.

Charlie turned to face us, and squealed, "Wast one to the hill is a rotten egg!" and took off toward the hills illuminated by the park lights. Will tossed me the smaller red sled and went after him, the larger silver sled flopping wildly behind him.

"Not fair!" I yelled as I raced as fast as I could toward the boys.

My lungs burned, ready to burst by the time I reached the edge of the first hill. Will waited for me, breathing easily, and Charlie stood with a toothy grin at the top.

"Come on, swowpokes!" Charlie teased.

I didn't even dare make eye contact with Will. I took off and reached Charlie just before Will did.

"You're the rotten egg, stinky rotten eeeegg," Charlie taunted, pointing at Will with one hand and plugging his nose with the other. I couldn't help but laugh.

"That's enough, Charlie. I've got the sled, remember?"

"Wanna ride with me first, Charlie?" I asked, readying the plastic sled as I winked at Will.

"Totally, Widdy! Wet's go!" I loved how he said my name.

Charlie and I went down a few times together before I decided he could go down this hill alone. I wanted to sled with Will instead.

"Hey, Will! You ready to tackle the next hill with me?" I called out to him. He came running over.

"These are for you." He handed me a small bouquet of Christmas roses.

I giggled in delight. He truly had a knack for finding the roses. "And where did you find these?"

"By the bottom of the storm grate over there burrowed into the side of the hill." Will pointed to an area virtually hidden by the snow roughly ten feet away, the full moon illuminating the white Christmas roses. "I've never seen so many of them in one place."

I placed the flowers in my pocket and hopped into the front of the large silver sled. Will pushed the sled, running alongside it, before jumping in behind me. Charlie stayed at the smaller hill only long enough to give Will and me two trips.

"Hey, guys! I want to try *that* hill!" Charlie pointed past us to the largest hill Mr. Jamison had told us about and took off.

"Wait up, Charlie!" Will yelled as he ran after him.

Oh geez. I moved as fast as I could, dragging both sleds behind me. Will turned back to grab the sleds from me and took off again. Charlie had a bad habit of getting himself into trouble, being as curious as he was. Even with both sleds trailing behind him, Will caught up to Charlie.

"Charlie, why do you do this?" He threw the sleds down and knelt so he was eye level with Charlie. "How many times do I need to tell you? You can't just run off like that!"

Charlie's bottom lip quivered. I gave Will a pointed look and he sighed in his own exasperation.

"Charlie, I'm sorry. I didn't mean to yell. Mom and Dad expect me to make sure you don't get hurt. If something were to happen to you, they would never trust me again. And, well, I would never forgive myself."

"I'm not a baby, Will, and how can I even get hurt? It's just snow!"

"You'd be surprised," Will responded gently. "Look, I love you, little dude. Can you help your big bro out by playing it safe tonight? Please, for me?" Will gave his best puppy dog eyes, his hands clasped together in prayer, and pleaded with Charlie.

Charlie laughed hysterically and pushed Will over. They wrestled playfully and flung handfuls of snow at each other. I cleared my throat. "Ummm, are we going to rock this hill or what?"

The brothers got up and Will mussed Charlie's blond hair before pulling the kid's black knit hat over his eyes. Charlie laughed and picked up his sled.

I reached for mine and an icy breeze caressed my face. "Lydiaaa," a honeyed voice whispered from somewhere behind me. I whirled around, but no one was there. Like the wave at a sports arena, I could feel the hairs on my arm stand up section by section. "Lydiaaa, I've found you," she cackled gleefully.

No, no, NO! I must be going crazy. I dropped and covered my ears. I recognized the voice this time. It was the one that had been haunting my dreams since the Jamisons moved in.

"Lid, what's wrong?" Will was by my side helping me to stand from my crouched position. He pulled his gloves off and gently removed my hands from my ears. His eyes poured into mine, pleading with me to answer.

"Nothing, I'm fine," I stammered.

"Since when do we lie to each other?"

"What's her prob?" Charlie asked. "She wooks wike she's seen a ghost."

"Charlie, could you be like the best bro in the world and

take the red sled to that hill?" Will pointed to the one right next to us. "I promise I'll ride this one with you before we leave."

"I guess," Charlie huffed.

"Thanks, I owe ya one."

As soon as Charlie was on his way, Will turned to me. "Liddy, talk to me."

"I'm fine. It was nothing. I think I just got too cold from standing still for so long."

He lifted his eyebrow, clearly not convinced. "Fine, we don't have to talk. Want to go down the hill a few times with me before I call Charlie over?"

"Definitely."

"Will! Is it my turn yet?" Charlie yelled from his hilltop.

"Five minutes! I promise!" Will hollered back. Charlie clutched his chest like he was shot in the heart and stumbled backward. Will and I laughed.

"He's been so patient," I reminded Will. "How about we just go down one more time? I'll steer this time."

I climbed in the front of the metal sled. Will grabbed on the back and counted off our final run together for the night. "One for the money, two for the show, three to get ready, and four to goooo!"

Will hopped on the back and I laughed in delight as I steered us to the right where clusters of moguls pitted the landscape. Like a lunar eclipse, my eyesight instantly disappeared behind a wall of black. "Will! I...I can't see!" I screamed.

"I'm coming for you princessss." I released my grip on the sled to cover my ears, clutching them in pain as her voice seared my ear drums.

"Watch out, Liddy!" But it was too late. He pushed me out

of the sled and my sight returned just in time to see Will hit the steepest slope at full speed. Time passed in slow motion as he soared through the air. I rolled and braced myself, watching helplessly. Gravity snatched him from flight and pulled him to the end of the hill where no snow padded the piles of debris.

I gasped as Will crashed hard into the ground face-first before skidding a couple of feet.

"Will!" Charlie's high-pitched scream echoed in the night. But Will didn't move.

"No!" the shrill, haunting voice screeched.

I ran towards Will, my heart threatening to explode. Charlie stood frozen in fear a few feet from his brother's body. I got down on my knees next to Will and gently rolled him over, tears spilling uncontrollably from my eyes.

"Will, please say you're alright. Answer me!" But he still did not open his eyes. I could see a large bump forming above his left eye, and blood, so much blood, gushed from his face. From where, I could not tell. *Please be alive.*

"I'm alive," Will responded, barely moving his lips, though he didn't open his eyes. I let out a small laugh through my sobs, but then flinched and quickly backed away from him. *Did he just answer my thoughts?* I shook my head. *No way.* Trying not to panic, I envisioned Mom at my bedside helping me through yet another nightmare. I came back to Will's side since he hadn't moved, concerned he may be paralyzed. I ripped my gloves off to unwrap the scarf from my neck.

"Charlie! Come help!" I screamed, my eyes glued to Will. I grabbed some snow and rubbed it gently over Will's face to try and clear the blood. He moaned and I could hear a faint wheezing from his chest. I grabbed more snow and did it again.

I needed to see where he was bleeding from. I'd use my scarf to staunch the flow. "I'm sorry. I'm so sorry. This is all my fault." I cried even harder.

Christmas rose. The thought floated through my mind. I took a few out of my pocket. The first two I wadded up and placed in the small, but deep gashes near his left temple and cheek. The last one I laid on his chest. I closed my eyes and prayed, "Please, God, let him be alright."

Will's breathing became less labored. A gust of wind swept past us. The roses, red with his blood, flittered off of his wounds. The bleeding had stopped. His eyes fluttered open. "What happened?" he asked, confused.

"Oh, Will!" I choked, snot running down my face. I wiped my nose on the arm of my coat and almost crushed him with a hug. Charlie joined in.

"Ow," Will laughed. "What was that for?"

"You caught some kiwwer air and took a gnarwey spill," Charlie said.

"I'm so. Glad. You're alright." My voice caught with every other word as the sobs began to dissipate. Besides being bruised up, he seemed fine. But I took no chances when it came to my best friend.

"Don't move," I ordered. "Charlie, grab the silver sled, please. Will, Charlie and I are going to pull you back to the parking lot, OK? There's a payphone there we can use to call your dad."

It had been a week since the accident and still Will wasn't

allowed to play outside. His parents did, however, allow me to play at their house. Today, Mr. Jamison built a fire in their fireplace and Mrs. Jamison brought us hot chocolate. I could sense that they seemed a little on edge. Will's accident must have really freaked them out even though he'd completely healed. In fact, the medical staff at Northwest Community were perplexed. X-rays had shown newly healing rib bones and bruises that looked a week old. The gashes that I placed the flowers in were nothing more than fresh pink scars by the time he got there— a little star by his temple, and a cute crescent moon resembling a dimple on his cheek. I was just happy that Will was OK. I was so distraught that I had practically barged into the Jamison's home the next morning to see his miraculous recovery for myself.

Since the accident, his parents rarely let us out of their sight for more than a minute. Will kept hinting he wanted to know more about what happened at Huskie Hill, and I was finally ready to share. I trusted that he wouldn't dismiss me hearing the voice from my dreams, but I didn't want anyone else to know. Not knowing how much longer Will would be on house arrest made me restless. I needed to meet with him alone. My nightmares had changed since that night. It was like the angry witch knew what had happened and wanted to make me pay for it. I had a fresh claw mark from her razor-sharp, red talons on my arm to prove it. That afternoon before leaving Will's house, I slipped him a note concealed in a small origami flower that resembled a Christmas rose.

We need to talk.
Meet me at the end of my driveway.

8:45 pm tonight.

"Lydia! No going to the neighborhood hill tonight after what happened to Will. Stay in our yard. You have until nine but come in sooner if your toes start getting cold. Frostbite happens quickly and you don't want to lose them."

"OK, Mom!" I yelled out, but on the inside, I wanted to run back to my cozy house out of fear of literally losing my toes. However, the anticipation of getting to meet with Will squelched those fears.

I walked to the edge of my yard and stopped to stare at the way the light from the streetlamp reflected in the snow and made it glitter.

I looked at my Wonder Woman watch: eight-thirty. I laid down on the edge of my front yard to gaze into the night sky. Every star shone bright tonight, winking back at me. I squeezed my eyes shut, begging the universe for just one wish, a shooting star. Mom always said a shooting star symbolized hope and a promise that your wishes were heard and would come true. To pass the time waiting for Will, I thought about Christmas. In just a few short weeks, Santa would be coming and I had my heart set on getting a Dream Phone game and a Skip-It toy. I opened one eye and cautiously scanned the night when a falling star, with the largest tail I'd ever seen, soared purposefully through the sky. I sat bolt upright, a grin spreading across my face. My smile swiftly evaporated when I heard a deep chuckle off in the distance.

"Dad?" No one responded. "Here I go, hearing things again," I mumbled to myself as I fell back into the snow. I continued to scan the night sky, but my attention immediately diverted when I heard someone dashing through the snow. An odd bell-like melody rapidly grew closer.

I sat up. "Will, if you're trying to scare me, it's not funny!" I called out, my muscles involuntarily contracting as blood raced through my veins.

The invisible melody only seemed to come closer. Still, no one replied. My heart sped up, and my mind raced as I moved to stand. Darn my stupid snow pants! There was no way I could make it to my front door. I was as agile as Violet when she morphed into the blueberry in Willy Wonka. I tried to quiet the loud drumming in my ears as a soft whisper passed in a breath brushing my cheek. "Get inside. You are *not* safe."

Whipping my head around, I glimpsed a tall shadow—a flash of silver near the top of its coat—racing down the block and out of sight.

Mom always said I had an overactive imagination, but I knew this was real. My eyesight sharpened and, though my mind told me to get home, my legs already moved me down the driveway. I shook as I desperately tried to turn back home, fighting against a magnetic pull. One foot in front of the other— like a baby taking their first careful steps—I awkwardly crossed the street. The shadow disappeared behind Will's house at the end of the block. My eyes locked on Charlie's window as a green glow pulsed from it.

A familiar woman's sinister laugh pierced the night air as I shuffled down the sidewalk. My mind screamed at me to stop, but I wouldn't. Deep down, I knew my friend was in grave danger. I was one house away from the Jamison's when a desperate pain flooded my heart. *NOOO!* I clutched my chest right before a blinding, blood orange flash exploded from the window. Like a dying star, I was thrown back into the snow.

When I opened my eyes, it was already morning and I was in my bed. *How did I get here?* I shot up but quickly laid back down. My head spun as I began to panic. I could feel a weight sink heavy on my small chest.

"Just breathe, deep, slow, breaths. It was just a dream." I repeated the words Mom so often recited. I assessed my surroundings. My sister Paige snored away in her bed. I was in PJs—all tucked in—with absolutely no recollection as to how I even got home. I tried to recall the details of last night to reassure myself that it was indeed a bad dream, but my mind felt hazy. I needed to ask Mom. I started down the stairs, missing a few steps in my rush. *Ouch, I hate rugburn.*

In the kitchen, my little brother Mickey watched Bobby's World. I poured myself a bowl of Cap'n Crunch Crunch Berries, leaving a few pieces and a dribble of milk on the counter before joining him at the table.

"Dad, is it time *yet?*" Mickey whined as Dad entered the kitchen, wiping his tired eyes.

Syllables catching in his clenched teeth, Dad responded, "Mickey, if you ask me one more time when we are going to start decorating, you will not get to help at all."

Dad stretched and little popping noises released as he rolled his neck. He reminded me of a robot oiling his joints as he gradually awoke and attempted to operate the coffee pot. Meanwhile, the tea kettle whistled like an angry train. As if on cue, Mom came whizzing in from the utility room just off of the kitchen, turned off the stove, and gently nudged Dad out of the way with her hip to take over his coffee mess.

"You guys are so annoying! Can't anyone sleep around here?" hollered my oldest sister, Kylie, from the balcony upstairs before slamming her door.

Agitated, Mom snarkily apologized as she shouted back, "Oh, I am soooo sorry for living in my own house! Maybe the prima donna would like to join us today?"

Dad wrapped Mom in a very handsy embrace, smiling as he pacified her temper with a nibble of her ear. I averted my eyes. *Ew.* I bit my lip to keep from complaining about their disgusting PDA. I didn't want to be the next to get scolded.

"Liddy, hun, be a sweetie and take your brother outside... Build a fort or something."

"But Mom, I wanted to ask you something. What time did I come in from playing outside last night?"

"You didn't go out last night." Mom dismissed me with a flick of her wrist. "You begged me, but I said no because I didn't want you out alone, especially after Will's accident. I tucked you into bed myself. Of course, now that I want you to go out, you're giving me trouble about it. Just take him out please."

Mom's story confirmed it was just a nightmare. Sighing in relief that nothing actually happened at Will's house, I got up and tossed my bowl in the sink, relinquishing the events of last night with it. Ten minutes later, with full snow gear on, Mickey and I clattered outside.

As soon as we stepped over the threshold, I knew something was wrong. It wasn't the odd, exotic scent that permeated the frigid air. It wasn't even the knotting in my stomach when my boot first crunched in the snow just off my porch. It was the flashing red and blue lights that stalled us in our yard.

"It wasn't a dream." I collapsed to my knees.

Down at the end of our street, neighbors gathered among the many police cars. My best friend's house was wrapped in yellow tape. I could read the bold letters from where I stood:

POLICE LINE DO NOT CROSS.

After

Eight Years Later...

THERE WERE ONLY TWO THINGS THAT SAVED ME from the long and painful torture that was winter—Christmas and a snowfall that stuck. The after effects of a fresh snowfall, before anything could disturb the brilliant-white blanket enveloping everything in its path, was simply breathtaking. Though it was just a dusting this morning, flakes the size of cotton balls silently fell in droves throughout the early afternoon and into the evening. Sitting at the dinner table, I couldn't help but gaze out the French doors at the trees bowing under the weight of the snow as I planned my escape.

Thanksgiving was just last week and my home officially shifted to full-on Christmas mode. I felt cagey being stuck inside these past few weeks, especially since I had to dance on thin ice. Preparing for the big Christmas Eve dinner we hosted every year always dialed Mom's anxiety to an all-time high.

My knees still ached from washing the baseboards and cabinets with Murphy's Oil. I walked into the family room and plopped on the couch hoping for a little T.V. and rest. I sighed at the pile of gifts that needed wrapping and groaned when I noticed my little brother playing Nintendo.

"Hey Mickey, care to quit playing Mario Kart and help me with these presents?" I asked my little brother.

"Nope," he quipped, not even bothering to look my way.

I bit back my frustration and chose to stick my tongue out at him rather than start an argument, pulling myself off the couch to start wrapping. This kid always seemed to get away with not helping.

Pins and needles stabbed my feet and I checked the time on the VCR. I'd been wrapping presents for over an hour. With a satisfying tear of the tape, I placed the two-inch piece on the present for Auntie Ang and placed it on the done pile. *Only about forty more to go.* I needed to get out of the house for a little bit. Besides, Christmas was almost a month away. The rest could wait.

I asked Dad to help me convince Mom to let me go for a walk. Dad conveniently praised me for all the chores I'd done in front of her. I knew she wouldn't mind, but I didn't want her to suppress any stress. Mom smiled and I smiled back knowing I could break free for a short walk without guilt.

The neighborhood was still, only the sound of snow crunching beneath my feet as I traipsed across my yard. Cherrywood Drive normally bustled with kids playing, people shoveling their driveways, and adults rushing to get an early start on their holiday checklist, but not tonight. I sucked in a deep breath. The crystalline air always helped me clear my head. The subtle sparkle of the snow illuminated by the streetlamps caught my eye. I smiled. *How cool would it be if snow really was magical?*

The snow absorbed all sound and the silence afforded me a peace I really needed. Junior year was stressing me out, but at least college prospects kept me distracted. I was probably the only Wildcat with plans to leave the state and never return as soon as I graduated. The truth was, I never really felt like I belonged in Illinois, more like I was destined for an entirely different place. Definitely somewhere warmer.

As I neared the end of the block, my heart fluttered for a split second. There it was, that oddly familiar house. My eyes scanned the empty, two-story brick home, but no memories surfaced of who once lived there. Whoever owned it never visited, but it remained well-manicured. With a crackle, the streetlamp above me flickered and died. Prickles traveled up and down my arms as the brown exterior of the house was swallowed by shadows. Alone in the dark, the cold seeped through my jacket and my instincts warned me to leave.

I took a few careful steps towards my house, trying not to disturb the pristine canvas by placing my boots in the marks I had already made coming this way. I noticed another set of footprints, larger and parallel to mine. I was not alone. Sucking in my breath and willing my heart to quit freaking out, I scanned for the footprint's owner. Nothing. I squeezed my eyes shut, recalling the mantra Mom would murmur in my ear, cradling me when I felt a panic attack coming on:

Just breathe

It was just a dream

Just breathe

No one is out to get you

Just breathe

You are safe

Breathe

Opening my eyes, I kept my gaze laser-focused on the safety of my wide front porch. I reached the edge of my driveway and a unique sound, like soft bells on a sleigh, rang through my ears. My heart tightened and I staggered back. As the melody stirred something deep within the confines of my mind, I raced to my door, kicking up snow behind me, and slammed it shut. Clutching my chest, I slowed my breathing before my parents could notice something wrong. I wouldn't allow panic to control me...not again.

"Lydia, is that you, hun?"

I sat, struggling with my boots. "Yeah, Mom!"

"I'm turning on *White Christmas* in a minute. Care to join us by the fire?"

"Umm, sure. Just let me get changed." I tossed my coat on the banister and bounded up the stairs. Gripping the smooth knob of my tall dresser, I paused. *Where had I heard that sound before?*

"Lydia, hurry up! If we don't start it now, you won't be able to finish it with us...school's tomorrow!" Dad called from the bottom of the stairs.

"Coming, Dad!" I threw on my flannel pants and favorite plain t-shirt, then hustled to meet him.

"You OK, sweetie? You look like you've seen a ghost."

"I'm fine, Dad. Just chilled from being outside."

He wrapped his arm around me. "Well then, this ought

to warm you up." He smiled, presenting a steamy cup of hot chocolate. Dad wasn't necessarily intuitive, but he was there when you needed him.

He led me into the family room. Dad snuggled Mom on the couch and I enjoyed my cocoa on the hearth of the fireplace, savoring the warmth. It wouldn't feel like the holidays if we didn't kick off the season with Mom's favorite Christmas movie. I secretly loved it too. Completing our family tradition may have infringed upon everyone's bedtimes, but it was worth it. I zombied up to my room and passed right out.

I smacked the alarm. My eyes rebelled and refused to open more than a crack. I shut them again giving them a stern warning that they had five minutes to get it together. *Ugh, Monday.*

The weeks between Thanksgiving and winter break always seemed to drag. *Why couldn't it just be the weekend again? No, why couldn't it already be spring semester of Senior year?* I craved a place where I could start my own life. But first, I needed to get out of bed. Peeking out the window, I noticed the overnight temps morphed yesterday's winter wonderland into a frozen tundra. I was back to officially hating winter.

After finishing my cereal, I popped back upstairs to finish getting ready. The creepiness from last night had unsettled me and I figured getting a little dolled up would help me feel better. Grabbing the mauve handle of my curling iron, I styled my long, dark hair into flowing curls. I dug out my Extra Lash mascara from my makeup bag. My spirits lifted with each coat

I applied.

I paused and leaned in closer to the mirror—my irises glinted back at me. *They changed again?* I opened my eyes wide and resisted blinking to further inspect them. Taking in the new vibrant violet that stared back at me, the mascara wand fell from my hands. *What the actual heck? It's fine. I'm fine. Everything's fine. No one seemed to notice the first change. Maybe no one will notice this one.* When my eyes first changed from bright blue to periwinkle a few weeks ago, I came up with many reasons to justify this—lack of sleep and poor lighting were my first go-tos. When they didn't change back, I chalked it up to hormones. I stuffed my panic away and made a mental note to ask Mom about an eye doctor appointment and continued to get ready. A little blush and tinted *Covergirl* lip gloss completed my look. I whipped on my new favorite jeans and purple sweater and looked in the mirrored closet doors for a final once over.

I was in the foyer tying up my Doc Martens when I heard the distant beeping of Mrs. Parekh's approach. I slung my Jansport over my shoulder and headed to the end of my driveway. My friend, Preethi Parekh—everyone called her Pree—lived down the street, and we often took turns carpooling.

I made it to the end of my driveway right before she pulled up. Pree wrestled to get her mom's horn-happy hands to quit honking. I squeezed in the back next to my friends Sara and Dani.

"Morning Libby," Mrs. Parekh sang.

"Mom! How many times do I have to tell you? It's LID-DY. You're so embarrassing."

"That's what I said, LIB-BY!"

"Just go, Mom," Pree said, hiding her face from her mom and mouthing, 'I'm so sorry' from the front seat. I just laughed and brushed it off. I dug Pree and her mom. Their relationship was so chaotic, but they did love each other. I wondered how many times Pree would "run-away" this coming week to my house.

"So, we were all just talking about the Winter Formal that's in a few weeks. You're gonna go, *with a date*, right?"

Dani knew I hated the whole dating scene. My plans were to graduate completely unattached. I wanted to take no chances of my heart being swayed to stay in Illinois. "Can we all just go stag? You know, just us girlfriends," I responded.

"Yes! I like that idea very, very much," chimed in Mrs. Parekh looking back at me as she swerved, sending my hair flying.

"Mom!!! Keep your eyes on the road... You almost hit the crossing guard!" Pree shrieked, wildly holding onto the 'oh schnikies' handle and her large, dark chestnut eyes nearly popped out of their sockets.

Sara fixed her blonde locks. "As if, Liddy! My source tells me that you are so going to be asked, and by a *senior*."

"Does this source happen to be your boyfriend, Matt?" I teased. Secretly, I was nervous. I wasn't close with many seniors. What if I didn't like who asked me?

"Maybe." Sara laughed. "And he's not my boyfriend."

"Yet," Dani chimed in.

Sara rolled her blue eyes. "But really, what are you going to do if he asks? Say no? You and I both know you are too nice for that. We all know you get weirded out with attention from guys, but letting someone down makes you feel worse."

Sara knew me too well. "I suppose if I am asked, I'll probably say yes, but I'd much rather skip this whole scene and just go with you girls."

Dani paused from inspecting her curved eyebrows and maroon lipstick in her compact to interject. "Well, rumor has it that Alex is asking you too."

My stomach turned as I digested the possibility of being asked by more than one guy. I would have to say no to someone. Even more disturbing, how would saying yes be interpreted?

"What's your damage? Daydreaming about your blonde lover, Alex, and his perfectly spiked hair?" Dani laughed.

I jumped. "Heck no! Just I...I was thinking about all the homework I've gotta get done."

We pulled up to Wheeling High School just in time to hear the warning bell. We all hustled out of the black Mercury Sable wagon, careful not to slip on the ice, and busted through the doors running.

"Morning, Ms. Rutledge," we all said in unison to the Vice Principal and headed in different directions. I bolted left up the stairs with Pree. Sara and Dani sprinted right through the main corridor.

"Write me a note!" Sara yelled as she disappeared around the corner.

Yeah, right! She knew I hated doing that. I hadn't written to her once in three years. Hello! I needed to pay attention in class or I might miss something important. *What if we are quizzed on it? What if I get caught?*

"Bye, Liddy! See you in AP Chem.," Pree squeaked.

"See ya!" I ran to World History and narrowly escaped getting squished by Ms. Mullens closing her door.

"Pree's turn this morning," I explained, hoping this would be enough reason for a reprieve. Ms. Mullens shook her head, grinning. Though Pree was the star of her debate team, she was also well versed with Pree's tardiness. She ushered me in and headed to the front of the classroom to turn on the projector, a clear indication for everyone to start taking notes.

I pulled out my favorite gel-pen and my notebook. At about the third bullet point, I literally couldn't write anymore. Frozen, like last night, an icy chill spread throughout my body. I couldn't focus on the board. My chest tightened as my breaths grew shallow. *Not here Liddy. Don't panic. You're probably just anxious about being asked to the Winter Formal.* After all, Alex was in the back row of this class with me.

My pen rolled off the desk, a welcomed distraction. I stooped to pick it up as the door opened, revealing two pairs of shoes. The outrageous pair obviously belonged to Jackie, a senior-student ambassador whose platform-yellow Skechers I'd know anywhere. She was very popular among the athletes and belonged to a group of girls who called themselves "the Double Dees"—seriously! They only dated athletes.

Distracted, I accidentally pushed my pen a little further away. I practically hung upside down now, my eyes transfixed on the vintage, designer men's boots. My gaze continued traveling up his body as I slowly sat up. Dark slim jeans with a slight roll at the top of the boot gave way to well-shaped, muscular legs. A leather cuff with an embedded metal piece circled the strong wrist. The turn-down collar on his cream sweater emphasized his chiseled jaw. Straightening my spine, I could now see a little star-shaped scar near his left eye.

That scar! Why do I feel like I've seen it before? I leaned towards him to get a better look.

His hair was as dark as mine; a perfect mix of tousled and styled. It wasn't the bleach- blond, *Sun In* hairdo most of the guys sported these days. His piercing blue—no wait, green— no wait, teal—eyes were striking against his bronzed skin. And they were locked on me. He smiled and radiated confidence.

The loud clatter of my desk knocking into Joy's seat filled the previously silent room as I fell to the ground.

"Ms. Erickson! Are you alright?" Ms. Mullens gasped.

I scrambled back into my seat. *Oh, crud! Now everyone's looking!*

"I'm fine," I mumbled, heat filling my cheeks. Ignoring the snickers, I got straight back to work.

I pretended not to notice as the new student took the empty seat a row over. I couldn't see him behind me, but I knew he could see me and I felt exposed. My foot wiggled as my thoughts raced. The warmth of my cheeks flooded down to my neck as my desire to look at him once more drowned out Ms. Mullens' lecture. I'd be mortified if I'd looked back and he caught me checking him out. I grabbed the collar of my sweater and began fanning it in hopes that the small fire in my belly would simmer down.

Where do I know him from?

He seemed so familiar, but I couldn't place him which was weird. I had a great memory and never forgot a face or name. One thing was for sure. His presence was as tangible as the humid air in Florida's summer, and it felt good—too good. *This can't be possible. I'm losing it.* The bell rang and I held my breath as he passed, purposely taking my time collecting my things. When I reached the doorway, I peeked out hoping to catch a glimpse of him, but he was gone.

I Know

As soon as I got to second period, I wrote a note to Sara, ignoring Mr. Dunbar scrawling math problems on the blackboard. He wouldn't notice I wasn't copying them down.

Hey Chica!

So, I don't really know what to write in these things, but something crazy did happen in first period. I figured you'd want to be the first to know. That is, if you haven't already heard about it. I dropped my pen and when I stopped to pick it up, I literally fell out of my chair. FELL! On the ground! It was absolutely heinous. I was so embarrassed and of course, everyone laughed. If I had the superpower to disappear, I so would have. Anyways, maybe Dani was wrong about Alex because he didn't stay after class to ask me to the dance and that's our only class together. Not that I'd be upset if he didn't ask me.

Oh yeah, one more thing. There is a new guy in my World History class. I think I know him from somewhere, but I can't quite pinpoint where. Anyways, I can't believe I'm saying this, but he is pretty dang cute. Pree or Dani should consider asking him to the dance, though I am still hoping we all go stag. He probably needs someone, someone other than Jackie and the Double Dees, to help him get to know the school and make some friends. If one of us doesn't ask him, it looked quite obvious to me that Jackie will!

-Liddy

I left out *why* I fell out of my chair. During passing period, I slipped Sara the note. Her eyes widened and her jaw dropped as I handed it to her. She skipped off in anticipation of what its contents would reveal. I knew she would be disappointed that it wasn't three full pages front to back like she normally wrote, but details weren't necessary since we'd talk at lunch.

Third and fourth periods dragged on. No matter how hard I tried, I couldn't stop thinking about the new guy and his gorgeous smile. At the sound of the bell, I booked it to the cafeteria and spotted Pree as soon as I walked through the doors. A mischievous grin emerged on her face as she waved me over. I was almost to our table when Pree's eyes suddenly widened and she quickly tried to stand. Her sudden change in demeanor gave me pause. Less than a second later I flew through the air, the blue and white checkered floor coming at me fast. I squeezed my eyes shut, clutching my head to protect it from slamming into the leg of a nearby table. The loud thud of my side hitting the floor could be heard over the silent lunchroom before a chorus of gasps erupted.

"Ow," I moaned as I slid to a sitting position. My hip throbbed and my ribs stung as if they'd been run through with a sword. I opened my eyes and startled when two voices next to me shouted over each other.

"Will you go to Winter Formal with me?"

Clutching my side, I attempted to stand, but then Alex Schramm and Justin Lindor came into view, fighting like two children over who got the last iced rose on the cake. I ignored their extended hands and stood on my own. Other than the stabbing pain in my ribs, the stiffness of my hip, and the extreme embarrassment for the second time today as everyone stared, I was fine.

"Liddy! Aw, daaang. Are you cool?"

"Dude—" Justin shoved Alex's shoulder— "I was going to help her up. Now she got up by herself. Liddy, I'm so sorry. Alex tripped me on purpose, and I fell into you. You alright?" Justin asked his dark, gentle eyes wide.

Everyone in the cafeteria whispered to each other while keeping their eyes locked on the three of us. The pinks of my cheeks deepened. I looked once more at Justin, who worried at his bottom lip. "I'm OK, thanks... Ummm, can we sit down, please? Everyone is kind of staring."

Alex spun to address the entire crowd. "Nothing to see here folks! She's fine. Mind your own business!"

Taking a seat across from Pree, the guys sandwiched me at the table like I was peanut butter in a do-si-dos cookie. Alex wasted no time and pasted his baby blues on my face. "Liddy, you've known me since elementary school. I had plans to ask you in a much more dope way, but here it is. I would really love it if you chose me to go to the dance. I'd definitely show you a good time." He winked.

Justin slid his strong hand into mine, a familiar gesture to garner my attention. "Liddy, I know Alex just asked you, but we've had some good times working together at the aquatic center over the summers, and well, since I'm a senior, and this *is* my last Winter Formal, there isn't anyone else I'd really want to make those memories with. I would love to take you." His defined jaw highlighted his slight, crooked smile and chin dimple.

"You're gonna go there, dude? Seriously. So desperate." Alex scoffed, crossing his arms and legs revealing *Adidas* symbols from head to toe.

Justin shot Alex a warning look, but Alex just laughed it off.

I thought the girls must have been joking this morning with all those rumors or maybe I just wished they had been. I couldn't breathe. I wasn't used to much male attention and it made me super uneasy. Even more, the thought of disappointing someone had my adrenaline buzzing like a swarm of bees whose hive was under attack. I didn't know what to say. Pree stood there gawking at us, like we were stars in a sitcom rehearsing for tomorrow's taping. Dani had seen everything from the end of the lunch line and strutted up to our table, her movements so fierce that I sometimes forgot she only stood five feet tall. Dani took one look at me and came to my side in an instant.

"Guys, you don't really expect her to answer you right now, do you? Puh-lease! Besides seriously lacking in your approach, you plowed her over, injured her, and both shouted at her at the same time. Lame," Dani lectured, her hazel eyes pinpoints as she stared the boys down.

Thank you, God, for my loyal friend, Dani.

Scarlet swept Justin's cheeks as he dropped his gaze and pushed his warm brown hair back.

"Sorry again, Liddy," he mumbled. "You know I'd never do anything like that on purpose, right?"

"I know. It's OK, Justin." He normally didn't start fights.

Alex noticed me rubbing my ribs while *I* noticed his lingering gaze on my chest. "You straight, Liddy?"

If only I had the guts to scream: I'm not OK!

"Umm, I'm fine guys, really," I said as I crossed my arms to cover my chest. I suppose they hadn't meant to publicly humiliate me and I should be grateful I was asked to a dance, let alone by more than one boy. It's just unfortunate it was at the s*ame exact time*. Alex and Justin still sat there waiting for an answer. Nausea threatened to send me to the nurse.

"Let me think about it and I will get back to you both by the end of the day." Alex huffed a little as he stood while Justin locked eyes with mine, gently squeezed my hand, and smiled before walking off in the opposite direction of Alex.

Just then Sara tapped across the cafeteria. "OMG, what's the dealio? I knew I should have just gone back later for the cookies." The Wildcat Snack Shack did have the best, partially cooked chocolate chip cookies ever. They were like eating buttery, warm cookie dough.

"Oh, not much, Sara. Only that Liddy was almost murdered while being asked to the formal," Pree said in exasperation, pulling her black, silky hair over her shoulder.

"Pree, that's not exactly what happened," I corrected.

"Isn't it?" Pree asked, genuinely confused.

"OK, OK. So, who are you going to say yes to?" Dani interrogated. Her purple eyeliner exaggerated her widened eyes which focused on me.

"We don't have to worry about who Liddy says yes to, that's her business. What we do need to help her with is the real possibility she might agonize herself to death having to say 'no' to someone," Sara commented.

"Ugh! Don't remind me," I squeaked.

Sara laughed. "OK, I won't. So, tell me *all* about this mystery guy."

"Mystery guy?" Pree gasped.

"Yep. Liddy had something interesting happen to her in first period with him and I'm dying to hear about it before lunch ends," Sara added.

I pulled my sandwich out of my brown paper bag and took a bite. I chewed slowly and took another bite.

"You're killing me!" Dani blurted out.

I couldn't help but laugh. "Well, he's in history with me."

"What's his name?" Pree asked.

"I must have missed it, but here's a detail you all will like. When he walked in, I literally froze. Like, couldn't move if I wanted to and then I got all tingly. He stared right at me and then, I fell out of my chair."

"Why?" Dani asked.

"I was leaning too far forward, inspecting his face and..."

"Nothing more important than a cute face and hot bod, am I right?" Pree interrupted, elbowing Dani and waggling her perfectly threaded brows.

"Pree, chillax. Pull yourself together girl! Your mom better think about letting you date soon, or your hormones are gonna get us all in trouble one day." Sara laughed.

Pree's face sank a little. "Yeah, right. I just succeeded in getting her to agree to not force me into an arranged marriage. Dating won't be allowed until I'm at least in college."

"Cheer up, Pree. You know, this guy looks more like a well-developed college graduate than a high school student," I offered.

A devilish grin rose on Pree's face and I knew that could only mean one thing. The bell rang before Pree had the chance to share any undignified remarks.

"We'll see ya in dance," Sara called to Dani. It took me a few tries to stand. *Crud.* I was already hella sore.

"Whoever you choose better make it up to you for that brutal show earlier," Sara said. She gestured to my side. "And your injuries."

"Let's not talk about it, OK?" I deflected a little saltily.

We walked together to English Lit. *Stupid boys.* My side throbbed, but I refused to go to the nurse and get an ice pack. As soon as I turned the corner to walk into Mr. Hurley's classroom, I stopped short. Sara and Pree didn't notice. They continued to chat as they walked across the threshold. My body froze as an icy chill soothed my muscles. As it traveled, the overwhelming cold stole my breath. My head grew fuzzy and my knees buckled, but before I hit the ground, a strong arm swooped around my waist.

"Ow." I breathed. I turned to see who caught me. It was *him.* He squeezed my bruised ribs. But in a blink of an eye, a warmth emanated from him, radiating directly into the spot and an involuntary sigh of relief escaped my lips. An apologetic smile crossed his lips and he released me. As soon as he did, my knees gave way, but he was right there and caught me once more. In a flash, his arm looped around my waist again.

"Where do you sit?" he asked. I pointed to the left side of the room and he assisted me to my seat. *What is wrong with me?*

"OMG, Liddy! Are you sure you're alright? Should I take you to the nurse?"

"It's OK, Sara. Please don't make a big deal of this," I whispered, barely moving my lips and flicked a glance towards the guy who still held me.

Sara smiled at him and then moved closer to my ear. "Is this him?" she whispered. I nodded and then drew my attention to Pree, who's open face gaped at the new guy.

"Hiiiiiii, I'm Pree," Pree purred, dragging out her greeting. She grinned, twirling her hair around her finger.

The boy shook his head and laughed before responding. "Nice to meet you, Pree."

She giggled again and stumbled over herself as Sara dragged her to our desks.

Sara turned and simply mouthed *wow* to me before getting in her seat. I could feel his body shake a little with laughter again.

"I'm fine, really. Thank you," I blurted in mortification. I would have wriggled out of his hold if I wasn't so nervous about falling again.

"Which desk is yours?" he asked, still not letting go of me.

"Next to Sara and Pree."

He flashed a genuine smile, his perfect teeth practically

glinting in the fluorescent lights. "I don't remember you being quite so accident-prone. You really ought to be more careful." He winked as he helped me into my seat.

His voice was smooth like honey, not super deep and gruff like I'd imagined. I wanted to tell him he must have me confused with someone else. I knew I should at least ask him his name, but when I looked up, he was already at Mr. Hurley's desk in the back of the classroom. I dug out my notebook channeling my inner Agatha Christie to try and solve the mystery of this boy. He seemed confident that he knew me, but I couldn't place him. I could feel Sara and Pree both staring as if I held the last golden ticket for entrance on the Polar Express. Their eyes held a million questions and I braced myself for the onslaught.

Mr. Hurley walked to his podium with a pep in his step. "Good afternoon, my favorite class! Today, I am going to give you all one more writing assignment that will be due the Friday before break starts. It will be a ten-page research paper."

A collective grumbling from everyone in the class resounded, which only seemed to make Mr. Hurley even happier before he bellowed, "Psych!" and belly laughed to himself for a full minute. "OK, in all seriousness, you will be getting one more assignment but will work on it with a partner. Look directly to the person across from you. This person will be your partner for the remainder of this assignment. You will be co-authoring a short story together that centers around the topic of True Love." He pronounced it *twu wuv*. More collective protests from the male students whereas many of the girls started chatting excitedly. "Calm down, calm down. You will be choosing a famous love story and re-writing it. We will be watching *The Princess Bride*, the most epic love story ever, for the next few class periods for inspiration. Go sit by your partner now and exchange contact information."

Mr. Hurley had the desks arranged in an almost fully enclosed circle claiming this facilitated better discussions. I looked up and noticed *he* was on his way over. Butterflies flooded my stomach. Every step he took towards me only intensified the fluttering.

"Looks like maybe *you* should be saying 'buh-bye' to Alex and Justin and ask *him* to formal." Sara smirked as she moved from her seat. I flushed.

Pree could barely compose herself and whispered, "I am so coming over tonight!" before she scooched to sit on the other side of Sara.

When he sat next to me, goosebumps traveled from my head to my toes. I turned to greet him, and his gorgeous eyes already twinkled back at me.

"Hi, I'm Will. I guess we're partners."

"I guess we are. Hi, I'm Liddy."

"I know."

The Dance

THOSE LAST WORDS CAME ACROSS ALMOST PLAYFUL. A sincere smile lifted the corners of Will's mouth. As it grew, the smile pressed the apples of his cheeks up until they reached his eyes, those enchanting eyes that whisked me away and left me breathless.

How does he know who I am? Did he ask about me? No, he wouldn't have. Besides, I don't have time for boys.

The lights went out, signaling the start of the movie. I quietly took out a piece of paper writing my name and number down before folding it up. *Oh wait!* I unfolded it to include my AOL Instant Messenger *Liddy1020* in case he preferred to message online about our English project.

I wanted to hand it to him, but his attention was on the movie, not on me. *He does kind of seem familiar.*

I shifted to get more comfortable, my arm accidentally resting against his. My blood pulsed. *Oh no! I'm turning into Pree! Dang these hormones.* Keeping his face on the screen, Will cleared his throat and moved his entire body away from mine. His face pinched, each of his muscles flexed and the veins in his exposed forearms and hands popped to attention. I turned my head discreetly so I could do a pit sniff test. Nope. I was good. I continued to work on the puzzle that was Will. *Why would he go out of his way to toy with me that he knows me, but then act like I have the plague?*

The movie's witty humor distracted me from Will and my bruised ribs, but I was careful not to laugh. I was so into the movie that I failed to pay attention to the clock like everyone else. When the bell rang, I didn't have all my stuff packed up, and everyone, including Will, was already out the door. *Dang it!* I didn't give him my contact info for the assignment. But when I looked down, an origami Christmas rose sat on my desk. *How'd he know I loved those?* A hint of neat writing peaked out from one of the petals, but I didn't have time to open it. Stuffing everything into my bag, I bolted to my next class.

Seventh and eighth period whizzed by. I couldn't contain my smile. In just a few minutes I would be stretching, leaping, and shaking what my momma gave me in my favorite and last class of the day—dance. When I got to my gym locker, I placed my bag on the hook. Opening it to grab my hoodie, the origami flower floated out. I quickly unwrapped it like a present on Christmas morning: *Will Jamison 386-555-3344 AIM: WLJdunes17*

Slightly disappointed there weren't any hints as to how we might know each other, I shoved the flower back in my bag and changed into my dance clothes. Putting on some strawberry Lip Smackers, I pulled my hair back, gave myself a once over and headed to the other side where Sara got ready.

"I would kill for your body," I lamented, leaning against the cinderblock wall.

"Are you kidding? I literally have no butt. There aren't enough squats I could do to compete with yours. It's totally unfair," Sara said as she pulled on her black tank. "But I do have a nice rack," Sara stated as she looked down, appreciating her hills. I giggled.

"Are we ready to shake our groove things?" Pree chimed in, Dani right next to her.

"Definitely," I said eagerly.

Dani checked the back door with her hip and we entered the fieldhouse. "So, did you make a decision yet?" she asked, looking at me.

I shrugged.

"Are you leaning toward one of them?" Sara implored.

"I don't know. Today has been insane enough already."

We made it to the top of the stairs and walked over to the shoe cubbies.

"Liddy, it's no big deal. Whoever you choose is fine by us, right ladies?" Sara suggested, placing her shoes into the cubby and slipping on her jazz shoes.

"Ugh, it's totally Justin, isn't it?" Dani blurted out. "Even though Alex is way more fun *and* he'll actually dance with you."

"And what if it is Justin? I'd think you of all people would support my decision knowing that Alex is a bit of a player."

"You don't have to date him. I just want to make sure my BFF has fun. I know you love to dance, and I'd hate for Justin to keep you on the bleachers all night," Dani said, giving me a quick hug.

We seated ourselves on the far end under the famous dancer's gallery wall and could see Coach R. in the window of her office, her neck kinked holding the phone and hands arms flapping.

"But Liddy," Pree whined, "Alex is so cute. Seriously, you guys would look so good together in pictures."

"I haven't decided yet. And Justin is very cute, too. He just doesn't let everyone know he is," I countered defensively. "Plus, I'm better friends with him." Right now, I was so glad they all had no idea how hard I had crushed on Justin the summer before Sophomore year.

"I think anyone you want to go with is fine." Sara shrugged in an attempt at keeping the peace.

"Well, how are you going to break the news to the boy you don't choose?" Pree asked.

My stomach churned again. If only I could borrow Bill and Ted's phone booth, I would go back in time and skip lunch altogether.

"Oh, Pree! Now look at Liddy. She's practically green!" Sara complained.

"Guuurl, they are big boys. Whether or not they take it well is not your problem," Dani stated.

"Actually—" Sara smirked— "why don't you consider going with that new guy and saying no to both of them? What's his name?"

"Will!" Pree exclaimed.

"How do you know?" Sara asked.

"Um, everyone's talking about him," Pree responded.

"OK, so, Will. Why don't you ask him?"

"Well, Sara, I guess because...well, that would be rude considering I was already asked."

"Who cares! They practically killed you today."

"Stop exaggerating, Pree." I laughed. Will was a stranger and I sure as heck didn't know what to think of him, but I couldn't deny being drawn to him. "I was actually thinking maybe one of you should ask him. He is pretty hot."

"Whoa! You totally admitted a guy was hot." Dani feigned shock. "So, who is this Will? For you to even admit that a dude is hot is worth talking about."

"Oh my gosh! Willlllll, so yummy," Pree sang. "He's only *the* hottest guy at our school—scratch that—in our entire state!"

"He is definitely a cutie patootie," Sara agreed.

I smiled. "So, it's settled. One of *you* girls ask him and help him get acquainted with the new school."

Dani lifted a thin brow. "When do I get to meet him?"

The tingles that traveled up my spine could only mean one thing. "Uh, right now... That's him," I whispered sheepishly as I quickly ticked my chin in his direction.

And there he was. *O' Holy Night.* My body sang with a longing to be near him. Will wore a black V-neck that hugged every chiseled angle of his body. He still wore the brown leather cuff. I closed my eyes to mentally check myself. *Stop this right now! Get a hold of yourself!* When I opened them again, Will had me transfixed in his gaze. My heart leapt and Will bit his bottom lip, tearing his eyes from me.

"I hope he can actually dance or that will dock him some serious hottie-points. And look, you can practically see his abs through his shirt. I'd like to press my body against—"

"Shhhhhh... Chill out, Pree!" Sara giggled.

"Will, care to sit with us?" Pree called out, scooching over before I could say anything. He walked over and settled between me and Pree.

I glanced at him, utterly confused. I wanted to be friendly, but with how he shifted away from me in English, I wasn't sure that's what he wanted. I was also annoyed at my body for betraying me and my mind for not letting me remember who he was. When Will caught my eye again, he tilted his head down, running his hand through his dark, full hair. As he turned his head, I noticed that what I thought was a dimple was actually another scar. My heart spasmed and Will stopped short. He turned to look at me, his eyes wide, and continued to work his bottom lip. *Did he feel what I did?*

Just then, Coach R. came sashaying into the dance studio. "Sorry I'm late, ladies and gents. We are going to skip warm-ups today so after we break off make sure to stretch on your own. We have a new student joining our ensemble." All eyes shifted back to Will. "I know we are an audition only group, but his former instructor, Ms. Waters, submitted a VHS tape of some of Will's work. After reviewing it, I have determined that he fits our ensemble perfectly. Plus, I am sure Scottie and Kiyo wouldn't mind the added testosterone in this sea of twenty-nine talented, determined women." Everyone laughed. "Will, would you please come stand by me and tell us a little about yourself?"

Every single girl in the room gaped at him as he joined Coach R. on the mirrored wall. *Were they even blinking?* He's just a guy. A nice, attractive guy who made me second guess the dating rules I imposed on myself, but nonetheless, a guy.

"Hey, I'm Will. I'm a junior. I lived here a long time ago in the Kingsport neighborhood behind the school, but my dad got a new job and we moved to Hammock Dunes, Florida. My parents still live there, but I wanted to come back north, so now I'm living with my uncle."

No wonder he was bronzed in the middle of our winter. *Wait, did he say he lived here before? In my neighborhood?*

"Thank you for sharing with us, Will. OK, everyone stand up and find a partner. You will have twenty minutes to improv and create a dance phrase with a minimum of five sets of eight. You must be connected in some way, shape, or form the entire time. We will be sharing these dances at the end of class."

As if he didn't notice any other girl in the room, Will fastened his gaze on me and made a gesture that asked if I'd be his partner. My dang nerves prevented me from responding. When I didn't get up and walk over to him right away, Will bounded towards me. There was a flurry of activity around me and yet, it was like he moved in slow motion. I swallowed hard.

"Care to be my partner?"

"Er, are you sure? I mean there are so many other girls who you haven't had a chance to meet yet." I quickly scanned the room, an army of scowls meeting my gaze.

"I'm only asking you, Liddy. I wouldn't have asked if I didn't want to. Besides, it gives us more time to...talk."

Pree, Dani, and Sara all eyed each other in wonder and then looked at me. I suddenly found the grey Marley flooring very interesting as I traced circles with my fingers. "Then, um, sure." *I am so going to regret this later.* I just made every girls' hate list in the room, except for my friends, though Pree did look a little disappointed.

"Um, sure? You don't care to be my friend anymore?" he teased with a bright smile.

His friend...anymore? I stood up. Okay, it was essential that I found out who Will was to me. While everyone partnered up, I moved a little closer to whisper. "Listen, I think you must have me confused with someone else."

Will's smile vanished and the light of his eyes seemed to dim. "Wow, so you really don't remember me at all?" he asked, his voice sad and distant.

I peered up at him through my lashes. "Should I?"

"Never mind. Sorry if I've come on a little strong. Do you want to change partners? Now that I'm thinking about it, seems like you didn't want to partner up."

"It's not that..." I peeked over my shoulder again. Everyone was already paired up and chatting excitedly, but continued to glance our way. "It's just, well, just about every girl in this room is staring at you and I don't care to start any drama with anyone over a dude, no offense."

"None taken. Even if everyone is staring though, why do you care so much?" He leaned in, careful not to touch me.

"I just like to live a no drama lifestyle."

"OK, good. Because I thought maybe I had freaked you out with me mistaking you for a long-lost friend of mine."

"Not at all. You didn't 'freak' me out. I just felt like a jerk for thinking I was supposed to remember you." Changing the subject, I continued, "I'm quite shocked that you're a dancer. You seem to be more of the jock type." Was I really this comfortable with him to be this bold?

"I have lots of hobbies; dance just happens to be one of them. Try not to be one of those people who judges a book by its cover," he taunted as he stretched his hamstrings.

"Who me?" I shrugged my shoulders innocently placing a hand on my chest and then rolled out my ankles, shoulders, and neck.

He laughed. *He has the best laugh. I've always liked his laugh.* Suddenly, I didn't feel quite so confident that he'd simply mistaken me for someone else. I was frustrated with these tricks my mind played on me. Did I know him or not?

I snapped out of my thoughts when Coach R. yelled, "Your time starts now!" She cranked the music and retreated to her office.

"Mind if I try something?" Will asked.

I nodded my permission. Will closed his eyes and took a deep breath. He walked behind me and gently grabbed me low around my waist. As a joule of energy flooded me with heat, we both let out a sigh. Will abruptly let go.

"Don't stop," I found myself saying. Will tried again, and this time I was ready for the blitz.

"If you stand in arabesque, I can lift you for a fish dive," Will suggested.

I grabbed his hands to remove them from my waist, but an image of a faceless boy blinded me. I shook my head to regain my vision and took a step away from Will.

"Is everything alright?" he asked.

"I'm fine." I breathed, my vision returning quickly, and came up with an honest excuse. "I don't like to be lifted."

"Oh, may I ask why?"

I dropped my gaze. "I'm too heavy. I would feel bad." Will laughed. I glared at him.

"You're serious? Liddy, you are not too heavy. Far from it."

Will closed the gap between us and brushed my shoulder with his thumb. *Wham!* I stumbled as another image, this time a faceless boy sledding down the hill with me was all I could see.

I sat down and rubbed my eyes. "Maybe we can start on the ground? That would be unexpected."

"Are you sure you're alright?"

"Yep!" I said, a little more chipper than I felt. "Times a tickin'. We better get moving if we are going to get the choreography done."

The assaults continued anytime Will came into contact with my skin. With each of his touches, more forgotten memories of my childhood came flashing back. In them, front and center, was a faceless boy.

What is my mind trying to show me?

More than fifteen minutes had passed and I was no closer to figuring out the mystery boy. At least my ribs no longer bit with each movement.

We were almost finished when Will asked, "Hey, Liddy? Since you won't let me do the lift, mind if I try out a new ending?" He took my hand in his, bringing my right arm up around his neck. Again, Will took a deep, wistful breath. He stepped forward, lightly pressing his abdomen against mine. As he leaned me back, he let his hand travel across my ribs to the small of my back.

"OK, now you grab my shoulders...good. I'm going to move my hands to your shoulders and slide down your arms until our hands are locked. As I do this, you'll extend your legs straight and put your head back. Ready?"

"I...I think so."

When he started sliding his hands down my bare arms,

I couldn't control the tidal wave that crashed into me. Remembrances too vast to count flashed before my eyes making me dizzy. I forgot what I was doing and let go while jutting my legs out and kicking Will's out from under him. I let out a yelp and we tumbled to the ground.

Keeping my eyes closed so as not to acknowledge my clumsiness, I couldn't help but notice Will's minty breath on my face. When I opened them, his eyes bored into mine and I averted my gaze. Will hovered over me in a push up position. My cheeks flushed when I heard some snickers from afar. In one swift move, he sat next to me, giving me the room to sit up. When his eyes skimmed my exposed torso, he grimaced. *Was that expression annoyance or disgust?*

I immediately pulled my tank top down. "I'm sorry."

"What are you apologizing for?" he asked softly, moving the piece of hair that had fallen out of my pony behind my ear.

I pulled away. "For falling and embarrassing you."

He stood and extended his hand to help me up. "That's what you think? That you embarrassed me? Liddy, this is dance. Falls happen all the time."

I politely refused his hand. "I can get up myself, thank you."

"Of course, Miss Independent. I apologize for looking, but what the heck happened to your side? It looks like you cracked a rib."

So, he wasn't disgusted. He was concerned. "Oh, it's nothing really. I accidentally got knocked into at lunch today. I'm fine, just a little sore."

"That looks more than a little sore." His brow furrowed. "I've seen a nasty bruise like that before on one of my football buddies. Turns out it was cracked ribs. Let's just try a different ending. One that won't aggravate your injury."

But my reason for crying out wasn't because of my ribs.

Will stepped into me, but this time he held my gaze before clasping his fingers in mine. I saw his jaw tense and his eyes seemed to flicker from teal to aqua. *I must be hallucinating.*

"Do you remember?" he whispered.

My head tingled as it grasped his words. I nearly jumped as shivers ran down my spine, like my body told me the answer I came up with was correct. Somehow Will knew I was seeing things, things from my past. But no, that was impossible.

"Liddy?" Will looked at me pleadingly.

Grappling for something to say, I unhooked our hands and decided to ignore his question. "So, there is this dance coming up. Have you heard about it?"

Will dropped his jaw and then snapped it shut. "Uh, yes... Not sure I am going to go though. Don't really know anyone here yet to ask. Unless you're asking me?" he said as he nudged me a little.

"Ouch."

"Sorry!" He looked alarmed, his eyes flicking to my side and back to my face.

I smiled. "I was already asked, but I was thinking that maybe you could ask one of my friends?"

Will looked down and ran his hand through his hair again. He seemed to do that a lot when uncomfortable.

"Look who's all self-conscious now," I teased, ruffling his hair. *Why did I just do that?* When he only offered a hint of a smile, I added, "You don't have to if you don't want to."

"No, it's fine. So, who do you think I should ask?"

"Times up! Everyone, sit upstage. Liddy and our new student—"

"Will," all the girls chimed at once.

"That's right, thank you very much. You're up first. I'm going to play a random piece of music and count you out. Change the tempo of the piece you created to the beat of the song that's played for you."

"Pree," I whispered to Will, nodding discreetly in her direction. "Ask Pree."

Will smiled back at me.

We assumed our starting position. Those brief moments waiting for the music felt like an eternity. I wiped my clammy hands on my dance pants. Everyone's attention stayed hyper-focused on the two of us. The acoustic guitar and smooth sax solo filled the air. I knew the song immediately—"I'll Be" by Edwin McCain—and my cheeks flushed. *Great, why'd she have to pick a love song?* I closed my eyes tight and said a mental prayer. *Please let this be over quickly, don't let me embarrass myself by tripping again or something worse.*

Will gave my hand a little squeeze. I blinked and focused on his lips. "Just breathe, Liddy," he said, flashing his beautiful smile. "This is the fun part."

"And five, six, seven, eight," Coach yelled out.

His guiding touches calmed my anxiety and it was like the rest of the room disappeared, leaving just us. Our movements flowed effortlessly, as if we'd been dancing together our entire lives. Midway through, Will brushed my hand with his lips and I found myself in a sudden dream-like state. In an instant his face appeared in the flashbacks I had earlier, the missing piece to a puzzle. As we finished, we paused and stared at one another, both of us breathing heavier than choreography justified.

Did he feel and see it all, too? I searched his face, gasping when I landed on the scar by his temple and absently reached to touch it.

Remembrances

S OMEONE CLEARED THEIR THROAT. I dropped my hand and Will took a step back. We both turned and were met with an audience of gawking students. A handful of girls glowered at me like I was a newly discovered threat to their pride. I cast my gaze to the ground hoping no one would see. My stomach twisted, and it took all my mental and physical strength to not collapse. My mind continued to sew Will's face in place of the blank mask of my dreams, the rush of images overwhelming me. I forced a smile in the direction of my friends and a single bead of sweat trailed over my forehead.

Coach R. waltzed over to the stereo system and with a big wave of her arm and flick of her wrist, pressed pause on the CD player as if she were an orchestra conductor. "That. Was. So. Moving!" she exclaimed. Her hands clapped wildly, encouraging the rest of the class to join in. "You two—" she pointed to me and Will— "see me after class for a minute."

I scurried to Pree and Will followed suit.

The next pair got set up. Once they started their dance, Will leaned over me and I involuntarily breathed in his woodsy, citrus scent. Distracted, I almost didn't notice him ask, "Pree, would you do me the honor of being my date to the formal?"

I don't think I've ever seen Pree speechless before. Dani gave Pree a hard shove before she gave a hard nod. Sara looked at me, her eyebrows raised so high, they almost reached her hairline.

"Awesome. Liddy has my number. She can give it to you."

The sudden ache in my chest was unexpected. This was silly. No one, especially a boy, was going to distract me from my plans.

Pree fidgeted, unable to sit still through the rest of the dances. When it was Pree's turn, her movements were rushed, no doubt flustered by Will's invitation.

Pain licked at my temples and my muscles ached from the stress of the day. I was dreaming of an Epsom salt bath when Coach R. called out from behind her door, "Will. Lydia. My office please. I've got to run to the coach's lounge. I'll be right back."

Will grabbed my hand as calm as ever, relief etched in his face, but his touch only furthered the process of my mind weaving him back into my memories. Waiting for the crowd to pass, he called "see ya ladies" as all the girls giggled, and then he twirled me across the hall into the office.

"Liddy, are you coming over after school?" Sara called after me.

I peeked my head back out. "Duh, I pretty much always do," I yelled back, trying to conceal the quaking in my voice.

"OK, good. Meet you at the back doors." Sara sped down the stairs, but Pree made a bee-line to me.

"Oh. My. Gosh. My mom is gonna totally freak." She smiled deviously. Pree hugged me, waved bye to Will, and headed out.

Will and I stood next to each other in Coach R.'s office, but it seemed neither of us could find the words to say. I did my best to ignore the enigmatic waves between us. The pulsing at my temples intensified and I closed my eyes as I massaged them in tiny concentric circles. I really didn't know what to say about what happened between us when we danced. It was ethereal and foreign. Every touch brought back more memories that had been tucked away somewhere for years. But it was during that brief, fleeting kiss on the back of my hand when his face became clear within those memories.

He was Will! My Will! My best friend who disappeared all of those years ago. How could I have forgotten him? I glanced up at his face. Wow, he had changed. Besides the tiny scars that had been there since our sledding accident, it was hard to see his features as I once knew them. I continued to study his face. His heart shaped lips were definitely the same, his scars, his hair color. *People change, but that much?* It must have been about eight years since I had seen him last. A ripple of sadness, uneasiness, and fear crept over me. Beginning in my gut, it made its way to my throat, slithering its hands around my vocal cords, and squeezed.

Will looked at me. "What's wrong?"

But I couldn't answer. It was his house that I stopped at last night when the light flickered out. His brief kiss brought back the memory of a green pulsing light, a woman's angelic, but oddly sinister laugh, a flash of blood orange, and...police tape. My hands searched for something to grab hold of, anything to find purchase... I finally latched onto the back of Coach's desk chair. I dropped my head and took a few deep breaths.

"Liddy, say something please," Will pleaded.

"I'm confused. I mean...I don't understand," I rasped out between short breaths.

"Do you remember me at all?"

So many questions raced through my mind, stumbling over each other and preventing me from formulating any coherent thoughts. I was mad at myself for not remembering who he was right away and equally mad at him for disappearing eight years ago without so much as a goodbye. How could I forget an entire period of my life?

"Sorry to keep you waiting." I stood up straight as Coach R. sauntered into her office. "Liddy, I know you don't ride the bus, but do you Will?"

"No, ma'am. I have a car."

"OK great and don't call me ma'am. That's for old ladies," Coach R. razzed. "Well, I called you both in here because I was positively moved by your performance today. Your working chemistry is so electric you could light up all of Broadway for a month! I would love for you both to perform a duet in the Spring Showcase. Do you both accept?"

"It would be my pleasure," Will said first, directing the response at me.

Coach cocked an eyebrow at him. "Well, aren't you just a little Gene Kelly, practically dancing in the rain already...and Liddy?"

"Hmmm?"

"Are you ready to be his Debbie Reynolds?" she asked, gesturing to Will.

If I was being honest with myself, I was looking forward to working with Will and getting some answers. I wanted to know what happened that night and why his family made such an abrupt move. A lot could change in eight years. How could I be sure he was still the Will I knew? Not to mention, it unsettled me how every touch sent me on a wild roller coaster. And, even weirder still, it was as if Will *knew* these memories were gone and recognized the *moment* they returned. These questions threatened to overshadow this coveted honor of dancing in the showcase usually reserved for seniors. I never imagined I would get a role like this, especially as a junior. My nerves were frayed, ready to spark a raging fire at any moment.

I looked Will directly in the eyes and said, "Yes, I accept." His chest fell as he let out a long breath.

"Great! The piece can't be more than four minutes and should tell a story. The more emotional the better. We'll talk more after winter break. Now, off you go."

As we walked through the corridor leading to the fieldhouse, Will broke our silence.

"What did Pree mean earlier?"

I laughed. "Pree's parents won't let her date or have any guy friends. They've backed off talking about it with her, but they believe in arranged marriages."

"What! So, why'd you tell me to ask her?"

"Because Pree doesn't get asked to dances considering most of the guys already know this. Her parents will only let her go if they know she is just going with girlfriends. But since you and

I are...friends—" I flinched again at an unexpected ache in my heart— "and Mrs. Parekh loves me, I can vouch for you." My eyes wandered over to the hall clock, five minutes until school ended. *Shoot!* All this talk about the formal reminded me of another impending disaster. I frowned. In just a few minutes I'd have to face Alex and Justin.

"Will, I've really gotta pick up the pace here. I need to get changed out and—"

"Can we talk about the elephant in the room?" Will interrupted. "Something happened when we danced. My guess is that you remembered—" his voice dropped low— "me."

My hands grew clammy. "Yes," I breathed, barely a whisper. "I'm not sure what to say or ask. I..."

Before I could finish, his arms were around me and, lifting me off my feet, he interjected, "That's great! I'm sure you must be freaking out." He set me back down, releasing me from a bear hug.

"I don't know, I... Yes. Yes, that could describe one thing I'm feeling." Nauseated from sensation overload, I could hardly form a coherent thought.

"Believe me, I am too. Liddy, there is so much I want—no, *need*—to tell you."

He had no idea just how much I wanted to sit and talk with him, but I wasn't sure I was ready. Not now anyway. I needed a hot minute to process some of this.

"Actually, I can't do this right now. But we should definitely talk soon...when we have more time and privacy."

"Agreed. So, what's the real scoop about your ribs?" Will asked as we entered the field house.

"I told you it was an accident." When Will stopped walking

and crossed his arms, I continued. "Ugh, fine. Well, the guys that asked me to the dance are kind of the reason I had that accident." Will's eyes darkened. "Let me explain. Just keep walking. I don't want to be late."

"Fine. Please explain why the guys who did this—" Will's knuckles grazed my bruised ribs— "get to take you to a dance."

I rolled my eyes. "It was an accident!" I said, frustrated. I could feel the impatience rolling off of Will. "The one I'm saying yes to is a good guy, truly. You'd like him," I finished, biting my lip.

"So why are you hesitating then?"

"Well, I hate the idea of hurting someone's feelings and there's something else... Never mind, I don't know why I am even talking to you about this."

"Try me. We were best friends once upon a time, remember?"

I sighed. He was right. Even though he'd just reinserted himself into my life, I couldn't ignore our unnatural connection. But that wasn't something I was emotionally ready to unpack at this moment. "Well, I don't want the person I say yes to, to get the wrong idea. I've kind of sworn off guys for the remainder of high school."

"I see... But, does it matter who you go with? I mean at my old school, we had our date, but we also went with a group of our friends. Do you guys do that here?"

"Yes."

"Then you aren't tied to just your date. I am sure whoever you choose won't mind if you were to, let's say, dance with others."

What was he insinuating? Will's bright eyes lowered to

meet mine. My heart quickened. I took a step away from him in hopes the distance would lessen the magnetic pull between us.

"And I'm sorry to hear you have sworn off *all* guys. It hardly seems fair, but maybe you should try to date men," he teased. And with that, he disappeared behind the blue locker room door.

Decisions

EVERYONE ALREADY HUDDLED BY THE DOUBLE DOORS in the hall while I still needed to change. I snatched off my black tank and slipped on my sweater. Whipping off my yoga pants, I shimmied into my jeans and spritzed myself with *Fuzzy Peach* body mist just as the bell rang. Turning to face the mirror, I slid my scrunchie out of my hair and gave my locks a good shake.

I flung my bag over my shoulder and darted out into the crowded hallway. I dodged and weaved bodies like Luigi avoiding banana peels and turtle shells. As I made my way to the bustling commons area, flashes of Will kept blurring my vision. My temples throbbed in response, pressure increasing in my head as if stuck in a vice, and someone cranked the handle.

I stopped just after the row of dark-wood doors leading to the administration offices. Placing my right hand on the faded, white wall, I pressed my other hand to my stomach and closed my eyes. *In...two, three. Out...two, three, four. In...two, three. Out...two, three, four.* I didn't want to linger too long, but I needed my adrenaline to simmer down. I shoved aside flashbacks of Will and focused on the onerous task at hand.

As I approached the back entry, a small group of familiar faces waited for me. Sara held hands with Matt. Chatting it up with Eric, Justin's baseball teammate, was Pree and Dani. Alex and Justin stood off to the side, brooding, the tension visible. My initial gut choice of Justin hadn't wavered, but that did nothing to relieve my apprehension about turning down Alex.

"Hey guys, sorry I'm late." Everyone fell silent and stared at me. *Let's get this over with.*

"'Sup, Liddy?" Alex asked, arrogantly.

"Hey, Liddy." Justin cut in, stepping in front of Alex, and giving my hand a quick reassuring squeeze.

Oh. My. Gosh. I might throw up. Maybe if I say it fast enough it might hurt less, like ripping off a band aid. "Alright guys, so I know you have been waiting all day for an answer. Please know that it was difficult for me to choose, but I'm saying yes to...Justin." Gasps of disappointment from Pree and Dani intermixed with whoops of joy from Justin and Eric.

Justin smiled big and patted Alex on the shoulder. "Don't go postal, homie." He hugged me and I bit the inside of my cheek so I didn't scream out in pain. "Sorry I have to jet, or I'll be late to training. I'll call you later!" Justin continued as he walked back towards the field house, Eric giving him congratulatory slaps on the back.

"Uh....sure. Bye, Justin," I responded as I looked for Alex. He retreated down the opposite hall and kicked a large garbage can in the corner. *He's angry.* It was apparent Alex wasn't used to being told no, but as cocky as he was, I still felt bad. Thinking of what Will had said, I had an idea. "Alex, wait!" I yelled as I ran towards him. "I didn't get to explain."

He stopped and turned to face me. "I don't want to hear it, Liddy. I can't believe you chose that buzzkill over me." He started to walk away again, but I grabbed his arm.

"Well, I'm going to tell you anyway. It's because this is his last Winter Formal at Wheeling High. You and I'll have plenty more dances. Besides, does it matter who our official date is to the dance? Can't we dance with anyone we want to?"

Alex cocked his head, staring at me. A ghost of a smile appeared on his face and he stood to his fullest height. "Will you save me a dance then, Liddy?"

"Of course!"

"Promise?"

Dang you, Alex. I didn't make promises lightly. I never entered into one without honoring them, no matter what. Justin wouldn't like this pact I made with Alex, but I'd have to cross that bridge when I got to it. "I...promise."

"Come on, Liddy, our ride is waiting." Sara grabbed my arm from behind, pulling me away from Alex.

"Well, that was uneventful," Dani complained.

"Yeah! Thank goodness! I got myself all worked up for nothing," I sighed. I still shook from the adrenaline rush.

"Smart move promising Alex a dance and agreeing to be his date to another," Pree said.

Schnikies. Did I actually say I'd go with him to another

dance? "Dani, I was thinking that since you were all like *Team Alex*, that maybe he could take you to the formal?"

"I'd say yes if he asked me," Dani assented. "It's not like I'm crushing on anyone at the moment."

"Great!" Sara chimed in. "I'll be sure to talk to Matt and slip it into the convo when he calls me tonight." Sara's mom pulled up. We hugged Dani, who was off to work, and hopped into the big blue conversion van.

"How was your day?" Mama L. asked.

"Matt asked me to the Winter Wonderland dance in the sweetest way today." Sara presented the dozen pink roses Matt had given her. Her voice rose an octave as she shared how three of the four of us, so far, were asked to the dance and how Alex would probably ask Dani.

"So, when are we going dress shopping ladies?" Mama L. asked, patting her perfectly styled hair.

"Mom, uh, I kind of just wanted to go with the girls, if that's alright."

Mama L.'s lips turned down, but responded, "Sure, I understand. It's not cool to go shopping with your mom anymore. Can I at least still do your hair?" Mama L. was a hairdresser and had a little hair studio in her house. She always cut our hair and styled it for special occasions.

"Mama L., I, for one, absolutely love when you do my hair," I chimed in, and the corners of her bright red lips curved back up.

"Agreed," Pree interjected.

"Thank you, ladies." She nodded, her dyed crimson locks swaying in the rearview mirror.

We got to Sara's house, grabbed a snack, and marched upstairs to her room. Sara turned on MTV so we could watch the daily countdown while we hurried through homework.

"Who are you guys partnered with for the English project? I didn't get a chance to see."

"A little preoccupied, were we? Lucky you, getting to spend so much time with our newest Wildcat." Sara waggled her brows at me. "Pree and I cheated, and we're partnering up."

"Yeah. Mr. Hurley was totally OK with it, because I was supposed to be partnered with Brandon, but you know how my mom would have flipped her lid," Pree reasoned.

I giggled, remembering that just a few years ago, Pree would get grounded if a neighborhood boy happened to walk on the sidewalk in front of their home while Pree was outside. Forget Mrs. Parekh allowing Pree any alone time with a boy, even if it was for school.

"OK, we seriously need to discuss Will and dance ensemble. So, don't get all salty, but what *was* that today?" Sara questioned.

"What do you mean?" I asked in mock ignorance, looking up at the TV pretending to be mesmerized by the latest No Doubt music video. I needed my solitude to think about how I felt about Will and my strange, literal attraction to him. Not to mention the mystery surrounding my forgotten memories.

"Oh, come on, Liddy! First, you're falling all over yourself around him according to this note right here. And yes, I figured out that *he* is why you fell."

"He made you fall too?" Pree asked, looking confused.

Sara ignored her. "You almost fell again in English. *Miraculously*, you guys get partnered for the assignment and then *somehow* get paired again in dance class! I've never seen you dance like that before and then Coach gives you two a coveted duet slot."

"Truth? I think I was hit harder than I thought with the whole debacle at lunch. See?" I lifted my shirt to show her. Sara squeezed her eyes shut, scrunching her face. The bruising on my side looked nasty. It extended from my bra line to my hip, the black spots outlined in various shades of maroon, purple, and blue. "That's most likely why I was a little clumsy today. Second, we got partnered in English because he was directly across from me. Some of us are not cheaters when it comes to picking partners," I teased. "And as for dance, well, he asked me to be his partner."

"If he lived in our neighborhood, how come Sara and I don't remember him then?" Pree wondered. Sara cocked her eyebrow at me.

"I don't know. It's weird." I shrugged, not ready to share. Although, I did wonder what they would think of the bizarre memories that coincided with his touch. But I had a hard time rationalizing all of this to myself. It was like magic, an illusion not explained by science. I couldn't imagine how it would sound to my friends if I even tried to explain it.

"I figure it's because he's changed so much. Besides the scar near his temple and his cheek, he looks...different. He's like six-foot-three when he used to be shorter than me and... well, he's got a man's physique. Not even his eye color is how I remember it." Thinking back, Will used to have green eyes, and now they were vibrant teal. Little bits and pieces of the Will I knew were in this new, souped-up version.

"Noticing a very small scar... Liddy, are you sure you're not into him as more than friends?" Sara posed.

"Yeah, 'cause it'd be weird for me to go to the dance with him if you both are, like, a thing," Pree agreed.

"I'm sure." I smiled.

"I mean, you should've seen yourselves! You were all over each other in dance," Pree continued.

"We are *just friends*. And besides, the assignment in dance was to be touching each other the entire time, remember?"

"Well, I will be making sure that he and I don't lose *touch*, if you know what I mean." Pree snorted and laughed hysterically at herself. "But wow! That dance was getting me all heated if ya know what I mean." I laughed as Pree fanned herself.

"Well you should, that is, think about considering it. He seems like a nice guy. I mean, even the way you guys just look at each other is something straight out of *Romeo and Juliet*, like when Leonardo DiCaprio first sees Claire Danes."

"Sara, you can't be serious."

"Oh my gosh, that was sooo romantic," Pree swooned.

"And then when you're around each other, like during that dance, I swear everyone could feel it too. My hair was on end, like I was touching a plasma ball! I've never seen you dance like that before. It was amazing. I've been telling you for years that you should let go and have more confidence with it. It's no wonder you got the duet spot."

I blushed, burying my face in some homework.

"For reals, Lid... You have real talent and the passion to match. Stop being so afraid to be you," Pree added.

"You should talk," I ragged, nudging Pree's shoulder.

"Welp, if you need any choreo inspiration, I'd love to teach you Raqs Sharqi sometime. Maybe you can add some of this curry spice into it." She laughed while doing a shimmy.

"Belly dancing? Pree, I would love that!" I laughed, looking up from the floor where I lay sprawled, flipping pages in my math text.

We were quiet for a little while, finishing our homework when Pree broke the silence. "So, what's really going on with you and Matt!"

Sara glanced at me and bit her lip as if debating what she wanted to say next.

"Just talk already, Sara," I prompted.

"OK, but don't get your panties all in a bunch. What would you say if I told you that Matt didn't just ask me to the dance? What if I told you that he also asked me to be his girlfriend?"

Pree and I both shrieked in happiness, nearly toppling Sara over as we hugged her.

I pulled back. "Why were you nervous to tell me?"

"It's just that after freshman year with Brandon, you've been kind of anti-relationships. You're always saying how pointless it is to date in high school because it doesn't last and how all high school boys just want one thing...yadda yadda yadda. I guess I just didn't want to hear anything negative about it."

"I'm so sorry if I made you feel that way." And I was. I never realized how my past had hindered even my friendships. "I'm super happy for you guys though. Matt is a great guy and of course, you're awesome. If anyone can make it work for the long haul, it'd be you guys. I'm just happy you're happy."

"Sheesh, you guys really know how to have a Hallmark

moment and make a girl get all teary eyed," Pree joked. "Now on to business. When are we going dress shopping?"

"What about Saturday?" Sara offered.

"I work, but I'm sure Bob would let me off early if I go in early."

"I wish you didn't have to work Liddy," Sara pouted.

"I don't mind it. It's good money and you guys know how badly I want my own car."

"OK, so we'll leave around lunchtime. Should we go to Woodfield or Northbrook Court?" Pree rattled off, as if checking boxes in her mental checklist.

"Woodfield since it has so many more unique dress shops," I suggested.

We spent another hour chatting and looking at dresses in magazines. Sara and I ripped out a few dress ideas, whereas Pree folded the corner down on just about every dress in *Seventeen, Cosmo Girl,* and *YM.* This was the first dance that Pree had a date for, I couldn't blame her for being excited.

"Singled Out's" theme song played on the T.V. *Wow, it's 5:30 already.* "Pree, we better head home. I'm sure dinner is ready and your mom is probably bugging."

"Oh, she totally is. She needs to take a chill pill," Pree scoffed.

Sara laughed. "See you tomorrow."

Christmas Rose

"**A**RE YOU SURE YOU DON'T WANT A RIDE HOME, GIRLS?"
Mama L. asked as I tied my black Doc Martens in her
foyer.

"I'm sure. Thanks though," I responded. Pree shot me a
dirty look and I shrugged back at her.

"OK, sweeties. Get home fast, it's cold out there."

"Have a good night," Pree responded, popping her
bubblegum pink hat on her head and flicking on her matching
scarf so it hit me in the face.

I ignored her goading and took a step to the side. I zipped
up my buttery-yellow puffy coat, pulled on my gloves, and
stepped outside.

"I hate this weather," I groaned as I pulled up my hood.

"Oh Liddy, spring break will be here before you know it.

Just think about all things warm, you know, like Will's body."
Pree licked her finger and as she pressed it to her bum, she
made a sizzle sound. "I know I am." She laughed and I joined
her.

"Watch for black ice," I cautioned when we reached the
driveway.

"Yes, mom," Pree teased.

As I walked, the icy wind made my eyes tear and pierced
my bones. "After graduation, I am so heading west towards
Arizona or even south to Florida."

"You're the one who dismissed Mama L.'s offer of a ride
home."

"Of course I would have liked a ride home. But come on,
she was busy making dinner."

"Whatever. Sometimes, you are just too nice."

"I can't help it. So, what are you going to tell your parents
about Will?"

"I'm going to simply tell them that we all talked and
decided to humor you by going stag. My mom heard you say
that this morning so I think she'll buy it."

"But, what about pictures?" I asked as we turned onto
Cherrywood Drive.

"Liddy, you're always such a worrier. I'll think of
something."

"I have no doubt you will," I giggled awkwardly, my face
half frozen.

We walked a few more paces and stopped before Pree's
white-washed brick house. Mrs. Parekh, her arms crossed in
protection from the cold drafts, frantically peered through the
glass storm door.

"Ugh, why is she such a worrywart?" Pree lamented. "Pray for me that I can handle her tonight, otherwise you may find me sleeping over." I laughed. Pree ran away to my house at least twice a month.

"Youuuuu...cannn...dooo it." My teeth chattered and I gave her a hug goodbye. I waved at Mrs. Parekh, turned, and walked past the seven houses it took to get to mine.

I passed three homes when suddenly, my chin stopped quivering. An energetic rush of blood heated me in seconds and my constricted muscles uncoiled. A subtle airy sensation plucked at my right shoulder as if someone tapped it, but no one was there. I walked faster. *My mind must be playing tricks on me.* I peeked out of my hood every few seconds to make sure no one followed me. I didn't want to be caught unawares like last night. My paranoia kicked and my body resumed shivering.

"Forget this," I said aloud and bolted, running the rest of the way. I glided into the safety of my front porch, yelling, "I made it!" *OW!* I clutched my ribs and immediately regretted the run.

Mickey, who happened to be inside walking past the front door, opened it, and laughed. "You're so weird."

"Bite me." I dropped my bag, carefully took off my coat, and hung it on the banister newel. Walking into the kitchen I inhaled deeply. "Yum, Mom! That smells great!" She made my favorite, mashed potatoes and meatloaf.

"Hi, Lydia. Dinner won't be ready for another thirty minutes. Got a late start tonight. How was Sara's?" Mom asked, not turning around while she poked potatoes and steamed green beans at the stove.

"Sara's was fine, just did homework and listened to music.

I'll be in my room. Call up when it's ready?"

"Sure thing, hun."

I snatched my bag and trekked upstairs. As I got to the top, Mickey jumped out from behind his door just off the landing and shrieked, "Ha!"

I screamed at a pitch higher than fireworks whistling to the sky and slipped down a few stairs. "Dang it, Mickey! Mom told you to stop scaring me!"

He burst into uncontrollable laughter as he slammed and locked his door, avoiding the beating I would have given him. *He's going to be responsible for my first grey hair, I just know it.*

I slammed my bedroom door and turned the bolt with a satisfying click. When Kylie left for college, Mom helped me paint it purple before I switched rooms. Dad had put a bolt on the door two years ago when Paige kept *borrowing* my stuff. Though my room was on the smaller side, it had become my own personal sanctuary. The all white bedding, canopy, and drapes my parents bought me for my last birthday made it feel a little like an island retreat.

I dropped my Jansport at the foot of my white desk and crawled onto my bed. Reaching for the cordless phone on my nightstand, I jumped when it rang.

"Hello?"

"Hey, Liddy."

"Justin?"

"Yeah. So, uh...thanks again for saying yes to me today."

"Of course. Thanks for asking me."

"I'm sorry again about what happened in the cafeteria. I hope you're OK."

"Let's just forget about it. Accidents happen," I said as I laid back down trying not to wince.

"Sure, that's very decent of you. Uh, about the dance. Can you, uh, just let me know what color your dress is when you pick it out? My mom wanted me to ask," Justin added.

I put my hand over the receiver, turned my head away, and snickered. That was sweet. "Of course."

"Cool." An awkward pause made me shift in my seat while I waited for him to continue. "Yeah, so I just wanted to say that you looked pretty today."

Yeah, right. I've never been good at accepting compliments and his little attempt at flirting surprised me. Since *that night* at the pool, Justin had remained safely tucked away in the friend zone. I was about to respond when I heard his mom yell something indiscernible in the background.

"Hey, I have to go, but I...I was...I was wondering who that guy was that I heard you danced with in ensemble?"

Why does word have to travel so fast? "That'd be Will. He's a friend and he just moved back here from Florida."

"Oh, OK. Just a friend."

"Lydia, dinner's almost ready! You've got ten minutes," Mom called from the bottom of the stairs.

"Hey, I have to get going, too."

"I'm glad we got to talk, Liddy. See you at your locker in the morning."

"OK, bye." I placed the phone on its receiver, snatched my pajamas and robe, and rushed into the shower. As the suds foamed on my hair, so did the anxious feelings. *Why was he gonna meet me at my locker in the morning? He never did that. Was he expecting we'd become more than friends now that I was his date to the dance? Why choose now to make it awkward?* I rinsed my hair, hoping my anxious thoughts would slip down the drain with the suds.

"So, can I borrow the van to go shopping with the girls Saturday?" I took another bite of potatoes.

"Sure, honey. Just be safe and make sure you are back before curfew," Dad cautioned.

Mom smiled wide, her eyes bright. "You work so hard and are such a good student. I want to buy your dress for you," she said as she placed another slice of meatloaf on Dad's plate.

"Thanks, Mom!" My parents weren't poor, but with two children in college and two more on their way, money was tight. "Oh, and I forgot to tell you! Guess who moved back and now goes to Wheeling with me? You guys remember Will?"

"Will who?" Dad asked.

"Jamison. He lived down the street, you know, in the house that's been empty since I can remember?"

Mom bit her lip and caught Dad's furrowed gaze. She raised her brows, clearly trying to tell Dad something from across the table, but he shook his head with the teeniest 'no'.

"What's with the look, guys?" I asked, confused by the sudden weirdness.

Dad cleared his throat. "Nothing honey, we just haven't heard you mention him in a very long time, that's all."

"If you say so," I responded. I didn't believe them, but until I knew more, I didn't want to rock the boat.

"They moved back in down the street you say." Mom

smiled, but it looked more like a grimace as she poured some two percent milk in her tea.

"No, I think he said he moved in with his uncle."

"I wonder who owns that house then. It's clear someone does since it's been so well maintained."

"I have no idea." And I really didn't. They posed a good question though. I would have to figure out a way to ask. "In any case, we were chosen in dance class by Coach R. to do a duet together in the Spring Showcase."

"A duet, Lydia, I'm so proud of you!" Mom gushed, tears welling in her eyes.

"Please don't make a big deal out of it," I said, relieved at the change of topic. "Can I please be excused? I have to get started on an English paper." With their nod of approval, I cleared my setting from the table, made my lunch for school, and headed upstairs. In my bag, I found the now crumpled paper flower that Will had given me. I tried to swallow the lump that had formed in my throat. I felt a small ripple of grief wash over me. Why had I jammed it into my bag? It was so thoughtful of him. I tried smoothing out the crinkles and wished I would have remembered how special the Christmas rose was to us sooner.

I partially dialed and hung up the phone at least five times. *What am I so nervous about? Maybe I'd be less anxious if I messaged him on AIM instead.* I put in my screen name and password and listened to the dial-up connection. *Darn it, busy signal!* I tried several more times, but each attempt resulted in an abrasive tone that taunted my nerves, saying: *call Will, call WILL, CALL WILL!*

"Liddy! It's garbage night. Can you please take it to the curb for me?" Mom called up, a much-welcomed disruption.

"Sure, Mom!" I hollered from the landing, not bothering to complain that Mickey should be the one doing it.

"I'll open the garage for you," Mom said as I slipped on my snow boots and bundled back up.

I braced myself and opened the front door. The frigid air shocked my lungs and my breath hitched. I hustled to the garage and rolled the heavy, over-stuffed bin to the curb. When Mom saw I was clear, she closed the garage again.

Before turning back to go in, I peered down the street at Will's empty home. Why had he left so suddenly without even saying goodbye? I know we were just kids, but he was old enough to at least write or call. From the moment Will moved on to Cherrywood Drive, we became best friends and every second of our time spent together. I loved that each winter, he would pick the white flowers near our sledding hill and give them to me. They were so beautiful, only blooming in the Winter despite the snow. On one of our trips to the library we discovered that they were called *Helleborus niger* or the Christmas rose. As the image of the last rose Will had given me faded, I realized I stood on the edge of his old driveway.

The moon, a few days shy of being full, cloaked the street in a luminous glow. *What the heck am I doing here?* I took a deep breath to try and alleviate the small ache in my chest. I knew I could zone out when focused sometimes, but it was so strange. Why would I forget Will, and Charlie for that matter, and only remember them now when Will returned? My subconscious tried to justify it—*you were just a kid; it's been a long time, and he's practically a man now*. But the ache my heart felt when his touch brought back my memories told me there was much more to this story, and I needed answers. How could his touch bring back my memories? *Is that even possible?* It wasn't logical or rational.

I closed my eyes and pressed my gloved hands to my face. My mind pictured today's events with Will. Each time he was with me, he was careful to avoid skin to skin contact. My heart nudged me towards the truth, but my mind couldn't process something so impossible. I removed my hands from my face and laughed at myself.

"I'm losing it," I said aloud to no one. I started to turn back towards home when I heard a breathy woman's voice call my name. The voice, soft and enticing, sounded distant. Lured by the coaxing song of my name, I made my way around the side of the dark house when I spotted them.

There, thriving at the edge of the window well, was a small garden of brilliant Christmas roses. Like the ones at the sledding hill so long ago, they glowed in the moonlight. Bending down to inspect them, the voice waned, and I felt the urge to grab one for Will. I don't remember making the decision, but I watched as my arm pulled back, fingers slowly curling into a fist. Before my brain could register the panic from my lack of control, I punched through the ice over the base of the flowers. After a moment, I scraped away the crushed ice. Wrapping my hand around the base of one of the flowers, I pulled, but it refused to budge. I felt out of control, a puppet on strings, surprising myself with frantic attempts at breaking loose a single rose. Again, and again, I punched and clawed, every hit sending further stabs of pain up my arm, scooping out the softer snow and finally hitting dirt. I wrenched at the flowers again, this time pulling a few with some roots and disrupting the now glittering, warm soil.

A muffled, sinister laugh echoed from beneath the earth. My mind screamed at me to run, but my muscles clenched so hard, they would spasm at any moment. My legs and arms were dead weight. I was a prisoner in my own body. I had heard that same laugh the night I saw the blood orange flash, the same night my best friend was ripped from me. I looked around to see where it was coming from, my eyes drawn back to the ground where I had dug at the flowers. *Wow, how had I dug so deep?* I looked at my hands. Dirt covered them and fresh blood pooled under my nail beds. Everything hurt. Beneath the patch of flowers, I noticed something bright white peeking from the disturbed dirt. So stark against the black soil, it seemed to radiate light. *What is that? A folded piece of paper?* No, more like a fancy envelope. It remained pure despite having been buried in black earth.

"Lydiaaaaa," the familiar ethereal voice purred once again. My hair stood on end and fire coursed through my veins. My body desperately tried to get away from it. My breaths came in short bursts. I told my body to *get up* and *run, run home!* I reached instead for the envelope. Another sound weakened the tug of the puppet master's invisible strings and made me pause. A faint bell-like song stirred memories from that night long ago. I closed my eyes. If I didn't control my breathing, I'd hyperventilate, and I didn't want to pass out here.

"Get it together, Lydia. There is no one here but you. Just take the flowers and go home." I spoke out loud in an effort to reassure myself. The chiming grew nearer, and the woman's voice now begged me to grab the envelope. My eyes snapped open and I saw that my fingers trembled as they reached for it.

"STOP! Don't touch it!" yelled a man's gravelly voice from

the shadows. I turned, but saw only a flash of icy blue light.

I awoke on my front lawn to Mom screaming my name from the front porch. It was snowing, which was weird because I could have sworn there hadn't been a cloud in the sky when I walked with Pree. Sitting bolt upright, I looked around and noticed that I had been laying in the indentation of a snow angel and right next to me were the Christmas roses. *How did I get here? Was I making snow angels? Where is the envelope?* I ripped my gloves off. My fingers were sore and the nails looked terrible. My heart sank. I hadn't been dreaming. The Christmas roses were right there, and my hands were jacked. My stomach clenched as adrenaline surged. I tried using my arms to get up but fell back, the soreness of them and the pain of my wrists biting.

"Lydia Andra! Get in here now!"

Crud! Mom would not like knowing that I heard voices again. *Think of an excuse.* "Sorry, Mom! Got carried away. You know how I love a fresh snowfall." I shot to my feet, looking up and down the street. A shadowy figure strode in the direction of Pree's house. Their silvery hair shone in the lamp light. I shivered and put my gloves back on to hide my hands from Mom.

"Lydia! Come on, it's late and I am not paying to heat the outside!" Mom bellowed, hands on her hips.

I bent down, grabbed the flowers, and booked it into my house. Not giving Mom a chance to lecture me further, I kicked off my boots and ran up the stairs. As my feet hit the landing, my phone rang. I briskly locked the door behind me, ripped off my gloves, and threw them at my desk.

"Hello?" I gasped, clutching my sore ribs.

"Liddy! I've been calling and calling. Are you OK?"

I would know the richness of that voice anywhere. "Will?"

"Yes, it's me. Are you OK?" he asked again more urgently.

I pinched myself. "Ow!"

"Lydia, what was that?" I couldn't speak. I knew I hadn't been dreaming and yet, I also couldn't tell what was real and what was fiction at this point. "Liddy...that's it, I'm coming over."

"Will, I'm fine. Don't come over. How...how did you...?" I couldn't seem to formulate a coherent sentence. One that would ask him how he got my number, how he knew something was wrong while at the same time hinting at how impossible that was.

"I got your number out of the student directory Jackie gave me." When I didn't respond he seemed to know what I was trying to ascertain. "I can't explain it, I just... I felt...like you were in trouble or something."

I didn't know how to respond to that.

"Liddy, please say something."

The thudding in my chest was the only thing I could hear. I closed my eyes, took a deep breath, and let it out over a handful of heartbeats. "Will, I'm OK. Can we maybe talk about this tomorrow?"

"Of course. Is my place OK?"

"That sounds great," I responded, but my mind was on overdrive. How could I tell someone I heard voices and not sound like I lost my mind? The fact that Will openly admitted that he knew something happened freaked me out further. This was all overwhelming.

"Are you sure you are safe, not hurt?"

"Yes." I huffed as I shrugged out of my jacket.

"Alright then, see you tomorrow. Oh, and Liddy?"

"Yes?"

"I..." He trailed off, a long few seconds passing before he continued. "Have a good night."

She's Back

"**L**YDIA, MY DEAR. THIS WAY," the angelic voice beckoned to me.

"I can't see," I called back as I took small steps. I tried to find something to grasp in the pitch black, but the smooth, damp walls provided no such help.

"Oh, I am so sorry. Here, let me help." In a matter of seconds, a warm amber glow filled the space. I had come to the end of a tunnel. In front of me was a small circular room with five passages tunneling from it like the spokes of a wheel. The ceilings in the round room were so high, I couldn't tell where they ended.

"Hello!" I called out, tiptoeing into the room. Silence. *Weird, where is the echo?*

The serene voice giggled. "Follow the light to me, sweetie."

The leftmost tunnel emitted an amber glow, so I hustled towards it. After a few moments, the light guided me left again into a shorter passage, then followed with a right. This final tunnel dragged on forever, the light fading with each step. Just as I reached its end, the amber light disappeared altogether, leaving me in darkness. My heart sped up.

"What happened to the light?" I yelled, my voice quivering, reluctant to proceed. A faint emerald glow appeared in front of me. Encouraged, I continued walking and emerged into another circular room. I stood before a large set of double doors encrusted with marcasite jewels. I marveled at how the black stones sparkled, just like snow under moonlight. The emerald light emanated from the cracks and crevices around the silver-plated frame and down the center where the doors met, pulsing as I drew near. My fingertips grazed the cool, elegant handle. My gut prickled with caution and I hesitated. That brief moment of stillness hummed with energy and I couldn't shake the feeling that I wasn't alone. The light reflected off several pairs of small orbs that disappeared back into the shadows and reappeared with each blink. My breath hitched when I realized the orbs were eyes, watching me. I frantically pulled the doors open and entered a stark room. An ethereal figure sat perched on an elaborate throne, her white gown in direct contrast to the chair's tufted wine fabric.

"I'm so glad you could join me, Princess." The most gorgeous woman I'd ever seen rose, gracefully shifting the train of her dress that draped from her chair and down the few stairs leading to the smooth slate floor. She smiled at me as she placed her hand on one of the oddly familiar flowers carved into the throne's silver leafed frame. Flower carvings stretched into a canopy over the throne. I rubbed my eyes. I could have sworn they stirred at her touch. She giggled.

My eyes were drawn back to the woman. "Are you an angel?" I whispered, enthralled by her beauty.

She erupted into laughter. This time I couldn't deny what I saw. The flowers twinkled and moved in rhythm with the slight shake of her slender body. "Thank you. It's been a long time since I've laughed like that. You must excuse my manners. I am Mara, and I am not an angel," she said as she crossed her right arm over her chest. Bowing, her platinum hair draped across her white, feathered gown.

"Nice to meet you. I'm Liddy."

"Correction. You are Princess Lydia, and quite the celebrity to boot." She snapped her fingers.

A spotlight shone down on me. Glittery purple dust floated and swirled around me like a flurry of star-lit snow. Within seconds, a purple gown adorned my body and something heavy pressed uncomfortably into my scalp. I reached up and pulled off an ornate crown encrusted with jewels and pearls. At the flick of Mara's wrist, it was forced from my hands back to my head and I curtsied at the swish of her fingers. My stomach knotted and twisted, demanding that I back out of the door. I loathed her intrusion into my mind and puppeteering of my body.

An almost imperceptible darkness crossed Mara's brilliant sea-green eyes and her cheek twitched. "You are fine. I am not here to hurt you. I just want to talk." Her voice exuded calm and I relaxed a little. "That-a-girl." She smiled, her pink-champagne lips curled up, accentuating her perfect cheekbones. "Have a seat." She sat back down and with another flick of her hand, something dark raced out of the shadows, bringing me a steel, high-back chair before the blur scurried back to where it came from.

I sat, a coldness creeping through my body, yet another warning to get the heck out of there. Something about this place didn't add up. The dark surroundings didn't match their angelic mistress.

"Princess, I see that your William has entered back into your life. I'm grateful. It means I get to speak with you again."

"Again?" I stammered.

"Oh, dear. Please don't tell me you have completely forgotten about all of our little visits when you were younger. That would make me so sad. I've gone through a lot of trouble to be able to speak with you." She drummed her silver nails on the arm of her throne.

"So, my dreams when I was little, those were...real? I wasn't just imagining all of it or hearing voices?"

"Of course not! I am very real, I assure you."

"What does Will have to do with it?"

"You poor thing. Has no one told you how special you and William are? Your people of Cristes would be so happy to have you both there."

"Cristes?"

A look of sincere shock crossed her creamy complexion. The flowers hummed green. A few heartbeats passed before she regained her composure and the flowers went dark. "What *do* you know, Lydia?"

"I guess not much."

She stood with force and turned. "Ugh! How selfish they can be, even locked in Mortalia!" she yelled to herself as she threw her hands up. Fear struck me like a punch in the gut as I watched a few white feathers from her gown flit to the ground.

"I should be going. I'm sure my parents are looking for me."

Mara brought her arms down and looked back over her shoulder at me. "I apologize for my outburst. I never believed that my efforts from when you were a child could be so easily erased." She sat back down annoyed, dropping her head into her hand. "I assume this was Nicholas' doing."

"Nicholas? I'm sorry. I don't know him." My veins pulsed at my temples and neck. Beads of sweat trickled down the nape of my spine to the small of my back.

"Interesting. Well dearie, we don't have a lot of time to catch you up, but I guess I could give you a reason for all of this. You are *Princess* Lydia Erickson of Cristes. Though some debate that, I have no doubt. Prince William Jamison is your betrothed. It is prophesied that once united, you two will save and restore Cristes to its former glory, blah, blah, blah."

"Betrothed? Save Cristes...from what?"

"Why, from me Princessss," she hissed.

I stood with an overwhelming desire to flee. But a new, warming sensation drizzled over me and charmed my mind into wanting to fight back.

She cackled. "What a pathetic waste of such gifting. Such a shame that a natural-born warrior doesn't even know how to wield their own power. I'm afraid your loved ones have left you woefully unprepared to fight me. You will not win." Her voice, now shrill, pierced my eardrums. I clamped my hands over my ears and backed away. Scampering noises sounded from behind, reminding me of the eyes lurking in the shadows that engulfed most of the room. I froze.

"None of you move! She is mine! How humiliating it must be that you don't even get to know what you are dying for."

I needed to stall her. "So, can't you afford a few more moments to just tell me?" I pleaded.

"You weak creature. I wish I could, but I've waited long enough... I could at least show you my true form, not this apparition of the fragile girl I once was."

The emerald light transitioned into a pickled green as Mara's platinum hair burned to floating ash. Her once bright, big eyes fell back into their sockets, revealing bottomless pits. I heard high pitch screaming and scanned the room feverishly for the victim of torture before realizing I was the one shrieking. My fear seemed to ignite her efforts. Coal-black shadows extended from her eyes, threatening to grab me and drag me back to her. The glittering eyes all around me whimpered.

"Silence!" she hissed. "It's nothing personal, Princess. It's just that I should be next in line to be Queen, not you. If he hadn't..." She trailed off, a single blood-red tear dripped from the corner of her dark eye socket. Shuffling backward, I dared not take my eyes off of her and watched the tear as it traced down her cheek. Her lips swirled from champagne to marcasite with the touch of the bloody tear.

"Make this easy on yourself, Lydia. I promise it will be painless." She held out her slender arms. I watched in horror as deep-green veins sprawled all over her creamy skin, creeping like a time-lapsed video of weeds growing after a rainy day.

My body moved towards her. "No!" I screamed, planting my feet in an attempt to stop myself.

She cackled again as my feet continued to slide over the

smooth surface of the cavern towards her.

"Fine, have it your way," she threatened. Her silver nails transformed into claws, the now red nails sharp as knives.

Fear threatened to drown me, and an intense rush of heat swarmed my body. A spear of light burst from me, a straight shot through Mara's chest, breaking her hold on me. I bolted towards the doors, but they slammed shut.

"That was unexpected," Mara wheezed. "I guess you are stronger than I thought. I won't make that mistake again." She limped towards me. I turned around and banged desperately on the doors. They refused to budge. I could feel her close, too close. Whipping around, I pressed my back into the doors. She was right in front of me, her eyes no longer gaping sockets but a vibrant orange.

"Please," I begged. "I've done nothing to you."

"Not yet, you haven't." Mara smirked and reached for me. "I'll get straight to the heart of the matter." Just before her red-tipped talons touched my left breast, the door opened. I fell back and it slammed shut. A loud banging rattled the doors. The last thing I remembered, before everything went black, was the witch's infuriated shriek.

Drinking the Warmth

I WOKE GASPING FOR BREATH. A bead of sweat trickled down the base of my neck and followed the curve of my spine, soaking into the elastic of my flannel pants. I slammed my hand down on the blaring alarm clock. It had taken me forever to fall asleep as my mind refused to get off the merry-go-round. Over and over again a woman's angelic voice hailed my name, a familiar bell chime, a faceless figure who yelled at me to stop, and then a call from Will because he *felt* I was in danger. But all that was nothing compared to the nightmare I'd just fought to wake from.

Now that I was up, I couldn't recall details of the dream except for one: *she wanted to kill me.* I shook my head as if that would rid the image of her from my mind, the face of a witch etched in hatred and pain. *Why is this witch haunting my dreams?* Shivering, I dragged myself out of bed and quickly dressed. I didn't care to spend time on my hair. So up it went in a messy bun with a few pieces remaining down to frame my face. After the second round of concealer, I resigned myself to the fact that nothing would hide the puffiness under my eyes.

It was Mom's turn to drive us all to school this morning. "Mom! We've gotta leave in ten minutes!" I shouted from the banister. Mom had no concept of time. I can't blame her though. She was always doing a million things at once and most of it was for everyone else.

"Thanks, Lydia!" she yelled back. Mom's kitchen chair scraped across the floor as she scuttered about the kitchen. I left the hall and returned to my room when Mickey emerged from his. His hair stuck out all over and he slumped down the stairs.

"Hey, Mickey," I said before I got into my room.

He grunted in acknowledgment.

I untied my robe; my ribs, though still bruised, were not nearly as sore this morning. I tugged on my fitted, red turtleneck, slipped into my soft yoga pants and headed to the front door.

I had just reached the foyer when Mom rounded the corner with my lunch bag. She paused for a moment, her right arm hugging herself as the back of her left hand rested just under her chin. Tears welled in her eyes.

"What's wrong, Mom?" I asked while lacing up my Sketchers.

"Don't mind me. I am so proud of the woman you are becoming. I can't believe how fast the time has gone." Mom wiped her tired eyes. She was a beautiful woman. Even behind her disheveled appearance, it was impossible to miss her electric smile and youthful cheekbones. She cared enough to try to be part of each of our lives, always willing to talk or help.

"Mom, what the heck? No crying!" I protested.

"Alright, alright, I am done with the mushy stuff," Mom agreed as she fanned the air in front of her face with her now mittened hands. "Let's go."

We picked up Sara, Dani, and Pree before heading off to school. Mom always blasted music whenever she drove us to school and today wasn't any different. We all sang along at the top of our lungs to *All I Want for Christmas is You* and arrived at school with ten minutes to spare. On the way to our lockers, Dani revealed that Alex had called last night to ask her to the Winter Formal.

A.J., a senior who I'd had a few classes with over the years, leaned against my locker. He was well known as the editor of our school newspaper and yearbook, but we'd never hung out. He groomed the spikes of his hair with one hand and clutched some papers to his chest in the other. A small crowd formed around him and, when they spotted me, fell silent. Alex was propped against the wall directly opposite my locker, a smirk on his face.

"Good morning, everyone," I said, uncertain of what to make of this little gathering.

"Hey, Liddy, can I talk to you for a sec? I wanted to show you something." A.J. handed me some computer paper, folded in half, that still had the perforated edges attached. I dropped my bag at my feet and opened them. I observed the bold red and blue names alternating on the left side of the paper; a chat over AIM between ajWHSeditor in red and curvygrl82 in blue. My eyes followed the conversation, my three best friends reading over my shoulder.

curvygrl82: Hey, you're A.J. Payne, right?

ajWHSeditor: Yes, I am. Do I know you?

curvygrl82: Aw, don't tell me you don't know who I am. That hurts my feelings.

ajWHSeditor: I'm sorry?

curvygrl82: It's me, Liddy.

ajWHSeditor: Liddy Erickson? But this isn't her screen name.

curvygrl82: Yeah, felt it was time. My other one was so lame. After all, I did choose it in seventh grade.

ajWHSeditor: I didn't think it was lame. What's up?

curvygrl82: I know I can be annoying... Annoyingly shy LOL. It's easy to talk to you on here. Easy to tell you things, things I'm way too shy to ever say to you in person. Promise me you will act like nothing ever happened between us on here when you see me next. I want to tell you something.

ajWHSeditor: On or off the record? I promise to keep your identity as a source a secret.

curvygrl82: Off the record, definitely off.

ajWHSeditor: OK, I'm all ears.

curvygrl82: Well, I wanted to get off my chest (sorry, they aren't real) that I like you and I've had a big, fat crush on you since Freshman year.

ajWHSeditor: Weren't you with Brandon then?

curvygrl82: Since Brandon, there has only been one boy to cross my mind and my dreams.

curvygrl82: It's been a long time for me, and I want you. In my dreams, I now imagine you doing things to me that Brandon used to. For example, when he'd...

A graphic description forced me to stop reading. I sucked

in a breath, choking on the rush of air and attempted to hide it behind a throat-clearing cough. I calmly folded and placed the printout in my bag. I would burn it later. Mortified, I rose to my fullest height and stared A.J. in the face.

"That was not me," I said matter-of-factly. "That was *not* me," I said again, louder to the rest of the onlookers, my hands vibrating.

Alex looked disappointed, like he had hoped some of those words could have been a true, alluring secret about me.

"I know. I know," A.J. responded, taking a few steps back, his hands up in surrender. "If you had read the rest, you would have seen that I only pretended to think it was you for so long before I started pressing them, hoping to trick them into revealing who they were."

"A.J., that's really decent of you. Any luck finding out who it was?" I asked.

"No luck. I so wish they would have cracked. It would have made a great front-page story, but they spooked when I started asking too many questions. If I ever find out who it was, I will smear them all over the paper for impersonating a peer."

"You don't need to do that," I insisted.

"Believe me, I do. This is a perfect example of just how dangerous chat rooms are. You can't be too careful talking to people on there. See how easy it was for this person to just create any name they wanted and say they were you?"

"I guess you're right. Thanks for letting me know."

"No problem." I watched A.J. and his friends travel across the lobby towards the commons.

"You OK, girl?" Sara asked.

"Not really. It's been a crappy week." My blood boiled.

"Babe, go on without me. I'm going to stay with Liddy," Sara said as she touched Matt's shoulder.

"No, you're not, Sara. What happened is horrifying, but I'll be alright. You can console me at lunch."

"Are you sure?"

"Yes, I promise."

Sara gave me a tight hug before placing her arm in Matt's and walking off.

"I'm going to join Sara!" Pree spotted Will glide past the cut through and ran after him.

Dani stuck around for a minute. "Lid, I will help you find out who did this and then we're gonna have a little chat of our own with them," she said, flicking her shoulder-length hair. She may look innocent with her locks flipped out and part in a zigzag, but she could take anyone down in a hot minute.

"Thanks, Dani. I'm blessed by your friendship and loyalty." I grew quiet trying to imagine what I could have done to encourage someone to do that.

"Stop it," Dani ordered.

"Stop what?" I asked, confused.

"Stop thinking about how this could somehow be your fault. Even if you were the biggest biotch on the planet, it still wouldn't have made it right."

"I just wonder who is that angry with me."

"You mean jealous. Well, that's not hard. It's Jackie."

"You think?"

"Uh, yeah," Dani scoffed. "She's never forgiven you since Brandon dumped her for you." I hadn't known Brandon did that until after we started dating. "What did he say again to you our first week at school?"

"'I didn't really date anyone my entire freshman year because I've been waiting for you to get here.' That one?" I responded. As a freshman I had no reason not to believe him. I didn't even know who Jackie was.

"Yeah that was it, that manipulative jerk. I just don't understand why Jackie blames you and not Brandon. He did the same thing to you the following summer."

"Just leave it alone, Dani. Thanks to A.J., everyone will know it's not me."

"Yeah, *this* time, but next time that may not be the case. It's not cool Liddy, not cool."

"OK, fine. If I ever get proof it is Jackie, I will let you know, and you can come with me when I talk to her." I sighed in resignation since I knew Dani would never live it down. Satisfied, she gave me a hug.

I closed my locker and jumped. "Justin! I didn't see you there."

"I've been here the whole time." He gave me a half smile.

"You were here for that heinous show?" I grimaced.

"I admit that I was a little intrigued as to why there were so many guys at your locker, but I was here because we had plans to meet here this morning, remember?"

"Oh my gosh! I'm sorry. I guess I forgot thanks to that whole scene. Walk me to class?" I could see that he wanted to ask me something, but we only had a few minutes before the bell rang.

"Sure thing." He beamed.

We walked down the hall, following the cut through Sara and Pree had taken. I saw Pree and Will still talking by his locker and decided to introduce the guys to each other. "Sorry to interrupt," I cut in. "Justin, this is my friend Will. Will, this is Justin."

"What's up, dawg?" Justin asked a little too loudly.

Will smiled. Will had at least three inches and twenty pounds more muscle than Justin, which was saying something since Justin's one of the most cut guys at Wheeling. Will offered his hand and Justin took it. "Nice to meet you."

"Justin's gonna walk with us to history," I chimed in. "Pree, are you coming?"

"Sure!" she squeaked.

When we arrived at history, Pree gave Will a drawn-out goodbye. After she gave me a quick hug, she skipped off to chemistry. Will gave a short wave and ducked into the classroom leaving me alone with Justin.

"Thanks for walking me to class, Justin. See ya later." Justin stepped forward, blocking my path to the classroom. "Everything OK, Justin?"

"Yes, I just wanted to—" Justin stepped forward and wrapped his arms around me *and* my backpack. My arms were awkwardly pinned at my sides, unable to return the gesture.

He cleared his throat. "See ya, Liddy."

I walked into class just in time to catch Will watching me. He quickly turned back towards the projector and studiously copied down notes. I had hoped today would be better, but A.J.'s revelation was the cannonball that sunk it. I didn't have the energy to patch the gaping hole.

Today, I played the role of perfect student engrossed in lessons and work to avoid my friends and peers. At the end of each class, I became a sloth while packing my bag. My deliberate movements helped me to avoid the crowded halls, especially Will. That ensured me a break from the murderous gaze of lionesses on their hunt to capture him. I even skipped lunch and just hung out in the empty biography section of the library to ensure my privacy. I just needed to get through the day and get to Will's so we could talk in private. My questions from yesterday lingered, unanswered. All I could think about was Will. He seemed to know so much about me. Things he shouldn't.

By seventh period, the looming dance class set my nerves aflame. I didn't think I could stomach another dance with Will. The onslaught of repressed memories. The questioning glances about my intentions with him. Coach with the dramatics again. Thankfully, dance was actually yoga today. Coach R. felt we all needed to chill.

"Lid," Will said in a soft, but concerned voice. I hadn't realized he'd caught up with me. His voice pulled me out of my mental fog. He grabbed my hand and saved me from bumping into students who converged in the hall as we all walked towards our respective locker rooms. His touch radiated a warmth that brought a contented smile to my face, a pleasant surprise compared to the intrusion of images and memories his touches brought yesterday. When my eyes found his, I righted myself as he asked again, "Are you sure you're OK?"

"I'm just a little tired you know, from..." I trailed off. I didn't want anyone to overhear. "Guess I just zoned out."

"All right then," Will stated, one heavy brow slanted in strong disbelief, as he stepped back and crossed his arms. "Would you prefer to meet at your locker or mine after dismissal?"

I shut my eyes and visualized each locker, methodically

LAURA DETERING

mapping whose was closest.

"We'll meet at your locker," I reasoned, trying to sound chipper. "It's closer to the parking lot."

Will laughed. "Of course. Efficiency wins."

I stuck my tongue out at him and then giggled. "I'm sorry. I can't help who I am."

"Exactly, nor should you." Will smirked, retreating backward through the guy's locker room door as I walked into the girls.

After changing, I hurried back to the junior hallway, excited that the day was over with no more surprises to report. I attributed the shaky feeling I had to skipping lunch, but quite possibly, it had more to do with my curiosity and angst at seeing Will's house. Not to mention, I'd be alone with him. I yanked down hard on my combination lock. *Shoot! I* checked my nails. *Thank goodness.* The purple nail polish I applied last night still hid the cracked nails and remaining bits of dried blood too deep under the nail beds to clean.

I eyed the paper lunch bag sitting at the bottom of my locker. It held the Christmas roses I picked last night. Shivers wormed down my spine just thinking about how I got them. This morning, I debated not bringing them. I wanted to show Will I remembered his sweet, childhood gestures. Then again, he could think I'm a total dork. Sentimentality won out in the end. I gripped the paper bag, slammed my locker, and swung my Jansport over my shoulder. A loud "oomph!" filled my ears. I had decked Justin with my backpack square in the gut.

"Sorry, Justin! I didn't see you there." *Again. What the heck was he doing back at my locker anyway?*

"It's...tight...Liddy," he stammered out between gasps

while holding his stomach. "I guess I...deserve that after... yesterday." He smiled, though it was tight on the edges. It was obvious he was in pain. "Where are you off to in such a hurry?"

"I was trying to catch up with my ride."

"Don't you always go home with Sara? She wouldn't leave without you. I was going to ask..."

"Dang it! I haven't even told Sara I wasn't going home with her! I've gotta run! Sorry again!"

I booked it to Sara's locker. I only made it halfway down the hall before stumbling upon Sara and Matt enthralled in a very flirtatious conversation. He leaned in to kiss her! His lips lingered on her cheek. I slowed down to give them more time to say goodbye. When I reached Sara, Matt had just left and she was swooning, clearly over the moon.

I smiled at her as I walked up. "Welcome back to Earth," I giggled.

"Welcome back to you. You're the one who has been M.I.A. all day."

Pretending not to hear her, I asked, "Did I just see Matt turn the corner?"

"He finally kissed me," she marveled, grey eyes sparkling.

"I can't wait to hear all the details," I replied.

"OK, let's go. My mom should be here soon."

"I'm so sorry I forgot to tell you, but I'm going home with Will."

Sara's eyebrows shot up.

"You're going to Will's?" Pree squeaked in my ear.

"Dang! Pree, you scared me. You can't sneak up like that. And yes, I'm going to Will's," I responded. Sara and Pree eyed each other, like they communicated telepathically. "Stop that.

I'm just going so we can work on our English paper. Hey, this will give you two the opportunity to work on the assignment too."

"True," Pree said, deflated.

"Pree, I am not interested in Will in that way, remember? We're just friends," I reassured her, even though I wasn't exactly confident in what we were to each other. It's true that we were close as kids, best friends even, but that had been eight years ago. Now, these new feelings? They shot through me, all too tempting and intimidating. I'd promised myself just before sophomore year that I wouldn't get involved in *that way* with any guy for the duration of high school. Was I so easily swayed?

"I didn't think that," Pree answered a little too quickly. "I mean he's cute and you would have first dibs and all since, well, whatever you two got going on, but that's not what I was saying."

I didn't quite believe her. Even though I didn't want to lay any claims to Will, I selfishly didn't want anyone else to have him either. I gave Pree a quick hug. "No worries. We'll talk later." The hall had cleared out when I caught Will gazing my way, not doing a good job of paying attention to Wheeling High's most admired ambassador, Jackie. *What an oxymoron.*

Will was at the very end of the hallway, leaning against his locker looking like a GQ model. *Why was he still staring at me and not her?* I approached him cautiously. I didn't want to give Jackie any more ammo against me. The nearer I got to him, the more rapid my heartbeat fluttered. Will stiffened just enough so I could see the slightest outline of his muscles through his thin pullover as the material stretched. Jackie noticed his lack of focus as he smiled at me. She stood on her tiptoes, her bright yellow sneakers creasing, and caressed his cheek attempting to regain his attention. Will caught her hand and brought it down and away from his cheek. I could see his lips move and Jackie pouted. She attempted to give him a hug, but his gaze was on me. Jackie stomped off, but not before she narrowed her eyes at me. Will wrapped me in a hug when I got near enough and all my tension from Jackie's small threat melted away.

"Hey, Liddy," Will said, his temple pressing to my head. I didn't move away. Instead, I squeezed him a little, accepting the greeting. "Are you ready to go?"

I nodded before we walked toward the student parking lot, doing my best not to give into the temptation of lacing my fingers through his. *Control yourself, girl. You are just friends.* I moved a few inches away from him right before pushing open the door. We reached the parking lot and my foot slipped out from under me on black ice. Will caught me around the waist, cradling me in his left arm with minimal effort. I couldn't keep my cheeks from burning.

He steadied me, cautious of my ribs though they didn't really hurt, and offered his arm for me to take. "There's some black ice out here. Mind if I see you to my car?"

I giggled. "Do you have to be so formal?"

"On the contrary, it's not formal. Haven't you ever heard of chivalry?"

"Heard of it, yes. Seen it? No."

"Well, let me be the one to show you how it's done." His smile revealed perfect teeth. "I'm parked over there." Will pointed to the end of the next row over.

Halfway to his car, Jackie's bright yellow mustang came speeding down the aisle. It slowed down just enough for one of the Double Dees in the back to yell, "Slut!" from the open window. A supersized styrofoam cup flew out the window. I hadn't zipped my coat. Blue Slurpee exploded as the cup smashed against my chest. I could feel the frozen slush as it seeped through the knitted holes of my favorite red sweater, onto my bra and stomach. I started towards Jackie's car as the group of girls laughed, but Will held me back, his eyes wide.

"Bye, 'curvy girl'!" Jackie jeered and peeled off. I advanced again.

"It's not worth it. It's *not* worth it," he repeated, thwarting my efforts by stepping in front of me, arms outstretched. "Let's just get to my car. You can get cleaned up at my house."

"Fine," I hissed, steam escaping my ears. As we approached his car, I instantly forgot about the cold Slurpee that had made its way through my bra. In front of me was a vintage, limited edition, Jeep Wagoneer. The outside was white with real wood paneling. Will opened the passenger door for me. I closed my jacket and climbed in. As he walked to the driver's side, I glanced around. The inside was just as cool as the outside. Almost every inch of the dash and ceiling were covered in wood veneer.

"Cool car," I said to him as he got in.

"Thanks, it was a gift from my Uncle when I got here. It can drive in all types of terrain so it's perfect for here or even Florida."

"Florida?" I asked, surprised.

"Yes. For when I visit my parents."

"Oh, that's right. Hammock Dunes. Where is that?"

"It's a small community in the North East of Florida, near Palm Coast. You'd like it."

"How I'd love to spend spring break somewhere warm," I sighed, closing my eyes and picturing the sun warming my skin.

"I'm planning on visiting my family then. You should join me."

I popped my eyes open. "Don't tease me."

Will stopped at the red light at the school's exit and turned to me. "I'm being serious," he persisted.

"For one, I don't think my parents would go for it. For another, I'm not sure I can afford to miss work, I've been trying to save for a car."

"Well, the invitation never expires. I know you would love it and I'd love to show you around."

We were quiet for a few minutes as I took in the direction we traveled down Elmhurst Road.

"So, what was that all about in the parking lot?" Will asked.

"Let's just say they don't like me very much."

"Seems a little extreme for just not liking someone."

"I agree, but I can't pretend to understand Jackie and her little minions. I mean, who would ever think the name *Double Dees* was a good idea for your girl squad?" I mocked.

"Seriously? That's their name?" Will responded, cocking an eyebrow.

"Yeah, don't ask. I'm surprised you didn't see the name on the back of her shirt, 'Double Dee #1'. I will venture that Jackie likes you and that she wasn't too thrilled to see us together. What was she doing at your locker anyways?"

"She was asking me to the dance. I told her I was going with Pree. Then she wanted to go grab a bread bowl sometime, but I told her I was going to be tied up working with you on projects."

"You didn't," I moaned.

"Why, did I do something wrong?" Will asked, innocently.

"Sort of, but it's not your fault. You don't know the back story."

"Well, whatever it is, it seems pretty immature."

"Immature is Jackie's middle name. She's hated me since freshman year. I try to stay out of her way. However, the crud she pulled today is a first."

The muscles of his jaw flexed and relaxed. "Are you OK?" Will reached over and grabbed my hand.

"I'll get over it. I just have to make it 'til the end of the year when she graduates." I yawned and snuggled into the grey and navy flannel part of the bench seat. I rested my head on the window, gazing at the heavy grey sky, and closed my eyes.

Promise

SOMETHING TICKLED THE BACK OF MY HAND. "We're here," Will murmured.

"We are?" I answered groggily. I sat bolt upright. "I mean, already?"

Will continued drawing letters on the back of my hand and chuckled. "You fell asleep. I didn't have the heart to wake you right away, so I figured I'd let you nap for a little bit."

"I'm so sorry!"

"It's cool. It's only been like twenty minutes."

"Twenty minutes! What have you been doing this whole time?"

Will's cheeks turned the slightest shade of coral. "Would it be creepy if I said watching you?"

"Yes."

"Then good thing I wasn't," he responded, light-heartedly turning off the car and tossing the book he was reading in the back seat.

We were silent for several, long breaths before I broke it. "I'm so sorry. I feel so stupid. Honestly, I got like no sleep last night."

"Nightmares again?"

"How did you—?"

Will cut me off, the iris of his eyes sparking green. "Yeah, about that. We are definitely going to talk, but first, let's get you inside so I can grab you a change of clothes and some food. Then I'll show you around. Wait here for a sec."

Will jogged around to open my door. *Could he be any more perfect?* I marveled. *Focus, Liddy.* Even if I was open to dating, I doubt he'd want to be with me considering the *wonderful* reintroduction to myself I'd given him over the past thirty-six hours.

I stepped out of the car onto a light gray, stone-paver driveway. I looked back in the direction we'd come from, a long drive stretched endlessly, trees hugging its outline. It curled up to the house in a circular drive complete with a water fountain in its center.

"See the tree lines up there?" Will pointed. I looked out at the flat, snow covered grounds that extended a few acres before a massive forest walled the property in.

"It's beautiful," I responded.

"Everything beyond those trees is protected lands, ten acres in any direction from the house. My uncle owns all of it and no one can build within ten miles of his house." We had parked off to the left side of the home in front of the four-car garage. The house, equally massive and beautiful, glistened with its clean, whitewashed brick. As we walked towards the house—scratch that—mansion, I noticed a balcony right above the covered porch entrance. The front entry had two oversized wreaths adorned with large red bows. I smelled their warm, earthy fragrance from the bottom of the steps. Just before we got to the knotted-wood, double entry doors, they flung open. A gangly, yet handsome, middle-aged man, groomed to perfection with every salt and pepper hair in precise place, stood ready to greet us.

"Good afternoon, Master William," he said, crossing his arm over his chest and bowing. I'd never heard an accent quite like his before, not-quite-British and lilting. I couldn't place it.

"Nolan, how many times do I have to ask? Please call me Will."

"My apologies, Master Will."

Will dragged his hand down his face. "Nolan, this is my friend, Liddy."

"Good afternoon, Madam Liddy," Nolan said as he gave a slight bow. Behind his heavy framed specs, his hazel eyes lingered on my stained sweater. I fought the urge to close my coat again.

"I'm going to find something for Liddy to change into. Do you mind if I bring you her sweater so we can get it cleaned up for her?"

"Of course, Master William. Ring for me straight away when it's ready. There are snacks laid out for you in the kitchen." Nolan smiled wide, softening the chiseled contours of his face. I could swear his eyes even twinkled.

"Thanks, Nolan." Will said as he grabbed my hand and

guided me through a speedy tour that would lead us to the kitchen. The foyer, with its wood inlaid ceiling, opened up into an atrium. Plush velvet couches lined the large rectangular room. A balcony encircled the upper level where frosted garland with glittering pinecones and twinkle lights hung. The ceiling gave the illusion of extending to the sky with its exposed white beams that crisscrossed below numerous skylights.

I caught him watching me; he looked like he suppressed a laugh. "What's so funny?" I asked.

"Nothing. It's just... You should just see your face." He struggled to keep his composure.

"Can you blame me? Look at this place!" My face reddened. "Just how many doors are there?" I gestured to the numerous archways that opened into the dining room, another living room, and a library.

"I may have seen it once or twice," he teased. "It's no big deal. It's just a house and I've never counted. You can blink and close your mouth now." He laughed, unrestrained.

Normally, I would have joined him. But today, his laugh pushed me over the edge. My eyes stung; their salty tears threatened to expose my weaknesses. As my throat tightened, so did the walls around my aching heart and as they squeezed, my vision blurred. I blinked rapidly, but it was no use. The tears flowed hot and fast.

"I'm sorry, Liddy! Please don't cry."

"I didn't mean to," I sniffled and quickly swiped my cheeks as I turned from him.

"I was just teasing."

"It's just been a wild few days. Plus, I haven't eaten since breakfast. I guess it's all gotten to me a little more than I thought," I said, my back still to him.

Will closed the gap between us, turned me, encasing me in a secure hug. I half-heartedly tried to pull away. He loosened his arms and offered me the chance to leave his warm embrace. When I didn't move, he enveloped me once more. After a moment, I snuggled into his chest and wrapped my arms around his waist, allowing myself a moment of vulnerability with him. He'd been gone for so long, but right now, in this moment, I was afraid to get too attached yet at the same time fearful of letting go in case he disappeared again. While my mind warred with my heart, I let my body drink in his warmth and relaxed with each stroke of my hair. Will cupped my chin, deflecting my ability to retreat. He broke through a layer of my walls leaving me unsettled. Raw emotions streamed down my face. It had been a long time since I'd let anyone other than my parents witness such a private and vulnerable moment.

I tried to look away, but Will persisted, not letting go of my chin. His eyes locked on mine, drawing me in as he whispered, "You didn't deserve any of that today. You are beautiful, caring, gifted, and more special than you know." Will released my chin and joined his fingers with mine.

My breath caught as we just stood there, my body shaking. After a few, pattering heartbeats, Will stepped back and I exhaled.

"I think some food may lift your spirits. Let's grab some and head upstairs to my room. I'm sure you want to change out of that wet sweater. We have some much needed catching up to do. I am sure you have a lot of questions."

My heart continued to flutter even after he let go of my hand. He balanced a cheese and fruit tray in one hand and grabbed a couple of cans of pop with the other.

Will walked to the back of the kitchen. "Follow me," he said as he walked through the swinging door and held it open for me with his foot. Each step he took was like a shot of espresso straight to my heart. Each step brought us closer to Will's room, where we'd be alone...*very* alone.

The back hall was short, a blank wall on our right and a wooden staircase on our left. We climbed until we came to another hallway with a small alcove and black, spiral staircase at the far end.

"My Uncle Shai's office is behind there," Will said, nodding to the middle of three doors when we walked past. "He's in there most of the time and only comes out for dinner and to catch up on my day. Maybe you could stay for dinner sometime so I can introduce you?"

"Sure. I'd like that. So, your uncle works from home. What does he do?"

"I don't really have a clue. He doesn't like to talk about it." Will gave an honest shrug. "Here we are," he announced when we reached the iron staircase. "After you."

Climbing to an attic, I expected it to become cold and stuffy, but when I reached the top, a warm and airy wide-open space greeted me. Large windows adorned the wall at the far end of the room and even though it was not yet four o'clock, evening already claimed part of the sky.

"*This* is your room? It's more like a loft apartment!" I gasped, eyeing the exposed brick wall to my right that held a small entertainment center with a large screen TV.

"There are other bedrooms in the house of course—" he looked up— "but Uncle Shai thought I would like this more." I followed his gaze to the ceiling; black walnut beams emphasized its incredible height. "I have to admit, it is pretty sweet."

Will walked over to the living room and I followed.

"Mind if I look around?" I asked and set my belongings down on the end of the Chesterfield sofa.

"Be my guest," he answered as he placed the food and drinks on the steamer trunk and took a seat.

At the far end, his queen-sized bed was immaculately made and inviting. It wouldn't have felt right to go through his bedroom, especially with him present. I scanned over to the kitchenette directly in front of me, small with top of the line finishes. But the area that pulled at my heartstrings was the mini library, a short wall full of books from floor to ceiling. I walked over and ran my hand along some of the books. The feel of three of them stood out to me, all wider and softer than the rest. I pulled one out and carefully inspected it, the bindings old and worn from use. I placed it back on the shelf and turned to head back to Will when a map above Will's desk caught my attention.

"What's Cristes Adventus?" I asked, pointing to what looked like a fictional landscape.

Will shrugged. "No idea. That was there when I moved in."

I studied the map for a few more minutes. When I meandered back to Will, pristine Christmas roses were sprinkled around his feet and the paper bag crumbled in a ball.

"Where did you get these?" he whispered, glaring at the flowers.

"Why are you looking through my things?"

"I accidentally knocked the bag over."

"I picked them for you last night. After dance yesterday, I

remembered how you used to give these to me all the time, so I thought..." I stopped short, distracted by his fisted hands, his knuckles now white. "Do you not like them?"

Will's head whipped up. He gently grabbed me by both arms, leading me onto the couch, and vehemently demanded, "Don't pick these ever again. Do you understand? You can never touch this type of flower again. Never again!"

I felt like a child being scolded. His words stirred in me a rebellion, simmering, ready to boil over if he continued. "What's your problem?" I asked defensively.

"Promise me you won't touch them!" Will pleaded, his eyes intent on mine. I stared back just as intensely; I wanted to scream at him and disappear all at the same time.

These last two days caught up to me faster than a roadrunner. His reprimand struck a nerve. "I'm sorry, why are you so angry? I thought I was doing something nice. They were a special memory for me and I...I *thought* they were for you too!" Will let go of me and sat back. Hot anger burned bright behind my eyes. When he didn't respond, my lip quivered, threatening yet again to expose my inner fragility. Besides physical injuries, harassment at school, and serious lack of sleep, this boy returned and my reality got turned upside down. I squeezed my eyes shut and refused to let one tear slip. "I need to change. Can you just grab me one of your t-shirts?"

"Liddy, let me explain."

I took a deep breath but kept my eyes closed. "Oh, you will explain...after I change."

Will walked to his dresser and pulled out a plain, black t-shirt. "Liddy, I'm sorry. I didn't mean to come across as angry. There's a lot to fill you in on. It's important to me for you to understand. Can you please trust me on this?" he pleaded, pushing open his bathroom door.

"I don't care what is going on," I snapped back, picking up my bag. "Don't ever raise your voice at me like that again. And don't think for one second you can ever order me around." I snatched the tee and stomped past him, slamming the bathroom door in his face.

My mind and heart performed fouettés, whirling round and round, unable to meld this version of Will with the one I once knew. The Will I remembered from childhood was still there and yet, sometimes this grown-up version of him was like a stranger to me. Will, my gentle Will, just yelled at me and it sucked. Sinking into a crouch on the floor, I brought his shirt to my face and muffled my sobs as they tore through my chest.

As much as I wanted to leave, to be alone and just think, I couldn't. I needed answers. Slowly, I reined in my tears and pulled myself up using the pedestal sink. I forced myself to look in the mirror. My eyes were red and puffy. I opened the door of the small chest in the corner and found a washcloth. I soaked it with cold water and rested it on my eyes hoping it was enough to reduce the puffiness. I tried to wipe off the black streaks of mascara without disrupting the rest of my makeup but failed miserably. *Whatever.* I scrubbed my whole face, leaving my cheeks a raw pink. With how this day was going, I didn't care anymore if I looked cute or like dirty snow on the side of the highway. I bent down to pick up the t-shirt Will gave me and began taking off my sweater when a knock sounded at the door.

"Lid? Nolan just rang up and was wondering if your sweater is ready?"

"Just a second please." Coolness infused my tone. I

continued trying to peel off the sweater where the dried slushie stuck to my skin. Frustrated, I gave it a good yank up and sucked in my breath. I tried to maneuver, but the more I moved, the more it hurt. "Dang it!" My sweater caught on my stud earrings.

"Everything alright?"

I stood silent, hands and sweater stuck over my head.

"Are you alright?" Will knocked again.

My mind raced to find a way out of this mess. *Suck it up. You can get out of this on your own.* I took a deep breath and gave it one more good tug. "OWWWW!"

"Liddy, I'm coming in!"

"No! Wait! Don't overreact, just—"

"You just screamed. I'm not overreacting."

"Give me one second!

"One..."

"Not funny Will!"

"Two..."

"Who are you, my dad? OK, fine! Promise you won't laugh at me." There was a long pause. "Will?"

"Only if you promise about what I asked before," he responded coyly.

"Fine!" I yelled in defeat. I couldn't see where I was in the bathroom, but I prayed I was facing away from the door. "You can come in."

I heard the door handle rattle. "It's locked."

"I can't open it. I'm sorta stuck."

"Stuck?"

"You'll see, just, hurry up."

"I gotta grab something to pick the lock." A few seconds

later, I heard a pop and then the door opened. Will drew in a deep breath.

"You said you wouldn't laugh."

"Believe me, I'm not laughing." His voice, deep and raw, awakened desires I thought I'd long ago snuffed out.

"I'm stuck on my earrings. I can't see, so I'm believing that my back is to you."

Will's warm hands wrapped gingerly around my waist. Shivers traveled up and down my abdomen leaving goosebumps as he turned me.

"What are you doing?" I shrieked, ducking down, hoping my knees would conceal me.

"I, uh... Your back is all I can see now."

What does he mean now? Oh no! Did he... Did he see the girls? My stomach dropped.

"I promise, I can't see anything."

"Let's just hurry up and get this over with," I whined, standing back up.

Will reached his hands up the neck of my sweater and his long fingers worked on the caught threads. With his body so close to my indecently exposed one, feeling his quickened breath sent my heart into a sprint it was woefully unprepared for. Seconds later, I breathed like I had just run the five-hundred-meter dash. My cheeks flamed, probably brighter than the sweater I was wearing. *Thank God he can't see my face.* After what felt like an eternity, I was free. I dropped down to grab the t-shirt he had given me and held it over my chest and face.

"So, I...I—" Will jumbled his words and backed up towards the door, stumbling a little over his feet— "I'm going to just, uh, get this...get this sweater to Nolan. I'm sure he can to-totally get this stain out. He's really good with..." Will pointed to my red sweater clenched in his hand.

I peeked out from his shirt. "Laundry?" I offered.

Will stumbled again when he backed through the threshold. "Um, yeah...laundry." And he closed the door.

I groaned into the shirt and muttered, "Could this day get any worse?" I changed and re-did my messy bun. Will waited for me on the couch, flexing, and balling his hands. I wondered if he was as mortified as me. I sighed. I needed to not think about what just happened.

When I sat down, Will took a steady breath and spoke first, breaking the tension. "Maybe we should work on English for a little bit before we dive into the more complicated stuff?"

"Sure. So, what epic love story should we do?"

"What about *Cinderella*?" Will asked. "I know she's your favorite."

"Let's not try and rewrite perfection," I said.

"But it's not perfect."

"Uh, excuse me, but it is."

"No, Liddy. Cinderella could have saved herself."

"I feel she did. Dude, with all the hardships she faced, she still chose love and joy every day. She chose to stay in that house full of hope that her stepmother and sisters would come to love her as she loved them with all she had to give."

"No, she was a doormat waiting for the prince to come save her."

"How dare you!" I gasped, throwing a decorative pillow at him.

"OK, OK! That was harsh. Let's move on. What about

Romeo and Ju—?"

"Cliché," I spat out, still ruffled about him dissing Cinderella.

"Woah, you didn't even let me finish the title."

"Sorry, I just think everyone else in the class will choose it," I said with contempt.

"*Pride and Prejudice,*" Will tried again with caution.

"Sorry, I've never gotten into that story." It was Will's turn to throw the pillow at me and I laughed. "I know, I know...it's a classic." I rolled my eyes.

"Too bad there isn't time to both read it and write the paper. I think you'd like it," Will remarked.

As we worked, we fell into the familiar rhythm of our childhood, and the awkwardness subsided. We continued back and forth throwing out more ideas. *The Notebook, Emma, Far and Away,* and *A Walk in the Clouds*, were all vetoed. We sat in silence for a few moments, our faces screwed up in thought.

I sighed. "I'm ready to give up," I grumbled, placing my head on the arm of the sofa.

Will had his head bent, hands in his hair. "This is frustrating, but we've got to be close to agreeing on something."

I bit my bottom lip and sat up. "What about..."

"Princess Aurora!" I yelled as Will shouted "Prince Philip!" We laughed.

"Don't you find it lame that she slept the whole time?" I asked.

"Definitely. How much better would it have been if the fairies trained her to be a warrior?" Will's eyes glinted in excitement at the idea.

"Of course! Which would then allow her to fight side by

side with Philip."

Will cracked a smile. "I think we've finally agreed on our retelling assignment," he said as he held up his hand for a high five.

"You're such a dork." But I returned the five anyways.

We worked for a long while and created a brainstorm web and then an outline for the paper. Will wrote in his planner and I stole glimpses of his strong, beautiful face. Despite our earlier incident, being here with him now, laughing, working together—it felt natural, like time froze and he'd never actually left. I pretended not to notice the uncertainty in his eyes when he glanced my way, but I sensed we both were holding back. I could no longer concentrate. A question I'd been wanting to ask Will kept resurfacing, dragging my attention away from English.

"Will, can I ask you something?"

He turned to face me and something about his eyes rendered me speechless. One second, his eyes were a serene green and the next, they flickered like embers smoldering after a blazing fire. He gazed at me with such intensity, drawing me in with a gentle pull as he maneuvered his body closer to mine. Our faces mere inches away from each other, I closed my eyes and parted my lips, eager for Will's to brush mine.

The moment never came. I opened my eyes and discovered Will at the far end of the couch, his head in his hands, and I was left kissing air.

Why?

"**W**ILL?"

He stood up and paced the floor. "Wow, this is going to be *so* much harder than I thought," he mumbled to himself. "Sorry, I shouldn't have—"

"I'm sorry, maybe I should go. We can talk later." Embarrassed yet again, I started to pack up my stuff. *What the heck was I doing anyway?* This went against every rule I had set for myself regarding boys and I was ashamed that I had even thought about kissing Will. I could certainly show more restraint. I mean he'd been back in my life for like two days!

"Please don't go," Will whispered, coming to stand by me. As I zipped up my bag and slung it over my shoulder, he cleared his throat and tried again. "*Please*, sit down with me. You think I *wanted* to pull away? I will explain everything. Just, be patient with me. I am still trying to figure it all out myself and—" he ran his hand through his hair— "I don't want to freak you out. What did you want to ask me?" He sat on the couch and patted the cushion next to him.

I inhaled deeply through my nose, letting my shoulders relax as I exhaled slowly. A moment of silence passed and I dropped my bag to the floor. A pressing question needed to be answered, something more important than my wounded ego.

I stood before him. "Will, why did your family leave so suddenly? I mean you didn't even say goodbye, not a phone call, not a letter. Why?" My throat burned as I fought to restrain the tears. I couldn't bear to look at him. "I don't recall much about the time after you left, and my parents have never talked about it. I faintly recollect overhearing my sisters mention I was *broken* for a while. The weird thing is, I didn't even remember them saying that until you came back. There's this chunk of time missing between you leaving and that Christmas. The memories I have of you before you left are still a little hazy."

"What do you remember about the day before I moved away?" Will asked, placing his hand on top of mine to still it. I hadn't even realized I was shaking.

"I remember playing in my front yard after it had just snowed and then seeing a burst of light shooting out of your house. From Charlie's window."

Will squeezed my hand and looked down. "Please, continue."

"The next thing I knew, I was knocked to the ground. There was this horrible laugh. And then it was Christmas morning weeks later. What happened?"

"What did happen? *That* is the question. I know we left

because of...Charlie."

Will whispered his brother's name with such hushed sorrow. Charlie. The boy's sweet face laughing in the snow drifted across my mind. My heart ached. I still don't understand how I could have forgotten him. I squeezed Will's hand urging him to continue; *my* grief was replaced by something much stronger, a grief that nearly suffocated me. *Will's. Was I actually* feeling *Will's grief?*

I flinched and Will quickly let go of my hand. "What happened to Charlie?" I whispered.

"He was taken."

"Taken? By who? We need to find him."

"Believe me, I know, Liddy. A man took him, but I don't know who."

"Why did you come back to Illinois?" I raised my hands in disbelief.

"You led me here."

I cocked my head at him.

"For a very long time, until recently, it was like you were more of a hallucination. You appeared in my dreams, a lot, but I had no idea who you were, until this summer. My last memory in Wheeling is you visiting me after my sledding accident. We drank hot cocoa together expecting to see each other the next day. The next day came, but instead of seeing you, I was living with my parents in Hammock Dunes. It was like you were an imaginary friend I outgrew, never real. I am glad that my memories have returned and that you are in fact very real." A soft smile lifted the corners of his lips, that hypnotizing, otherworldly glint kindling in his eyes again.

I let a few breaths loose. "You still haven't mentioned how

it is you came to be back here."

"Promise me you won't freak out." He screwed up his face.

"I can't make promises before I know what it is I am promising, but you can trust that I will do my best to not freak out." I brightened my tone, hoping to set him at ease.

Will gave me a half-smile. "OK, then. At the beginning of summer break, I received an unusual letter." He walked over to his desk and reached underneath it. Producing a key, he inserted it into a black satin globe with gold trim. From where I was sitting, I had no idea it was anything other than a decorative piece—one solid piece with no visible seams. Will used both hands to lift open the top and pulled out its contents. He sat back down and handed me a piece of thick, worn parchment with a dried Christmas flower attached.

"I thought I wasn't supposed to touch these?" I razzed, pointing to the Christmas rose.

"It's dead now," he said directly as if this was a given. "It's all dried out and doesn't seem to be working anymore."

"Working anymore?" I asked incredulously.

"It's kind of the reason I was able to remember you. Keep reading."

I looked back at the letter. Handwritten in red ink was a very regal and old script that read:

Dear Prince William Lucas Jamison,

As you have come of age and the necessary transformation nearly complete, the time has arrived for you to learn about where your talents and gifts in this historical tale all began. But before you can return to your rightful place, you need to depart and restore your life in Wheeling, Illinois. Your betrothed, Princess Lydia Andra Erickson, is almost of age and her transformations are just beginning. It is time you join her, for the battle has breathed new life and is strengthening once again. She will need you, and you her, as you take up arms to save our people and those of Mortalia—the land you currently reside in. All will reveal itself in due time, but for now, you are to stay close to Princess Lydia. Once you reconnect, you may begin to endure a deepening, alluring pull towards her, but you must heed my warning. Do not yet act on these prepossessing feelings as they can truly be your downfall as well as lead to the collapse of all realms as we know it. I will be in contact with you once you have made it to your Uncle Abishai's, but do not mention this to him. Tell no one.

Sincerely,

Nicholas G. Klaus

P.S. Touch and smell the enclosed Christmas rose. It will help you remember.

I put the paper down on the steamer trunk and laughed. That letter couldn't be real, and yet when I stopped laughing, Will's face paled as white as the flower he held. Realization dawned on me. Absurd as this all was, I couldn't negate the fact that it brought Will back to me.

"I'm sorry. I didn't mean to laugh. This all just seems..."

"Absurd?"

"Exactly."

"I felt the same way at first," Will reassured me.

"So, who is this Nicholas Klaus?"

"I don't know."

"How did he know where you lived? How did he know where I lived for that matter?"

"I don't know," Will said again.

It was becoming harder to swallow as the terror crept up. "And why is he calling you a prince and me a princess? Why did you..." I trailed off as I paced the room. This whole princess business wasn't true, but it scared me that this guy knew our names, our history, and succeeded in convincing Will to move back to Illinois.

"One question at a time." He smiled, but it didn't reach his eyes.

"Easy for you to say. You've had a little extra time to process all of this," I reminded him as I rubbed my forehead trying to make sense of this letter.

"I get it. I may have had extra time, but I didn't have anyone else to talk to about it." I frowned at my own lack of sensitivity and looked back at Will, encouraging him to continue. "That's why I am trying to be protective of what I share with you, Liddy, and when. I have no idea who Nicholas is, but as soon as I smelled that Christmas rose, memories of Wheeling, of you, almost crushed me—like wiping out on my surfboard and getting hit by a ten-foot wave."

"I know the feeling." I sighed and sat down next to him.

"I'm sorry for that. I tried to be careful in helping you remember. I didn't want it to disorient you as much as it did me."

"You...you gave me back my memories?"

Will turned red. "I'm not sure how it all works. But I went searching for a Christmas rose when I first came back here. I crushed one in my hand right before dance class started and while we were dancing, I made sure to get a little of the dust on your skin."

"But I didn't remember you... Not until you kissed my hand."

"As I said, I have no idea how this all works. It was so strange watching you as your memories hit. If I'd known..."

"Known what?"

"If I'd known a simple peck would have brought it all back at once, I would have done it differently, somewhere more... private."

"Well, I did get partial memories back when we had skin to skin contact. Your face didn't appear until you kissed my hand, though I haven't gotten all of my memories back. Some are still hazy, and pieces seem to be missing. It could have been worse. I'm just thankful no one noticed." On the outside I was calm, but inside my heart hammered so hard, I could hear the *swish-swish-swish* of my pulse. I didn't know what was more outrageous, his belief in magic flowers or the fact that I started to believe him.

"I'd originally hoped that when you first saw me it would spark your memory, but I knew immediately that it didn't. That's why it didn't hurt my feelings when you didn't know who I was."

"That's not totally true."

"It isn't?" He looked amused.

"No. Your scars did stir something."

Will reached for the scar on his cheek and then temple. After a few moments, he continued. "That flower Nicholas gave me, for whatever reason, helped me to recall my forgotten past while at the same time bringing more clarity to the images in my mind that were once weak. I thought since it worked for me, it could do the same for you, only not as drastically. The rose brought up things that..." Will trailed off as sadness clouded his face, the corners of his mouth turned down and his eyes went blank.

"Will?"

He remained silent, his gaze transfixed on something only he could see.

"Anyways," he persisted, as if he hadn't just zoned out, "this letter, at first, seemed like a sick joke...far-fetched and sent by someone who just wanted to hurt me. I tossed it in my wastebasket and continued to enjoy many days at the beach surfing. But each day proved to be harder and harder to not think about..."

"Your brother?"

"Well, yes, but also about—" Will studied me— "you."

His eyes followed me as I paced again. Finally, I shook my head and went for it. "So, you tossed that letter—" nodding my chin towards the steamer trunk— "and thought it was all crap. Then how'd you end up back here in Illinois?"

"Well, about six weeks after having tossed the letter, I found it smoothed out and lying open on my desk with the dried Christmas rose affixed to it. Next to it sat another envelope." Will handed me the second envelope. "Just know, despite Nicholas knowing stuff, my physical changes, and what the flower did, I wasn't convinced. Well more like, I wasn't ready to accept it all." Will let go of the letter.

The writing style of this letter was the same but written with less care as if the author was in a hurry.

To: Prince William,

I see that you have not taken my first letter seriously and have chosen to spend your days surfing and charming young women on the beach. I do not think you understand the vast importance of what I said before. What is being asked of you and Princess Lydia is cruel and more than anyone should have to bear. However, you must take this first step of faith or everyone you have ever loved, including Charlie, will die. That's right, Charlie is alive, and it is imperative that we find him. You must move to your Uncle Abishai's as soon as possible. You cannot let your parents, or your uncle know the real reason why you want to move. I trust you can make something up.

Sincerely,

Nicholas G. Klaus

P.S. I do suspect that, by now, the Princess is consuming your every thought. It will only be a matter of time before you are unable to resist what is ordained to happen in the future, but the timing needs to be just right. And time, my Prince, is running out.

"Charming women on the beach, huh?"

Will's face was redder than I'd ever seen it. "That's what stuck out to you? Liddy, I already told you."

"I know." Nervous laughter escaped my chest. "I'm just messing with you. It's none of my business. In all seriousness, this is quite ridiculous and a little creepy," I mumbled. "If I were you, I'm not sure I would have returned." Ordained? Death to all? "I mean come on! This is messed up."

"You're right. I didn't know if this letter was for real or not, but for one, it mentioned my brother and that he is alive. For another..." He paused and averted his eyes. "Well, this Klaus guy was right. Whatever was in that flower made it so I could no longer stand to be apart from you."

"You don't need to feel obligated to me Will. We've been separated a long time."

"I know. And, I don't feel obligated. The rose may have awakened my memory of you, but I'm not convinced it's the reason I feel..." He trailed off and looked up. "Gosh, I know that sounds insane." His widened eyes found mine. "I hope I'm not freaking you out, but last night, it was almost like I could feel how you were feeling; I felt like you were in trouble and that I needed to get to you, to help protect you." He drew in his lower lip between his teeth as he examined my face.

My jaw slackened. His honesty was refreshing, but I didn't want to admit to him just yet that I too felt the captivating lure, though mine hadn't been from across the country. I snapped my mouth closed. "So that's why you called last night. You knew I was scared. No, you *felt* that I was scared?" My eyebrows rose with skepticism.

"Would you be frightened of me if I said yes?"

"Not frightened of you, no. More baffled how it's even possible."

"I wish I could give you a reasonable explanation. It's more that I just sensed you were frightened but I had no idea why. Before when I was in Florida, it was nonstop images of you in my mind and each day desire built, like a craving, to be near you again." He cleared his throat like he had shared a little too much and continued. "But, last night, feeling your fear so intensely, that was a first."

"Have you, um, felt anything else I've felt?" I gulped.

"No, and I'm not sure I want to." He laughed. "You've had quite an interesting few days."

Thank heavens! my mind screamed. I didn't want him to know how I felt when near him. My relief loosened the tight muscles in my neck. "So, you still haven't answered how you got here."

"I will, but I've done all the talking. Now it's your turn. What the heck happened last night?" he questioned.

I felt a little faint as thoughts of last night bolted through my mind as quickly as flashes of lightning. Will grabbed my hands, and in an attempt to steady myself, I fixed my eyes on his. They flickered and I felt as if I'd just entered a warm jacuzzi. I slid my hands from his. If I was going to talk, I couldn't have Will be any more of a distraction than he already was. I stood and moved around the room, putting distance between us, allowing my heart to steady.

I finished recanting the story, minus the part about hearing voices. "And then I woke to my mom calling my name. I lay there perfectly still in the snow, my vision blurred. I thought I saw the silhouette of someone with silver hair all the way down the street. They moved with inhuman speed and passed Pree's house in an instant, disappearing into the shadows. I went inside, heard my phone ringing and voila—it was you."

"I tried calling you, *a lot*, but you never picked up. I got all the way to my front door and tried one last time when you finally answered."

"Why? Were you going to drive around looking for me, come to my rescue?"

"Yes," he said, shrugging his shoulders. "I couldn't just sit there and do nothing knowing you were in danger. I'm sorry if that seems a little intense."

"What are you apologizing for?" I pried.

Will's eyes flicked to the roses still on the floor. "You were put in harm's way picking Christmas flowers, to surprise me with a sweet childhood memory, and then I yelled at you for it."

"Yeah, what was that about?" I teased.

"Well, after the flower that Nicholas left, things have gotten...interesting for me and I just don't know what would happen to you...me...us if you inhaled their fragrance or if I did, again. I mean, I am glad it made me remember you, but there are other things I am still processing that I'm not comfortable talking about quite yet."

I inwardly shuddered at what else he possibly had left to reveal. "You're forgiven then." I gently touched his shoulder to reassure him. As I did, he looked up and I swore I could see the green of his eyes shimmer again. I moved my hand and pretended to rub a fuzzy off my jeans. "So, how were you able to convince your parents to let you come here?"

"I'm getting there." He laughed. "I needed to take a chance. I've never been a person who lived a life of *what ifs* and *could haves*. So, I spent the rest of the summer and the beginning of the school year trying to figure out a way to come back up here. My parents and I may have left, but my uncle still lived here and I knew he was very well off with plenty of space. He'd been asking my parents for years if I could come visit. I think in part because he may have been lonely since he never got married or had kids of his own. When I asked him if it was alright, he was very enthusiastic about the idea."

"Your parents were cool with it?" I asked in disbelief.

"On the contrary. It was quite difficult to convince them to let me come. I assumed they were reluctant because they'd already lost one son and weren't too eager to let go of me too. But then I realized they never spoke of Charlie and there was not one picture of him in our house. Maybe they didn't remember either, so I played it safe like the letter advised and didn't mention anything."

"So then, what convinced them?"

"My uncle. I don't know what was said between them, but they relented. I did have to promise to call them often and return home on school breaks. Since I just moved here though, my next trip home won't be until spring break."

"Wasn't your uncle the least bit curious about why you wanted to come back?"

"I just told everyone that I wanted to live where it wasn't so hot all the time, where there weren't giant tropical storm threats and oversized mosquitoes and that I was considering colleges in big cities due to the prestige and career opportunities. I told Uncle Shai that it had been far too long since I had seen him and I wanted to make up for lost time."

"Was any of that true?"

"Heck no! I love Florida. It *can* get a little hot and humid and I can't say that the mosquitos aren't a problem, but it is so beautiful I don't care. Can't wait for you to visit with me."

"You're so lucky. I can't wait to get out of Illinois. What's that third letter?" I asked, eyeing the last piece of parchment.

"This one was delivered in a package the day after I moved in here along with some books."

My curiosity peaked as I turned and walked to his library.

"It doesn't happen to be these three books, does it?" I asked gesturing, with my best *Vanna White* impression, to the leather-bound books with gold inlay. At his nod, I grabbed one at random and brought it back to the couch. I set the book on the steamer trunk and took the letter from Will's hands. Written in the same ink as the other two with barely legible handwriting, it read:

> *Prince William,*
>   *Keep these safe and hidden. Cristes needs you.*
> *-Nick*

"That's it?"

"That's it. I've looked through all three of the books. Some are blank, others are filled with partial maps. The rest I can only make out the words written in green. I can't make sense of any of it."

I flipped through it. The smell of the pages reminded me of a fresh snowfall. "I don't see anything written in green," I commented squinting at the pages.

Will got closer to me, careful not to touch me, and pointed to random spots on the page. "This one, this one, that one... They are all green."

"Whatever you say."

"You don't see it? Are you colorblind?" He gave me an astonished look.

"No, I'm not colorblind! Besides, being colorblind would mean I would see the words, just in a different color. I see words, but they are purple."

He pondered for a moment. "Weird."

Will stood and walked back to his library nook. I watched, admiring his strength as he placed the book back on the shelf. With nimble fingers, he carefully placed the letters back into the velvet globe. My mind wandered and I imagined those fingers caressing my skin with the care he showed in opening the globe. I turned away before Will could catch the pink in my cheeks and my eyes landed on the clock in his kitchenette.

Oh crud! "Will, it's after five. Do you mind taking me home now? My mom will have dinner ready and I need to get home before she goes berserk."

"Why would she go berserk?" Will asked while I focused on tying my shoes. "You didn't tell your parents you were coming here." Will stated. "Why?"

Uh oh. It was my turn in the hot seat. "Well, I told you earlier that I went through a hard time when you originally left. When I told my parents that you had moved back, they gave each other this apprehensive look. I didn't let on that I'd noticed, but I did. Normally, I go to Sara's every day after school anyways."

"So, what if your parents find out you were here and not at Sara's? Would it help if I dropped in sooner rather than later to at least say hi? I mean, according to Nick, we are ordained to be together and I'd rather not upset my future in-laws by being caught up in a lie," he razzed.

The air felt too thick and I choked on it, coughing violently.

"I'm kidding, Liddy," Will said, patting me on the back.

"I didn't lie," I insisted.

"Omitting is essentially lying."

"Fine." I rolled my eyes. "I will let my parents know at dinner that you are coming over tomorrow so we can work on our project. Though, I do love that working at your place is like being away at college and having your own apartment. It's so nice to not have anyone bother you."

"It's fine, I guess. Who bothers you?"

"My brother, Mickey. Remember him? Ugh, he can be so annoying."

"I do, he was just a toddler then. Can't wait to see him! I don't think it would be such a bad thing though to have a brother who cares enough to tease you." Will frowned and looked away.

"I'm sorry, Will. I didn't mean..."

"I know, Liddy. It's no biggie. I'm just hoping there is some truth to these letters. I mean crazy, inexplicable things have happened already so maybe Charlie really is alive."

Radio static filled the room. "Master William. Madam Lydia's sweater is ready. Shall I bring it up?"

Will walked over to the side of the door and pressed the button to reply. "Of course. Bring it on up. And Nolan, how many times do I have to tell you? Please call me Will."

"Right away, Master Will."

I packed up my bag and sat on the couch tapping my foot. I didn't want to be late getting home for dinner. A few minutes later there was a knock at the door. Nolan came in quick as a cat and handed me my clean sweater, bowing before walking back out. "Thanks, Nolan!" I shouted back in his direction as I rushed to the bathroom to change.

When I came out a minute later, Will already had his jacket on and assisted me into mine, his hands sliding my hair out from under its high neck. The brush of his fingers raised tingles all over my body, extending out to my arms and legs.

I shuddered slightly. *Would I ever get used to whatever this was?* The faint hope that Will wasn't aware of my attraction to him was something I clung to. The light in his eye and quirk in his smile left me with a hint of doubt.

A light snow fell, dusting the path that curved around through the backyard, as we walked to the detached garage. He opened the wood-paneled car door for me, and I got in, brushing some of the snow from my hair. Will started the Jeep and placed his hand behind the headrest of my seat as he backed out of the driveway.

I touched his arm. "I'm sorry again about Charlie. I never got to tell you that. If you are looking into whatever happened to him, I want to help."

Will put the car in park and pressed his hand against my cheek. "Thanks, Liddy. It's nice to have someone I can trust with all of this. I was starting to feel a little crazy."

"You are crazy," I teased. Will's eyes popped and his chin dropped in mock dejection. I closed my hand over the top of his. "Relax, I'm just messing with ya. I'm not sure if I believe all that this dude wrote in those letters, but there have been *some* strange things happening lately. I do believe your brother is out there—somewhere." Will sighed and dropped his hand from my cheek. "Maybe we can spend some time tomorrow in those books you were sent?"

"That seems like a good place to start."

We didn't talk much the rest of the way to my house. As Will turned onto my block, the color faded from his face and sadness glazed his eyes. I never paused to think what effect being near his old house would have on him. So, I did what I do best and diverted around the complicated stuff. I took my thumb and index finger and measured the distance from his nose to his forehead. Before he could figure out what I was doing, I placed my pointer finger at his knee, thumb at his thigh to find the perfect tickle spot and squeezed.

Will let out a startled half-scream, half-laugh. "Liddy! What the heck? I could have swerved us right into a lamppost!"

I cackled. Will joined in a moment later. "So, my house tomorrow?" I asked with a devious smile.

Will threaded his hand through his hair. "Sounds good."

"Cool. Meet you at your locker then?" I grabbed hold of the door handle.

"You sure Justin will be down with that?" Will asked, plucking at the neck of his coat.

"Of course. We're just two friends going to a dance together."

"If you say so." He rolled his eyes.

"Goodnight, Will. See you tomorrow."

"Sweet dreams, Liddy." He waited until I got through my front door before driving away.

I smiled as I remembered how much of an effect those simple words, *sweet dreams,* had on me when they came from Will's mouth. He used to say them to me every night before he moved away. I never realized how much I missed those two words.

Unfair

"LYDIAAAAAAA," the voice hissed. Disoriented, I opened my eyes and found the voice. The dark cavern imprisoned me once more. I tried to walk away from her, but my feet were frozen in place.

"Answer me when I address you!" Her orange eyes flashed.

"Ye-ye-yes, M-m-mara," I stammered, barely a whisper. My throat burned as I choked down the screams that tried to escape. The new violet gown I wore constricted me from my shoulders to my hips. With a flick of her wrist, Mara forced me to curtsy and a gasp escaped my lips as the boning of the dress pinched me.

My heart was beating so hard, my ribs felt like they would crack under the pressure. "This is just a dream," I said aloud to myself. "Just a dream." The witch cocked her head at me, the tendrils of black smoke around her head flicked wildly, and she cackled as if I'd said something funny. "Wake up, it's just a dream!" I closed my eyes and repeated the words like a mantra, trying to wake.

"It's not a dream, Princess. Sure, your body is home in your bed, but your soul is mine. Right here, right now."

Off in the distance, I heard a faint echo. "Will?" My vision swayed. *Sweet dreams,* his echo called to me again.

"Pay no attention to his voice, you silly, naïve girl. If you willingly sacrifice yourself, I can make it painless and I'll even free Charlie. I can't have Prince William upset, now can I? If you refuse, I will still end you myself." Her voice was as sharp as her razor red nails.

I knew I should say no. *Sweet dreams* echoed in the dark cave again. The witch growled in agitation. Steadying myself, I glanced around. Those blinking eyes within the shadows were more numerous than last time. They were on me again, pleading and begging. I opened my mouth, prepared to say the simple word *no*, but I closed it again, choosing my next words carefully.

"Why do you hate me?" I asked. Tears threatened to escape but I wouldn't let them. Mara paused and returned to her innocent form—soft blond curls with bright sea-green eyes.

"I don't hate you. You are a means to an end. A victim just like me."

"So, I've done nothing wrong?"

"Well I'm sure you have not lived a perfect life, but if you are asking if you've wronged *me* the answer is no."

I let that sit for a moment. *What is it with girls wanting to hate me for no reason? First Jackie and now Mara?* "It's so unfair," I whispered.

"Quit feeling so sorry for yourself," the witch snapped, a blazing orange now snuffing out the green in her large eyes. "I felt sorry for myself once, but then I learned just how powerful I was and how I could have everything I've ever wanted."

"And what's that?" I asked.

Mara clicked her tongue. "I won't divulge all of my secrets in case you somehow escape again like last time—a simple oversight I remedied for tonight. I can say that killing you not only advances, shall we say, my political position, but also fulfills my desire for sweet revenge."

Sweet dreams echoed again. My muscles reacted to those words, filling with blood, readying my body for a fight. "That's not a good enough reason to take my life," I stated boldly while I glared straight into Mara's cold eyes.

"I don't need to explain myself to you," she quipped as she transformed back into the terrifying witch. An unseen, but tangible ripple blasted through the cavern. I couldn't be sure, but I thought I heard whispers of *run* coming from the shadows. "Silence!" the witch screamed. "Jamie, come here please, and bring one of my toys with you."

A young man with ashen skin stepped out of the shadows, his hand entwined with a young boy's, maybe eight years old. A thick iron cuff enclosed Jamie's ankle. My eyes followed its bulky chain to where it attached to the base of Mara's throne. I turned my gaze to the young man and to my surprise, he stared back at me. *I know him.*

I cocked my head studying Jamie, trying to fit his face within my memories when Mara stepped in front of him blocking my view. "Like what you ssssee?" she hissed through her blood red lips, looked over her shoulder at Jamie and then back at me. I shook my head, noticing for the first time something heavy was stuck in my hair. "Careful, or you'll knock your crown off." Mara stalked towards me, taking her time like a cat playing with their prey until she rolled her shoulders and cracked her neck ready to pounce. "I am growing bored. Let me just end it for you."

Sweet dreams resounded again.

"Will! Help me!" I ran as fast as I could toward the large doors, the boning of my dress crushing my ribs.

"*Ceástaté!*" Mara shouted. An orange flash illuminated the cave. *BOOM!* The doors slammed, the sound reverberating through my bones. My body froze mid-sprint. A million invisible hands forced me to stand straight and face Mara at her throne.

"Whatever the hell that protection spell is, I am going to have to break it." The witch unfastened her shimmering, inky cloak and it floated to the ground. She held her arms out, palms facing up. Jamie reached across her chest from behind, grabbing a sharp, glinting object from the boning of her dress as she licked her lips in anticipation. I tried to scream, but her magic muzzled me. Jamie traced the branching, putrid-green veins on her pale arms with his fingertips until he found a desirable one. He readied the winged device he'd retrieved from Mara's bosom and slid it into the swollen vein with care, leaving it in the crook of her arm. "If she moves, you strike," Mara ordered the faceless eyes in the shadows.

Jamie then sat the child in front of her. "Hold out your arm," he ordered, his voice void of all emotion. The boy whimpered and shook. *What can I do to help him?* My gut twisted and tightened, scared for his well-being. The boy, so young and innocent—I wanted to, no *needed* to save him. "Now," Jamie commanded, and the boy obediently held his arm out.

I tried to scream, *"Stop!"* but only air came out.

Mara closed her eyes and for a moment all was still. Too still. It was impossible not to feel the weight of her magic fall over the room. I watched in horror as Mara's lips moved with supernatural speed, but no audible words resounded. Her heart lit up first, its green-orange glow extended outward, feeding a black vine as it snaked its way from her punctured vein to the boy. He gasped as soon as the thin vine punctured his arm and fell silent. With the connection secure, Mara floated a few inches off the ground.

Tears streamed down my face. *What is this witch doing to that innocent child?* I closed my eyes and reached for Will again. *Will! WILL! WIIILL!* My mind screamed over and over again.

Sweet dreams! Will's voice reverberated, filling the cave.

Mara glowed even brighter, the light transforming to a blood-orange. I tried moving again with all my might and only managed a single step toward the doors. My eyes flicked to Jamie's. He nodded his head with an almost imperceptible 'yes', telling me to go. I didn't know why I chose to trust him, but I whipped around and bolted towards the heavy marcasite doors. Footsteps rushed after me.

Sweet dr... But the sound of Will's voice cut off, replaced with cackling. I dropped to the ground, clutching my head. Pain. There was so much pain. Breathless and panting, I stood up and ran again.

"It worked," Mara celebrated. "It worked! Your prince

can't save you now."

I was almost to the heavy doors when a crowd of young children blocked my way. Hundreds of echoes—*sorry, she made us, help us*—filled my ears, but they continued to push me toward Mara. I couldn't stand to look at her. Her deranged, orange eyes thirsted for my blood. Her body blazed and a searing pain stabbed my brain. I fell to my knees and clutched my head. It took every ounce of strength I had to hold my hand up to shield the light from my eyes. My pulse thundered in my ears. Mara floated back to the ground and Jamie tied her cloak back around her neck. He lifted the boy from the ground. Somehow, he appeared entirely unharmed. *Thank God!* They both bowed and disappeared back into the shadows. Mara flicked her hands to shoo away the children and they scattered.

Stall her! Stall her! I thought to myself.

"Why do you have all these children?" I asked.

"That's my business. Speaking of business, let's get back to it, shall we?"

"You make me sick," I dared.

Anger distorted the witch's face. "Sticks and stones, my dearie. Pain it is. And, oh. I will definitely enjoy it." She licked her lips again.

She threw an invisible lasso and caught me around the waist. I panicked, thrashing, struggling to free myself. Warmth smarted behind my eyes, insufferable. The scalding pain held no mercy and I lost control. I cried out as it boiled over and squeezed my eyes shut.

"No!" Mara screeched.

Wet and cooling, an ointment nourished my eyes. In less than a second, the torment subsided. I opened my eyes as Mara was thrown back, somersaulting through the air. She landed on her side with a loud *CRACK!* I was released from her hold and dashed for the doors.

"Stay where you are!" I ordered the children in the shadows. "I don't want to hurt you." *Wake up, Liddy, wake up!* My hand reached for the door handle and upon contact I immediately ripped it back. "OWWW!" A small 'M' with a line above and below was seared into the first few layers of skin on my palm; tears freely fell as burned flesh filled my nose. I glanced behind me to find Mara stirring.

Smoke roiled off of her. This was the end. I knew it. When she got to her feet, Mara skittered towards me, her body moving fast and disjointed like a praying mantis snatching its meal. But I would not go down without a fight. A battle cry erupted from deep within me and I barreled towards her.

A cloaked figure appeared out of nowhere, dressed from head to toe in emerald green. I caught a flash of glittery green eyes. Moving as fast as lightning, it rammed into an unexpecting Mara. She flew through the air, her back cracking on the arm of her throne. The slender figure grabbed me and flung me over their shoulder, blasting the doors open, then slamming them shut. The mysterious person set me down. Familiar green eyes poured into mine. "Wake up, Lydia! Remember nothing," a woman's voice lulled as she pushed on my forehead with her hand.

Just Friends

I WOKE GASPING, grabbing my comforter for dear life as my legs thrashed about. Vertigo upended me, my body exhausted like I just ran a marathon.

"Not again," I moaned, slumping back into my pillow. Night terrors hadn't been a thing since I was a kid. I'd hoped the other night was just a fluke. *Why can't I just sleep like a normal person?* My alarm wailed and I slapped my hand on the snooze button. *"Ow!"* I looked at my palm and a faint outline of the letter 'M' stared back at me. *What the heck?*

"Liddy!" Mom yelled. "You alright?"

"Just stubbed my toe!" I lied. I tried to recall more details from the nightmare, but they vanished quickly. I knew it was just a dream, but dang it felt real. Too real. *Why am I dreaming about dying?* I shook my head as the image of a witch stalking me faded behind my squinched eyes. Peeling sweaty hair off my forehead, I rushed into the shower then headed downstairs.

I greeted Mom and Dad with a hug. "Morning!" I sang, a feeble attempt to hide my anxiety over my nightmare.

"Must have hit your toe pretty bad," Dad said from behind his paper.

"I hope you can still dance," Mom added sitting down at the kitchen table.

"It felt better after I showered." I didn't love lying to my parents, but I didn't want to worry them. "So, Will and I will be taking turns on whose house we'll be studying at after school. Today is our house." Not giving them a chance to react or comment, I shot right up, leaving my bowl on the table, and headed back to my room to finish getting ready for school.

"Lydia, come back here please," Dad called after me.

Here it comes. "Yeah, Dad?" I responded from the middle landing of the stairs.

"When Will is here—" Dad appeared from around the corner and crossed his arms over his chest— "keep your bedroom door open."

"Daaaad, it's so not like that. We are just friends."

"Yeah, right, and I'm JT and Mom is Britney Spears." My eyes about popped out of my head and my chin hit the ground.

"How do you know who they are?"

"Oh, John, stop messing with her." Mom wrapped her arm through one of Dad's. "So how are the Jamison's? It's been so long."

"Will's parents didn't move back. He's staying with his uncle on Mistletoe Lane."

"The estate?" Dad said, sounding surprised.

I ignored him and continued. "Anyway, I bet you won't even recognize Will." I smiled.

"Can't wait to see him." An undertone of uncertainty glazed Mom's words. I knew something happened after Will left that made my parents worry about me, but it wasn't Will's fault. I just needed to figure out what happened.

In the meantime, I hoped my family behaved during his visit. "Just be cool guys. I'm gonna go finish getting ready before Mama L. gets here."

After Mama L. dropped us off, we all headed straight to Sara's locker where our formal dates would be waiting.

"Happy hump day," Alex bellowed from down the hall.

"OK guys, here's some four-one-one for the dance. My friend Joey is having an after-party at his crib. Do you all want to go?" Matt asked.

I hated high school parties, especially when alcohol was involved. It gave an excuse for bad choices and there was always at least one fight. Before I could even suggest anything else— a concert, cosmic bowling, movies and games at one of our houses—my girlfriends all jumped in with a resounding, "Yes!" Justin eyed me, waiting for me to respond, but didn't comment.

"I guess that's settled then," I muttered, plastering on a fake smile so I wouldn't sour everyone else's excitement.

"Joey's parents are letting everyone stay the night so I can take home anyone who sleeps over," Matt offered.

Will added, "I won't be staying the night, or drinking, so I will do the same and take home anyone who is not staying over." He looked at me and gave me a coy smile.

"Cool, you and I can leave our cars in the school parking

lot before the dance so we can drive to Joey's from there," Matt replied.

The warning bell rang, and we all headed to first period. Justin again joined Will and me on the way to class. When we reached the door, Will walked right in leaving me alone with Justin. I wish Will had *sensed* that I didn't want to be alone with Justin right now, the way he sensed other things about me.

"Liddy, we don't have to go to Joey's if you don't want. I know that's not your scene. We can do whatever you'd like, maybe go see a late movie somewhere."

Wow. That was big of him, and selfless. He was buddies with Joey and some of the other baseball team members that would be there. "Thanks, Justin. I'm fine with it. We're only young once. I guess I should see what all the hype about a high school after-party is."

Smiling, Justin said, "Sweet, Liddy. I won't sleep there if you don't plan on it. I'm happy being wherever you are."

"Thanks. I probably won't stay, but I'll let you know if I change my mind."

"Liddy, I wanted to ask you yesterday, but never got the chance. Can I...take you out on Friday night?"

Dang it. What's changed since that summer? I thought he'd made it clear he didn't want to date me, so I put him in the friend zone. It took me a little time to adjust, but it worked and now I couldn't see him as anything but a friend. However, formal was just around the corner and I didn't want any awkwardness.

So, naturally, I said, "Umm sure, what do you have in mind for two good friends?" Meanwhile, I was sure I'd have pit marks, my nerves had me sweating. I hoped throwing 'friends' in there clarified things.

"I'll call you tonight." Justin grinned, his face losing the uncertain expression he'd been wearing. "I've gotta bounce to class. Talk to ya later." He capered down the hall.

Maybe a casual date wouldn't be too bad of a thing if it made someone that happy. I'm capable of going on a date and keeping it platonic. It might also be a great reminder to both of us why we didn't work out before. *If nothing else, it might get Jackie and any other Will-loving haters off my back,* I thought to myself as I found my seat. I looked behind me and Will cocked his head.

I mouthed in return, "Tell ya later."

Every teacher was in full on lecture mode today and my hand ached from all the notes I'd taken. I was relieved when sixth period came so my hand could get a break.

I arrived a little early, eagerly anticipating my escape to the world of *The Princess Bride.* As I sat waiting for class to start, a fleeting thought poked my heart. *I want adventure. Like Wesley. Fighting for love.*

I peered down at my hand. The faint 'M' from this morning was now a light pink.

Shortly before the bell, Will got to class and sat down next to me. Leaning into me, he whispered, "So what was that all about this morning with Justin?"

"You don't have to whisper." I poked his shoulder. "It was nothing much. Justin just wanted to know if he could take me out on Friday and I...sort of said yes."

"Sort of?" he asked, raising his brow.

"Yeah. As friends. I guess it couldn't hurt to just go on one casual date with him. Maybe this will keep my haters from literally throwing trash at me for even talking to you."

Will was about to say something in response, but Mr. Hurley shut off the lights and started the movie. I kept glancing over at Will, who slouched over and rested his chin on his forearm, hoping he'd finish what he was going to say, but he never did. Will wore a look I'd not seen on him before. I could see the clench in his jaw and the rigidity of his body, and the warmth I usually felt being near him was gone. As if he knew I was looking at him, he caught my gaze, but then just as swiftly returned his eyes back to the screen. In that brief moment, I noticed his bright, sea-green eyes went dark. *It's just the lighting. No one's eyes just change color like that.*

Forty-five minutes passed in a blur of uncertainty that revolved around Will. The lights flickered on, assaulting my eyes. By the time they adjusted, the bell rang, Will fled, and I could only wonder what the heck was wrong.

"Wow, Will seemed to be in a hurry," Sara noted as she stood by my desk, waiting while I zipped my bag.

"Totally! I was all 'Hey, Will' and he was all 'Psyche'! He just bolted out of class and didn't even acknowledge my presence," Pree pouted.

At least I wasn't the only one that noticed Will wasn't his normal, gentlemanly self. I made it through study hall and then to the locker room for dance unscathed by any more unwarranted attacks from the Double Dees. I hadn't realized how on edge I was about yesterday's Slurpee and AIM chat incidents. That relief lasted all of two seconds. When I opened my locker, I discovered that someone had squeezed ketchup and mustard through the slits.

"Woah, these girls are straight clownin', Liddy."

"You have any extra gym clothes, Pree?"

"I don't, but you can put your stuff in my locker. I'll get changed out quickly and let Coach know you'll be a minute."

"Thanks, Pree. Please just tell her that somehow my condiment packages from lunch exploded in my locker."

"Why not just tell her what happened? These girls can't get away with pulling crap like this."

"Because I don't want to deal with more drama for being a snitch. I'm gonna go see if Sara and Dani have clothes I can borrow."

Luckily, they did. The pants I borrowed from Sara hugged me more tightly than I'd have liked. Since Dani was short, the tank fit the girls but left some of my abdomen exposed. I grabbed my hoodie and wrapped it around my waist to help conceal my midriff. I threw my hair up and made my way to the studio.

I was anxious to see Will and fussed with my hair. We walked into the dance room and there he was, his head thrown back in laughter, comfortable with the attention of the many girls around him. Before I could try to even talk to him, Coach R. cha-cha'd in and started our warm-up routine.

"Spread out, arms width apart! Plié, breathe in two, three, four, release out two, three, four."

Afterward, she separated us into small groups to work on shaping. I was relieved Will had a chance to work with other dancers in the class. With five minutes left in the period, Coach R. partnered everyone up to work mirror exercises.

"Sit on the floor across from your partner and mimic what they do. Just like your reflection would in a mirror." Coach

R. linked arms with Will, walking him over to me. She gave us a wink and continued her quick partnering of ensemble members. Will didn't look at me as he sat down. As he kept his gaze cast to the ground, I lowered myself to the floor, my agitation rising.

"I'm sorry, did I do something to offend you? You've been acting like a jerk since sixth. I mean, yesterday I get trash thrown at me and today my locker was torn up probably for dumb reasons like having the audacity to talk to you. Now I'm paired up with you again adding fuel to the fire, but please, continue to brood," I spat, steam practically seeping from my nostrils. When the pang of my own nails bit into my already tender palm, I uncurled my clenched fists.

The hard line of his mouth softened. He tilted his head up at me and moved once Coach started heading our way. I was thankful we didn't have to touch. I needed to be mad at him and touching him would hamper that.

"I'm sorry. I...I guess I owe you an explanation." He bit his bottom lip and I copied the gesture. "Can we talk about it at your place?" he asked, his right arm forming a large circle as his eyes shifted to my abdomen and lingered. I repeated the movement and self-consciously tried to make the tank top extend a little lower. I succeeded in covering my abdomen only to reveal my cleavage. He averted his eyes. I unwrapped my hoodie and pulled it over my head.

"Fine," I huffed, blowing a strand of hair from my face. "I have stuff to tell you too, but let's meet at Sara's locker, so we're seen as a group. I don't think my wardrobe can take these assaults much longer."

"How are you so sure it's because of me?"

"Are you saying that *I* did something to warrant these attacks?"

"No, that's not what I am saying. Maybe they are just jealous of you, what with getting the duet and all the attention from eligible guys you've been receiving," he replied.

"First of all, that's not true, and secondly, I just know it's about you, trust me." *I mean my gosh, have you seen yourself?* "Besides, if girls were the least bit jealous of me, this all would have started before *you* got here," I chided as I poked him hard in the chest.

The bell rang. I rushed to join the girls on the descent to the locker room and joined them at Pree's locker.

"Hey, um, I sort of told my mom that Matt was going to start bringing me home from school. Matt said he's cool with dropping you guys home too if you want, but I figured Pree has debate, Dani, you work, and Liddy, I figured you'd be going home with Will." Sara spoke like she'd rehearsed this.

"Of course!" I exclaimed, a little more bubbly than usual to put Sara at ease. "I'm so happy to see you guys are hitting it off so well. I do have plans with Will for the next week or so, while we finish up our project, but even when we're done, I can always walk home."

"No, we'll give you a ride home."

"Yeah, because when I don't have debate, I'm still going with Sara, because, like, I am so not walking home," Pree cut in.

I laughed.

"Are we all still good for Saturday dress shopping?" Dani inquired. "Holy cannoli, Liddy. Did your boobs grow again? You're, like, barely in your bra."

"Dani!" I screamed in embarrassment as I threw on my baseball tee.

"For reals, girl. I thought for a second maybe the rumors of stuffing might be true, but after seeing it with my own eyes..." Pree laughed.

"Rumors?" I fumed. "My body is not something that should be anybody's topic of conversation. I don't stuff, but if I did, who cares! That would be nobody's business. Pree, you should have backed me up," I chastised.

"Take a chill pill! I did back you up, silly. Don't let them get to you. Think of it as a compliment that they are talking about your body. They are just jealous that you are fabulous, and that Will only has eyes for you." Pree batted her lashes at me and whispered, "It can be a little intense the way he stares at you."

"Whatever, he does not stare at me," I muttered back. I'd never caught Will staring at me. If anything, I was the one fighting the urge to look at him.

"As if!" Dani guffawed. "He looks at you like you're all that and a bag of chips and he'd about just die without you and if you don't kiss him already he'll wither away in a slow, painful death and..."

"Alright! Enough." Dani's unusual dramatics amused me. "But for real, I am *not* with Will. I...I agreed to go out with Justin Friday night."

Crickets. Mouths open wide enough to hit the floor. Eyes bugged out. All generous ways to describe the looks on my friends' faces.

"What?" I teased as I shimmied into my jeans and shoved the borrowed clothes into my bag.

"Did I miss something? I mean tell me everything!" Sara

exclaimed.

"Spread that news around, Pree. Get these haters off my back," I half-joked. I looked around to make sure no one was in earshot. "It's nothing serious. He's been hinting about asking me and he's gotten more persistent. I'm just over dodging it and feeling awkward around him."

"So, you're going on a pity date," Dani said, fitting her shirt over her head.

"It's not a pity date! We may or may not have almost gotten together once upon a time when we first started working together. Anyways, I figured I should be taking all of my chicas' advice and have a little more fun. Justin's a nice guy and I suppose I ought to give him a chance before automatically signing off."

"Girls, we are starting to rub off on her! This is a proud moment for us." Sara used her index finger to fake swipe a tear from her eye.

We exited the locker room together laughing. As Jackie and her clique walked past, my foot hit something hard and my body launched like a bullet through the hall and into the commons area. I caught myself, my wrist buckling under the strain and belly flopped to the ground.

Dani rose to her fullest height, all five feet of her vibrated. "Hey! Step off, Jackie! What's your problem?"

I laid on my stomach, processing what just happened. While my friends stood guard, I sat up. *Only a bruised wrist. Could be worse.*

"Seriously Jackie? That was uncalled for!" Sara snapped.

Pree gave the Double Dees her best stare down.

"Oops, sorry. Did I do that?" Jackie laughed wickedly, her

cronies following suit.

That's it! I've had enough! "Jackie, are we seriously traveling back in time? What the actual heck! Have you distorted reality *again*, believing I've done something to you?" Jackie just stared down at me. "This better not be about a dude again," I scoffed.

"And if it is?" she coaxed.

"Then you're losing it. Everyone knows I don't date, but even if I wanted to, you're not dating anyone! Everyone is fair game, and I don't need your permission."

Alex was right behind us and swooped in, offering his hand to help me up. I grabbed it and he pulled me from the floor, his strength causing me to fall into his arms.

"You alright, Liddy? You hurt?"

"I'll be fine," I assured him, pushing against his chest to create some space and trying to ignore the prickling pain in my wrist. "People just need to watch where they are walking."

"Yeah, stupid hoochies like you," one of Jackie's clones hissed.

"I said, *step off!*" Dani bellowed as she wound her arm back to throw a punch, the girl cowering under the threat.

Alex wrapped his hand over Dani's fist, stepping in between her and the Double Dees. He spun, looking Jackie dead in the eyes. "You are straight up wiggin'. You need to apologize to Liddy right now for hurting her."

"Ugh, as if," Jackie sneered with disgust.

"She's done nothing to you. Apologize to this fine specimen or I will be forced to tell everyone what you did last summer," Alex threatened in a low voice.

Jackie paled. "Whatever. Sorry, Lydia," she growled.

"Now, I think you can do much better than that," Alex drawled.

Jackie seethed, her voice dripping with artificial sweetener. "I am deeply sorry for *accidentally* bumping into you, Lydia. Please, forgive me."

"That will do, for now." Jackie seemed to cower slightly under his command. "I don't want to hear of you bothering Liddy again. Off you and your *Pound Puppies* go." Alex dismissed them with a smug flick of his hand.

"Alex to the rescue," Pree cooed.

"That was pretty generous, Alex," Sara agreed.

"Walk me to my locker?" Dani asked as she hooked her arm in his.

He looked at me. "Are you sure you're alright?"

"I've had worse; nothing a little ice won't help." I half-smiled. "Thanks again for what you just did. I appreciate all of you sticking up for me."

"We got your back girl, always," Dani promised. Loyalty was something I never had to worry about with my handful of close friends.

Dani walked on ahead with Alex while Sara and Pree walked with me to my locker. I wasn't expecting to see Will there leaning against it, an anxious look on his face. As soon as he saw the girls with me, he switched on a charming smile.

"Hi, ladies. I hope you don't mind if I steal Liddy from here so we can get started on our paper? I have to get home earlier today than I anticipated," he explained to them, but his eyes gave me a concerned glance, searching for something.

"Of course, it's no problem!" Pree said, stumbling over her words and touching his arm as she spoke. "We know our Liddy is in good hands with you."

Will placed his hand over Pree's. "Have a good afternoon, ladies."

They walked away, Pree practically drooling.

I opened my locker and went to grab my history textbook. "Ouch!" I hissed as the book fell, grabbing my wrist. Will said nothing as he leaned down to grab the book, placing it in my bag.

"Anything else you need in here?"

"I don't think so."

He slung my bag over his free shoulder, slammed the locker, and placing his hand at the small of my back, hurried me towards the parking lot. We stepped outside, but not before Will held his hand out to stall me for a second.

"What are you doing, silly? You're acting weird."

"I'm just looking to make sure I don't see a yellow mustang."

We got to his car and he opened the door for me, then the trunk to place our bags. As he sat in his seat and closed the door to the Wagoneer, he turned to look at me, alarm etched in his face. He gingerly grabbed the wrist I cradled. Immediate relief washed over it. I let out a teeny, involuntary sigh.

"So, what happened?"

"It's no big deal," I insisted, slipping my wrist from his hands.

"Is this because of *me* again?" He looked horrified.

"No," I answered a little too quickly.

His head dropped. "This is all so unfair," he whispered.

"What's unfair?" He wasn't making any sense.

"They can't keep us from being friends. I *have* to fix this."

I looked out the window. *Have to?* I got it. He felt obligated to me because of the letter.

"Don't worry about it. The girls and Alex took care of it."

"I'm sure he did," Will muttered.

"Excuse me?"

"Let's just say that Alex only does things that benefit him. And since you have a hard time saying no—"

"And just what are you implying?" I spat out.

"Nothing."

As You Wish

WE DROVE THE QUICK FIVE MINUTES TO MY HOUSE in silence. I wished I'd let him continue to hold my wrist though. His touch was like an IcyHot balm—both soothing and healing. Will parked the Wagoneer next to the curb across from my house. I didn't wait for him to open my door this time and helped myself out—a gesture I knew he'd be miffed about.

"Liddy!" Will called. I continued walking towards my house. In a flash, he grabbed the bags from the trunk, ran ahead, and stopped directly in front of me, forcing me to a halt.

"What?" I crossed my arms and popped my hip.

"This is maddening." He took a half step, closing the gap between us, and brushed my hair from my face. Will wrapped his arms around me. He took a long, slow inhale and an even longer exhale before he spoke. "Can we just get on the same page?"

"Sure. Quit being so difficult to read."

He laughed. "I was not implying anything. I just don't want Alex to try and take advantage of your good heart." He released me, stepped aside, and with an *after-you* sway of his arm, followed me through the front door.

"What are you looking at?"

Will pointed at the wreath hanging on the wall. "Your mom still puts this out every year?" Will walked to the wreath and leaned in close to the wooden Merry Christmas sign attached to it. "I remember when she first made it and how I accidentally broke the M with my basketball. She never even got mad." Will looked back at me and smiled.

I hung our jackets in the coat closet and cut through the dining room to the kitchen. I grabbed us some fruit and drinks while Will stayed in the foyer.

"What's with the goofy grin?" I asked him, his smile extending from ear to ear.

"Last one to your room is a rotten egg," Will challenged. I dodged under his arm and up the stairs, taking them two at a time. He chased close behind. As I neared the entrance of my room, I turned my head. Will tried to grab my shirt in an effort to hold me back. I evaded his grasp, but accidentally dropped one of the apples that was tucked in my arm. Will tripped on it, flying into me. I braced myself. We landed with a thud. I opened my eyes, shocked that no new pain registered, and found myself on top of Will, who sheltered me in his arms.

"I'm so sorry! Are you OK?" I wiggled out of his grasp and placed my hands on the floor near his head. I searched his face for any sign of pain, our gazes anchored to each other.

"First comes love, then comes marriage, then comes..."

"Shut up, Mickey!" I yelled after the retreating form of my brother. I rolled off Will and sat bolt upright in an attempt to go after him.

Will grabbed my good arm. "He's just being a kid. Don't be too harsh on him."

I let out a frustrated groan and laid back down. Will laughed and settled next to me while stroking my injured wrist.

"I've never been in Lydia Erickson's room before."

"You haven't? We hung out every day and you never came upstairs?"

"Nope. Your dad would not allow it." He smirked.

"Well, you didn't miss much. It's nothing special, especially compared to where you live." I laughed.

I closed my eyes concentrating on the warmth and tingles that ebbed and flowed through my body in rhythm with each caress of my arm.

"Liddy?" Will whispered in my ear.

"Mmm?" I responded.

"You fell asleep."

"No, I was just relaxing."

"It's been an hour," Will murmured as he stroked my hair.

I shot up and almost headbutted him. "What!"

"Liddy, are you still having nightmares? Like when you were a kid?"

"Maybe... Why?"

"Well, I've noticed how tired you are. I mean, you did just fall asleep at the drop of a hat."

"I'm so sorry, I know we have important stuff to get to and

I just wasted a bunch of our time."

"It's OK. I'm just sorry I had to wake you." He got up and sat on the bed.

"Shall we get started on our assignment?" I suggested.

"Yes, but first, I should tell you something."

My cheeks burned and my ears went red. *Was I snoring or something? Am I narcoleptic now?* "OK, shoot," I said as I got up and closed the door. He patted the bed for me to sit next to him.

"Do you remember how I told you last night that Christmas roses make me, uh, feel things?"

"Yes." *And how very relieved I was to learn that you didn't know how I was feeling all the time.*

"The reason why I got so worked up when you brought them with you was because—"

"You don't have to explain."

"But I do. I need to share what happened yesterday at my place when we almost—"

"Stop. I know you are only in Illinois because the letters told you to be and of course, you need to find what happened to Charlie. I promise, you owe me no further explanations." I did *not* need to hear his reasons for rejecting me.

Will looked baffled. "Man, you really don't seem to know me anymore, but I can't blame you for that. It has been a while."

"Yes, it has been. And excuse me. You're nice to me one second and frustrated with me the next. Who wouldn't be confused?"

"You're right. You worried me again today. I knew you got hurt, but had no idea what happened to you. I wasn't angry. I was worried."

There it was again. He openly shared the absurdity of knowing I was hurt. I shook my head. "I was referring to English class. Ring a bell?"

"First we need to address what you just said. Is that what you believe? That I'm only here because the letters told me to be?"

"Yes. Now, today in English, what *was* that?"

Will threw his hands up in exasperation and the bed springs squeaked under the shift of his weight. "Can you blame me?" He raised his voice. "You had just told me you agreed to go on a date with Justin!"

"I'm just going out with a friend. Why would that matter to you?" I snapped. Will's disapproval got under my skin more than it should have.

"It's definitely a date and it matters a great deal to me," he shared as he stared down into my eyes. "I have always felt something more than just friendship for you. Heck, even as a scrawny little eight-year-old, I knew our future—"

The lump in my throat grew three sizes too big and I cut him off before the tears welled. "Well, then you left, and I never heard from you again." Earlier today he ignored me and now he's talking like he thinks about us...as something other than friends?

"Yeah, and you and I both know there is more to that story and I don't know about you, but I care enough to find out."

"I do care," I muttered, but I wasn't sure he heard me.

"Whenever I figure out who this Nick guy is, I'm gonna find out what that flower did. It changed everything, like bringing back all of these wonderful memories—" Will gave me a half smile— "but many are also very painful."

He stood and walked to the window. I got up from the bed and stood next to Will. My shoulders dropped as the tangible weight of Will's pain in losing Charlie washed over me. "I'm mostly glad for it, but Liddy, I wish you could feel what I feel..."

I can feel it, Will. "Feel about what?" I asked, giving him the opportunity to confide in me.

"You."

My chin dropped. I closed my mouth quickly and hugged myself.

"Don't you want to talk about Charlie?" I whispered.

"I wish there was more *to* talk about. Trying to live in the past is just tripping me up. I want to focus on my future, on finding Charlie and my relationship with you."

I'd never met a boy before, well any teenager really, who was so open with their emotions. That is, *if* he was being truthful. "And...what do you feel about me?"

A small ember ignited his eyes to a brilliant green in response, the same color they were yesterday, when he leaned in for what I thought was going to be a kiss. He took a step towards me and my body stiffened.

I don't think I could handle putting myself out there and Will deny me *again*. "Listen. I'm sorry if I gave you the wrong impression. Yesterday, I went against every rule I have set for myself and for some reason, I faltered and almost let you kiss me. I think it was just a rough day and my emotions were all tangled up. We've always been friends, nothing more." I stepped around Will and moved toward my dresser, but he caught me by my belt loop and pulled me close, leaning in like he planned to kiss me again. I resisted closing my eyes out of spite. If he got any closer, I would be the one to pull away this time. I could feel his sweet breath on my face. My lips grew more rebellious as seconds passed until they were heavy, throbbing under the rush of blood.

"Tell me you don't *feel* this." His voice was hoarse. "I mean, I am not even touching you and yet my lips feel as if we've already been making out."

I wouldn't tell him I felt the same. My stubborn streak fought hard, trying to win this one.

He continued, "For me, it feels like a growing heat that starts deep within my chest and increases in pressure with every second. It feels like I will burst if I don't act on it, taking every ounce of self-control and strength I have to *not* kiss you."

He inched closer and I held my breath. His cheek brushed mine and his lips grazed my neck. My skin tingled where his lips touched, an invisible imprint. He pulled away just enough for me to see his beautiful face donned with a look of complete and utter satisfaction. I finally exhaled. He had no idea how much strength it took me to not kiss him.

"Good," he murmured. "I'm glad to see I'm not the only one who feels this way."

"I...you...you don't know that." I turned and fumbled with the CDs at my dresser. His eyes, glowing, left me both enamored and a little spooked.

"Fine." His face fell. "I apologize for being so forward then. By the way, how does your wrist feel?"

Little guilt monsters reared their ugly heads, but I smashed them back into their holes. I wasn't ready to open myself to someone again. "It feels—" I rolled my wrist around and examined it— "good, like new."

"I didn't want to move and wake you so, I continued to

hold your wrist, even after you fell asleep."

"What are you trying to say?"

"I think I may have discovered another...ability thanks to Nick and his Christmas rose. Can I try to convince you of one more thing?" I nodded. "Close your eyes and don't move," he instructed.

"I'm not closing my eyes."

Will guided me back from my dresser to stand in front of him. "Alright then. Keep your eyes on mine and hold out your hands, palms up. I noticed your palm looks like it got a little hurt in the altercation with Jackie."

I probably needed to talk to Will about my dreams, but what was the point? I could barely remember them. I stood still and held out my hands and Will placed his on top of mine. A few anxious heartbeats later, he dropped them to his sides and sat down at my desk.

"OK, and the point of that was...?" I wondered not quite certain what he expected from his hand experiment.

He was silent as he looked at me. *Why is he staring?* I couldn't help but fret with my hair, fix my shirt, and eye the small flaws in my nail polish.

"Doesn't it alarm you that we didn't even physically touch and yet it felt like we did?"

"Yeah right, you totally just put your hands on top of mine."

"No, I didn't. Look at your palm." The pink had disappeared, and my skin was back to normal. "Liddy, I think I can heal you, to a small extent anyway."

My breathing went ragged and I slumped onto the edge of my bed. There was no real explanation I could think of. I don't know which was stranger, waking up with what looked like the letter M branded on my palm or that fact that Will somehow magically healed it. I swallowed hard. Will needed me to be strong for him.

"Well, I mean, I wouldn't say it alarms me. I would say interests or intrigues. But, if I were to be honest, if it were anyone else, I would probably be totally panicked." I hoped my face didn't give away my half-truth. I sat back down on the bed. "These past few days have been a lot to handle, but at least..." A moment of realization hit me. "I think I now understand why my ribs healed so quickly."

Will ran a hand through his hair. "Do you remember feeling any of this, whatever this is, when we were kids?"

"I don't. Not to this extent anyway, but I do remember wanting to just be by you all the time."

"Same." Nervous laughter caught him briefly. "I'm debating asking you something. I do not want you to think I am going postal though."

I walked towards him. I took a soothing breath and grabbed onto his clasped hands with my left and used my right to lift his chin. Skin to skin contact still assured my body with a torrent of sensation, but at least it no longer surprised me. "Just say it."

Will grasped my hand and rested it on his lips. After a long pause, he sighed, moving my hand to the side of his chin, but he didn't look at me. "It's my eyes. Have you noticed anything... *different* about them?"

There had been a few times where I thought they did seem to ignite though I reasoned away the possibility every time. But he asked which meant I had to face reality. The slight tremble of his hand assured me he was just as uneasy about this as I was.

"I thought I was imagining things, your eyes changing color with your moods."

Will closed his eyes and sucked in his lips. "I wasn't sure I could believe what I saw in the mirror. I needed to know if you saw it too. Are you scared of me now?"

I placed my hand on his shoulder. "Nothing I've seen scares me. So what if the color changes and they glow sometimes? I'm only more drawn to you, I mean *them*, I mean, no I am not scared." *Chill, Liddy!*

"Do you think other people notice?" Will asked, his grip tightening on my arm.

"Umm...Will?" I gestured to my arm, and he let go.

"Sorry."

"With the way gossip travels so fast at this school, if people noticed, I'd have heard from Pree by now." He seemed relieved. We were silent for a moment. "I was nervous when my eyes changed colors."

Will snapped his head in my direction and searched my eyes. "I don't see anything."

"You can't see that they're violet?"

"Weren't they always?"

"No, they were blue!"

"Huh. I don't remember that. They are gorgeous all the same and I haven't seen them change." Will smiled.

I should go through Mom's photo albums to prove it to him, and myself. "Did you by any chance bring those letters or books with you?" I asked Will.

"I didn't. I wasn't sure who all would be at your house... It said to keep everything hidden. I thought for at least this first time with seeing your parents again, we wouldn't get the opportunity to go through it all anyway."

"So, English paper then?"

"Yeah, let's get it done so tomorrow we can start making a plan on how to contact Nick and get my brother back." Will sat forward on the edge of his seat, excitement lighting his eyes at the mention of Charlie.

It appeared that Nick gave some sort of magic to Will, something I was still trying to wrap my head around. Maybe Nick poisoned Will and used the flower to do it. As awful as that sounded, it meant all of this would soon fade.

I smiled. "Sounds good. I've just got to open my door, so my parents don't get the wrong idea."

I opened my door and propped myself on the floor at Will's feet.

We'd been working for a little over an hour when my phone rang. Before I could grab it, Will answered.

"Princess Lydia Erickson's phone... One second... It's Justin." He let the phone slump on the bed.

I shot an annoyed grimace at Will. "Hi, Justin."

"Hey, Liddy," he greeted. "I heard what happened to you earlier. I wish I had been there to take care of it. Between me and Jackie, are you going to make it to the dance in one piece?"

I laughed and turned my back while trying to sound casual. From our conversation earlier, I doubted Will wanted to hear me talking to Justin. "I'm fine. Alex saw it happen, so he helped move Jackie along."

"Alex *rescued* you?" he exaggerated.

"I wouldn't say he *rescued* me. Alex has some sort of dirt on Jackie and threatened to come out with it if she harassed me again. I am hoping it's good enough that she'll stay away."

"That's decent of him I guess." He cleared his throat. "So, yeah, about Friday night. I was thinking I could take you to dinner and a movie. Have you seen *Ever After* yet?"

Dinner doesn't last forever, and movies don't require talking in case things get awkward. "That sounds nice." And, it was sweet he picked a chick-flick. "I do have to work early Saturday though."

"How about we get started earlier then, say five-thirty?"

"Sounds good. Hey, I don't mean to cut this short, but Will's here and we are working on our English paper, so I need to get back to it."

More silence.

"Justin?"

"Uh, yeah, my bad. I don't want to keep you from homework when you've got someone at your crib waiting on you. See ya tomorrow."

"Bye."

I hung up with Justin and turned to see Will packing up. His eyes were dark, that deep green again, and sparking.

"Are we done?" I asked, confused.

"I am," Will declared, nearly ripping his zipper off his messenger bag as he closed it.

Can he just be done with me so easily? An unexpected ache in my chest hit me. "Can you chill for a second."

"I've gotta get going."

But I wasn't ready for him to leave. *Why does he have to be so difficult?* "Your eyes are the darkest green I've seen them yet and—" he stopped short and I got close to his face— "and I haven't been honest with you." He turned away from me.

"You still going on a date with Justin?" Will asked, looking over his shoulder, a muscle in his jaw twitching.

"Are you seriously leaving right now because I am going on a casual date with a friend?"

Will wheeled around. "You can say no, Liddy."

"I can't say no *now*. I already said yes, and I don't want things to be weird before the dance."

"You don't have to do something just because someone else might feel bad."

"I wish I could, but that's just not me! I care about how I make others feel. As I said before, I'm sick of feeling bad about making him feel bad. I know it's not fair of me, but he was there for me when you weren't." Will winced and he caught his breath. He looked away from me and took another step towards the door. "Besides, everyone is always telling me to not be such a straight edge and have fun. I doubt my feelings will change for him, but he's put in the effort and is a nice guy. I feel I owe him at least one date."

Will gritted his teeth. "You. Owe. Him. *Nothing.*"

"What's it to you?" I said stepping towards him, thankful my parents weren't home yet to hear us squabbling. "You come back to Illinois and start revealing all these crazy things to me. I'm trying to be patient and not freak out because I have no idea what all of this is, and I want to be there for you."

"I appreciate that, but—"

"I'm not finished. You say you're interested in me and I'm supposed to believe you, but that nothing can happen, fine. But then, what? Am I just supposed to sit here and wait? Wait for what? Some lunatic named Nick to dictate your life? And then you get jealous when I accept a casual date. I'm not yours and I think I am doing a pretty darn good job of trying to understand all of this."

"What's it to me? Are you seriously asking that?" Will challenged, striding past me and spinning around to face me again.

"Yes, yes I am," I said, turning to face him fully, hands on my hips. "How many times have we almost kissed and you pull away or change course? *You* tell me how right this all feels—" I pointed my finger at him— "show me letters about our destiny and then, nothing. We talk about our childhood friendship and nothing more than that. What are we?" I relaxed my shoulders, curious where my boldness erupted from.

"We are friends, but it's complicated."

"Well, there ya go. Back to square—"

"Of course, I want to be with you!" he yelled, throwing his hands up in exasperation. "I know you are super sensitive to caring about what others think of you so how could you *not* know? What I don't know is how *you* feel. Do you remember what the letters from Nick said? We can't be together, not that I don't want to be, and it is *so* unfair."

I busted out laughing. "So that's what this all is? You seriously believe that dude?"

His jaw dropped, then he snapped it shut, setting his mouth in a tight line. "Laugh all you want. You and I both know there have been inexplicable things happening. I have to believe that my brother is alive and if I believe that, then I have to believe what it also said about us taking this to any level besides friendship." He sighed and sat back down at the desk, placing his head in his hands. "Not to mention, I respect you and wouldn't want to do anything without a more important commitment."

I laughed and even though guilt struck me, I wasn't holding back any punches. I was tired of this merry-go-round already. "What the heck does that mean? Important commitment?"

"You, Liddy. It's always been you." Will groaned, lifting his head to me. "I know this is going to sound crazy to you because it sounds completely and utterly ridiculous to me every time I've thought about telling you. I know technically we've been apart for many years. But for me, when my memories came back, it felt like I'd just woken from a deep sleep, one without any dreams. What I'm trying to say is that it feels like we've never been apart. Earlier, when I said that I've always felt that I've wanted to be with you, I was *not* kidding. I am not sure when the transition from best friend to wanting—no, realizing—we were made for each other happened, but it did. I believe we'll be together, forever."

My stomach both flipped and sank, legs so weak I had to sit. My heart wrestled with my brain. Was he saying what I think he was saying? *Marriage.* I wasn't ready to deal with a conversation of that magnitude. This was all impossibly fast, and I was only seventeen. I counted fifteen heartbeats before I managed to speak.

"Listen, Will, I too choose to believe your brother is alive and I promise I will do whatever I can to help you find him."

"You do? So, then you understand what I am saying!" He dropped to his knees, my hands now in his.

I focused on his warm hands. If I agreed, it meant that I believed this psycho guy Nick existed and everything he put in those letters. Not just the stuff about Will's brother Charlie, but also the parts about Will and me. If I said I didn't, well then, I would break any glimmer of hope that Will had about finding his brother and I'd possibly lose him again forever. He looked so happy just now; I didn't want to screw that up. I needed to suppress my growing feelings towards him, for his *and* Charlie's sake. Will's happiness involved playing along with this notion that the world would come to an end should I act on my desires. That was more important to me than testing out any relationship. I wanted to let him know just how sucky this all was, but I knew this wasn't the right time.

"Yes, I understand. Which makes it all the more reasonable that I said yes to a date with Justin."

Will's face sunk. "I suppose you're right. I just didn't expect for this to even be an issue until I figured this all out. I thought you didn't even want to date. Something about it being a waste of time, keeping you from your goals."

"Listen, I didn't think I wanted to date either and I'm still not convinced that I do." Will didn't need to know that it was because my heart was telling me I didn't need to. Because, my body knew it wanted *him*. "Justin is a standup guy and a friend. I don't plan on this going anywhere and I want to give him a break, but at least attempting a date makes saying no easier in the future."

"Always so calculated, Liddy," he said as he came to sit by me again.

"Will, you've made it clear that we can't take this friendship anywhere and I'm good with that. I haven't had time to even assess if that would be something I'd want," I added for good measure, hoping to help keep us at a safe distance. "I have been assaulted all week by girls who want to date you and hate that I'm even friends with you. You'd be better off dating one of

them since they don't pose such a threat to human existence."
As the words rolled off my tongue, they left a bitter taste.

"Have you not heard a word I've said? I don't want them! I
know it's unfair of me to ask, but wait for me," he said resting
his hand on my knee. "I know you are meant for me. I can feel
it." He leaned in close, his eyes light and pleading. "I need you
Lydia Andra and I hope to be with you as soon as I can find
Nick and figure out why we can't be together..."

I scratched at my neck, but felt no hives to explain the
itching. He hadn't even been back in my life for a week, and he
already had plans for our future. I just knew that the more we
kidded ourselves the more we would just wind up getting hurt.
Not to mention, I was scared. I couldn't get hurt again, and
especially not by Will. I had to be lovingly honest. "Can we step
back for a minute? Your words of being *with me* seem like they
have a much larger connotation attached."

"They do," Will proclaimed, exasperated.

"Well, that, *that,* scares the crap out of me!" I said standing.
I paced. "I can't even think about that right now. I *just* turned
seventeen and I need to get into college and get out of Illinois.
I know you feel differently, but for me, we barely know each
other as we are now. Yes, we were best buddies once upon a
time, but—"

"I didn't say we'd get married right now, just that I know
you are who I want to spend my forever with. I can't explain
why or how I know that. I just do. I'm sorry I said anything."

I closed my eyes and rubbed my temples. I must have
opened and closed my mouth at least seven times. He was an
emotional tornado. He seemed hurt, angry, and frustrated all
at the same time. I took a deep breath. I didn't want to hurt

him, but I wasn't ready to open myself up in that way yet and it was too easy to do with Will. I also didn't want to keep this *we're dating but we're not* charade up. He believed Nick, and if temptation got the best of us, I wouldn't want Will to resent me. "Can we *just* be friends?" I implored. I came to sit by him again. "I know we have this assignment, but I think it'd be best if we weren't alone together anymore."

"As you wish." Will shot up off the bed. Without looking my way, he threw his messenger bag over his shoulder and hurried out the door.

I hesitated at the door, debating whether or not I should follow him. But what else could I say? I needed to do this for our sake. Deflated, I locked my door instead and collapsed in a heap on my bed. The tears that built up flowed like a raging river, free after being dammed for far too long.

The Date

T HE NEXT EVENING I WALKED TO CLEAR MY HEAD. Will kept his distance the next day, ignoring me in our shared classes and made himself scarce during passing periods. He slipped a note in my locker letting me know that he couldn't work on the English paper today, nor tomorrow after school, and wanted to make sure I had a ride home. *Whatever.* I exhaled; the rush of air passing my lips left a cloud of steam.

His coolness frustrated me more than the frigid air I walked in. This was about way more than the English assignment. We were supposed to figure out a game plan for tracking down Nick and finding Charlie. After all, it was the main reason for all the drama between us. *Ughhhh!*

I slowed my pace, trying to enjoy the satisfying sound of snow crunching beneath my boots when a distinctive chiming caught my attention. My foul mood was extinguished and a new fire, one made of fear and fueled by adrenaline, surged through me. Like a frightened mouse recognizing a predator near, I wanted to scurry right back to my house. I picked up my pace, glancing over my shoulders, trying to find where the tinkling sound came from. I gasped upon spotting the source. Across the street, about a yard and a half away, a man strolled toward me with silver hair and a long, black coat. Like a practiced speed walker, I pumped my arms closing the gap that separated me from my house.

"Wait, Princess, please!" he yelled, the chiming growing louder.

Run, Liddy, run! I was so close, one house away from mine, the bell-like tone growing louder and louder.

"Lydia, stop!" the man ordered. A bright light lit up the sidewalk in front of me and then it was gone. I skidded to a halt, not sure if I'd stopped of my own volition or if this man made me. I turned, heart pounding, to face him. The silver-haired man walked closer to me and my body vibrated with the desire to run away, but I couldn't move.

"I am not here to hurt you." He lifted his arms to signal a truce, to show that he had no weapons in his hands, as he came to stand with me under the light of the next streetlamp.

"Can I help you?" I shouted and he flinched. When he did, a familiar melody sounded again. My eyes searched him for what could possibly be making such a unique sound. Three gold chains glinted from the pocket of his Christmas-green vest. He brushed a dusting of snow off his arms and what looked like at least fifty tiny charms and trinkets jingled and jangled against each other. I went rigid realizing I'd heard them the other night...the night I lost control of my body and dug up the Christmas roses for Will.

Fear crept in, but I held my ground and forced my voice steady. "Sorry, can I help you?" My eyes located the fresh, glittering Christmas rose in the lapel of his high-necked peacoat.

His charming face with trimmed white beard followed my gaze. He smiled, his voice surprisingly smooth. "Indubitably, you *can* help, Princess Lydia." He bowed. "I have been waiting for you. You'll have to excuse my chagrin, but every time I have tried to seek you out, it—hmmm—hasn't ended well." His smile widened pushing his ruddy, prominent cheekbones to his crystal, blue-grey eyes.

"I'm sorry, who are you?"

"How egregious of me. I thought you may have recognized me. Alas, I should have been more fastidious, but there has not been much time for pleasantries. My name is Nicholas Gabriel Klaus, Nick, and it's a pleasure to formally meet you, again." He winked and gave a slight bow.

"Again? So, so that *was* you the other night down the street."

"Yes, but I was also referring to when you were a little girl, around the time William lived here."

I couldn't speak. I knew the sounds of his chains seemed familiar beyond last night, but he definitely was not in any of my memories, including the ones Will helped restore.

"You may want to breathe before you pass out. I'd hate to have to carry you home again." His voice was soothing and accent unique.

"You could have just introduced yourself instead of being

a creeper," I replied, lifting my chin and rising to my fullest height. I knew better than to let my guard down. After all, I had seen just about every episode of *America's Most Wanted.*

He let out a deep chuckle, his eyes twinkling in the night. "I apologize for the poor timing on my part for...complicated reasons," he stated as he glanced at his pocket watch. "But I do need your assistance if you'd be so willing. Please look at these and go over them with Prince William." He held out his leather gloved hand and produced a large manila envelope. Attached to his wrist was a thick bracelet, the leather worn and embedded with a charm resembling an old compass. It reminded me a lot of...*Will's.*

I snatched the envelope from Nick's hands with a little more force than intended, never taking my eyes off of him. Though his eyes were kind and bright giving him a more youthful appearance, a few battle scars on his cheek and eyebrow suggested he had a fierceness not to be tested. I wasn't sure what to make of him.

I clutched the envelope to my chest and took a few steps back, continuing to stare at Nick in disbelief. So, he did exist. Nick had an oddity about him. He seemed harmless, but the worn look of his face shadowed an impressive man. His bright eyes, his clothes, his accent, all led me to believe he was not from around here. The letters to Will were obscure, enough to bring Will and I closer together and yet keep us apart.

"Princess Lydia, did you hear what I asked?" Nick questioned, a look of confusion on his face.

"What's with the few and far between cryptic letters? And why only to Will? And why are you sneaking around all the time? And how did we first meet?" I rambled faster than the guy in the *Micro Machines* commercials when Nick cleared his throat.

He pulled up his white shirt cuff, looked at the inside of his leather bracelet, and frowned. "I've had to be discrete, more than I would like, but alas I have had no choice. I'd love to answer all of your questions, but at another time. For now, I must be getting back. I know this is a lot to process, but please study the papers in the file I handed you. In there you will find a thick stack of articles about missing children."

"Missing children?"

"Yes," Nick pinched the bridge of his nose as if this pained him. "I have something of importance to attend to at this moment, but I don't want these to wait while I'm gone. This small collection of news clippings may be Mara's undoing."

"Mara...that name rings a bell."

"It does?" Nick asked, concern laced his words.

My mind refused to produce a face to fit the name. "Never mind, I guess it doesn't."

Nick studied me before continuing. "I need you and William to research children who went missing around Christmas time as far back as 1982. I need to know if there are any connecting factors as to why they were abducted and for what purpose. Don't neglect the books either. Do you understand?" I nodded. "Excellent." He turned to start walking away, but whipped back around. "Oh, I almost forgot. They are to be read *with* William. That is very important. We will talk soon." He turned once again and stalked away in the direction of Pree's house.

That's it? That's all I get? We'll talk soon and research... *with Will? That's crap.* I started towards him and hollered, "Don't just walk away from me!" but Nick continued on.

Frustrated, I tried again with a nicer tone to my voice. "Please, can you at least...tell me how I can get a hold of you?"

Nick turned around to look at me and I stopped. Walking backwards, he responded, "Not to worry, I will seek you out when I need to. Oh, and one more thing. I've heard that you and Prince William haven't been speaking. You will need to maintain your friendship with him if we are to be successful. Your *close* friendship." And with that, he turned back around, his long strides gaining speed.

"Hey, this is a two-way street! I'm not at your beck and call..." I protested but trailed off as Nick stopped and whipped around. *Crap. Did I just anger this dude?* I took small steps back, flinching from him as he bounded towards me, his eyes alight with what seemed like annoyance.

He abruptly stopped a few feet away. "Yes, Your Highness?"

"Remind me again what we're trying to accomplish here."

Nick dragged his hand down his face. "In rescuing Charlie and the children! And of course, restoring Cristes."

"Just so you know, you don't have to worry about Will and I. Of course we're friends."

"You're a terrible liar," he interjected.

"How dare you!"

"I know you and Will are in a disagreement at the moment."

"How did you—"

"How I know is not of importance. It's *what* I know that truly matters."

"Whatever. What did you mean by close? I thought your letters said to keep it free of the *close stuff*," I said, gesturing with air quotes.

Nick smiled. "I am confident you can figure out a way

to be close and nothing more. *Teenagers*," he mumbled and he shook his head with a slight chuckle. "Your powers are amplified when you are together. Young Watchers need that amplification especially here in Mortalia, but too much contact and KABOOM!" He clapped his hands.

"Kaboom? Like, we'll explode?"

Nick belly laughed. "No, but let's just say Mara, someone we are trying to keep you and William from, can more easily locate you and she's already too close. Not to mention, you may give your human friends something to talk about, if you don't scare them away first. Either way, we don't want that attention."

All I could do was stare, my mouth hanging open.

"I bid thee farewell." Then he gave another quick bow and sped off. Keeping my eyes glued to his movements, I backed in the direction of my house until Nick vanished into the night.

The next day after school, I woke with a start hunched over my bedroom desk and checked my alarm clock. It was just after four thirty. *Dang.* I fell asleep finishing my homework. My date with Justin was in two hours. I yawned and stretched. *Time to get ready, I guess.*

I went to the bathroom, turned on my hot rollers, and hopped into the shower. The heat melted away the stress of my impending date with Justin. I used my favorite body wash that smelled of coconut and hibiscus, the scent transporting me away from the cold and dreary to the warm and tropical. I wrapped myself in a towel and headed to my room where I turned on Ace of Base. I bent my head over and sang along to "I

Saw the Sign" as I blow dried my hair. I turned off the dryer and as I flipped my hair back to stand up, I let out a startled scream, nearly dropping my towel. Will leaned against the door jamb, arms crossed, a huge grin adorning his face. I heard Mickey belly laughing through the vents from somewhere in the house.

"Sorry to startle you. Mickey let me in and, since your parents are gone, offered to walk me up. Nice singing by the way," Will commented.

"Yeah, right," I sneered.

"I'm not joking."

Still red faced with both embarrassment and anger, I retorted, "Whatever, would you mind turning around for a second, please?" Will did as he was asked and I raced into my robe. "You can turn around now. Why are you here?"

Will stepped into my room. "I got an email from you saying to stop by. Something about you having something to give me from Nick?" he said, eyeing the ground and running his hand through his hair.

I'd almost forgotten I hadn't told Will everything that happened last night. *Almost.* "I didn't email you."

"Yes, you did." His head snapped up. "Don't know if you noticed, but I wasn't at school today. I'm a little, *eh hem*, under the weather." I rolled my eyes at his poor acting skills. "But shortly after two-thirty, I received an email from you saying to stop by tonight a little before five, that you had something to show me."

"Will, I swear I did not write that email." *It had to be Nick!* "But in any case, yes, I do have something for you," I said, going to my desk drawer. "Meeting Nick last night was crazy... He's an interesting dude. Here it is," I said holding out the large manilla envelope. "I waited to open it with you." Will snatched it.

"What?" he asked. "You met Nick and didn't tell me?"

"Well—" I hesitated, noticing the deepening color of Will's eyes— "it was late, and I didn't want to wake you."

"Something tells me that's not the case."

He was partly right. He had angered me the previous day, acting like anything but a friend, but I thought it better to tell him in person. "Believe what you want. I felt that meeting Nick was something we should discuss face to face. Since you weren't too keen on speaking with me yesterday, I decided not to call, and today you weren't at school." I crossed my arms and popped my hip.

"I'm sorry about yesterday." Will glanced down at the envelope. Peering at me through his lashes he continued quietly, "I still wish you would have called, knowing how much this means to me." He turned the envelope in his hands, examining it, and ran his long fingers over the crimson red seal. "Do you mind if I have a look?" he asked, his eyes glued to the package.

"Not as long as you don't mind me getting ready," I replied as I headed to the bathroom.

"What did Nick look like Liddy?" he asked just as he sat down at my desk.

I walked back to my room and leaned on the doorframe. "He was a little shorter than you, silvery hair, white beard, and light blue eyes."

"Anything else?"

"Oh! And he wore posh clothing that no one from around here would wear."

"Posh. How so?" Will asked.

"He wore this black pea coat that had a high neck and large buttons. And underneath was this Christmas-green velvet vest with an elaborate pocket chain and a Christmas rose in the lapel. I think the chain may explain why he jingles when he moves."

Will made a deep throated sound under his breath and brought his eyes back to the envelope while I disappeared into the bathroom.

"What color is Christmas-green?" he yelled after me.

I came back into the room with my hair in hot rollers, and explained, "Christmas-green, like the color of a Christmas tree, duh." I finished getting ready in front of my mirrored closet doors, but changed in my bathroom. I looked at myself in the mirror. *Why did I agree to let Pree pick out my outfit?* When I returned, Will still sat at the desk, hands folded, staring at the grey computer screen. I gave myself a final once over, trying to recognize the once short and far less curvy girl from last summer.

I grabbed my favorite perfume, *Exclamation,* and spritzed the air. I walked through it to stand next to Will at the desk. Placing my left hand next to the keyboard as I leaned in closer to Will, I observed the scattered contents of the envelope— newspaper clippings from disappearances in Illinois and surrounding states over the past twenty or so years, including the one about Charlie.

"You smell nice," Will said softly.

"Thank you." I gave him a quick smile before returning my attention to the clippings. "Nick mentioned he was providing us with information to start our research on what happened to these kids. Maybe it's all connected to Charlie?" I suggested.

"I never thought there would be so many kids. I guess I just assumed it was only Charlie."

Will's eyes went dark, the anguish in them a pit of despair in my stomach. I swallowed hard and studied the pictures in the articles. Some were just a crowd of onlookers with police tape while others included parents of the missing children in the background; the deep circles under their eyes and the dead stares on their faces broke my heart. I found the one with Charlie and gasped.

"What is it?"

"Nothing, I just didn't expect to see me in a picture. That is, I don't remember it." My eyes were wide and a man's fingerless, leather-gloved hand was on my shoulder. He wore a leather cuff...like the one Nick wore last night.

I looked through the rest of the images. Nick was in every single one of the photos, though only parts of his body were visible, never his face. Normally, he wouldn't stand out, but there were pieces of his attire that just didn't fit in with the rest of the crowd. The leather cuff, the high-necked pea coat, the back or profile of his precisely styled white, wavy hair, or the rose in his lapel.

I jumped as my clear cordless phone rang. Will sat back at the desk as I answered.

"Hello?"

"Hi, Liddy, it's Justin."

"Hey, Justin, everything alright?" I lost track of time and forgot about my date!

"Yep, just letting you know I'm about to leave to come pick you up. Are you ready?"

Through no fault of his own, Justin's timing sucked. My

heart warred with my brain. On the one hand, I wanted to stay with Will and look more into this. But I couldn't back out on him now, especially since I had already fought with Will about it.

I surreptitiously glanced at Will, his eyes a dark but vivid green, and rolled my neck, willing the creeping tension away. "Yes. I'll see you soon." I hung up. I busied myself with straightening my already made bed as I mentioned in passing, "Will, that was Justin. He's coming to get me soon."

"Yeah, I know, for your date," he said coolly.

I walked over to him and placed my hands on his shoulders. Staring into his face, I prepared to drink in the good feeling I always got from touching him, only this time, a cold, sinking sensation overwhelmed me. I let go and Will dropped his face.

"Will look at me, please." But he would not move. "Look. At. Me," I articulated, using the best grown up voice I could muster. He acquiesced to my request and I smiled down at him, placing a hand on his cheek. His eyes shifted a shade lighter. *Cool.* "You are my friend and very important to me. I want nothing more than to help you find your brother and we'll figure this all out. I promise. It's just that I gave my word for tonight and I can't back out. How about tomorrow?"

Will was silent for a moment, searching my face, and as his eyes lightened more, my heart quickened. His hand covered mine as he responded, "Tomorrow evening sounds great. My place?"

I sighed in response to his touch. His eyes phased back to their normal color and that scrumptious joyful feeling coursed through my veins.

"Is that a yes?" he murmured.

I will not succumb to this feeling. I removed my hand. "How about the library?" I proposed, the corner of my mouth turning up. I wanted to stay true to our hanging out in a group or public setting until I could trust myself to be able to resist the temptation of him. I missed Charlie so I could only imagine how hurt Will must be. I didn't want to be the one to muck it all up by dooming his brother and quite possibly the entire world. Meeting Nick had given me pause to consider the slight possibility that this all might not be so far-fetched after all.

"As you wish." Will smiled, using that line again from *The Princess Bride*. When Wesley said it, what he was really saying was *I love you* to Princess Buttercup. *There's no way he means the same thing.* "But I am picking you up. You are not walking anywhere with this Nick dude hanging around."

"I'll call you when I'm done shopping with the girls, OK?"

"As you wish." His smile grew and at that moment his eyes turned a beautiful aqua. I froze as if I were made of stone, perfectly still, except for the butterflies flapping wildly in my stomach. *Is he saying he loves me?* For a fleeting moment, my eyes tingled, like they twinkled back at him of their own accord. But if they did, he didn't say anything about it.

"Let *me* try something," I challenged as I closed my eyes and placed my hands on top of his shoulders. "Ahhhhh." A deep sigh beyond my control rang out. I opened my eyes and saw his eyes spark.

"What?" he asked, his voice rough.

"Your eyes... It's cool when they change like that." Will dropped his gaze, but I caught his chin. "It's quite amazing. Depending on the shade of your eyes, when I touch you, I can feel different vibes course through my body. Like just now, your eyes are a lovely aqua and when I touch you, it feels nice, comforting." Will blushed and I laughed. "It might not just be me that feels this, so be careful with *touching* others," I teased.

"I don't plan on it," he bristled. "*You* should be careful of the effect *you* have on others," he cautioned, and as if he saw me for the first time tonight, he caught his breath. "Are you wearing that? I mean, this poor dude doesn't stand a chance."

"What is that supposed to mean?" My black shirt and red cigarette pants may have hugged my curves a little more than usual for me, but they were still modest.

"Forget it." Will gathered the clippings to put back in the envelope. "I'll get started on looking into these more tonight."

"OK. Nick said we should focus on what, if any, connections the kids had and why they were taken. Oh, and to see if we could find any more kids who disappeared."

"Got it. Well, I guess I should be going."

"Great, you can walk me down."

Will helped me into my coat first. I yelled to Mickey to let Mom and Dad know when they got home that I had gone on my date.

"Mickey can stay home alone?" Will asked.

"Believe it or not, but he's eleven now. Plus, my parents will be home in like thirty minutes. He'll probably just play *Punch Out* on Nintendo until they get back."

"Mind if I wait until Justin gets here?" Will asked, looking at me through his lashes. "I'd feel better knowing you weren't out there alone."

"I don't think anything will happen on my front porch." Truth was, I was nervous about how Justin would react. When I saw Will's face fall, I said, "But, as my friend, you're welcome to keep me company."

We stood in silence for a few moments more until Justin pulled up. Will walked me all the way to Justin's Bronco, his mouth twisted and jaw clenched as he stared Will down. Justin was midway through getting out of the car to open the door for me, but Will got there first. Justin sat back in the driver's seat and slammed his door.

"Take good care of her," Will said with a slightly patronizing tone before walking off to his Jeep.

Justin drove in silence, the veins in his neck popping as he clenched his teeth.

"I'm looking forward to our date. Thanks again for asking me."

"Thanks for saying yes." His jaw relaxed. He patted my knee. "I have a surprise for you."

"I can't wait."

We walked into Wa-Pa-Ghetti's Pizza. The owner led us to a red and white checkered table set up in the back adorned with two taper candles and flowers just for us. But Justin's surprise didn't end there. We were led to the kitchen for a private pizza making class, where Justin helped tie my apron, fingers lingering at my back. The owner winked at Justin and left us to our own devices. I tossed the dough with a little too much force. I must have used too much flour because when it landed on Justin's head, a puff exploded out covering his face and shoulders.

"I'm so sorry!"

Justin retaliated by laughing and swiping flour on my nose and cheeks.

I'd forgotten how funny he was. Two summers ago, I got

my heart broken by my first and only boyfriend. Justin was there to help me pick up the pieces. He was nice to me, always lending a listening ear, and could make me laugh no matter my mood. I can't pinpoint when the shift occurred, but I realized at one point that I liked him as more than just a friend.

Luckily, we didn't have to eat our own pizzas. Justin paid the bill and we headed to the theater.

I started to stress halfway through the movie when Justin's fingers entwined with mine. Unfortunately, I felt no chemistry with him now. What if he tried to kiss me? Did I owe him at least that for the wonderful dinner and movie and paying for it all? *You owe him nothing.* Will's words echoed in my head. But would Justin expect me to kiss him? No. The Justin I knew would never expect that. Besides, I told him we were just friends. However, some peers might argue I was leading him on if I didn't kiss him. The date was suddenly marred by societal pressures. Why did a kiss, or even the idea of it, have to be so complicated?

When the movie ended, we walked back to his car and Justin opened the door for me. As he drove me home, I worked myself into a tizzy, allowing anxiety to simmer just beneath my skin. I couldn't even speak and the silence didn't help. I glanced at Justin who worried his bottom lip.

We pulled up to my house and he put the Bronco in park; he kept the car running but turned off the headlights.

Justin unbuckled his seatbelt and twisted to face me. "I had a nice time with you tonight Liddy—" he leaned in— "kind of like old times." His wintergreen breath was cool against my cheek.

Oh gosh, here it comes. "Me too. It was fun." My voice

shook.

"I would like to take you out again sometime," he said, grabbing my hand.

"Well, we do have the Winter Formal next week," I reminded him.

"Of course. I meant after that," he countered with a smirk and leaned in even closer.

I panicked and gave him a quick kiss on his warm, smooth cheek and blurted out, "Thanks again, but I've got to get going. My parents are probably waiting for me at the kitchen table." *Why did you kiss him, idiot?*

Justin reached for my arm. "I'm sure they won't mind just a few more minutes."

His warm eyes momentarily tempted me. *No, Liddy. This wouldn't be right.* I politely pulled away. "Sorry, I really should be going."

Justin sat back. "OK, then. Can I walk you to the door?"

"Sure." *Friends walk friends to their doors all the time.* Hopefully, Mickey would be his normal annoying self and be at the window ready to jump out to scare us or make some sort of crude comment.

While I tried to reason away my anxious thoughts, Justin came around to open my door and offered his hand to assist me out of the car. He tugged upward, but the seatbelt caught me. My cheeks flushed. "Sorry, I guess I forgot to unbuckle." Justin laughed. He let go long enough for me to unbuckle and then grabbed my hand again.

I tried to rush while he walked at a snail's pace. We made it to the stoop right before the porch, just out of the light peeking through the door's windows, when Justin stopped and turned to face me.

His eyes bore into mine. I'd forgotten just how charming and attractive he really was. "Liddy, I can't help but feel I made a huge mistake that night at the pool. My feelings have never gone away. Did I wait too long?"

Did he? In those final weeks of summer, Mom was routinely late picking me up from work. One night, Justin sat with me on the bench next to the bike racks for over thirty minutes. We were alone and the only light visible came from the few lamps in the parking lot. He'd sat so close that I could feel the heat from the day's sun radiating off of his tanned skin. The glazed muscles of his bare chest smelled like pink sunsets and coconut oil. His gaze lingered on my lips and we both leaned in, but at the last second, he pulled away. I remembered it like it was yesterday...

"I'm so sorry," my voice quivered as I put my face in my hands.

"Liddy, it's not that I don't want to, but you are clearly not over Brandon."

"Yes, yes I am!" I pursed my lips.

Justin sighed. "If you were, you wouldn't still talk about him every single day."

Justin's truth stung. He was right but I was so ready to move on. "But I do like you," I whispered.

"And I like you, but I don't want to be the rebound."

"Liddy, you OK?"

I focused my attention back to Justin. "You told me you didn't want to be the rebound, but I've been over Brandon a long time. Why now?"

"Well, you made it very apparent you had sworn off of guys

after that."

"I was hurt."

"I know, and I just wanted you to have time."

When Brandon cheated on me, I was the last to know. Justin's rejection only amplified my embarrassment and shame. When Mom pulled up that night, my emotions ran wild. A wall built itself around my heart and I made an impetuous decision. I vowed that I would never put myself out there again. A silly thing to promise myself in the midst of heartache, but I've kept it anyway.

"OK, but still... Why now?"

"I'm graduating at the end of the year. I would have regretted not taking the chance and seeing if you had changed your mind at all."

Your timing stinks, Justin. "I...I don't know what to say."

"Don't say anything. What if we just...picked up where we left off that night in the parking lot, just to see if maybe you did change your mind?" His hands traveled around my waist and started pulling me in for a kiss.

Right before his lips touched mine, I turned my cheek and leaned back, his lips awkwardly landing on the edge of my mouth. Keeping my head turned away from him, my body leaned back and stiff as a board, eyes clenched shut, I floundered for words. "Sorry! I'm so, so sorry. I'm not, I'm not ready for that," I said, a little too loudly.

"It's OK, Liddy. I'm sorry, too." He righted me to standing and dropped his arms. "You can't fault me for trying, eh?" He shrugged, and his face fell, my heart along with it. *I feel terrible.* "Is it alright if I give you a hug goodnight?"

"That...that would be fine." I said and relaxed. He enveloped me in his arms, lingering for a minute before planting a soft kiss on my forehead.

"Thanks, Justin. I really did have a great time tonight. It's just not the right timing." I withdrew from his arms, not meeting his eyes.

"Maybe it's just a no, for now." I looked up into Justin's bright face, alight with hope.

"Goodnight," I responded and closed the door. *It's over. I handled it OK. For me, anyway. He didn't seem like he was going to give up. I will cross that bridge when I get to it...after the formal.*

The Dress

"LYDIA... LYDIA," the angelic voice called. "Where are you?" it asked sweetly.

"I'm right here," I responded, looking around trying to find her.

"Lydia, come to me my dearest," she beckoned. "I can't seem to bring you to me, and I need you."

"Where are you? I can't see anything." A brilliant white light burned bright in the distance, green at its center; green like Will's eyes when he was angry.

"Come to the light. Come to me."

I tried to walk towards the light, but couldn't. My legs felt like they were encased in cement.

"Lydia, don't go. Stay with me here where I can keep you safe," Will implored, but I couldn't see him either. The white light shone even brighter, eating the edges of the pitch black encasing me.

"She's not dangerous, she needs me!" I shouted towards Will's voice.

"She's preventing you from remembering her vileness, playing tricks on your mind. Don't go to her." Another woman's voice, familiar and pleading.

A siren wailed in the distance, sounding off over and over again. I realized I was in a dream, but when I tried to open my eyes, they wouldn't budge. I could still hear the first woman's voice clear as a bell, her fervency rising.

"Lydia!" she wailed. "Stay with me. I've been waiting a *very* long time. Come to me now, please! I need you." At the same time, I could hear Will's voice fading, beseeching me to stay with him. I was confused, both seemed to need me. I could only go in one direction. I fought against the pull of the light and commanded myself to turn towards the darkness in the direction of Will's voice. I shouted, "Will!" and my eyes snapped open. I bolted up as my phone's blaring ring assaulted my ears and I answered with an exasperated, "Hello?"

"Lydia, thank God!" It was Will. "What's going on? Are you alright?"

"Yes, I'm fine. It was just a bad dream. You sound all freaked out. Are you OK?" There was a long pause. "Will?"

"I'm here. I had a bad dream, too. I can't remember any details except you were in danger."

Goosebumps ran down my arms. "Do you want to talk about it?"

"No, I'm just glad you are alright. Don't you have to get ready for work?"

"Holy crap-ola, I almost forgot! Talk later tonight?"

"Of course. Looking forward to it. Have a good day."

"See ya."

"There's a spot!" Pree pointed out from behind me.

"I see it, Pree. That's why I am stopped here with my blinker on."

"Ugh, this person is taking forever to pull out! Move it lady! We have dresses to find and don't have a ton of time to do it!" Pree reached over me and honked the horn.

"Pree!" Everyone shrieked in unison.

"Oh my gosh! I just became my mom." Pree sank back into her chair, and we all laughed.

It took me a few tries to park the van but I finally succeeded and we all rushed into Woodfield Mall. We entered through Carson's, since they usually had the best dresses. Christmas music and large red bows strung with twinkle lights greeted us when we walked in. Immediately to our left was the formal dress section.

"Well, I found my dress!" Dani beelined to a sale rack in the middle. How she even saw the silver dress with black mesh overlay from where we stood, I had no idea. We followed her over as she took it down and checked the tag. "Just my size as well!"

"You should still try it on," I suggested.

"Wait for me," Pree said. "I'll go to customer service and grab mine so we can try ours on together."

Sara and I sat and waited by the mirrors near the entrance

to the dressing room.

Dani walked out first. Sara and I held up our hands, wiggling our fingers.

"A solid ten from us!" Sara shouted.

Dani's smile was huge. "That was easy! And it's a perfect fit. That like, never happens! My mom is going to love that she doesn't need to hem it."

Pree came out next and we sat there, gobsmacked.

"You hate it, don't you," Pree whined.

"Just the opposite, Pree. You look radiant," I responded and walked up to her to check out the intricate details of the gold and cornflower-blue sari-inspired gown.

"Now you're just exaggerating." Pree shrugged.

"She's not," Dani chimed in.

"And your mom will totally approve," Sara added for good measure.

Dani and Pree purchased their dresses and we headed into the crowded mall.

As we walked to our fifth store, my stomach rumbled. We were slammed at work—I fed everyone but myself. "Hey guys, I'm starving. I'm going to the food court. You guys go on ahead. I know you have shoes and accessories to find."

"OK, but hurry because we're running out of time to find your dress," Sara cautioned.

"Meet you at Claire's in thirty?" I suggested.

"If you'd listened to me and picked the one from Jessica McClintock where Sara got hers, we'd all be done," Pree interjected, sounding annoyed.

"Sorry, Pree. The red dress is beautiful, but I'm just not feeling it. I'll be back in a jiffy." I waved and headed towards the food court. It was a lovely dress, but I couldn't afford it. Well, that's not true, more so that I refused to pay one hundred eighty dollars for a dress when I could save that money for a car.

On my way to the food court, I dodged around families with straying toddlers as they struggled to keep them happy while waiting in line for a photo op with Santa.

I headed straight to my favorite Chinese restaurant and ordered chicken teriyaki with fried rice. Grabbing my tray from the worker wearing an elf hat, I headed to a secluded table so as not to attract attention while I people-watched. Some seemed genuinely happy to be Christmas shopping, but the majority looked stressed and annoyed. *So much for it being the most wonderful time of the year.* I savored my final bites when Nick sat down across from me, placing a large garment bag over the back of the chair next to him. "You don't need to stop chewing on my account," he teased.

I closed my mouth. There had been no warning this time that he was near. No familiar tinkling and plinking. I swallowed and continued to stare.

"I come bearing gifts." He smiled as he gestured to the bag. I flinched at his movement. "I'm not going to hurt you." His brow furrowed as the grin faded from his face. Holding his hands up in a show of good faith, he said, "Let me show you." He unzipped the lower part of the navy bag, pulling out gorgeous shoes: clear, peep-toe booties with three-inch heels, all encrusted with Swarovski crystals. If Cinderella was set in today's world, I'd imagine her glass slippers would have looked like these. Placing them back at the bottom of the bag, he then pulled the zipper all the way up and held open the sides to reveal the most gorgeous gown I'd ever seen. Eyes wide, I leaned in to get a better look as he slid his arm under it. The draped ombré dress was saturated with a dark shade of plum near the hem and chest. The color faded into lilac at the waist where the fabric gathered, creating an hourglass shape. Deep purple beading dusted the bust of the sweetheart neckline.

I sunk back in my chair. "Wow," I breathed out.

"I'm glad you like it," Nick exclaimed, eyes twinkling as he stowed the dress back in its bag. "I was thinking these could go with it." He presented a black satin box to me and opened it. Inside was a gorgeous silver and amethyst bracelet with matching earrings, both glinting in the light. Upon closer inspection, Christmas flowers etched in the metal of the jewelry caught my eye.

"Are you the real Santa Claus?" I joked.

"Something like that," Nick grinned.

"Thank you, but is this why you are here—to give me a dress?"

"Partly, yes. I knew you needed a dress and it should be one befitting a Princess of Cristes."

"How do you—" I started, but Nick held his hand up.

"Unfortunately, I am not quite at liberty to discuss how I know just yet." Nick's jaw twitched. "The person doesn't want their identity revealed."

I slumped back in my chair, dejected, and crossed my arms.

"I also wanted to remind you how important William is, but for now, keep a safe distance, romantically speaking. I understand you guys have a date tonight."

"Romantically? Who even says that?" Nervous laughter in the form of a short giggle escaped my mouth. Nick cocked an eyebrow at me. I fell silent and composed myself. "It's not a date. We are just going to the library."

"I sent William one of these—" Nick touched the Christmas flower attached to his velvet vest— "to help remind him why he needed to come back here. Did he tell you about it?"

"Yes," I remarked. *And, according to Will, it did some pretty funky stuff.*

"Then he mentioned that it—ahem—physically and emotionally changed him."

"Something like that."

"I expect it had a great effect on him which will make keeping your friendship platonic a lot harder for him than you," he stated.

"I know. Will showed me the letters. I've picked Christmas roses before. How come it's never changed me the way it's changed Will?"

"All Christmas roses contain magic, but the ones you picked had not yet been to Cristes or altered by a skilled Watcher. The rose William received *was* altered for him—*by me.*"

"Do I get one of your roses?" I was somewhat surprised by my boldness. Though Will may be freaked out about his new abilities, I enjoyed the idea of the adventure.

Nick studied me for a moment. "Yes, but I'm holding out until it is absolutely necessary."

"*OK,*" I drawled. "Can I ask you something?" Nick nodded, folding his hands on the table. "I think I can feel what Will is feeling sometimes. Is that—normal?"

Nick paused for a minute. "At what distance?"

"What do you mean?"

"I mean, what distance are you apart when you can feel

this?"

"Only if I'm touching him. But I can also sort of sense what Will's feeling by looking at what his eyes are doing."

"That's...interesting. This is going to be harder than I thought." He stroked his beard with his thumb and index finger.

"What is?" I pondered.

"Well, it can be normal for our people. All Watchers are born with giftings, as can be foretold by their eye color. Every so often some Watchers are born and they exhibit signs that they have a soul match. This could be likened to a birthmark that vanishes or colorless irises that change and adopt a color after a few days to a few weeks; a clear indication to the parents their child is destined for another. Others develop a strong bond with another Watcher over time or after marriage. A very select few physically display their magic before their abilities have fully matured."

"And what are Will and me? Our abilities that is."

"Will is all of them. You, dear, are a strong theory." Nick shifted, straightening his back, as he surveyed the crowd. "I have to get going. Just remember what I said when you see William tonight and stay away from Christmas roses for now." He stood and pushed in his chair. "By the way, Princess, stay away from the white light." He bowed his head.

"What do you mean I'm a theory?" I asked, but he was already across the court and disappearing into the crowd. I should have been more shaken than I was at his speed, but I was more unnerved at myself for keeping my cool with all this Cristes magic talk. I tossed my garbage and stacked my tray. Taking the garment bag, I met up with the girls in time to pick out temporary rhinestone tattoos.

"Where did you find it again?" Pree asked.

There was no way I'd be able to explain Nick. "Well, I saw it a few months ago at this little dress shop here and placed it on hold. I've been making layaway payments on it and wanted to surprise you guys when we got here."

"Then why did you try on so many dresses?" Dani accused.

"Well, I wanted to still make sure this was the one."

"Well, I'm dying to see it on!" Sara exclaimed.

To be honest, I was too. We ran into the nearest store and dashed into the women's dressing room. I made the girls wait outside my stall while I changed into the gown. As I slipped it past my knees, I noticed my name embroidered into a tag.

Like water caressing a rock in a riverbed, the dress flowed around my shape; every curve accentuated, every line the perfect silhouette. I stepped into the viewing area and onto the short, cylindrical podium, waiting for their reactions.

"Good heavens, Liddy. I don't see how Justin is going to keep his hands off of you. That fabric screams 'touch me'!" Pree blurted out. I twirled, the whimsical fabric floated about me.

"First of all, Justin is a perfect gentleman. And second, all of my lady parts are well covered," I defended.

"And the slit?" Sara cocked an eyebrow.

"It's only slightly less than modest." I poked my right leg out and showed how it only came to mid-thigh.

"Gurl, you are lying to yourself. That dress is totally see-through when the light hits it," Dani remarked.

"It is?" I gasped, covering all of my lady bits.

"Only from the mid-thigh down, simmer down." Sara laughed.

"Whatever. It's gorgeous. I think I'm girl crushing on you,"

Pree gushed.

I sashayed back to the dressing room and changed so we could leave. We walked through the still full parking lot to the white conversion van. Even though my friends all loved it, this beast was embarrassing to drive. I couldn't wait to get my own car, which would *not* have a mauve interior. *Gag.* I opened doors and we loaded our dresses carefully across the back seat.

I turned on the radio to Bing Crosby crooning another Christmas classic.

"Puh-leassse, anything but Christmas music," Dani beseeched.

"What's up your butt, Miss Grinch?" Sara laughed, turning from the passenger seat to look at Dani.

"Um, you'd hate it too if you'd heard nothing else for the past three weeks."

"No problem," I responded and flipped the station. Screeches of excitement filled the van when "MMMBop" started playing.

I got home a little after five and called Will to let him know I was home. Scarfing down my dinner, I then booked it upstairs to touch up my makeup and hair. I finished just as I heard knocking on the front door. Seeing Will through the window on the way downstairs, a wave of relief hit me. He looked especially handsome tonight and I was thankful we'd decided to hang out at the public library. Before I made it to the entryway, Dad got to the door.

"Dad!" I scolded.

"Sorry. I've got to meet Will and see who's driving my precious cargo around." Dad opened the door. "Hey, Will, do you remember me? John Erickson," Dad boomed as he stuck a hand out.

"Good evening, Mr. Erickson. It has been a long time, but yes, I remember you." Will smiled as they shook hands.

"You've got quite the handshake. Come on in. Oh, and call me John." Dad beckoned Will to follow him into the living room.

"OK, John." Will bit his lower lip and glanced at me with a shrug before trailing after my dad.

I leaned against the wall, pretending to admire our Christmas tree while Will and Dad sat on opposite ends of the sofa.

"Liddy tells me you've been living in Florida. What brings you back to Illinois? That's quite the change."

"My uncle is here. He does pretty well and he offered to let me to stay with him. He believes the school system here is better and that would help my future career path."

"And what is it that you want to do after college?"

Will glimpsed at me, but I kept silent. I wanted to hear his plans.

"I would like to return to Florida, or somewhere warm. I want to be physical therapist or athletic trainer."

"Respectable careers. I understand you're taking Liddy to the library tonight and that you both will be spending a lot of time together, for school projects of course." I rolled my eyes and Dad chuckled, the tree's lights coloring his face in blue, orange, and green.

"Yes, sir... I mean, John."

"Make sure to bring her home by curfew."

"Of course. What time is that?"

"Eleven."

"Dad!" I whined. "Can we go now please?"

"Sure, just one more thing. He stood up and Will followed his lead. "Will, come here." Will obediently closed the gap. About four inches shorter than Will, Dad placed his hand up onto Will's shoulder. "If anything happens to my little girl, just remember, this world isn't big enough for you to hide from me." Dad grinned and gave Will a few hard pats.

I dropped my face into my hands. *I can't believe he just said that.*

"Of course, Mr. Erickson. I would be lost without her—" Will glanced my way— "and I would never let anything happen to her." Will's eyes flashed as emotional intensity filled his words.

"Well, I know I'm ready to go. Shall we, Will?" I didn't wait for his answer before grabbing his hand and leading out the front door.

The Search Begins

ELIEF SIMMERED THROUGH ME as we stepped onto the
front porch. I held Will's hand as I practically dragged
him to the Wagoneer—anxious to be free from Dad's
watchful eye and his embarrassing *tough dad* moment. Even
though Will and I decided to be "just friends", I wanted this
time with him. As much time as possible.

"How was dress shopping?" Will inquired as he reversed
out of the driveway.

"It was actually great! We all found everything." And then,
at a speed that would rival any auctioneer, I added, "Oh, and
Nick surprised me at lunch and gifted me all of my stuff for the
formal."

Will slammed on the breaks.

"Ow!" The seatbelt caught me around the waist and

pinched my collarbone.

Whipping his head towards me, Will blurted, "What do you mean Nick was there? Liddy, he's dangerous."

"First of all, we were in a very public, crowded area. Secondly, I don't remember you becoming the authority over my life and third, it's not like I invited him," I argued. Will had his eyes closed and gripped the steering wheel, his knuckles turning white. I placed my hand over his and closed my eyes, focusing on him. He wasn't angry. Emotions that weren't mine flitted through my veins, my nerve endings testing them, sending messages to my brain. Dark colors with sparks of red swirled through my mind and my adrenaline started to respond. He was scared. I twined my fingers in his and attempted to push all images and feelings of calm his way. When I saw the swirling colors slow down and lighten to blue, I brought his hand to rest on my stinging collarbone. "Ahhh." I closed my eyes in sweet relief.

"Does it really feel better when I touch you? You made that same sound when your wrist was hurt and I held it," he said, his eyes alight with curiosity.

"Sure does," I told him, contentment softening my voice as I kept my eyes closed. I was nervous that making eye contact would cause us to fight, and I didn't want to argue again. A sane person would probably be more concerned with the science behind this whole healing touch thing, but it felt so good, I didn't care to know what deadened the pain as long as it helped. "Listen, I didn't plan on seeing Nick, but I didn't leave because I felt safe around him. Besides, I was in a crowded mall in an even more crowded food court."

"You're right. I know you didn't plan for this. I'm…I'm

sorry I overreacted."

"Ya think?" I laughed. "So, why is it Nick freaks you out so much?"

"You're not going to let this go." Will sighed in resignation.

"Nope."

"Fine, I'll tell you, but after we get to the library." Will lifted his hand from my shoulder. "I'm glad this helps you, but please only do that when completely necessary," he groaned. I could see his eyes begin to ignite like they do when he is happy as he returned his hand to the steering wheel. "Are you going to wear the dress he gave you?"

"Heck yes! It was free and it's sweet!" I exclaimed. I snatched his hand with reckless abandon and placed it back over my collarbone. I didn't mind seeing him struggle to maintain his composure, resisting whatever urges coursed through him.

We walked through the library doors, the familiar scent of old and new books tugged at my memories. Will and I walked up the stairs side by side in silence. I recalled how my younger self would contemplate hiding out here after hours, convinced that the books contained magic and would take turns coming alive at night to act out their stories.

In the back of the second floor, Will emptied his bag on the table nearest the archives. Splayed on the wooden table were the three old books from Nick, the manila envelope, and some notebooks and pens. He was in the process of putting up pocket folders around the perimeter of the table.

"That's a little third grade-ish, no?" I asked, gesturing at the folders.

"What, I don't want anyone to see what we are doing," he

said, sincerely.

"Don't you think it draws a teensy bit more attention this way? People might think we are making out or something rather than doing some research. Besides, no one is even up here except for the librarian at the circulation desk who, by the way, is currently staring at us for probably talking too loud." I waved at her and hustled into the seat next to Will who placed the folders back in his messenger bag. "So, did you look more at the newspaper clippings Nick gave us?"

"I thought about it, but I wanted to wait for you. It's, uh, a little difficult to look at." His lips turned down and he looked away. My heart sank as I thought about Charlie. I placed my hand in his and gave it a quick, little squeeze.

A few breaths passed as I watched his shoulders move with each inhale and exhale. "You can talk to me, Will." I rubbed the top of his hand with my thumb.

"I never told you what happened the night Charlie disappeared," he mumbled. I leaned in closer. Clearing his throat, Will continued quietly, "The night Charlie vanished I snuck outside because we were supposed to meet, but I also thought I heard Santa's sleigh. Pretty dumb right? Thinking Santa was outside on my roof when it wasn't even Christmas Eve."

"There is nothing silly about a kid hoping to see Santa."

Will continued on in a robotic tone; he must have run this nightmare over and over in his head millions of times. "I believed Santa was on my roof. I exited through the basement window and crawled out of its well. I remember my hand pressing into something soft and when I looked down, there was a patch of white Christmas roses. Some of them were turning black."

"I think that's where I grabbed the roses from the other night," I whispered as I reimagined Will's steps with him.

"A crisp, white envelope sat tucked into the ones that were black. When I reached down to pick it up, I could swear I saw my name flash across it. I was about to open it when I heard my mom yelling out the front door... 'So help me, William Lucas! If you are outside, you are grounded for a month, young man!' I fell back in surprise. She never yelled, but I remember she had been on edge that whole week. Both my parents had. Scared about getting caught, I grabbed the envelope and a handful of Christmas roses I wanted to give you the next day. I army crawled back into the well and booked it to my room. I made it upstairs without being spotted and just as I reached the top, I heard my mom and dad at the base of the stairs. Since Charlie's room was closest to the top of the stairs, I dashed in there and said to him, 'I was here the whole time,' my eyes pleading for him to go along with it. I jumped in his bed and pretended that I had been reading to him. My dad bolted in the room a second later, presumably having checked my room first, my mom right at his heels. My parents' faces softened at the sight of their boys reading a Christmas story with each other and snuck back out of the room. I ruffled my brother's hair, said thanks, and left.

"I had trouble sleeping that night. Something kept calling my name, a voice so desperate; she needed me and if I didn't come to her, she would die. It woke me up. I got out of bed to get a drink of water, but when I opened the door to my room, the voice seemed to be real, coming from Charlie's room. I pinched myself to make sure I wasn't still dreaming. I took a step into the hall towards his room when a green glow emanated from under Charlie's door. That angelic voice, pleading and calling me, transformed into one of the most demonic sounds I've ever heard." Will shuddered at the memory. "And then there was a man's voice. He yelled, 'You will never win! Let it go, I beg of you. I can still help you!' Then the green light flashed, changing to blood-orange in symphony with her sinister laugh and all at once it went dark and quiet except for the sound of tinkling sleigh bells. I rushed into Charlie's room as a figure dashed through the window. He held the white envelope. I don't remember much after that. It was so dark, but I do remember his eyes."

"His eyes? How could you have seen them if it was dark?"

"That's the thing. Despite the pitch-black room, his eyes were not only bright but glowing icy blue. I've never seen anything like it."

"Glowing?" Goosebumps ran down my arms as I pictured Will's eyes doing the same.

"Yeah. Anyway, he saw me and tried to come back into the room, but I screamed. As he scrambled out the window, I caught a glimpse of his black coat thanks to the Christmas lights attached to our roof. It covered most of his face except his glowing eyes. I screamed again for my parents which I think surprised him because he stumbled and fell off the roof. I raced to the window expecting to see him lying on the ground, but he was already up and disappearing around the side of my house."

"When did you remember all this?"

"I started remembering once I got back to Illinois. I thought I was crazy for thinking this mystery figure had eyes that glowed, but here I am with a similar eye situation. Though, I'm still not sure if I saw those lights coming from under Charlie's door or if I truly heard a woman's voice."

"Will, you coming back into my life brought back some of these memories for me too. I was out in my front yard that night, waiting for you. Something forced me to head to your house. I was only halfway to you when I saw those flashes of light and heard a woman's voice."

"You heard the voice halfway down the street?" Will's eyes widened.

"Yes. Do you remember anything else about this figure with glowing eyes?" I asked, turning to face Will. I so badly wished to help him find Charlie. It unnerved me that this sounded very similar to Nick, but the Nick I knew didn't seem threatening. I wouldn't tell Will for now. I didn't want to give Will any further ammunition since Nick was our only lead to helping find Charlie.

"Nothing." Will looked down, placing his head in his hands.

"So, what does this have to do with Nick?"

"I don't trust him." Will looked at me, his eyes hardened with conviction. "He's pulled me from my family and hasn't offered me any help or guidance in dealing with whatever the heck it is that he did to me."

"True, but..."

"No, Liddy. Think about it. He's shady, elusive, hasn't even introduced himself to me, and he claims to know where Charlie is yet he's not bothered to tell me how to save him. And isn't it weird we can't tell anyone?"

"Shhhhhh!" the librarian hissed at us.

We both sank into our chairs.

I waited a few moments before continuing. "Will, I've met Nick. He is definitely eccentric, but he's not a danger. Maybe there's a reason he hasn't seen you yet. And he has mentioned Charlie. That's why we are here, right? To look at the stuff Nick gave us to help find him. What do you say we get started?"

Will tried a smile. "You're right. I'll try and tackle these books."

"Great, let's divide and conquer. I'll start on the articles."

Silence seemed to hum in our ears while we poured over the materials. All six victims were boys between the ages of six and twelve. No one knew how the boys disappeared from their own homes, vanishing into the night. Each disappearance happened in the month of December, within the two weeks leading up to Christmas. Nothing else—not their hair color, not their school, not their family—connected them. I sighed as I leaned back and stretched. I stood up and headed to the card catalog to try and find Dewey numbers for reels to see if there were any follow-up newspaper articles to the ones Nick gave us.

"I'm going to head to the archives to try and find more articles."

Will grunted in acknowledgement as he flipped another page in the book.

I grabbed my change purse so I could print anything I found. I located some microfilms and placed the first one on the reader. It took me a good twenty minutes before I came across a follow up article on one of the missing kids. The boy who disappeared was an eleven-year-old named Noel Pickering. He disappeared a few days before Christmas 1981. The younger brother in this case was interviewed a few weeks after the disappearance and remembered—I scrolled to the next image—nothing, except a flash of green light. *Woah!* I clicked print.

I spent the better part of another hour looking through the microfilms. *What if there are more disappearances in addition to the ones Nick offered?* I expanded my search to the entirety of Illinois, not just the northwest suburbs, and the surrounding states.

"Attention patrons. The library will close in twenty minutes. Please make your final selections and bring them to check out."

Crud. That didn't leave me much time to read through any more articles, but I wanted this trip to be fruitful. I narrowed my search to the month of December, when all known disappearances occurred and went back ten years prior to the first disappearance. Some unusual headings caught my attention.

> *Six-Year-Old Megan Carson Claims She Saw Angels Picking Flowers from Her Windowsill Garden*

> *Joey Knasel Swears He Saw Angel Drop Magic Envelope*

> *Joy Lang Believes She Exchanged Mom's Vase of White Flowers for Wooden Toy*

Three more popped up and I printed them as well. The lights flickered.

"The Indian Trails Library will be closing in ten minutes," a librarian announced.

I quickly searched for all articles in December over the eight years after the disappearance of Charlie. Many more popped up and my breath hitched. *So many kids...gone.* I selected every article and clicked print.

The lights flickered again. "The library will be closing in five minutes. Please bring your selections to the checkout desk at this time."

I grabbed the used film rolls and walked to the copy machine. I danced anxiously at the printer whispering to it to hurry the heck up.

"Dear, we are closing now." The librarian that shushed us earlier had made her way over to me. "Your friend is already packed up and waiting for you."

"It's almost done, I promise." I offered a nervous smile gesturing towards the printer.

"OK, OK. Let me have the rolls you've finished with."

"Thank you! I'll bring this last film to you as soon as—" The printer stopped. "Right now, I guess." We both laughed.

I ran to get the last microfilm from the viewer and returned it to her. Grabbing the stack of papers from the printer, I offered my thanks again and booked it to Will.

He stood with his back to me, coat on and pack slung over his shoulder. Will held my coat, his head pivoting as he searched for me.

"Will?" I placed my hand on his shoulder. His eyes closed in response and as he covered my hand with his, a smile formed at the corners of his winter reddened lips. He opened his eyes and turned to me.

"Attention all patrons. It is nine p.m. and the library is now closed."

"Took you long enough." Will smirked. "Mrs. Baxter was getting anxious. She kept looking at me, then the clock, then back at me like I could just make you appear." Will smiled at the librarian walking past us. She waved and returned to her post at the circulation desk. I laughed and Will helped me into my coat.

"Looks like you found a lot of good stuff."

"Well, actually, I'm not sure what I have found," I said, picking up the stack and putting it in Will's messenger bag. "I didn't have much time to read a majority of them. Did you find anything?"

"Nothing... I found absolutely nothing in those useless books. They don't even make any sense." Will's voice was full of frustration as we reached the bottom of the stairs.

We left the library in silence. Will opened the passenger door and I hopped in. He grabbed the ice scraper from behind his back seat and set to work on the windshield. I took off my gloves and rubbed my hands together. "Huhhhh" I breathed onto my hands and my breath frosted in a cloud before me. Will came back and turned on the car blasting the heat. I thanked him before he ventured back out to finish the windows.

"Tonight wasn't a total loss," I commented, as Will got in the car and placed his hands near the heater.

"How so?"

"Well, though I didn't have much time to read the new stuff I found, I did discover from Nick's articles that there had been six other children taken shortly before Charlie. They were all boys aged six to twelve."

"That's...something. Were the boys recovered?" Will inquired, a hint of hope in his voice. I fidgeted with my scarf.

"I'll take that as a no."

"Actually, we aren't the only ones to notice the green light and it seems, after Charlie, the disappearances began to increase and included boys *and* girls."

"That's awful. How many kids is that?"

"A lot." I frowned.

"What does my brother's disappearance have to do with these kids? I mean, the kidnappings seem pretty random after Charlie."

"I believe Nick is showing us that whoever took all of these kids also has Charlie." A long pause filled the car.

"And none of them have ever returned." Will slammed the steering wheel with the palms of his hands.

"Will, this is a start and we've got a lot to go through. Maybe we should call it a night and meet back up here tomorrow?" I offered. It was hard seeing Will so upset, and I too missed Charlie.

"Please don't go yet. We still have a little more than an hour," Will pleaded.

"Do you want to sit here and read through some of the articles I found together?"

"No."

"No?" I repeated, confused.

"I know this seems extremely selfish, but I need a break from this. I need to do something fun. Any ideas?"

I looked around and stopped back at Will's perfect face. His eyes swirled a brighter teal. *Pure thoughts, Liddy, pure thoughts.* He shifted a little and the streetlamp rested on half his face, highlighting the crescent moon on his cheek and star near his temple; scars from our sledding accident when we were little. Our last happy time together with Charlie.

"That's it!" I blurted out.

"Come again?" Will asked.

"You up for some sledding? We can stop at my place and grab Mickey's sled."

"You're kidding, right?"

"Oh, sorry. Are you too cool for it now?" I razzed.

"No, that's not it. It's just, well, how weird is it that my uncle bought me a sled. I mean it's not a typical gift you give a seventeen-year-old."

"Agreed."

"That's not all. Nolan insisted I pack it and extra snow gear into my trunk tonight before picking you up."

"Weird, or confirmation that we are supposed to hit those hills tonight?"

"Both?" Will and I laughed together as we buckled our seat belts and drove the few miles behind the library to Huskie Park.

Sledding

WILL DRAGGED THE LARGE SLED, leaving a groove behind us in the snow as we trekked up the sledding hill.

With the park lights off for the evening, the moon and stars illuminated the park around us. Sparkles cascaded across the snow-covered hills and shadows draped around the trees. When we were almost to the top of the hill Will called out, "Careful, it's a little icy," just in time for me to slip and fall on my behind. We both started laughing. I crawled the few feet left to the top of the hill and sat myself in the front of the sled.

"You coming down with me?" I asked. In response, he grabbed the sled from behind and ran a few yards before he jumped onto the back and gripped me around my waist. We both screamed out in sheer delight. We couldn't get enough.

On the tenth trip, we decided to take the hill furthest back. Inky clouds rolled towards us in the night sky, taking with it some of our visibility as they snuffed out stars one by one in their path and encroached upon the moon.

"I think this may be the last one," Will hollered to me as he nodded his chin towards the sky.

"Two more? Please?" I begged with an exaggerated pout and puppy dog eyes.

"Well, with those eyes, how could anyone resist?"

On our final trip down, I eyed the large mogul at the bottom-right of the hill closest to the storm grate. Some kids must have built it earlier in the day. Feeling adventurous, I steered us toward it, heart pounding with excitement. We hit it and flew high into the night sky. I looked down. *Crap!* The sled was no longer beneath me. Will clutched me from the air, shielding me from the fall, and I landed hard on top of him. Shock paralyzed me and I laid there, motionless, staring at the stars who blinked back at me. Will moaned.

"Will!" I screamed, my mind racing. The clouds claimed half of the moon. I could barely see as I climbed off him and positioned myself near his head. Tearing my mittens off, I cupped his face. "Will! I'm so sorry! Are you alright?" Now, in the gloom, I could barely make out the details of his face, and my heart raced.

He didn't respond. I placed my ear in front of his mouth to check for breathing and felt his warm breath on my cheek. *Thank goodness!* I caressed my hands through his hair to feel for any wounds. No lumps or blood. I was about to assess the rest of his body for other possible injuries when I could have sworn I saw a flicker of a smile cross his lips. To be sure, I traced his face with my hands and sure enough he smiled.

"You jerk!" I gave him a good swat on his arm. A deep laugh erupted from his chest and he rolled with laughter. I went to hit him again, but he caught my arm and with one fell swoop, he hovered over me, holding both of my wrists with one hand. There it was. That luminous green color coming alive in his eyes. He clenched his jaw, contemplating his next move. I highly doubted the world would end if we kissed, and I hadn't found anything in the library that made me think otherwise. Neither had Will. But he was my friend and, according to Nick, I needed to be the strong one here. I wanted to honor Will's wishes no matter how dang much I may have wanted otherwise. I slid my arm from his grip and placed my hand on his strong chest.

"Will, let me make this easy for you. Do *not* do what you are thinking of doing. Remember what you told me. I'm not worth risking Charlie." But Will only moved his face an inch closer to mine. I could feel his breath, warm against my lips as he spoke. How I wanted them to touch mine, for his lips to melt away the cold.

"I never said you weren't worth it. You, my sweet Lydia, are worth more than you know. I can't help but think maybe I'm making a mistake by *just* being your friend. Last night was hell for me." I could see the strain on his face as he let go of my wrists and placed his hands against my cheeks, his weight resting on his elbows.

"What? What happened last night?"

"You. Justin. Your date. Ring a bell?" His eyes poured into mine, darkening a few shades. I moved my hand from his chest to stroke the crease between his brows. I only had to move a few centimeters and my lips would meet his. My senses fired so rapidly I could hardly focus on keeping my promise to him, or to myself for that matter. I closed my eyes and took a deep breath to try and calm my racing heart when I heard it. That angelic voice, calling my name.

"Did you hear that?" I whispered, as my eyes shot open. The voice called again. I pushed Will to the side as I sat up, searching for who summoned me.

"Hear what?" Will asked, his eyes returning to their normal state as he moved to sit next to me.

Another cry of my name echoed. "That woman, calling my name," I said as I stood. "There it is again!"

"Liddy, are you getting back at me right now for faking I was hurt?" Will protested.

"Shhhhhh!"

A gust of wind blew. The clouds snuffed out the moonlight, the sky a black hole. In the corner of my eye, a jade light distracted me. I turned back to Will. A small gasp escaped my lips as he stood there, a shimmering star in the darkest of nights. *How is he doing that?*

In the distance beyond, a brilliant white light demanded my attention. My heart raced. *But I don't want to leave Will.* Hazy memories from my dream came rushing back as Nick's words of caution echoed in my ears—*Stay away from the white light.* My need to follow the light overtook me and I ignored Nick's warning.

"Liddy? Liddy! Where'd you go?"

I could hear Will calling out to me over and over again, his voice growing more urgent. I heard him and yet my body was on autopilot. Each step I took toward the light was a step further away from Will. The closer I got to it, the louder I heard the woman's cry of my name. My hands reached up and clasped something so cold it burned my skin: the large storm grate.

As soon as my fingers touched it, my name echoed wildly, bouncing off the walls of the drain. On either side of the base of the grate, patches of Christmas roses scintillated in the light. I was about to reach down to pick one when Will seized my arm and pulled me back.

"Liddy, what are you doing? You're acting strange!" Will shouted. I blanched at the pressure of his fingers digging into my arm.

"I think I'm supposed to go in there," I said, unable to look away.

"Lid, this is crazy. It's a storm..." His hand stiffened. He gripped me harder, trying to pull me back. I paused, brow drawn, my hand around the base of a rose. *I was trying to pluck a Christmas rose, again?*

"Liddy, STOP!" he bellowed as he yanked me back with full force. His arms wrapped around me, pinning my arms to my sides. The fire in Will's eyes danced and I feared I would combust as he searched my face.

"I'm sorry," I choked out. "I have to go in there." The voice grew more and more impatient. "I need to get in there. Please, she needs my help!"

"No. We *need* to leave," Will commanded. "Liddy, I can feel that you are in danger!" He spun me around, released my arms and grabbed my wrist, pulling me back. I planted my feet and yanked my arm from his strong grasp. Everything in my body told me I needed to get in there.

"You don't have to come, Will, but I am going in there," I

declared.

"Liddy, no! You're acting like—it's like you're possessed!" I ignored him and continued again towards the grate. "Stop!" Will said with an air of authority I didn't recognize. A green light flashed.

Whatever had held me released. My body sagged. "What was that?" I whispered in disbelief.

"I don't know. You were...freakishly strong. It took all of my strength to prevent you from picking one of those things." Will jutted his chin towards the large patches of glittering Hellebore. "Come on, let's get out of here."

I was just possessed and he's terrified of dang flowers? "Seriously? That's what you're mad about? Will, the flowers won't hurt me. Nick told me so when he dropped off the dress. A Watcher has to tinker with it."

"What? A Watcher? You're not making sense." He shook his head. "You'd believe this psycho over me?"

"We used to give them to each other all the time as kids and I picked some the other night for you and look, here I am, completely fine," I protested.

"Do you even remember the other night? You blacked out! And every fiber of my being was on high alert letting me know you were in danger."

"But Nick got me home safe."

"How do you know? You said you woke up in your yard. The link here is the Christmas roses. Both times you've been around them you said you lost control over your body, like you were someone's puppet."

"It's not the roses... It was *her.*"

"Who?"

"The woman's voice. Whoever was calling me. I think she wanted me to grab a rose so I could get to her."

"Yeah, and again... Where did you say you heard that voice coming from?"

I looked back at the grate and trembled.

"Come on, let's get you home." Will slipped his hand back in mine and led me towards the sled. In the far distance, a muted tinkling sounded. I tried to find the direction Nick came from, but the clouds had moved across the moon again and covered all the natural light. I grew stone cold and stopped breathing as if I'd been hit by Medusa herself.

"Liddy, what's wrong?"

"Shhhhh... Listen!" I walked away and, feeling the tug of my hand, Will followed suit.

The chiming got closer. *We're moving too slow.* Continuing to hold Will's hand, I started trudging through the snow while simultaneously trying to hide some of our tracks. Will shuffled his feet to do the same. I could only hope we travelled in my intended direction. We needed to hide before the clouds moved again. *Please let the forest preserve be ahead.* We walked as fast as we could, trying to put as much distance between us and Nick as possible.

The clouds shifted, letting a sliver of the moon shine down and I could see the start of the small forest preserve at the edge of the field. We bolted towards the trees. We dropped to the ground and hid behind a large tree trunk before the clouds exposed the bright moon. With my back pressed against the tree, I twisted my head to peek around it. Nick stood at the base of the storm grate. He looked around surreptitiously, then dropped down on one knee. He opened the grate and disappeared behind it. Will and I let out a long sigh and sat there, our chests rising and falling in sporadic rhythm, trying to recover.

After at least ten thudding breaths I spoke. "I guess we know where to find Nick."

"That was Nick?"

Now, I had to tell him *now* what my suspicions were. "Just don't get mad, OK? I have to tell you something." Will frowned, gesturing for me to continue. "I think I saw Nick in every picture in those articles he gave us."

"Why didn't you tell me?"

"Well, I wasn't confident, but when you started describing what the man looked like who escaped out Charlie's window, it sounded a lot like..."

"Nick?"

"Yes, but Will. He's our only lead. It wouldn't make sense that he'd be the one—"

"Wouldn't make sense? His place is concealed by a storm grate near a hill *kids* sled on. A voice you claim called for help came out of it and possessed you."

"Not just any voice, Will. It was the woman's voice."

"Yeah, you said."

"But I've just realized. It's the same voice I heard the night Charlie was taken." *What is Nick doing with her in there?*

Will ran his hands through his hair. "And let's not forget that bell sound. Liddy, that noise is exactly what I heard coming from Charlie's room that night. It's what brought me outside in the first place! Nick had something to do with Charlie's disappearance, I can feel it."

Confusion settled over me. Everything Will said made

sense, and yet, it didn't add up with Nick's current actions. Nick seemed nice—showering me with gifts, helping me, offering to help find Charlie. None of it added up. My head throbbed. "I think we should head back to your car while we can still see."

Will nodded in agreement. We made it to the car in a roundabout way, trekking a wide perimeter back to the parking lot. It was near eleven when Will started the car.

"Crud. My curfew."

"I promised your dad I would get you home in time and I will."

Without another word, Will drove me home. When we pulled into the driveway, he angled toward me as if he was about to say something, but turned back.

"You OK?" I asked him.

"Can I pick you up tomorrow? We should get that English assignment finished."

"Sure, library again?"

"I was thinking of my place." Sensing my hesitation, he added without skipping a beat, "We don't have to go to my room. We can work in the library where I am sure Nolan will be keeping an eye out. Plus, my Uncle Shai is always home."

"OK, then," I responded. "I'm done with work around twelve. Pick me up from The Continental?"

Will smiled and nodded.

"Have a good night," I said, climbing out of the car.

"Sweet dreams, Liddy."

Betrayal

M Y SHIFT AT THE CONTINENTAL WAS ALMOST OVER. I glanced at the clock, the second hand drifting along. *Come on... There!* I rushed toward the landline behind the sundae counter. The bell attached to the front door chimed while I dialed. I turned and cringed as I watched the Andersons walk in. Notoriously bad tippers, I was relieved that I would not have to serve them today.

"Liddy," my boss whispered.

"Gah!" I dropped the phone. "Bob, you scared me." I turned to face him, his hands already clasped together, pleading. "Don't do this to me. I told you I had to leave on time today."

"Liddy, please! You're my best waitress." Bob hung up the phone. "I'll never hear the end of it from my mother-in-law if she has bad service here."

"You owe me," I whined and walked to the Andersons.

"This way please." We traipsed over the green carpet to a booth at the far end of the dining area. The Andersons made me hustle and I didn't get the chance to call Will. As I exited the kitchen with a full tray over my shoulder, my body tensed. Every fiber, every nerve ending sparked with anticipation. My mind directed me to the Anderson's table, but my body demanded I go in another direction, and I tripped over my own feet, nearly toppling the lunch for six. *Will!*

I looked up and caught him stifling a laugh. I sneered at him, pretending to be angry. I served the Andersons and, after two more trips to the waitress station for napkins, extra sauces, refills, and a third shaker of salt, walked to Will.

I sat across from him in a small booth near the window. "Sorry, Bob assigned me to his family's table twenty minutes before my shift ended and I didn't get a chance to call. I've gotta roll silverware and when they are done, we can head out."

"No rush. I'll wait here and have a hot tea if that's not too much trouble."

"Not trouble at all. Wait, hot tea?"

"Something wrong with that?" He smirked.

"Just an unusual choice for someone like you."

"Ms. Erickson, are you judging me?" His comment made me blush. "Relax, Liddy. I'm from the south and it's freaking cold out. I want something warm that also has caffeine."

"Got it." I smiled. "Coming right up."

In between tasks, I stopped in on the Andersons booth, trying not to grit my teeth at their constant requests. I checked in on Will whenever I got a free moment. After an eternity, the tension in my neck bit more than their poor attitude, the

Andersons got up to pay the bill.

"Bless their heart," I mumbled to myself clearing their table. Plates and trash everywhere, and not a hint of a dollar.

After saying bye to Bob, who gave me an extra ten dollars for my trouble, I headed back over to Will.

"Do you want to stay here for lunch or pick something up on the way to your house?"

"Nolan is making us lunch. Bob let me use the phone to call and let him know we'd be a little late."

"Nolan didn't need to go through all that trouble."

"Believe me, it's no trouble at all for him."

As we drove, the smell of the restaurant lingered over my skin and hair— a mix of french fries, Matzo Ball soup, and Saganaki. I hoped that Will wouldn't notice. Thank God I remembered a change of clothes.

"It's fun watching you work," Will remarked.

"How so?"

"You have such a stern look on your face when you are concentrating," he said sucking in his cheeks slightly and furrowing his brow. "But at the same time, you are warm and inviting. You really care about your customers."

"So, working hard and caring about your customers is funny?"

"I didn't say you were funny to watch, I said fun. Not a lot of kids our age tend to care so much about their work. No need to get defensive."

"Sorry. I usually get teased, not commended, for working hard or, how do they put it, being a *goody-two-shoes*."

"Idiots," he responded.

"I was made fun of in middle school. A group of guys were

making fun of another girl and I tried to stop them. I became their new target and it was almost two years of torture."

"I didn't know, Liddy. I'll never understand why people do that."

"I was naïve and let them make me feel worthless. They wrote nasty things all over my yearbooks. I still have them, to remind me to never make anyone feel like that; to make them feel like they are the ugliest thing to walk this Earth. At one point the teasing got so bad, I found myself wondering—if I disappeared, would anyone miss me?" I turned my head to look out the window, trying to conceal the unexpected pain prickling behind my eyes. *Why the heck did I share all that?*

I could see the uneasiness in Will's face. "They wouldn't know perfect if it hit them square in the face."

"Ha! There's no such thing as perfect." I perked my voice up and turned to him. "I'm fine now. Don't worry about me. I have a killer work ethic—" I winked at him— "and it made me even more determined to stick up for others who are being bullied. I have zero tolerance for those who think they are better than everyone else." We drove the rest of the way to his house in silence. When he pulled up in the driveway and placed the car in park, I turned fully to him. "Sorry for being a real downer. I—"

"Are you seriously apologizing to me?" Will unbuckled his seat belt and leaned towards me, collecting my hands in his. "I am glad you shared that with me because I plan on letting you know every day for the rest of my life just how special you are Lydia Andra Erickson. It makes me so angry that you ever felt that way and that I wasn't there for you. I wish I could go back in time and change that."

My neck tingled with embarrassment but my cheeks stayed mercifully cool. "Thanks. But, I'm good now. I promise. I don't need anyone. I can take care of myself."

Will sighed and shook his head. "I know you can, but that doesn't mean you should have to, and definitely not all the time. I don't think we were designed to be alone. Trust me. As someone who had a brother and then became an only child, true happiness can be found within yourself, sure, but having someone you can love and trust to walk alongside you makes the bitter in life all the sweeter."

"I'm sorry, Will. I can't even imagine what that was like for you."

"I was spared from that memory for a long time. But I am not sharing this so you feel bad for me. I want you to know that you don't have to have your walls up with me—you can trust me." He kissed my hand and teeny shock waves rippled across it.

Will came around to open my door. I started to exit the car, his hand extended out to me, but hesitated for a brief moment. *Do I really walk around with my guard up?* I took his hand and he intertwined his fingers in mine. As we approached the front door, Nolan stood at the ready and a wide smile donned his face.

"Good afternoon, Master William. Nice to see you again, Madam Lydia," he greeted us as we entered the grand foyer.

"Good afternoon, Nolan." I smiled. "You're looking well." I don't know why I said it. Maybe it was the extra glint in his eyes.

"We'll be in the library today, Nolan." Will gestured to a room on our right. "Would you mind bringing us lunch in there, please?"

"Of course. I'll just be a moment, sir," the lean butler responded with an enthusiastic smile while adjusting his vest with both hands and bowed.

"No need to bow to us." Will ran his hand through his hair, but Nolan did an about face, sending his coattails flapping, and went on his way.

"Which way to the nearest bathroom?" I asked.

"Go straight through the atrium, fourth door on your right."

When I got back from freshening up, Nolan had just finished setting up lunch. "Wow!" I exclaimed, surprised, my chin practically touching the floor.

The butler turned around with a grin on his perfectly angled face. "Enjoy!" he announced, his gloved hand tapped me under my chin as he strode out of the library and I closed my mouth.

Nolan's extravagant spread was like something straight from *Better Homes and Gardens*. A cream tablecloth embroidered with faint silver snowflakes draped across the coffee table set for two. A holly-berry-red linen napkin adorned the center of each plate at the perfect angle. Crystal glasses were filled with sparkling cider. A small fire burned and transformed the room into a cozy retreat.

"I am *really* sorry." Will grimaced. "Nolan doesn't get to entertain very much. Uncle Shai never married and has no kids of his own so he is super stoked that I am here now. I guess it gives him something to do, though I prefer to grab something for myself straight from the kitchen."

"I don't mind it."

"You don't have to fib to me. I promise, I tried. When I told him you were coming for lunch, I was unable to talk him out of this." Will gestured to the set up including the side table in the corner holding a colorful array of fruit pieces dipped in chocolate. "He did compromise at least with my request for *casual* foods."

My eyes zeroed in on a steaming, large stainless-steel pot. As I neared it, the scent of tomato soup made my mouth water. I lifted the top of the serving platters on either side of the soup and perfectly crisp grilled cheese sandwiches greeted me.

"It's perfect. I love it!" A squeal sprang from me. I was used to doing the serving and the spread made me feel a little like a real princess. I inched around the room touching all the fabrics and materials, admiring the Jamison's steward's eye for detail. "How'd he set it up so fast?"

"He had a cart in the corner with the stuff pretty much set to go out. And I helped as much as he'd let me of course. I got to light the fireplace. Care to sit?" Will gestured to the coffee table.

My stomach rumbled and I clutched it in embarrassment. "Sorry, I haven't eaten all day."

"What? Sorry for being human? Please, help yourself." I plopped down on a large plush-velvet pillow and dug in. Will chuckled as he sat next to me.

We ate until we were stuffed. I popped one last chocolate covered strawberry when Will reached over to his messenger bag and pulled out some paper. "I hope you don't mind that I finished the English assignment for us."

"You what?" I choked.

"Take it easy." Will raised a hand in protest. "I know you are busy with work and your other classes and here I am taking up so much of your free time with the investigation into my brother's disappearance. It's the least I could do."

I grimaced. "Thank you for thinking of me, but if you remember, I like putting my best effort into something and earning my own grade. Not freeloading off of you for it."

"Liddy, that's not what this is. And besides, you did almost all of it with me," he said.

Nolan sauntered in to clean up lunch. I tried to help numerous times, but on my last attempt the butler took me by the shoulders and sat me down on the soft leather couch behind the coffee table. He was surprisingly strong for such a slender, greying man.

As Nolan finished up, Will continued our conversation. "I left the ending for you to finish."

"That's fine, *I guess*. Thanks." I smiled as I started to look over the paper.

Will sprawled his hands over it. "Do you mind doing that at home? I kind of have other plans for us while you are here."

Will's teasing smirk flustered me, but I kept my face carefully blank. I placed the paper in my bag and calmed myself before saying, "So, what did you have in mind?"

"I was thinking we could figure out our next steps with Charlie and Nick."

"Of course." I went in his bag and grabbed the articles that I had copied from the microfilms last night. "Let's go through them and highlight what jumps out at us."

Will stood up and went to the desk in the back of the room, grabbing some pencils and a few highlighters. He joined me on the couch. Pointing a blue one at me he lifted his brows and asked, "Shall we?"

I handed him half the stack of the articles. Will and I sat next to each other in silence, pausing every now and again to highlight new information. I finished before him, sat back, and let myself take a long minute to study his face. Hanging out with him confused me. One minute, like now, for instance, it seemed no time was lost from our childhood friendship and things were easy and light. It was refreshing to be with someone who respected me and lifted me up, someone I could trust and openly cared for me. The next moment my senses were overwhelmed—like a raging blizzard. Yes, he was quite attractive and had a great physique, but something deeper stirred feelings I wasn't quite ready to explore. As if he could read my mind, his eyes locked on mine. He put his papers down and turned his body to me. Ever so slowly, he moved in, causing me to lean back into the arm of the couch. If he kissed me, I wasn't going to stop him this time.

He didn't. He grabbed the articles I finished from under my hip.

"I'll take these now and you can look over my half. Figured it couldn't hurt to have two sets of eyes looking in case I missed anything." Will handed me his stack and shuffled through the articles I already reviewed. "I don't see a follow up article on my brother's disappearance."

"I'm sorry, I didn't find one. I did get through most of the ones Nick gave us. I decided to go back further in time to see if there were other cases that Nick failed to mention."

"We've got to go back," Will stated.

"To the library? Of course. I kind of figured we would need to go back. A lot."

"No. Back to the sledding hill."

"Honestly, I think I've had enough sledding fun for now. I'm a little sore from yesterday and you scared the crap out of me with your prank. I really believed you were hurt. Sledding gets a little more painful when you're older and not properly dressed, but..." The sight of Will's face stopped me. "What?"

"I didn't mean actual sledding." He busted out laughing.

"Oh. *Ohhh!*" I bonked my forehead with the heel of my hand. Will continued to laugh and I smacked him on the shoulder. "You can stop now. I realize you meant the storm grate. Why do you want to go back?"

"Think about it. You said you heard a voice coming from it, a voice needing help. I know it's crazy. I know I've told you to stay away from Nick, and we will. I have a feeling that there is something in there that will get us information much faster than microfilms and these strange books."

"And just how do we plan on doing that?"

"I haven't figured out that part yet. And, I don't want you coming inside with me, but I do need your help as my lookout in case Nick comes."

"OK, I get that we need a lookout, but is that the only reason you don't want me coming in?"

"Let me rephrase that. It's not that I don't want you going through the grate with me. Liddy, do I have to remind you what happened last night? You were talking about hearing a woman's voice and moved with supernatural speed. And at one point you looked scared of me."

"I did?" I didn't want it to be true. Last night Will glowed. I was used to his eyes doing that, but as I mindlessly followed the voice, Will's whole body had been aflame. He looked both beautiful and dangerous. But looking at Will now, shame washed over me. How could I ever have believed he could harm me?

"Yes, you did." Will looked a little sad. "When you first started walking, I grabbed you and you turned towards me. The last bit of moonlight landed on your face, revealing an expression of true alarm. I let go and then you were running... running *from me*."

"I'm sorry. You were...glowing."

"My eyes again?"

"Your entire body. It was beautiful, but also..." I looked at Will and he worried his lip. "Never mind. I felt it was urgent that I get to the white light and that pleading voice."

"The white light?" Will asked confused.

"Yes! You didn't see that either? Man, I must be losing it. This is all so crazy and the crazy thing is, I have no one else to talk to about it because, well, they'd think I was crazy!"

"Yes, we've established that this is crazy." He smiled and grabbed my hands. "But you are *not* crazy. With so many, um, shall we say, *intriguing* things happening, I believe that if you heard a voice, you heard a voice. And I did not say I didn't see *any* light, but I didn't see a *white* light."

"But you saw a light, too?" I asked.

"I would describe it as more of a glow, a mix of green and a reddish-orange." Chills ran down my spine. "What?" Will asked, his brow cocked.

"Red-orange, like when Charlie was taken?"

"Kind of, but last night was very dim in comparison. Liddy, my senses were amplified last night and they told me to get you the heck out of there. That's why I don't want you going in there with me."

I knew Will only wanted to protect me, but I was growing increasingly impatient. How could he implore my help and then expect me to sit on the sidelines when the time came to spring into action? I opened my mouth to protest, but realized this would be an uphill battle if I didn't pretend to agree with him. For now.

"Fine, I guess I'll be your lookout."

"Really? That's it?"

"That's it." I grabbed my stack of articles and made a show of studying them.

"That was a lot easier than I thought it was going to be." Will frowned. "I am glad you trust me."

My stomach sank. I did trust Will, but I also wanted to be part of the entire adventure. I didn't want to be Aurora on the sidelines while Philip slew the dragon. Will sat back into the couch and let out a sigh of relief. After a moment, he sat straight up and turned to me. "Let's start planning this little excursion after I get us some refills on our drinks."

While Will was gone, I made notes in the margins of the articles. They all seemed to have the same thing in common. If there was a witness, they only saw a dim green glow. No one saw a blood-orange flash. Each kidnapping occurred overnight in the month of December. All the victims until Charlie had been the oldest boy in the family. After Charlie, the disappearances seemed random. Girls and boys alike were kidnapped—no matter their birth order.

After a while, I took a break and walked over to the window, the sky now painted in deep pinks and oranges. *What's taking Will so long?* I contemplated going to find him but wanted to save myself the embarrassment of getting lost. Instead, I moseyed over to the end table near the fireplace that held the old books from Nick. I picked up the thickest one. I started to flip through its pages, shuffling them back and forth like a motion picture flipbook. For as thick as the book was, it didn't have that many pages. I stopped flipping and sat in a nearby chair to really examine the front and back covers.

My fingers traced the gold inlaid letterings and down the rippled spine. The covers were beautiful, hand stitched leather and pliable. In the bottom right corner, etched in gold, was Nick's full name. Nicholas Gabriel Klaus. I turned to the back cover, my thumb catching on the corner's peeling edge. I ran my fingers over the blank velvety face, pressing down. *Is this hollow?* I would never purposely deface a book, but curiosity got the better of me. I peeled back the fabric at the corner, like I inspected an ancient artifact. The fabric lifted easily. A small white journal laid within a hollowed-out rectangle, a shimmering, sea green shell painted in its center.

I should wait for Will to go through this. Where is he? I peeked out of the small library and called out, "Hello?" Silence. I put the small book back and pressed the cover down. *Where the heck is Will?* I set the book on the end table and left the library.

Proud of myself for finding the kitchen on my first try, I opened the door, but no one was there. Maybe Will went to his room for something. Maybe I could find him without getting lost. I exited the kitchen in the back, the way Will had brought me last time. After a few wrong turns, I found the first staircase and headed up. Walking down the narrow hallway towards the spiral staircase, I stopped short when I heard a TV reporter announce "BREAKING NEWS" from behind the partially closed door of Shai's office. I tiptoed over and peeked in. Nestling my face close to the crack in the door, I spotted a man I assumed was Shai. I studied him out of curiosity. He looked a lot like Will, but with a clean-shaven beard and a few crow's feet. Shai sat in a chair with his attention glued to the television. Following his gaze, my breath hitched in my chest. On the screen was someone I recognized instantly—a brunette girl, bright blue eyes, full cheeks and the familiar mint green walls of the room behind her. Shai was watching an old interview...*of me.*

The date in the corner showed that this was less than a week after Charlie had disappeared. The girl—me—gave robotic answers to every question. It was weird watching myself explain how I was friends with Charlie and Will and that I didn't know why Charlie had run away. *Charlie didn't run away and why do I not remember this? What the heck happened when you left Will?* I focused again on the TV. After a few more questions in which the younger me couldn't answer, the news reporter lost interest and brought the attention back to the newsroom. Then it cut back to today.

"For you viewers at home that are just tuning in, what you saw in the clip was a series of interviews from neighbors of the Jamison family whose young son Charlie disappeared almost exactly eight years ago. This was the last time a child disappeared in the city of Wheeling until today. Nine-year-old Brandon Davenport joins the list of mysterious child abductions." As she spoke, a picture of a young, dark haired boy appeared over her left shoulder. "Let's see what our investigative reporter discovered during her visit this morning to the Tahoe neighborhood where the boy disappeared."

What played next was an edited compilation of the reporter interviewing the Davenport's neighbors. Each person she spoke with was only able to share their condolences and shock. As the reporter said her closing remarks to cut back into the live broadcast, I caught a glimpse of a familiar figure trying to rush out of the camera's view and gasped. Shai whipped around in his chair. Holding my breath, I ducked into the alcove until I heard him slam the door. I exhaled and peeked out to make sure he returned to his office. I hurried up the spiral staircase to Will's room and grabbed the cold, cast iron knob. I opened the door about halfway and froze.

There Will was, lip-locked with another girl. Her arms wrapped around his neck, shielding her face. They didn't hear me, so I backed out of the room, bracing the door until I heard its soft click, and bolted.

Off or On

SHOCK SLAMMED MY CHEST and took my breath away with it. I clutched my breast as piece by piece my heart splintered. I somehow made it to the second staircase and rushed down with a few missteps. I desperately reached for the banister and regained my balance. Breathe, breathe in...two, three, four, out...six, seven, eight, in...two, three, four, out...six, seven, eight.

What did I just see? I paced the library and tried to convince myself I was being irrational. Will and I weren't together, I had made that very clear to him and everyone else. I wanted to leave now, but with no car, I had no way to escape. I knew Will and I agreed to just be friends, and I've insisted that I don't want, or need, a boyfriend. *But Will shared his feelings for me.* The only reason he wasn't pursuing me was because of Nick!

Will even convinced me that his plans for a future together were sincere. At the moment he said it, the sentiment freaked me out a little, but it still meant something. Now, seeing him kissing another girl, my real feelings—stuffed deep in my own cavernous heart—flooded to the surface. *Why did I have to be so stubborn?* And now I couldn't help but feel double-crossed. Will told me I could trust him, but he was no different than anyone else.

It's a good thing I knew better than to put my faith in people. The hardest part of all of this? I did this to myself. *I had to make a point and go on a date with Justin,* I chastised myself.

I heard Will and the girl coming down the hallway. I ran to look out the bay window so my back would be to the entrance of the room and wiped the tears from the corners of my eyes.

Get ahold of yourself, Liddy. Just like you had a right to go on a date, he has a right to be with whomever he wants, however he wants. Congratulations Will, my guard is officially back up.

A few moments later, Will entered the study. "Liddy!" Pree's voice chirped. "Oh my gosh, chica, I totally forgot you'd be here. What's up?"

Surprised to hear Pree's voice, I turned around plastering a fake as heck smile on my face. My eyes flicked to Will for a split second. His face was flushed, the same as Pree's. His eyes shifted across the library, his eyes never quite looking my way. *Betrayal.* The word flashed through my mind as quick and powerful as a bolt of lightning. Pree, my best friend with... my Will. *You encouraged this Liddy. You set them up for the dance.*

"Hey, Pree! I didn't know you were here. When did you get here?" I asked, my voice pitched higher than usual.

"Oh, like ten, fifteen minutes ago. I surprised Will!" she squealed. "The formal is next weekend, as you know, and I wanted to give him a gift. I got him a tie that matches my dress and wanted him to try it on."

"That was very thoughtful of you. So sweet that you'll match," I stated, sarcasm dripping off my words.

"Right? And it looks hot," she whispered. "But seriously, where have you been girl? Sara, Dani, and I were saying how we feel like we've not really talked to you in a while. Well, actually just Dani. Sara's been a little busy with Matt." Pree used air quotes on 'busy' and giggled.

"Pree, we talked Friday at school. And went dress shopping yesterday! But, yeah, Will and I have been…" I paused as I saw Will waving his arms like a drowning victim behind her to grab my attention, then shook his head no. "…busy working on our projects."

"Tell me about it. You still haven't told me about your date with Justin." She elbowed me. "I've got to get going. My mom's been in the car waiting." As if on cue, I could hear Mrs. Parekh start honking in the driveway. "Ugh! My mom is so embarrassing. What time will you be done here, Liddy, so I can come over tonight and you can tell me all about your date with Justin?"

"I'm done now if I can hitch a ride with you."

"Of course!"

I threw the remainder of my belongings into my bags, careful to avoid Will's scrutinizing glare. I put Nick's books back. The white journal I'd discovered would have to wait. All

I knew was that I wanted to get out of Will's house as fast as I possibly could. I had my coat on and was in the hall before Pree. I turned, but Pree stood a few feet away, lingering near Will.

"Pree! Your mom is honking pretty incessantly. We should go."

"Finnnnnne. Bye, Will." She went to give him a hug, which he reciprocated with an awkward pat. I waved bye and walked towards the door, Pree at my heels.

"Liddy, wait!" Will came running after me. I was halfway out the door when he caught my arm. "Pree, would you mind giving Liddy and I a moment, please?"

"Of course. I will walk slowly to the car to stall my mother who apparently can't WAIT A MINUTE!" she shouted towards the car.

"Liddy, what happened?"

"Nothing, I've got to go."

"You've never been good at lying. You look pained when you do. What's wrong?"

"Nothing."

"You're lying again! You're angry with me and I deserve to know why. What happened in the fifteen minutes I was gone?"

"Apparently a lot."

"Care to elaborate?"

"You have a little pink gloss riiiiight there." I used my thumb to wipe off the gloss from his upper lip. I ran down the steps towards Pree's car without looking back.

Each step I took toward Pree's car was a step closer to my undoing. My heart sputtered in my chest, each beat a strain on the already weakened muscle that could break at any moment.

As soon as I shut the car door, Pree's mouth took off faster than a shooting star.

"So, like, can you believe the dance is only a week away?"

"Calm down, Preethi. You're too excited. You know I can't understand when you speak English quickly."

"Sorry, Mom. I just said I can't wait for the dance. Liddy, girl, why are you not excited? It's going to be the best night ever."

"What best night? Why are we talking night time with boys? You are making me nervous. I may change my mind."

"Relax, Mom."

"She's not wrong, Pree. You two do seem to be getting close. Will's a great guy and I'm sure you're going to have a lot of fun." Those words pierced like frostbite and a new pain ached in my chest. I knew I had no right, none at all, to be angry with Pree. I stated, quite adamantly that Will and I were just friends. I even believed it. *So why am I trying to sabotage my friend?*

Pree's eyes widened and she immediately changed the subject. "Sara and I finished our English assignment. We chose Lancelot and Guinevere's love story. We're definitely getting an A." The mention of school work and good grades always distracted Mrs. Parekh and I caught her smiling in the rearview mirror.

"Will and I should be finished soon." I remained silent the rest of the way home.

I turned to close the car door and Pree shouted at me, "Call you later for the deets on Justin."

I skulked up to my room, locked the door, and collapsed on my bed. I didn't want to finish homework. I didn't want to think, period. Turning the ringer off on my phone I closed my eyes, but sleep wouldn't come. Images of Will and Pree kissing played over and over again in my head like a stupid slideshow.

The smell of lemon dill chicken and rice wafted up through the vents. I dragged myself off the bed despite not being hungry. The last thing I needed was a lecture from my parents about how skipping meals wasn't good for you.

While in the kitchen, I cut a small chicken breast in half and placed it over an even smaller pile of rice. Before even sitting down I asked, "Mom, Dad? Mind if I take this upstairs? I need to finish up some homework and get ahead since formal is this weekend."

"Of course, honey," Mom replied before taking a bite of chicken.

When I returned to my room, I set my plate on my desk. My phone taunted me from its perch on the nightstand. *What if Sara calls and wants to discuss plans for formal?* I slid the ringer back ON and sat at my desk to eat. *But what if Will calls and wants to talk about the kiss?* I stormed over and turned the ringer OFF. I pushed the rice around on my plate and contemplated turning the ringer back on. *But what if Pree calls to talk about Justin?* I wasn't sure I could stomach that tonight. *But...what if there's an emergency? UGGHHH! Fine, ON it is!* While still in my hand, the phone immediately rang and I nearly dropped it.

"Yes?" I answered brusquely.

"Oh my gosh. I've called you at least a million times. Tell. Me. Everything!" Pree squealed.

"What do you mean?"

"Spill it... *All* of it."

"I have no idea what you are talking about."

"Your date with Justin. Now, what's the scoop?"

Might as well get this over with, I thought, knowing I would never hear the end of it otherwise. "There isn't that much to tell. Justin and I almost kissed a few years back, but now we're just friends. He was a perfect gentleman all night and was very charming."

"Woah, how did you *almost* kiss? More importantly, how about you answer this next question. Did you guys kiss *this* time?"

"No. He made a good attempt, but you know me. I panicked. I wasn't ready for that."

Now it was Pree's turn to laugh. "Liddy, it's only a kiss! You're allowed to let loose and have fun once in a while."

"Don't judge me," I snapped saltily. I was still angry at her for kissing Will. "Sorry," I said, "I meant to say I don't agree. I believe a kiss can mean so much more; an unspoken promise or maybe leading the other person to assume you want more."

"Oh please, Liddy, this isn't the forties. So, what did he do when you dissed him?"

"I didn't diss him. And he was understanding. Our situation is complicated."

"Are you guys going to go on another date?"

"He asked me. I'm not sure I feel that way about him. I'm pretty busy this week and then we have the Winter Formal."

"So, the dance is your next date then."

"Not technically."

"Technically, it is," Pree teased.

"Whatever. I am going with a group of my friends. Pree, I've got to run. I am exhausted and I've got a bunch of homework to finish up. We should all try and finalize plans for Saturday soon."

"I hope you don't mind, but we already picked the restaurant. Well, Sara sort of did. We're going to Buca di Beppo. Apparently, her brother is a chef there now and he helped make the reservation for us. He's going to hook us up with our drinks and desserts. Sweet, right?"

"That's great. Are we still going to do pictures at two separate locations?"

"No! I forgot to tell you! I was ruthless in begging my mom to let me go to the formal with a date. I told her a nice boy had asked me and I talked him up so much, she finally relented."

"Really? She gave into a date with a boy?" I asked, surprised.

"Right?" Pree laughed. "Once I told her where he lived, she jumped out of her chair asking when she could meet him. That's why I was at Will's. She came to my room less than two hours later with a tie that matched my dress insisting that I bring it to Will's right then."

"Woah."

"I know! After she saw Will's house, she was so impressed, she bragged to my dad about it."

"I'm...so happy for you." I forced the words. "OK, well I've gotta get going, so let's figure out everything else tomorrow."

"Word, Liddy. See ya tomorrow."

$\mathcal{F}$orgiveness

$\mathcal{A}$S I ROLLED MY HAIR IN DRESS SOCKS, the way Mama L. instructed for perfect curls, I tried not to think of Will. I tried to pretend he didn't exist all week, but that proved to be more difficult than I'd imagined. I busied myself with my girlfriends during the day and after school as if he'd never come into my life. I grabbed another section of hair. I never imagined I'd be the one who'd drop my friends once a boy entered the picture. True, the English paper was partly to blame for my disappearance, but more importantly, I wanted to help Will find Charlie. But still, another part of me, a part that would not simmer down, wanted me to admit out loud that it was because I wanted to be with him.

The CD player clinked and hummed while it changed discs. Dave Matthews Band crooned from my stereo as I grabbed the last section of hair. How could I let myself drop everything for him? I needed to be stronger than that, to keep my focus on my original goals—no boys, good grades, and move to a warmer state.

At my dresser, I set the sleep timer on the stereo. I snuggled into bed, sighing as my newly shaven legs met the cool sheets. The weight of Will's absence hung over me like a weighted blanket. Sleep lulled at my body when a shrill ring cut through the air.

"Hello?" I answered, my voice drenched with sleep.

"Good evening. May I please speak with Princess Lydia?" the man's voice asked.

"May I ask who's calling?"

"Nicholas Klaus."

My heart skipped a beat. I sat straight up and swallowed hard. "This is she."

"Glad I have the right number. Listen, Princess, I know it's late so I won't take up too much of your time. I wanted to say have a good time at the dance tomorrow and..."

"Uh, thanks?"

"I was not finished. I get the sense you and Will need a little shove toward reconciliation. You need each other now more than ever."

"Yeah, about that, listen. I don't know what kind of game you're playing, but this is all getting so confusing. You gave us books that we can't read, articles that we don't know what to do with, and you keep reminding me that we can't be together. Now you're telling me I need to be with him?"

"Children's lives are depending on this." He sighed. "I know I am not saying a lot and yet I am asking you to trust me.

I understand you have no reason to, but it will all make sense soon, I promise. I'm waiting for it to be...safe."

"If I am to trust you, then can you answer me one thing?"

"Anything."

"Why me?"

He sighed and almost sounded pained to respond. "That is a loaded question, Your Highness. I cannot presume it is entirely safe to tell you everything right now, but if you desire the truth in summation, know that you are one half of a solution that will restore all order and seal the pathways between Cristes Adventus, Mortalia, and Beldam."

"Pathways to the what and the what now?"

"I must retire for the evening and allow you to do so as well. Please remember how special Will is. Try not to let foolish teenage games interfere with much more important matters. Forgive him."

Why does he know everything? "Wait! I get one more question. Why can't we read the books you gave him?"

"These books are no bags o' mystery. I would have thought you both had figured that out by now. Seems like I am going to have to do more than I thought. Maybe I was too strict on the whole keeping your distance from each other," he mumbled to himself. "I was hoping the both of you would be able to at least figure some of these basic things of substance out together so I could spend time on more pressing tasks, such as finding the missing pieces of..." Nick paused and let out a huff. "Have you even tried to read any of it, Lydia?"

"Briefly."

"The next time you are both together, get close, but not too close. Try...holding hands and then open a book together. If still nothing, then and only then will I determine if everyone is prepared for the next step. I bid thee farewell."

"How do we contact—" The dial tone hummed in my ear.

Rude. I looked at my clock: ten-fifteen. I needed to go to bed, but my gut told me to call Will. Not because Nick had suggested it, but because if I was honest with myself, I wasn't being fair to him. Besides, I missed him. When we stopped talking—rather when *I* stopped talking to him—a part of me went missing again. But I was still hurt. Normally, I'd convince myself that the person who hurt me needed to make the amends first.

I picked up the phone and dialed his number. I could continue to ignore Will and be unhappy, or try to make peace and rest easy knowing that I tried, no matter the outcome. The phone rang and rang until finally his answering machine picked up.

"Hey, Will. It's Liddy. I wanted to talk and say I'm sorry about Sunday, and well, just about this week, I mean that we haven't talked this week. And um—I miss you." I swiftly hung up. A few seconds later, a knock rapped on my door.

"Lydia, sweetie. There is someone here to see you. Are you decent?"

"Just a minute mom!" I slipped on my purple robe over my tank and flannel pajama pants. I opened the door and Will filled my doorway, shoulders slumped. Shadows colored his eyes. I surprised myself by almost plowing him over with a hug. He embraced me just as tight. Lost in each other's arms, Mom cleared her throat and snapped us back to reality.

"I'm going to be right near the bottom of the stairs in the living room. Keep your door open please."

"Sure, Mom," I assured her. She gave me one last look and went downstairs.

I sat down on my bed and offered Will my chair. He ignored it, walked up to me, pulled me up, and gave me another lingering hug. I never wanted to let go.

"I'm sorry," I whispered into his shoulder. *I'd rather have you as a friend than not have you at all.* He squeezed me tighter in response and then pulled away, keeping hold of my waist.

"I'm sorry, too," he breathed, his eyes holding mine.

"For what? You didn't do anything wrong. I overreacted." I dropped my eyes. It hurt me to admit it aloud.

Will lifted my chin with his finger. "I'm sorry it didn't immediately register why you were upset. For the record, *she* kissed me. I am not sure what you saw, but it happened so quickly I didn't have time to move. It was a surprise attack! One minute she was showing me this tie and the next her lips were on mine. It shocked the heck out of me. I regret that my reflexes aren't as quick as my brain. I feel like an idiot for not anticipating it and moving out of the way. I would think Pree knew... What I mean is, I guess I haven't done a good enough job of letting people know how...how I feel about..."

"I'm not even sure what I saw anymore." I cut him off. *Why do I keep doing this? Why am I incapable of sharing my true feelings with him?* And as much as I wanted to be mad at Pree, I knew I didn't have a right to be. How many times have my friends suspected my true feelings for Will and yet I denied it? After all, I was the reason Pree was even going to the Winter Formal with him.

"Liddy?"

"Yeah?"

"You seemed like you were going to say something else and then got sidetracked."

"Oh, yeah." *Quick, Liddy, change the subject so you can try and forget this whole painful thing.* "I'm so sorry I avoided you all week for something so stupid. I've spent far too much energy on that."

"Are you sure you're fine?"

"Totally," I lied. Though I believed him, my heart still hurt. The images would be seared in my mind for a long time to come, but I was done talking about it. "Besides, I shouldn't have let my emotions get the best of me. We lost a whole week because of a misunderstanding that was none of my business anyway and I have something important to fill you in on. Like how Nick called me a few minutes before you got here."

"How did he get your number? How did he—"

"I don't know," I told him, my voice low. "He seems sincere in his concerns for the world, these lands, and his belief that you and I are somehow important to that. But I don't get how these children are involved. What I think we need to do is go on about our lives and act as if we don't suspect him." I started pacing back and forth as the hyper-focused portion of my brain planned out our next move. "Let's play his little game, but we need to be careful to be a step ahead of him. We won't get much done tonight or tomorrow obviously, but we should plan on getting back to it on Sunday. We've one week until winter break. We should plan how you're going to get into that storm grate. We need to hurry to prevent more kids from disappearing. Will, are you hearing me?"

"What? Oh, sorry. Is that the dress he got you?" Will asked, gesturing to the gown hanging on the back of my bedroom door.

"Yeah, why?"

"Are you still going to wear it?"

"Yes. I told you, I don't want him to know we are onto him."

"Good thinking. Have I thanked you yet for all of this? I mean if it was anyone else, they'd have thought I was—"

"Crazy?" I smirked.

"Yes," he breathed. "Being near you brings me comfort. I don't know what I will find regarding my brother and I do not think I'd be able to do this without you. You are a good friend Liddy."

"A good friend wouldn't have ignored you for a week. I truly am sorry."

"Don't be so harsh on yourself. You are an excellent friend."

I tried to smile, but a yawn escaped.

"It's late and you seem tired so I better be going. We have a long night tomorrow and I'm looking forward to seeing you in that dress," he said as his cheeks flushed. "Do you remember what you promised me?"

"No." I cocked my head.

"You promised me a dance." He smiled.

I walked up to him, stood on my tippy toes so I could wrap my arms around his neck and whispered, "I wouldn't miss it for the world." His eyes stirred and his grip tightened around my waist. Every fiber of my being wanted to press my lips to his. Drawing him in close, I leaned my head on his shoulder instead.

I walked him to the front door. "Goodnight, Will."

"Sweet dreams, Liddy."

I bounded up the stairs giddy as a kid on Christmas

morning and yelled, "Goodnight, Mom."

"What's in your hair you weirdo?" Mickey asked around a mouthful of toothpaste as I passed the bathroom.

"No, no, no!" I slammed the door to my room and locked it. I peered in the mirror. "Dang it!" I yelled as I examined myself. No makeup and socks rolled into my hair. *Great!* Well, Will had seen the real me and hadn't run for the hills screaming. I laughed to myself. Heck, he didn't even question for a second why I had socks in my hair. *Oh well, tomorrow, with that dress on, he'll forget all about it.* My head hit the pillow and I drifted off to thoughts of all things Winter Formal.

$\mathcal{A}$nticipation

$\mathcal{D}$ANI, SARA, AND I LOUNGED in men's button down shirts painting our toenails when Pree walked in sporting an elaborate bun.

"Love your hair!" Sara said.

"Thanks, girl. By the way, your mom said she's ready for you."

We watched *Clueless* and continued painting our nails until Sara returned. Half her hair was pinned up in pastel butterfly clips, the rest swayed in ringlets just past her shoulders.

Clueless ended by the time Dani returned with her hair slicked back and her ends flipped out. Rhinestone encrusted barrettes decorated the sides.

I skipped downstairs, eager for my turn.

"I have the picture here that you picked out for your hair,

but...will you trust me if I take creative liberty?"

"Of course!"

"Oh, thank you, Lydia! Your dress is so inspiring. I'm turning you around because I want it to be a surprise."

She gently pulled the dress socks from my hair as she hummed along to Dean Martin. By song sixteen, Mama L. unleashed her can of *Big Sexy Hair* hairspray on me, then turned me around.

She stood behind me with a mirror so I could see the hairstyle from all angles. My vintage inspired hairstyle had numerous pin curls on one side. On the other, waves swept my hair up into a cascading loose braid.

"I love it!" I hugged her. "Thank you!"

"You are so welcome. You girls need to eat or you'll all be famished. Your mom dropped off food earlier. Can you help me bring it up?"

"Of course." We grabbed the food and headed upstairs.

"Thank God, I'm starving!" Pree rushed to grab the water bottles and chips from Mama L.

"Dig in girls. Let me know if you need any help with makeup."

"We got it, Mom, thanks."

We ate and helped each other place a temporary crystal tattoo of one-of-a-kind snowflakes on our left shoulder blades.

"Ladies, it's time!" Sara rang out. She stood by her closet and grabbed each of our dresses, one by one, and handed them out.

"Liddy... You look like royalty featured in a magazine straight out of the 1930s!" Dani chimed.

"I mean, seriously...I might just kiss you myself!" Pree

planted a solid kiss on my cheek and we all laughed.

"Ladies! You have ten minutes!" Mama L. called to us.

"Quick! Someone help me with my head piece."

"I got it." I placed a gold circlet over Pree's bun. It came to a point on her forehead where a jewel hung from it, resting between her brows.

We packed our small purses with essentials, put on our lipstick, and slipped into our heels. Mama L. drove us to Matt's to take pictures with our dates.

"Welcome, ladies!" Mrs. Hyatt said as she led us to the large living room with a grand fireplace.

As we entered the room, all eyes were on us and a hush fell over the group. My body temperature rose with each click and flash of the cameras that nearly blinded us. I adjusted my necklace, its weight now too heavy and constricting, desperate for an escape. I quickly scanned the room and relaxed, letting go of my necklace when I found my parents. A hug from Mom always made me feel more at ease.

"Are you guys crying? You guys, please don't embarrass me." I spoke with a tight smile, careful to not move my lips.

"My baby girl is all grown up," Dad whispered as he stared at me.

"You are breathtaking." Mom shakily wiped a tear from her eye.

"I agree," Will said as he came to stand by me.

I peeked at Will and leaned in quickly to whisper in jest, "You can close your mouth now," like he'd done to me when I first marveled at his home. Will's uncle stepped around from behind him.

"My nephew is correct. That is quite a regal dress. It might overpower some women, but not you... It was clearly tailor made."

I stared at him. Will gave me a gentle nudge with his elbow. "Th-thank you, sir."

"It's a pleasure to formally meet you, Lydia. You may call me Shai," he stated as he gave me a small bow. "I apologize that I did not have the chance to introduce myself earlier."

"It's a pleasure to meet you, Shai," I responded as I curtsied. *Holy heck! I just curtsied!* He smiled in response.

"I expect I will be seeing a lot more of you at the house soon. You have made Nolan happy, keeping him busy doing what he loves, but I do hope my work slows down so I can—how do you teenagers say—*hang* with my nephew now that I am lucky enough to have him living with me."

"It's uh, time for pictures, Liddy." Justin appeared at my side, hand on my elbow. "Oh, and my 'rents would like to meet yours."

"Of course. Mom, Dad, this is my good friend, Justin." Shai seemed bewildered, but he regained his composure before anyone else took notice.

"Nice to meet you Mr. Erickson, Mrs. Erickson." Justin turned to wave his parents over. His mom choked on an hors d'oeuvre when she saw me.

"Liddy, you look so...different from when I've seen you at the pool," Deborah said.

I smiled at her. *Ya think? A fancy dress, elaborate hair, and full makeup compared to a swimsuit and hat at the end of a long day in the sun.* I bit back a *bless your heart.*

"Thank you, Mrs. Lindor." I turned my attention to Justin's dad. "Hi, Mr. Lindor."

"You look radiant, darling," he replied.

"Let's get this over with." Justin rolled his eyes and quirked a smile.

Alex did a great job of both looking like a runway model and making Dani laugh while they posed for the camera. Mrs. Parekh gave Will the best stare down she could muster since Pree kept finding every excuse to touch him. Every swat Mrs. Parekh gave Pree's hand was met with a quick prayer. Who could blame her for worrying? Will was striking. Of all the high school boys in the room, he was the one that stood out. Not because he wore an indigo suit compared to everyone else in standard black, but because he looked more like a young man than a teenage boy. In fact, he didn't look like he was from this time period at all.

The silky sheen of Will's three-piece suit tantalized me; the flawless tailoring tempted my hands. I wanted to run them over the smooth fabric and feel each ripple of his athletic body. Though his tie was made from the same fabric as Pree's dress, his purple pocket square matched mine perfectly. He had a platinum, double-chain pocket watch that hung from the center button of his fitted vest. I couldn't help but stare. Our eyes met for a brief moment and he smiled, sending my heart into spastic flutters. Commotion and chatter surrounded us and yet, in that moment when my eyes were locked with his, I heard nothing but my own heartbeat.

Justin wrapped his arm around me and the sounds in the room came alive again. "Our turn," he said as he led me to the mantle.

I hated being in pictures. I knew nothing about good angles or sides and every attempt felt unnatural. With so many people taking photos, there was no doubt I looked at the wrong camera. Justin was even more timid, his hands clammy and his smile dim compared to its usual brightness. A honk sounded from just outside.

"Limo!" Pree screamed out of sheer excitement and got everyone else riled up. We girls took a final, obligatory Charlie's Angel posed photo before we all hustled out to the limo and were off. The driver closed the window divider, and blasted the music.

Winter Wonderland

USTIN AND I EXITED THE LIMO FIRST. His hand shook like he had a tremor as he helped me out of the limo. *How sweet. Is he nervous about dancing with me?* Alex ducked out right after me, making some inappropriate comments about my rear end and Justin's arm tensed against mine. Will assisted Pree out of the limo with well-mannered charm. He moved with confidence and ease as he held out his hand to her. Pree's heel caught on the hem of her dress and Will swiftly dropped down to release the thread. He was truly, like Nick claimed, a Prince. He was way too well-dressed, well-mannered, well-intentioned, and well...too darn good looking. I reminded myself right then and there to be super careful to respect the friendship boundary tonight; one kiss could change everything.

Some of our teachers, barely recognizable in their formal

attire, greeted us at the school's entrance. They "ooh'd" and "ahh'd" at our dresses and made a fuss over the dapper guys. At the table just outside of the commons, we stopped to show our tickets. We checked our coats and purses. As I stepped into the commons, I sighed in wonder. *Kudos to Student Council.* The room, dimly lit, created an air of mystique. A white aisle runner lined with pre-lit trees guided us into the dance. We wandered closer, the trees around us finely dusted with snow and glittering beneath the lights. A smile stretched my lips. *Like fresh snow beneath lamp light. My favorite.* A sign pointed us to the left of the gym doors. *Framed Polaroids: five dollars.*

"Let's all take pictures first while there's no line," I suggested.

"Duh! And while our makeup is still fresh," Pree added.

They would be placed in a cute, white frame embossed with snowflakes that read:

Winter Wonderland
Wheeling High School
Winter Formal 1998

"On the count of three. One...two..."

Something grabbed my shoulders and spun me. I came to an abrupt stop and Justin's face was close, too close.

"Three!"

As the camera flashed, Justin closed the gap and lingered. It took me a moment for my body to register something warm— Justin's lips. I instinctively pulled away and swiped where he'd narrowly missed my mouth. He snatched me around my waist, my torso connecting with his as he laughed.

"Justin, come on. Can we take a real photo please?" I tried to play it off as though it didn't bother me since most of the group, except for Will, laughed along with him.

"Sorry, Liddy." Justin put his hands up. "Won't happen again." His words drawled as if they took a lot of effort for him to say. *That's weird. I don't remember him drinking.*

"Mrs. Harbaugh, would you mind doing a retake?"

"Of course, dear." She turned to Justin, her tone more serious. "Justin, quit acting like you've never been on a date before." We got into position again. As the camera flashed, Justin landed a kiss hard on my lips. *Ouch!* I recoiled from him, covering my mouth, tasting a hint of blood.

"Good grief, Justin! Don't make me rescind your title as my favorite student. You nearly toppled your date over."

Will's eyes ignited; they swirled into a deep green, a color I hadn't seen before and a warning to flee from Justin flooded my system. I tried to step away again, but Justin slid his hand down my arm and snatched my wrist.

Alex seemed less than thrilled and made an attempt to come towards me, but Matt stopped him. "She's not your date, Alex. Justin was just playing around."

"Excuse me. I need to use the ladies' room." I stated in the best unshaken voice I could muster.

"We'll join you," Sara remarked, catching the eyes of the other girls.

"No, I'm fine. I just need a minute."

"I'll wait right outside the door for you," Justin said as he kissed my hand. He pulled away, his lips lightly stained from my lipstick. I turned from him and forced a smile at Will before I dashed into the bathroom. I held onto each side of the white porcelain sink; my head lowered as I tried to regain my composure. *What's wrong with Justin?*

I lifted my face to the mirror. My lower lip was swollen. I grabbed a paper towel and wet it, pressing it to my lip. I sucked in a breath. The water stung a small cut decorating my lip.

Justin definitely let me know his feelings for me on our date. His approach was endearing and gentle. Unlike tonight. Whipping me around. Rough. Clashing his lips against mine. I was like a toy to be used. I shuddered.

"OK, you've had your minute." Sara announced as she walked in, Dani and Pree on her heels.

"OK, I will admit, that was a little forward of him," Dani blurted out.

"Yeah, one half-ditch attempt shows poor judgment," Pree stated, checking herself in the mirror. "I mean, you know he likes you so it's not so far-fetched that he'd try to kiss you, but two times, in front of everyone?"

"He's lucky you didn't deck him!" Dani rushed over and took my chin, inspecting my face.

"Damn right, Dani," Sara interjected.

"Sara!" I said, shocked.

"What, you're one of my best friends. He can't go around acting like a perv."

I sighed. "I should have punched him. I guess I was just too shocked to react. Justin has never done anything like this. Something's not right with him tonight."

Pree sighed. "OK, so he made a big mistake, huge. Maybe he had a little drink you know, to calm his nerves? It should flush out of his system soon. Let's not let his poor judgment ruin our entire night. We look too fabulous for it all to go to waste."

"She is so right," Sara chimed in. "I'll make sure Matt gets him tons of water and talks with him."

She was right. Up until now, Justin had always been kind and a gentleman. For as long as I'd known him, he'd been a solid guy and friend.

"That'd be great. I feel much better now, thanks girls. If you see him starting to get close like that again, can you..."

"Kick his butt?" Dani asked with a wicked grin. "With pleasure." We all laughed.

"Sara, Dani, do you mind giving Liddy and I a minute?"

"Sure, see you out there," Sara responded as she grabbed Dani's hand and walked out of the bathroom.

"What's up?" I asked.

"Let's discuss how you've basically been undressing my date with your eyes all night," Pree responded. I attempted to protest, but she shut me down. "It's OK. I know what's going on. The question is, are you going to ever admit how you feel about Will? I mean come on! It is *so* obvious. Anyone who has eyes can see it. Maybe Justin isn't drunk! Maybe he's making one last ditch effort because he's been driven mad by jealousy." Pree's eyes widened in excitement over the possibility of such a development.

I laughed. "I think your drinking theory is more plausible, but you have always loved a good soap opera drama."

"OK, and what about Will?"

I didn't want to lie to her, but I hadn't even told Will yet. Not to mention, how would I explain Nick or Charlie? "It's complicated, Pree."

She studied me. "Fine, have it your way. I love you, but you make things too dang hard on yourself. One way or another the truth is gonna come out. Now, let's get back to our dates." Pree smirked. "If you're not going to act on what we all know to be true, I for one have no problem dancing with that fine piece of..."

"Pree!"

"Art! I was going to finish with 'art'. Get your head out of the gutter." Pree snorted.

I rolled my eyes and laughed.

We checked ourselves in the mirror one last time and proceeded out of the bathroom.

I lagged a step behind. *You can do this Liddy. You've known Justin for three years now. He's harmless. And Pree is being...Pree. Ignore it and enjoy the night.* I took a deep breath and walked out. As promised, Justin waited for me right outside the bathroom. And Will stood next to him.

I avoided Will's eyes; they always said too much. At the very least, they stirred feelings that I desperately wanted to act on. I wasn't sure if the warning I'd gotten earlier was my own gut instinct or if Will had somehow sent it to me.

No, tonight was not the time for more theories. Tonight, I would take my friends' advice and have fun. Justin tried to grab my hand again, but instead I hooked my arm through his. "A true gentleman escorts a lady at a dance," I teased.

He smiled back. *Whew! Linking arms is way less personable than holding hands.* We walked two by two down the aisle and through the gym doors.

The gym was a larger version of the commons area. Each side had bleachers collapsed into the walls. The sections closest to the gym doors were partially pulled open to allow three long rows of seating. A few couples sat on the bleachers on each side, some talking while others held hands or rested their heads on each other's shoulders. White organza draped the walls with twinkling lights underneath. Randomly placed around the edges were more pre-lit, snow covered trees. Every few minutes, the fog machines placed around the gym took turns releasing a gentle mist to blanket the floor in white. Tons of white, silver, and pearl ornaments hung from the rafters at different lengths that cast the DJ's lights all over the gym. The small crowd grew as more and more students trickled in.

As we walked towards the stage, the song changed to "Wannabe" by the Spice Girls. The girls and I shrieked and ran the rest of the way to the front by the DJ. The guys followed us, but mainly hung back watching and laughing at our interpretations. I couldn't blame them for being intimidated by our hip bumpin', booty shakin', and over the top shimmies. Three more songs passed before the DJ played the first slow dance of the night, "Kiss from a Rose". Justin slid his hands around my waist and I rested my forearms on his shoulders, my hands dangled in the air instead of around his neck.

"I love watching you dance, Liddy. You're really good."

"Thanks. You're not so bad yourself," I lied. This boy did not have rhythm, but I loved that he didn't seem to care.

"Sorry about earlier. I don't know what came over me," he said as he wiped the small beads of sweat off his forehead with the cuff of his shirt.

"Thank you, Justin. You're forgiven."

He gripped my waist a little tighter, drew me into him, and guided my arms so I hugged his neck.

Relax Liddy, we're merely dancing. I peeked over his shoulder. Following the stares and glares of many girls in the room, I found Pree and Will. He appeared at ease and Pree glowed at his side. While I loved seeing Pree so happy and carefree, my heart sunk a little watching them. Jealous emotions crept up and, for a brief moment, I wanted to steal him away, maybe even share how I truly felt about him. I looked away and chastised myself for being a coward. *How would Will react anyway? It's not like he'd actually change dates in the middle of the dance.* I peeked back over. Like Fred Astaire and Ginger Rogers, Will turned Pree to and fro, and lifted her with ease, even sweeping her down into a graceful dip.

My body craved Will. I wanted to dance with him. I feared if I continued staring at them, envy would turn my heart to ice, and I'd steal Will away. I tore my eyes from them. Pree was my friend. I wouldn't ruin her first dance with a boy, no matter how desperately I wanted him. I excused myself from Justin's arms to get a drink. The music shifted back to an upbeat club vibe as I walked to the refreshment table. Someone came from behind me and grabbed me hard on my hips. I froze as they pulled me close and grinded against me.

"You promised me a dance, beautiful," he whispered huskily in my ear. My skin crawled. *Who the heck?* I whipped my head around and Alex grinned from ear to ear, a smug look on his face. Justin barreled towards me and shoved Alex, hard. Alex stumbled, regained his stance, and knocked into Justin, yelling, "Step off dude!" Justin went at Alex again, but I stepped in the middle of them, holding my hands out. As if I weighed little more than a delicate snowflake, Justin flicked me out of the way. My heel twisted and I stumbled. In a flash, Will came to help me up. His face locked on mine and I was distracted from the heinous scene unfolding before us by the glowing green embers in his eyes. I knew what that color meant. He was furious.

A muscle in his jaw flexed. "I'm OK, Will. I promise."

Justin looked shaken, his eyes wide in disbelief at his own actions. He looked at his hands, a perplexed look on his face, then rushed to my side. "I'm so sorry, Liddy! I didn't mean to—"

"To what? Shove her?" Alex accused. Justin shivered as if he literally tried to shake something off of him. A crowd formed around them.

"Oh no you two don't." I pointed my finger in their faces. "You guys are not going to get us kicked out. This is a special night for us and you will not taint its memory! Justin, I promised my friends I would dance with all of them tonight and that is what I'm going to do. Alex and I were just—" I threw a sneer at Alex— "dancing!" I practically screeched. Pree and Dani approached with twin frowns on their faces, cups of punch in hand. Pree stood wide-eyed while Dani looked ready to throw some punches for me.

"I guess," Justin mumbled, clearly still miffed. "Does he have to be quite so handsy though?"

"No, he doesn't," I reprimanded, shifting my attention to Alex.

"My bad," Alex apologized. "I was just dancing. Can we all get back to it?"

"Yes, lets! Alex, I'll give you the next slow dance and after that, Pree do you mind if I have that dance with Will?"

"Of course," Pree said.

"As you wish," Will responded with a wink.

THE WITCH IN THE ENVELOPE

"OK, now that we've got that all sorted out, let's get back to it!"

Another slow song made its way through the D.J.'s playlist and Alex wasted no time finding me. Alex, a better dancer than Justin, had looser hips and definitely more swag. I let my body respond to his movements, my hips swaying in time with his. I peered around the gym and saw Pree with Justin doing the guy-girl waddle. She kept getting tripped up and her face scrunched in apparent agitation. I laughed.

"What's so funny?" Alex whispered in my ear. His wintergreen breath wisped past my nose.

"None of your business," I teased.

About mid song, Alex's hands moved down my waist, following the curve of my body and rested on my hips for a second before starting their journey down the sides of my hips and around to my butt. I moved his hands back. A few moments later, he tried again. Will's threatening stare pelted over my shoulder to Alex.

"Dang it, Alex!" I'd been tested enough tonight. "Don't make me knee you in the little boys. Keep your hands back up where they belong," I lectured.

"My bad," he said as he reversed his hands over each inch of my body until they rested on my waist. "My hands couldn't help it. Clearly, they have good taste and a mind of their own." He grinned.

I rolled my eyes. "Why do you do this?"

"Do what?" he asked, blinking innocently.

"Act like a sleaze and treat everyone like an object, like they don't really matter."

Alex sucked in his lips. After a few lyrics passed, he leaned down to my ear. "Don't tell anyone, a'ight? I was bullied a lot when I was younger. Then I moved here and with a fresh start, I decided to try being a cocky jerk. It seemed to be what worked for the popular dudes at my last school. Suddenly, I was cool and dudes didn't mess with me. I guess I've never been confident enough to show the real me."

The Alex I knew was a lot of things, but being short on confidence wasn't one of them. This revelation took me by surprise. "Thanks for sharing that. You know, I think you owe it to yourself to show people the real you."

Alex smiled at me but didn't respond. I thanked Alex for the dance as soon as the song ended. He gave me a hug and walked away, his head down and a tiny pucker between his brows. "I'll Back You Up" by Dave Matthews Band crooned from the speakers: one of my favorites. I looked around for Will and found him near the pulled-out bleachers. He looked at me and his eyes gleamed that alluring bright green as I walked over to him.

"Can I please have this dance, Your Excellency?" I asked, grinning as I lowered into a curtsy.

Will smiled. "I'm glad you could grace me with your presence, Your Highness." He bowed.

"Gotta save my best friend for last," I reassured him.

"Ah, I see. Best friend, huh?" His eyes dimmed and his smile didn't reach his eyes.

I quickly added, "For now."

He inched towards me, a grin emerging on his perfect face. He reached one hand up to the side of my neck and, with a soft caress, he followed the curve of my spine. His left hand slipped around to rest on the small of my back. Deep, warm quivers consumed every place he touched and I let out an involuntary gasp.

Snow machines buzzed to life and white flakes flitted over the entire gym floor. My heart raced and my blood thrummed through my veins. Time stood still as he laid me back to dip me. His face never moved more than a few inches from mine. I couldn't help but stare at his lips and longed for them to touch mine.

As carefully as he had lowered me, he brought me back up, his hands encouraging my body to roll up: first my hips, then abdomen, then chest, and ending with my head resting on his shoulder. His hand trailed down my side with slight pressure and my body ached for more, more, *more*. He released my neck, followed the arc of my collarbone and shoulder, and traveled down my arm to connect our hands. He separated us a few inches and grinned, his eyes luminous.

"Lydia?"

"Yes, William?" I giggled a little. He never used my full name. He moved his mouth close to my ear and my body went taut. He nestled me close and, in an instant, the tension melted away as my body softened completely into his.

"You can always trust me," he whispered.

"Promise?"

"As you wish," he murmured.

We slow danced, two snowflakes flying on our own among a blizzard of many. When the song ended, we stopped moving, but didn't let go. We stared into each other's eyes, inhaling and exhaling in unison as we tried to catch our breath. I slowly slid my hands down the length of his arms and moved to step away. Will caught my hand and walked us to the bleachers.

"Thanks. I needed a rest."

"I thought you might," Will responded. "Care for a foot rub?"

"Ew, no! I've been dancing all night! They're gross!" I exclaimed.

"Your loss." He laughed. "I am quite skilled with these," he said as he wiggled his fingers in my face. I grabbed his hands and rested my head on his shoulder. I didn't want to let go. I had found my happy place, bliss settling over me.

"Uh oh, Justin looks a little putout," Will said.

"He'll have to get over it. You're my friend and I'm sitting here with you."

"Are you sure? Because he is on his way over here now."

I reluctantly lifted my head and asked Will, "You're coming to the after party, right?"

"Well, I am your ride. And besides, I don't think Pree would forgive me if I didn't." Will laughed.

Justin now stood in front of both of us. He looked peeved—his jaw twitching and his eyes scrunched to laser beams. "Liddy, may I please have this dance?"

"Of course. I needed a quick rest. Let me get myself a drink and I'll be ready to hit the floor again."

"I'll get it," he responded, but his enthusiasm didn't reach his eyes and he mumbled something under his breath.

"Liddy, please be careful around him," Will cautioned, staring intently at Justin's back, emerald darkening his bright eyes.

"It's not him you should be worried about," I teased as I nudged him and lifted my chin towards Alex.

"Yeah, well him too, but I'm serious. I get a bad...energy

from Justin tonight. Something's different."

"Yeah, something *is* different... Will, earlier tonight when Justin tried to kiss me. I could feel what you were feeling."

I froze as Justin returned, holding the drink out to me. Will dropped my hand. I stood, grabbing the cup from Justin. I took a few sips but sensed him growing impatient. I quickly walked my cup to the garbage can, gulped most of it down, and turned to Will. "See ya, Will."

I pulled Justin to the dance floor near the center of the gym, not wanting to give him a reason to start something with Will.

"Last one of the evening ladies and gents," the D.J. called out.

Halfway through the song my friends all came up to us. "We are going to head out now and avoid the crowd," Matt announced. We all shuffled out of the gym to the parking lot, Justin sticking to my side and holding my waist the entire way. I convinced Pree to sit in the back of Will's car with me. Justin attempted to squeeze beside me, but Will encouraged him to take the passenger seat. Pree chatted a mile a minute, but I barely heard a word she said.

I caught Justin's reflection in the visor. His eyes darkened, full of something I didn't recognize. My stomach squeezed tight and I ducked my eyes. My instincts told me something wasn't right with him as he continued to watch me through the mirror. And nerves stood on high alert the rest of the way to the party.

You Owe Me

WE PULLED INTO THE CIRCULAR DRIVEWAY; pale stones led up the steps to the front door. We packed onto Joey's front porch a little after ten. His dad stood in the entryway collecting everyone's keys.

"Matt! Glad you made it bro! Food and drinks are in the kitchen so help yourselves. Party is downstairs through this door. Ladies, if you need anything tonight, don't be afraid to ask." A tipsy Joey winked at us and led us down the Berber-carpeted stairs to the basement where the music was bumping and a group of at least twenty people already danced. He showed us the makeout closet he assembled complete with red Christmas lights, plush pillows, and blankets. My parents didn't allow me to sleep over, but they had at least given me a much later curfew. Fine by me; I hated the taste of alcohol and nothing good happened after midnight anyway.

Justin excused himself upstairs to get a drink and came back with one for me. I went to take a sip, but the smell made my face twist.

"Justin, is there alcohol in this?" I asked over the music.

"No, it's just coke."

"Oh, ah, thanks," I replied. I pretended to take another sip and smiled at him. I would get myself a new drink soon.

"Liddy, give me a sip!" Pree demanded. I handed her the cup. With only a few sips, she was chattier and even more bubbly. She took another deep swig.

"You better be careful," I warned. "Your mom will smell that a mile away."

"She never lets me have any fun," she whined and handed back the cup, joining the few people dancing in the center of the room.

Will came up next to me. "Can I see that for a sec?"

"Why?"

"I'm not going to drink it," Will clarified. I handed Will the cup. He smelled it and wrinkled his nose. "What's this?"

"A coke."

"That's not a coke."

"I know. I think it's flat or something. Pree drank most of it. I'm gonna go upstairs and grab myself something else."

"Good idea," Will said. "I'll go with you."

Pree came bouncing over and stumbled into Will. "Where are you two love birds going?" She bopped him on the nose while Will helped to hold her up.

"Oh no!" *That was fast.* "Will, can you keep an eye on her for me? I'll be right back with water."

I reached the base of the stairs. A second later, Joey stood on the coffee table and shouted over the music. "Let's get the realllllll party started." Everyone started cheering. "All zee guys circle up! I'm a gonna to spiiinnn this boddlle and whoeverrr it lands on, you and yourrr date will go into da closet forrr sevenn minutesss of heavennnnn," He drooled and nearly stumbled off the edge of the table.

Ugh! This is so juvenile. I want no part of this. I was halfway up the stairs when I heard Will and Pree's name get called out followed by lots of whoops and excited chatter. I ran back down and leaned over the railing in time to see Pree pulling Will into the closet. I looked at Will, whose eyes were already on me. He didn't seem panicked as he resisted Pree. He gave me a look that said he was fine. When Will broke free from her grip and helped her away from the closet, I dashed up the stairs. Poor Will would have his hands full until I returned.

I grabbed two plastic cups and filled them with ice water from the pitcher on the island. With the cups balanced in one hand, I reached for the basement's door knob when I was yanked by the arm. Both cups flew from my hands and sloshed all over the wood floor.

"Whoever you are, this isn't funny!" I yelled as they dragged me into a nearby room. The room was pitch black.

"Shut up, Liddy," Justin whispered as he cupped his hand over my mouth and pushed me into a wall, the back of my head slamming against it.

"OUCH!" My muffled scream barely registered over the noise coming from the basement.

"I said, SHUT. UP!" His hand crushed my mouth and my teeth bit into my lips. "I'm going to move my hand. Nod your head if you promise not to scream."

I nodded obediently.

"Good girl. You know, I don't know what he sees in you," Justin said, spittle hitting me in the face. I almost became intoxicated just smelling his breath, though that same sweet and rancid scent that had been in my cup earlier now pierced my nose.

"Justin—" my voice quivered— "what's wrong? You're scaring me."

"Liddy!" Justin's voice shifted. Panicked. "Don't listen to anything she says. She's forcing—" A choking sound escaped his throat.

"Somebody, help!" I screamed.

BAM! Justin punched me square in the face and silenced my scream. The copper tang of blood gushed down my throat.

"Shhhhhhh! We don't want to upset Prince William yet now do we? This can be quick and *painlessss* if you cooperate."

Justin mashed his hand against my mouth and nose. I whimpered through the searing pain shooting through me. "That-a girl. I've visited you many times before Princess, do you remember?"

My head spun. I would suffocate on my own blood if he didn't remove his hand.

Justin's new voice made a disgruntled sigh and he laughed in an oddly familiar and menacing tone. "Too many people are looking out for you. You see, they've been using old Watcher magic to protect you, even in your sleep. I guess they've slipped up this time," the voice cackled.

"Please, *please!*" I begged, my words muffled.

"What's that?" the voice asked and Justin removed his

hand.

"Justin, stop. Please! I don't understand what is happening."

WHACK! The second hit across the face sent me to my knees and stars sparkled within the blackness. My face stung and throbbed. Justin caught me around the waist and pushed me back up against the wall, gripping my shoulders and shoving me over and over again.

"Help!" I screamed as I ripped at Justin's hands attempting to get away, but he was too strong. One spot remained that offered me a small window to get away, a guy's Achilles heel. I kneed him in the groin.

"You bit—" I kneed him again, harder this time. *THUD!* He dropped to his knees like an anchor cast into ocean waters and I ran. He lunged at me, knocking me down. I clawed at the carpet, trying to gain purchase to get up, but Justin gripped my hair and pulled. I screamed as he dragged me to him. *Fight, Liddy. Get off the ground!* I kicked and punched. I pinched and threw elbows. Too strong. He twisted me around and pinned me beneath him. Trapped. Fear gripped me.

Justin's head quirked oddly as if hearing something I couldn't. He stopped and forced me to stand. "This can't all be explained away by a dream this time. It is so nice to be able to make contact with you outside of your subconscious. Now, I can finally do what I have wanted to all this time."

The music below seemed to rage even louder. My heart sank. I knew no one could hear me. I closed my eyes and conjured up Will's face. I hoped that even with the distractions and the noise of the crowd, he sensed my distress.

"Justin, *stop*! I know you don't want to do this. Let me

go." Tears slid down my cheeks as Justin pressed me against the wall.

"You're right, he doesn't want to do this. You're a smart princess trying to talk to him. He can hear you by the way. Alas, all it does is make him try to fight me. Wasted efforts don't you think?" Justin hissed as his irises swarmed a dirty orange and then a chuckle rang out.

"It's you," I whispered. Her face assaulted my mind, image after horrible image, and I flinched in fear. "You...you are...n-no-*not*...real!"

"I assure you I am very real. I'm also sick—sick and tired of waiting for an opportunity to strike. I'm done waiting. This ends tonight."

More pieces of my nightmares came back to me and a cold chill crept along my spine. Justin still pinned me against the wall. The witch would kill me and everyone would believe Justin did it.

"How'd you do it?"

"Do what?" she asked.

"Possess Justin."

"I have a lot of *friends* that work for me. Christmas roses can be manipulated in all sorts of ways. They also make humans very vulnerable. Justin should have been more careful about who he accepted a drink from. He may be cute, but he's a naïve idiot. Luckily, you'll both be dead soon."

I hoped that if I kept her talking, Will would come for me. *Where was he?*

"What do you want from me?"

"Ugh, I hate that they did not let you keep your memories. It is quite tedious to have to keep re-explaining everything.

What do you remember?"

I shook. "I know your name is Mara. I know what you look like. I know you're a witch and that you...want to kill me. But I don't know why."

"Years of visits and that's it? I'm going to make the Jamison's suffer for this," Mara spoke aloud to herself before Justin turned his glinting orange eyes back to mine. "I promised someone a long time ago that their firstborn white-lighter daughter wouldn't live to be queen. That title belongs to me without question. You do not get to have Prince William either. He is mine. Together, he and I will rule Cristes and produce a powerful heir."

"He'll never go with you." I blurted out and my heart thudded as I waited for a blow that didn't come.

"Oh, I think he will. You see, I have something of utmost importance to the Prince."

"Oh yeah, and what's that?" I demanded, trying to sound braver than I felt.

"Charlie."

I gasped. He really was still alive then.

"That's right. I've kept him well. You see, when William learns that I have killed you and that I will do the same to Charlie if he does not acquiesce to my request, he will come running."

"Liddy, stop talking and get out of here!" Justin, the real Justin, broke through Mara's trance. He struggled against his own grip on me.

I karate chopped his arm and made a break for it. The witch ensnared Justin once again in a matter of seconds. He lifted me over his head and flung me across the room.

"Not yet, Princess. I've scarcely gotten started." Mara laughed.

I landed on my side. For a brief moment I was completely numb. Discomfort turned to misery. Pain stabbed to the marrow and I shrieked in agony. I rolled onto my back, clutching my hip. Justin grabbed my foot and dragged me to him, my skin burning against the carpet. Mara cackled louder.

Anger flooded me. Heat rose from my toes and surged through my body. *Don't be the stupid girl in the horror movie who panics... FOCUS... Think of a plan to get out of this!* My desire to live sparked an adrenaline rush surged with potency. I closed my eyes and tapped into the fueling power that threatened to overwhelm me. The room hummed with a violet glow. The energy came as one swift jolt, and knocked Justin off of me. The room flared with light, drifting back to black as my adrenaline dissipated. I paused for a moment. *What the heck was that?*

"Liddy! Get out of here, quick! I can't fight this much longer!" Justin screamed. "Leave her alone!" he bellowed, but it morphed into Mara's wicked laugh. The same one I'd heard eight years ago on the night Charlie disappeared.

"He's a strong one. Poor baby—he must really love you."

I stumbled around the room trying to find the door. My hand found the cool metal of the handle, but as soon as I touched it, I was torn back and thrust into the corner. My jaw audibly cracked and my face went numb. Justin navigated the room like he'd been in it a million times before. With tears running down my face, I bit back the pain and screamed as loud as I could.

His hands snaked around my throat. As they coiled, they

squeezed just enough to cut off my scream. His muddy-orange eyes brightened and with a sickening smile, he licked his lips, squeezing harder. Tighter and tighter he crushed my neck as I struck his arms, gouged his eyes, anything to get his vice-like grip to release, but nothing phased him. It was no use. All I could do was hope, hope that someone heard me scream.

I reached out for Will, something I'd never tried before. *Will...please.* Tiny flecks of light danced before my eyes— little wisps that I couldn't look away from. Piece by piece I watched the tiny lights leave my body and go up and up, the pain dissipating the higher they traveled, until I felt nothing at all. Well, almost nothing. A new pain burned in my chest. *I'm dying. I didn't get to say goodbye. I didn't get to say I love you.* Tears rolled down my cheeks. I closed my eyes and collected in my heart the names of everyone I loved. *I'll miss you all.*

A bright light flashed behind my eyelids accompanied by a loud bang. I maintained one last thread of consciousness as I fell to the floor. And the world went black.

Cherished

EVERYTHING HURT. I thought once you died, it wasn't supposed to hurt anymore.

"Lydia, honey?" Mom's soft voice nudged me.

Mom? I struggled to open my eyes, but the exertion proved too much. Moments passed, too many moments, and I tried again. I forced myself to peel one eye open, but the bright light assaulted the small crack. I squeezed it shut again.

"Lydia, baby. It's Mom. Can you hear me?"

"She's hurt, not deaf," Dad joked.

With strained effort, my eye watered in protest of the light as I forced myself to keep it open. I blinked away the tears, Mom and Dad coming into focus at my bedside. I moved my hand up to my face and lightly examined it. My fingers brushed over puffed cheeks and swollen lids. *This isn't my face.* I couldn't tell where my lips ended and my cheeks started, everything at least three sizes too big.

"Can..." I rasped, but the sound was squashed. The ghost of Justin's hands still wrapped around my throat. Crushing it. Like it was caught between the jaws of a vice grip.

"You aren't supposed to talk for a few days. Here, use this," Dad placed a whiteboard and dry erase marker in my hand.

'Can I c mirror?' I wrote on the board.

"So, how was the dance?" Mom replied. She grabbed my hand and gave it a little squeeze. Something crumbled in my palm. I opened it and little flakes of something almost black scattered on the white linen. I stared at my hand encrusted in blood. Justin's blood.

Mom sniffled. "They will let you get washed up tomorrow."

I again showed her my comment requesting a mirror.

"Evie, hand her the mirror," Dad huffed, the circles under his eyes darker than I'd ever seen them. "Liddy, the doctors say you will be just fine and everything should heal up in a couple of weeks, maybe a month. We're so happy you are OK." He gave my shoulder a little squeeze, and quickly blinked tears away.

Mom handed me a small, rectangular mirror. Tension radiated off my parents and settled into my nerves. I lifted the mirror, hesitant, and froze when my face came into view. Tears slipped down Mom's cheeks; she stifled a sob and excused herself. The mangled face that stared back at me left no questions as to why Mom ran out of the room. A brace hid any visible damage to my nose. Nine stitches lined my upper lip where the doctors sewed it back on. I tried to give Dad a reassuring smile, but my jaw felt slack and my mouth drooped. I tried not to cry at the disfigured stranger looking back at me.

I angled the mirror lower. Black and blue bruises tie-dyed my neck.

I shifted to get more comfortable and winced. Dad sat at the edge of the bed. "You got pretty banged up. They still need a CT to check the extent of the injuries to your jaw and eye socket, but your nose was a clean break and should heal well. You do have some pretty good bone contusions..." Dad's voice trailed off. He looked shaken, but did a good job of maintaining his composure.

'When can I get out of here?' I wrote next.

"Hopefully in a few more days." Dad avoided my gaze. "They want to keep you for observation."

I tugged on his sleeve, knowing he hadn't shared the whole truth with me.

"You're too observant sometimes. You...you might need a little facial reconstructive surgery... There's a good chance you won't, though!"

I closed my eye and swallowed a cry, the pain in my throat flaring.

"You've got this, sweetie. You're the toughest kid I know," Dad said as he embraced me.

Mom knocked on the door and peeked in, her eyes puffy from crying. "You've had quite the crowd in the waiting room. Don't worry, I've sent everyone home, but Alex and Will insisted they stay. I'm only humoring them because they are a big reason you are still with us, but do you mind if they come in to say goodnight?"

I scribbled on my board, 'Alex OK...Will wait plz.'

Alex walked in shortly after. When he saw me, he stopped in his tracks and rubbed his eyes, as if trying to erase the horrifying image.

"Oh snap, Liddy. Those are some brutal injuries. I'm so sorry."

I looked at Dad. He got the hint and excused himself, but not before looking strernly at Alex, then addressing me. "You have the call button in your hand, Lydia? Good. I'm right outside the door if you need anything." He smiled back at me and closed the door.

The room was silent except for the steady drip of my IV.

"I should have stopped Justin," Alex whispered.

I wrote 'no' on the board and waved him over to the bed. This wasn't his fault.

"Yes, Liddy. At first, I guess I was jealous that you two seemed to be going upstairs together and I didn't want to cause a scene again. But then I got to thinking about it. It didn't seem right...how Justin came after you up the stairs. The look on his face was off, and I know, well anyone who knows you knows, that you two weren't off for some *alone* time. I should have gone up after you right away." He hung his head as he stood next to me.

I patted the bed for him to sit by me and he obliged.

"By the time I got upstairs, I couldn't tell where you guys went. I went left towards the dark library. When I didn't find you there, I turned around and saw what looked like a black light turn on—it's purple light flashed throughout the house and then quickly turned off. It caught my attention and then... And then I heard your scream." His face drained of all color and his head dropped again. "That's when I came running."

Alex saved me? 'U resqd me?' I scrawled.

"You could say that." Alex smiled, a hint of his cockiness

showing.

If I could smile, I would have. I was extremely thankful for Alex's help in saving my life, but...it did surprise me that he, of all people, was the one who had thought to come up after me. I shifted in an attempt to sit up, but my head spun, the dizziness forced me to lay back down on the inclined bed.

"Are you crazy? You shouldn't be getting up. I overheard the doc saying to your mom that you have a concussion." Alex leaned in and kissed my forehead. "You probably need your rest. I should get going." He walked away, pausing in the doorway. "I *told* you, you should have gone to the dance with me instead of Justin."

I attempted to smile back at him, only half of my face responding. I liked this new charming Alex; so much better than the annoying cocky jerk. I jotted on the board, 'G-nite. Thx again. Get Will plz?'

"You sure you don't want to just go to bed instead?"

I double underlined 'plz.'

"Sure thing, Liddy."

In the few minutes before Will walked in, I had a moment to think. *What happened to Justin?* I shuddered as the menacing laugh that came out of him replayed in my mind without warning.

I wrote down some questions for Will. Where had he been during my attack? Why hadn't his sixth sense kicked on when I actually was in trouble? Looking at the time, it was after one in the morning. A few short hours ago I had been dancing and then Will helped me with a drunk Pree. *Oh my gosh! Pree!* I scratched down another question.

Will shuffled in, glanced at me, and quickly cast his eyes

down. He sat in the chair facing my bed continuing to stare at the floor. *Why can't he look at me?* I reached out to Will with my mind and without speaking, I asked him to look at me. He lifted his face; his eyes looked pained and he dropped his chin to his chest. I tapped the board to gain his attention. He wiped his eyes and looked at me. *Had he been crying?* I pointed to the first question I wanted answered. It probably wasn't what someone else would ask first, nor was it a fair one.

'Where were u?' I settled back into my pillows, encouraging him to talk.

He cleared his throat and rolled his shoulders. "OK, so you last saw me guiding Pree away from the make-out closet, but things got chaotic after you went upstairs." Will paused but seemed to remember I couldn't respond. I crossed my arms. "I had gotten Pree across the room but she grabbed my hand and started pulling me back towards the closet. She was strong, like you were that night at the sledding hill, only worse. I narrowly escaped her efforts, but then Joey and his buddies thought it would be cool to ambush me and help Pree get me in the closet."

Will searched my face, his eyes dark and glossy, his skin pale.

"You want me to continue?" he asked.

I nodded in response, careful not to move too quickly.

"Liddy, I'm sorry. I am so, *so* sorry!" he pleaded. He leaned over and put his head down on my bed, his hand resting on my thigh. I stroked his hair, a gesture to reassure him he needn't be sorry. He looked up at me, his eyes wet, as he continued, "When we first got in the closet, I tried to be polite and not hurt Pree's feelings." He sat up and showed me lipstick stains on his collar. "As you can see, she was, uh, quite persistent with her advances. Letting her down was not easy."

Was that Pree or the alcohol?

"We all know Pree can toe the line, but she was...*different*. Her eyes, Liddy. They changed right in front of me. Do you think she could be one of us?"

I quickly scribbled back, 'I doubt it. Probs just drunk.'

"You're probably right, but nothing else makes sense. I mean her eyes did change and glow, not like mine, but just enough that she didn't look human."

I stopped writing to contemplate what he'd shared.

'P's eyes orange-ish?' I wrote down and showed Will.

"Yes, how'd you guess?" Will asked as I wrote feverishly.

I flipped the board over to show him, 'Keep going... Tell u after.'

"So, at this point, Pree was no longer...Pree. She attacked me, tried to bite me." Will showed me scratches on his arms and neck. "I hoped you'd come back down to help me with her, get her that water, and take her back to her house. I had Pree restrained, with quite some difficulty, but then..." Will's face paled and I feared he would crumble.

I placed my hand over his, reassuring him. His wet eyes met mine. "It hit me, so fast and hard, it nearly knocked me to the ground. I knew you were in trouble. Serious trouble. I've never felt anything like it. I've sensed before when you were in danger, as you already know, but this time... This impaired my soul. The fear, knowing that you were hurt and in pain made me...stronger. I held Pree back with one arm as I tried the door. The guys had locked it from the outside. I yelled telling them you were in trouble and begged them to open the door. They cracked jokes about how I couldn't handle Pree and how much time was left that I was wasting. I sensed you didn't have much time; infinitely less time than I had left in that stupid closet. When I felt you growing farther from me, something came over me. By the way...I think I freaked Pree out."

I held up my hand to stop him and wrote on my board, 'How?'

"I think she somehow saw my eyes do that...thing they do, only amplified."

I pointed to the freshly written word again.

"All of a sudden I felt this sensation start in my heart and spread throughout my body. It was as if every vein ignited. Pree had been making another advance, but suddenly backed away, and before I knew it, all the Christmas lights blew and the door literally exploded."

I scribbled on the board. 'I felt something similar.'

"You did? Did you...glow?"

I shrugged. I wasn't sure and the only person who'd be able to tell me was Justin. 'What about Pree?' I wrote.

"Pree's OK, Liddy. She snapped back to herself after the explosion. She wasn't hurt, but she was scared and confused."

Poor Pree. I scribbled down another question. 'Justin?'

It took Will a second to read it. His jaw pulsed and I could hear his teeth grind together as he clenched them. Will took my hand before answering. "Justin attacked you, Liddy. He is handcuffed to a bed somewhere in this hospital. The police say he almost succeeded in..." He couldn't finish as his voice caught. I patted his hand, urging him to continue.

"Killing you," he stated flatly, eyes flashing. I squeezed his hand to calm him and remind him I was mostly OK. "You put up a good fight, Liddy... You should see him. The police think that he attacked you after you resisted him and I guess that is when Alex found you. Justin was so doped up it took over seven men to restrain him before he came to. They are running some tests on him. His mother is convinced he was drugged or poisoned."

The guilt and anger coursing through Will washed through my veins like they were my own. My head spun, so I dropped his hand, laid back, and closed my eye. Without skipping a beat, Will was there gently stroking my hair and offering me some water. I opened my eye to the sensation of him caressing my arm, up and down, up and down, waves of warmth and pain relief ebbing and flowing.

"Do you mind if I sleep here tonight?"

I grabbed the whiteboard. 'Don't think Dad'll go 4 that.' *I want you to stay.*

"I'll sleep in this chair."

I again pointed to my board. *I wish you could stay. I want you to stay.*

"Please, Liddy. I don't want to leave you right now. I know it's selfish, but I don't think I'd sleep knowing Justin is somewhere in this hospital. Last time I wasn't able to get to you, I about lost my mind. I need to be here. I...I can't leave you."

He grabbed my hand and prevented me from pointing at my chicken scratch again.

"Please." I could feel his desperation.

I wriggled my hand free, erased the board, and wrote, 'Pretend to zzz in chair.' I quickly erased it. I might act brave for my family, but I was deeply shaken and scared. I wasn't going to let anyone wake Will and send him home. Not only did

I physically feel better and safer when I was with him, but...I loved him. Will's presence calmed me and, I fell asleep before I had a chance to talk with my parents again.

"Princess, wake and be well."

I woke with a start to an empty room and heard my parents' voices in the hall. *These pain meds definitely make for some interesting dreams.* My stomach growled loudly and I grappled with my sheets looking for the call button. Before I could reach it, Will walked back into the room carrying a tray of food. The thermal shirt Will wore hugged his body.

He set the tray down and brushed his hair off his forehead. "Oh good, you're awake. Your mom was getting worried and instructed me to wake you to eat if you were still sleeping when I came in." He brought over the bed cart and set the silver tray on it. "Compliments of Nolan." He sat for a second on the edge of the bed and then shot right back up.

I reached for my board, but he spoke before I could write. "Your eyes, the bruises...they're..."

I threw my hands up, frustrated.

"Liddy, they're practically gone!"

I looked around and reached for the mirror. My body didn't ache as much when I moved. I held it up. Will wasn't joking. My eye, swollen shut last night, was now halfway opened. My once bloodshot eye was only pink and the prominent bruises around my neck were more like swampy shadows—still ugly, but at least I was healing. The stitches in my lip were gone and it was fully healed. Only a thin, faded scar remained.

"Tell me I slept for like three days and am just waking up." My voice, though rough and shaky, was audible. "Hey, my jaw doesn't feel jacked."

Will, shocked, shook his head and sat back down next to me. His fingers traced over my brow bone and cheek, flowing over my lips and trailing down my neck, as careful as if touching a newborn baby.

"Incredible," he whispered.

I smiled. "I guess I'm a fast healer."

"You, my dear, are not supposed to be talking."

"Ugh. Yes, *doctor*." I teased Will.

"Seriously, Liddy. You could permanently hurt your vocal cords. I don't want you damaging that beautiful voice of yours." He smiled.

"I don't have a beautiful voice. Besides, it's so much easier to talk to you this way and there is a lot to talk about. How about I make a deal. You're the only one I talk to and I promise to whisper."

"If I say yes, will you let me stay here with you until you are released?"

"As you wish."

Will cocked his head, his eyes sparkling.

Nolan made me that amazing soup again along with my requested vanilla pudding and lime Jell-O. I scarfed it down while Will and I talked.

"Did you wind up staying the night? I have to confess that I passed out before even talk...writing with my dad."

"I did. Your dad woke me up around eight to let me know Nolan was here with a change of clothes and some breakfast. Uncle Shai also stopped by to check on you."

"Can you ask my mom to bring me my clothes? This hospital gown is hideous and I definitely need a shower. I look like I have literally risen from the dead. I'm ready to feel human again."

"They're in a bag there on the chair."

My phone rang and Will answered.

"Hey... She's doing much better... Maybe give it a few more days until she can talk? Alright, I'll let her know." Will hung up. "Sara, Dani, and Pree all say hi and they can't wait to see you."

I smiled. I loved my friends, but I was thankful for the alone time with Will. I grabbed my clothes and went into the bathroom to take a very long, very hot shower.

The rest of the day was a whirlwind and I was glad to have Will with me. Doctors and nurses were in and out, marveling at the speed of my recovery.

"Mr. and Mrs. Erickson, all I can say is sometimes miracles happen."

"Please, call me Evie. But Doctor, did her stitches just fall out?"

"We aren't sure. It's quite miraculous, isn't it?" the doctor said as he looked at me, his head tilted in thought. "Let's go over her testing results. Her carotid ultrasound was insignificant. The CT revealed no permanent issues and though we were prepared for reconstructive surgery on her eye socket and cheek bone, it seems they are healing in correct alignment."

"Let's just focus on how happy we are that she has healed so well," Dad chimed in.

"I agree, Mr. Erickson. Lydia should remain home for the next few weeks. I'd like to keep her another night for observation. Most likely she can be discharged sometime tomorrow on one condition, she follows up with her primary care physician by the end of the week."

Mom and Dad went for a long lunch while Will and I played some cards and watched a movie. A few hours later detectives entered my room.

"Mr. and Mrs. Erickson, we need to ask Lydia a few questions."

Will held my hand and my parents came to stand near my bed. I nodded giving them my consent to proceed.

I was prepared to have to rehash every detail of my attack, though it pained me to do so. The detectives were sympathetic and careful with their words, extending their patience when I needed breaks.

"Thank you for your time, Lydia. I understand how difficult it must have been to share those details with all of us," the detective shared. "I do have one more question."

Mom and Dad looked green. I peeked at Will and he was as white as the bleached hospital bed linen.

"Were there any drugs being used at the party?"

I shook my head and Will answered, "No, there weren't any drugs that we saw. Just alcohol, although Liddy and I were not drinking. Why do you ask?"

"We have reason to believe that Justin was drugged. Our toxicology labs came up negative, but the Unknown Poison and Toxin Analysis was off the charts. We are unable to identify the toxin at this time. Anyway, we will be by again in the morning to have you sign your statement and formally press charges."

I held up my hand. Quickly, I wrote on the board, keeping up the charade I'd promised Will. 'No, no charges.'

"Lydia, he nearly killed you," Mom stated. As if I needed

reminding.

Dad and Will leaned in as if they too had some protest to my decision, but I held my hand up to still them.

'He was drugged. A victim, like me.' I finished writing and showed everyone. Everyone averted eye contact, the detectives raised their brows and pursed their lips. No one really agreed with me.

"We will see ourselves out. Mr. and Mrs. Erickson, Lydia can take a few days to process. Here is my card. Call if you need anything."

My parents followed the police out while Will stayed at my side.

"Liddy, please reconsider—he tried to murder you!"

"Will, it wasn't Justin," I whispered.

"Lid—"

"Please trust me. I haven't shared the *full* details of what happened to me with anyone yet. You're the only one who would believe me anyway. The way Justin spoke and the things he said, he was possessed, like someone else was speaking through him. His laugh—" I shivered— "it was exactly like the night your brother disappeared."

"Are you sure?"

"I will *never* forget."

Will looked sick. His eyes quickly turned from his normal teal green to a menacing dark green, so deep they were almost black. "I will end whoever, whatever, it was that did this."

"Can I join in that?" I smiled, but Will didn't respond, his brows stayed furrowed. "I'm going to go get ready for bed."

When I exited the bathroom, Will was in the chair holding a piece of white stationary with the initials NK raised from the paper, a look of confusion on his face.

"What is this?" he grumbled.

"I don't know. Looks like another get-well card."

"It's from Nick. Were you going to tell me about it?"

"I had no idea that was even in my room."

"Really? It was under your pillow along with a Christmas flower."

"If I knew it was there, don't you think I would have told you?" I whispered back in defense. "Can I at least see this secret letter I'm being accused of hiding?"

Will reached to hand me the letter and I snatched it from his hand.

Dearest Lydia,

I am sorry to see someone so precious be treated in such a hideous manner. I got to the hospital as soon as I could. Please excuse my absence during your recovery, but now that I know you are alright, I need to continue seeking the one responsible, to break her target on you. I hope you can accept a Watcher's gift of healing instead of my company. I left this Christmas rose for you. Hold onto it. Only inhale its sweet fragrance when you are ready to remember everything. Continue to take care of Prince William, as he is taking care of you, and advance your research together. You both need to know your history. As you have experienced firsthand, it's of dire consequence that you help me find what I am looking for. I will be in touch very soon.

-Nick

"It really was him then."

"What do you mean 'it really was him'? He was here?"

"I had the most realistic dream that someone was here in the room with me last night. A pink light shone from their hands as they placed them quickly over my body, but I brushed it off as the pain medicine giving me hallucinations."

"How is it possible that Nick got in here without anyone seeing him?"

"Don't ask me. I mean, after what we've seen with our own eyes and what you told me happened with Pree, is it that impossible? How else would I have healed so fast? I guess all Watchers have healing powers." A faint memory nudged me. "Will, do you remember our sledding accident? I used Christmas roses to help heal you. I don't know why I thought to use them, I just...knew."

"Yes, now that you mentioned it. I do remember." Will was quiet for a moment. "So, are you going to use it?"

"Use what?"

"You're not going to use the Christmas rose Nick left, are you?"

"I'm not sure. I've had quite the weekend, so, at the very least, it would be a little while." *Is that relief in his eyes?*

"Wanna see what's on TV?"

"Yes, please."

I flipped through the channels and came across *Dirty Dancing* on WGN. "Care to lay next to me to watch the rest of the movie? I'm sure that chair isn't that comfortable and my parents have left for the night. You've made quite the impression on them." I smiled.

Without hesitation, he slid in right next to me. After a few moments, he raised his arm around me and I nestled into the nook of his chest. He smelled delicious, a tempting woodsy scent with a hint of sweet orange. A few scenes later, I drew hearts on his sternum with my index finger, enjoying the way his heart seemed to patter with each caress.

"So, since I won't be at school this week, I figure I could do more research for us. How would you feel about coming over after school to my house a few times so we can look at those books Nick gave you?"

"I would like that," he murmured. I tilted my chin up to look at him—his eyes were closed.

"Also, I have been thinking about our English paper."

"You have?" He tensed, though clearly exhausted since he didn't open his eyes. "What, did you, um, what did you think?" he asked, his voice low and quiet.

"I like what you've done so far—" I found his hand and intertwined my fingers into his— "but you've left the ending pretty open." I laid my head back down.

"Have you...thought at all about that?"

"Yes, yes I have."

"Liddy, you're killing me," he finally said.

"Well, I haven't written anything yet, but I have a feeling it will bode very well for Prince Philip." I pushed up on an elbow and watched a grin spread widely across his face. I leaned in and gave him a soft, lingering kiss on his temple. An intense, static-like electricity delectably zinged my lips. "Sweet dreams," I murmured in his ear. Goose bumps raised over his flesh as I slid back down and nestled into his warm body. The sound of his strong heartbeat lulled me into a cherished, deep sleep.

Inhale

Y THE TIME I WOKE IN THE MORNING, Will was gone. I closed my eyes and rolled over to where he'd slept. His scent, though faint, titillated my senses. I opened my eyes and saw a note left on his pillow; a slight indentation remained where his head laid next to mine all night.

My beautiful Liddy,

You looked so peaceful, I didn't want to wake you. I was extremely tempted to skip school and stay right where I was, holding you, having the absolute best sleep of my life. I know you are going home today, so I will be by your house after school. I already let your parents know I will bring all of your homework with me. With it being the week before winter break, I doubt we will have any. Can't wait to see you.

-Love, Will

With the letter pressed to my chest, I let out a tiny squeak of giddiness. I'd just finished dressing when Mom walked in.

"Oh good! You're awake. I was going to come sooner, but then I remembered Will was staying with you and, well, you slept so late yesterday, I figured I'd see Mickey off to school."

"It's OK, Mom. I just woke up. I promise you didn't miss anything." I smiled in an attempt to reassure her.

"Lydia, you're talking! You're not supposed to until the doctors say."

"I feel fine mom. I promise. But I'm hungry and want to get home."

"I'm so relieved at how quickly you have healed up, physically anyways. I suspect the other stuff will take some time to sort through, but we will take that one step at a time. Let me go find a nurse who can help us get you discharged and then I'll get you something to eat." She hugged me and hustled off.

I finished combing my hair and packed the clothes my parents brought me. I walked over to the get-well bouquet I'd received from my boss and co-workers at the Continental. *Good, still there.* I'd hidden the Christmas rose within the calla lilies and baby's breath that adorned the red roses. I'd just finished brushing my teeth when a soft knock rapped on the door.

I peered out of the bathroom and froze.

"Lydia, may we please come in?" Justin's mom asked, a hint of disdain in her voice.

"I'm not sure that's such a great idea," I responded, my

eyes traveling over Justin in the wheelchair.

"Please?" she begged. She kept peering down the hallways like a skittish rabbit.

"Fine, but leave the door open." I know I shocked Will and my parents with not pressing charges against Justin. I knew it wasn't really him who attacked, and yet, my mind warred with itself. It was still his face that I saw.

My body tensed as Deborah wheeled Justin into my room. "I told him that this was a bad idea, coming to your room with everything that has happened, and an investigation still underway, but he was insistent that he see you—"she paused looking me up and down— "which is funny because you look absolutely fine, unlike my poor baby who has barely begun to heal and..."

"Enough, Mom," Justin growled. "You saw the pictures. You saw what happened, what I did to her." His voice cracked. He put his head down, resting it in his hands.

"But sweetie, that wasn't you! You didn't even know what you were doing, seeing as though you were poisoned and—"

"Enough! Please go stand by the door. I'd like to talk to Liddy." His baseball cap hid his face, but when he lifted his head, the true extent of his trauma became apparent. He looked...awful; he had dropped at least ten pounds, his face pale and sunken. Deep scratch marks spread over his neck and face, interrupted by two black eyes. One eye socket was misshapen, and he had a busted lip. I gasped as I surveyed the damage I'd inflicted upon him. He tried to smile at my response.

"You didn't look much better you know, though whatever treatment plan they have you on, I'd love to get in on it." Justin smiled, revealing a chipped tooth.

I could only stare wide-eyed. I felt terrible for him—but I had to keep reminding myself it had been Mara, not him, who attacked me. In order for us to move on and heal from this, I would need to forgive him and he himself. But how long it would take to replace the horrible event in my mind with the real, kind Justin I knew was yet to be determined.

"Liddy, I am so, *so* very sorry. I don't remember much after getting into the limo and heading for the dance. It was like I was trapped behind a one-way mirror with something watching me, controlling me. I tried to fight it. Your voice, the screaming..." He covered his ears as if my cries still echoed in them. "I would never, *ever* in a million years..." He couldn't finish.

Deborah looked scared. "See, he's talking nonsense. That drug really—" I cut her off with a glare.

"I know this whole thing..." His voice broke and he pulled away casting his gaze to the ground. "I understand that you will most likely never be able to look at me again, at least not the way you used to. If it was anyone else who had done this to you regardless of how or why, I would kill them."

I didn't know what to say. He was right. It pained me to look at him, to not cower in the corner out of fear and repulsion. My skin recoiled, but I held my ground. This meant war, a mental war I was hellbent on winning. I forced myself to stay because I knew the true demon wasn't him. He was simply a vessel— used. I wouldn't let *her* win this one.

"I don't expect you to say anything, but I need to tell you that...I love you, Liddy. I have ever since that night at the pool." He moved his hands to his face. "I'm going to miss you." Silent tears streamed down his face.

I walked over to Justin and knelt before him. I shoved my fear and revulsion deep down in order to give him a long embrace. He clung to me, sobbing into my shoulder. "I forgive you," I whispered in his ear. "We will find who did this to you, to us, and get justice." *I would get justice.*

I would have to remind myself to somehow ask Nick to extend Watcher healing to Justin. "I pray he heals quickly." I wiped the tears from my eyes, moving out of the way for Deborah to wheel Justin out. Mom walked back in with breakfast, giving them a long, anxious glare.

When they were out of sight, Mom rushed over. "Lydia! Are you alright? Did they harass you? What were they thinking coming to your room!"

"Mom, calm down, please. I'm fine, really, I am. I mean, I know it will take some time to forget about all the details of what happened, but it wasn't Justin."

"Lydia, it *was* Justin."

"No, it wasn't!" I snapped, fresh tears spilling down my face. "I mean, it was him in the flesh, but...never mind." I couldn't explain to her the unexplainable; the blankness behind his eyes, and the words he'd uttered definitely belonged to someone else. He called me 'princess,' and that laugh... I shuddered at the memory of the foul words. I wiped my tears. "He came to apologize for something he had no control over and that shows courage. Mom, someone did this. Justin's torn up physically and emotionally over this horrible act he knows he committed. But you have to trust me; he doesn't remember. That's *got* to be scary, to know you came close to taking the life of someone you love."

Mom joined me as I sat on the edge of the bed and sighed.

"He's got a long road ahead of him. His recovery hasn't been as miraculous as mine and he'll bear physical scars forever reminding him of that night. I can only imagine the rumors that have started, and how that will impact him now and down the road. I don't even know if *I* will ever be able to look at him the same. I may have forgiven him, but that doesn't mean I can ever forget." I looked away as another tear trickled down my cheek.

Mom cupped my face in her hands, a look of admiration and sadness filled her eyes. "Sometimes, most times really, I can't believe you are only seventeen. We'll get through this."

Mom helped me gather my things so we could drive home. We walked through our front door and the old adage never rang more true. There's no place like home. Deciding to skip the hospital's breakfast, I ate chicken noodle soup from The Continental with Mom at the kitchen table and let her know that Will planned on coming by a lot since he'd volunteered to grab my make-up work for me over the remaining weeks.

"You two seem to be spending a lot of time together lately. Anything I should know about?" she asked as she dipped some bread into her soup.

"Nothing, Mom. We're just friends."

"OK, well then let me just say, make sure you are using protection and don't let your father catch you."

"Mom!" I spat, a few pieces of noodle hitting the table.

"Close your mouth, sweetie. You're practically an adult now and a rather mature one at that. It's not such a farfetched idea. I want you to be safe. If I had my way, you'd wait until marriage, but I'm here if you have questions."

"We aren't even dating." This was *so* not the convo I wanted to be having with my mother.

"Could have fooled me."

"Seriously we aren't. I...I don't have time to date. Dating is so messy and sex can lead to pregnancy, diseases, and broken hearts."

"Geesh, you make it sound like pure torture and not the beautiful, pleasurable gift it was intended to be." Mom laughed.

"Don't laugh at me." I smiled. "Seriously though, I feel like when you take it to that level, you give a piece of your heart away that you can't fully get back and...I'm not ready for that. Plus, I *am* saving myself for marriage. I'm not working this hard in school so that I blow my chances to—"

"I know, I know, leave our terrible city and go off to college, save the world and make something of yourself. I get it." Pain reflected in her eyes, but she smiled. "You know, Liddy, it's OK to protect your heart, but it's also important to love people and let them love you, even when it hurts and is hard. Always choose love. Don't sacrifice your happiness for limitations you put on yourself with titles and agendas. Be responsible, but live in the now. As we all experienced firsthand this weekend, none of us are guaranteed tomorrow."

"Wow, Mom. Thanks. That's beautiful, but also kind of morbid."

"I'm just saying. I know your first boyfriend...Brandon, right?" I nodded. "The point is, he set this negative tone for the rest of your relationships. Don't let a young boy who was still learning about himself steal your happiness. Life is so much better when shared with someone."

Well, this lunch took a weird turn. "Whatever, I'm heading upstairs now to finish my paper." I bolted upstairs as fast as I could. Back in my room, I closed the door and slumped onto the bed. I reached for my backpack, but it was at least another six inches from my fingertips. I had no desire to get up. I caved into my exhaustion, letting everything fade away.

I woke to a setting sun; its orange glow filled my room. I had fallen asleep alone, but now strong arms cradled me. I blinked up at Will, who wore a concerned look in his eyes as he said my name over and over.

"Will?" I breathed.

"Liddy, my gosh, you freaked me out. You started to call out for me and you were crying. So I came to you and held your hand. You started to thrash and plead and I thought you might be reliving the after party, but then you said a different name. Who's Mara?"

Something warm trickled down my cheek—another tear. I wrapped my arms around his waist, and hugged him close.

"Liddy, you're shaking."

"Mara is the witch who haunts my dreams and wants to kill me." Will started to let go, but I held onto him tighter. "Please, don't let go." I focused on the warmth of his body, diffusing through every inch of me. "She's the one who possessed Justin."

"How do you know?" Will asked, concern in his voice.

"Because she told me," I murmured. "Made me remember somehow. I think she used a Christmas rose and a drink to possess him. I'm assuming the first drink was at dinner."

"The first drink?" Will stroked my hair helping my body to calm.

"Yes, I assumed he had been given more than one because he grew worse as the night went on."

"You are right. Pree didn't even have a full cup and her

strength, the ferocity of her attack on me... I can't imagine what you faced with Justin." Will shuddered.

"Well, there's something else." He remained silent, and hugged me even tighter. "Will, that's a little too tight," I squeaked. He loosened his arms, but still held me. "Well, she knew where we were, where we both were, at Joey's house. I can't be sure, but I don't think Pree was trying to attack you. I think she, Mara that is, was trying to prevent you from getting to me."

"She tried to bite me," Will protested.

"True, but that still could have been a stalling tactic."

Will was silent for a moment. "When they first started the whole seven minutes in heaven, Pree was being...*Pree*, but as soon as we were locked into the closet, she changed. Come to think of it, she didn't actually change until I expressed my concern for you. I tried to leave and that's when she attacked me."

"That's because I was the bait and the message."

Will let go and waited until I faced him. "What do you mean by the message?"

"Her plan was to kill me—"

"You've said," Will interrupted, the deep green I'd come to know as anger flashing in his eyes.

"Because she wanted you to know the same thing would happen to Charlie if you didn't do as she said."

Will shot up from the bed. "Ch-Charlie? Justin, Mara, whoever it was, mentioned Charlie?"

"Yes, Mara said he's still alive and that she's kept him well," I replied, frowning.

Will sat down again and turned to me, "What are her

terms? I'll do anything to get Charlie back."

"For you to go with her."

"With her where?"

"I don't know, but she said something about...marriage."

Will paled. "All this time, she's been tormenting you. She doesn't need to do that. I believe what she says, what she's capable of doing to Charlie."

"Killing me would serve her two purposes. One I already mentioned. The other—" I gulped— "is that she promised someone she would kill me. I think it's why Nick wants us to dive into those books. To learn what happened and maybe figure out how to help stop this."

"So, no matter what I do, she will keep coming after you," Will said flatly.

"Yes." I needed a moment to myself. Fear crippled my chest, and I struggled to breathe through it. "I'm...going-to... fr-freshen-up." I stood and Will grabbed my hand as I passed and pulled me close.

"Just breathe, Liddy. In...two, three, out...two, three... That's right. Breathe again with me. I promise I'll do everything in my power to keep you safe."

When I got my breathing under control, I smiled at him half-heartedly and proceeded to the bathroom.

When I got back to my room, Will sat at the desk pouring over the books that Nick gave him, frustration written all over his face. My family had all gone to dinner. I didn't feel well enough to go out yet, and after my talk with Mom, my parents weren't so worried about leaving me alone with Will. It seemed like the perfect time to try Nick's suggestion before they came back with food for us. I closed the door and snuck up behind Will. I reached around him and slid my hands down his sculpted arms, then intertwined my fingers through his. His breath hitched.

I placed my chin on his shoulder, my cheek pressed against his. "Let's try looking at the books this way."

He tried to turn his head. *Or is he trying to kiss me?* Either way, I resisted and used my cheek to nudge him back towards the books. Will grabbed the one in the middle. Within moments words swirled onto the pages as if someone held a blow dryer to invisible ink. They came in slow at first. Red letters outlined by a bright white, shone brightly against the parchment paper. I dropped our hands and they disappeared.

"Whoa," Will breathed.

"Whoa is right," I responded. "Nick suggested we hold hands or touch in some fashion and try reading the books that way."

"When did you talk to Nick?"

"That night before the formal."

"Why didn't you tell me?"

"Well, I did tell you, but not about his advice on how to read those books."

"I wonder if we came in even, uh, closer contact, if we'd get more time to read the words."

"He said we couldn't get too close, but maybe I could try the flower?" I walked over to the floral arrangement that held it and plucked it out.

"Liddy, maybe we should wait on that. I mean, you just had a near death experience and after what you told me about Mara, we should think about how it will affect you."

"Will, we don't have all the time in the world. Don't you

want to find where Charlie is? What about these other kids?"

"Yes, but...Mara wants you dead."

"You don't have to worry about me. She can't get me in my dreams, not yet anyway."

"How can you know that?"

"Because something always rescues me."

Will hesitated. "Why do you trust Nick? What if this flower—"

I brought the flower to my nose and inhaled before Will could protest further.

All at once images rushed through my mind, a constant assault of hidden memories.

More vivid and detailed memories of my time with Will and his brother Charlie when we were kids. Charlie, a once distant, shadow of a memory came back to life. He was with Will and me a lot more than I previously remembered. And Nick was there. A lot. Whether we were outside in our yards or at the sledding hill, Nick was always there. In fact, I looked forward to seeing him. Almost every day Nick would peer in my mailbox looking for something and one time he pulled out a white envelope and tucked it away in his long black coat.

Sharpened memories came of the night Charlie disappeared. That flash of green light was almost blinding. Mara's sinister voice. It held me captive—frozen in fear. I saw the flash of silver hair whizzing by at superhuman speed towards Will's house. It was Nick! He was the one with me that night.

Flash. The scene changed again, another buried memory unearthed itself. I watched my parents come into view and my body crumple to the floor as they told me Will's family was gone. I could see the worry on their faces as they held me while I cried so hard I went numb. Mickey had been there, even as a toddler, trying his best to get a reaction out of me. But I was *gone*, mentally checked out. I watched as Dad held Mom, promising her I would be alright when I'd refused my eighth meal in a row since Will left. I was an empty shell, as empty as Will's house after they moved, staring at nothing. Until Nick walked up to me and gave my heart the Band-Aid it needed to survive. He handed me a flower and when I smelled it, my memories faded deep into the recess of my mind and I returned to my normal, though not complete, self.

"I remember," I whispered. My knees gave out and Will caught me. When he touched me, the usual sensation I felt from him, the one I was *just* getting used to, turned intoxicating. *How the heck am I going to resist that?* I shrugged away from him and backed myself in a corner. I needed to be strong. His normally teal eyes shifted to a piercing aqua. They told me he was desperate and I knew he'd felt the shift in my emotions. He moved towards me, and my body hummed. This was it. We'd ruin everything with one, forbidden kiss. Will, a mere step away, was about to be mine, but a knock jolted us from our trance.

"Liddy, it's Pree. Can you talk? Your front door was unlocked so I let myself in."

Pree! I rushed to the door.

"Liddy! OMG, I have been so worried. You look terrible!" I flung my arms around her, thankful for the interruption, and Pree returned the hug. "I've been dying to talk to you and see you to make sure you were OK. I've been so worried. Oh hi, Will." She shrunk back.

"Hello, Pree." Will cleared his throat, the glow in his eyes faded to normal. "It's nice to see you."

"Uh, yeah, you too. Listen, Liddy, I'll come back another time." Her eyes flicked to Will and then back to me. She slowly backed away as if she was scared of Will and couldn't wait to get away from him.

Will stepped to the side, blocking the doorway and looked to me. "Do you want me to give you ladies some time alone?"

"No. Please stay, Will. We should tell her what we believe happened at the party." I hoped Will sensed that I didn't mean the full truth.

"Um, I'm gonna go." Pree's voice shook.

I grabbed her arm and turned her to fully face me. "Pree, what's wrong?"

Pree eyed Will and then looked back at me without saying a word, but her eyes sure as heck said, *Danger, danger! Get me away from him!*

"Will, come sit in my desk chair. Pree and I will take the bed." I held Pree's hand and we sat down across from each other. "Tell me what's got you so shook up?"

Pree leaned in. "Not in front of Will," she whispered.

"OK, I'll go first. Will, jump in if I miss anything. Pree, you drank more than half of the cup Justin gave to me when we first got to the party. We found out that Justin was drugged with something and we think maybe you were too, though not to the same extent." Pree's hand flew to her mouth. "So, I went upstairs to toss my drink and get you some water. Before I made it all the way upstairs, seven minutes in heaven started and you and Will were called. I rushed back down, but Will let me know he had everything under control. He had you across the room away from the closet and was letting everyone know that it wasn't going to happen. So, I ran back upstairs and that's when..." My voice hitched.

"She was attacked," Will jumped in. "Pree, you were acting a little drunk at first, getting handsy." A blush filled the apples of his cheeks. "Once we were forced into the closet, you became aggressive and..."

"That's when Will made his escape," I chimed in.

"Escape? You make it sound like he waltzed right out of there." Pree scoffed.

"How do you remember it?" I questioned.

"OK listen, this is going to sound strange, but something weird happened with Will in that closet. First of all, you know as well as I do that Will is fine as hell," Pree turned to Will and gave him an annoyed look. "Don't get a big head now, Will." She returned her attention to me and continued. "And I wouldn't have minded kissing him, but I know, I *know* you two are together even if you won't admit it." Will cleared his throat and my cheeks burned. Pree looked at both of us and rolled her eyes. "Coming on to him was out of my control. My brain said stop, but my body did its own thing. I'm so embarrassed. I never dreamed I'd be such a lightweight."

I squeezed Pree's hand. "It's fine. No harm done." I smiled.

"Thanks for being so gracious. I do *not* deserve it. Anyways, I started acting crazy in there once Will tried to leave. I pinned his arms and forced him away from the door, trying to make him stay. But, the weird thing is, I don't know why. I'm so sorry you guys."

"None of it is your fault," Will reassured her.

Pree looked up at me. "That's not all. So, the super freaky part is that..." Pree trailed off and sucked in her bottom lip.

"You can tell me," I encouraged.

Pree bent towards me and whispered, "Mr. Perfect over there is a freak of nature. He's a supernatural." Pree's eyes were wider than a doe in headlights.

"Like that guy on *Buffy*?" I tried my best to keep from laughing.

"Don't laugh at me," Pree said as she looked down, her brow furrowed.

I sucked in my breath and immediately stopped. "I'm so sorry. That was wrong of me. I won't laugh again. What makes you think all that?"

"Girl, Will started glowing and then all the lights burst and the door exploded. What's creepier is he was screaming your name, like he knew you were in trouble." Pree shivered.

Pree may act like a hormone crazed airhead, but even while possessed she was too astute.

"Pree, don't be scared of Will."

Pree swatted me. She puffed her chest and stared daggers at him before turning back to me. "The question is, why aren't you after what I told you?"

"Remember, you were drugged the same as Justin, Pree," Will interrupted. "You were hallucinating. Yes, I did want to find Liddy, but only because I needed her help. I tried to get out of the closet because you were attacking me and I didn't want to hurt you. I kicked the door a few times. It was made of cheap wood and splintered easily."

Tears streamed from Pree's eyes. She sniffled. "I'm such an idiot! Everything you guys are saying makes sense. I can't believe my imagination got that far away from me."

Lying to one of my best friends was not something I liked

doing, but for her own safety I couldn't tell her everything.

Pree continued blubbering. "Oh my gosh, I could have been Justin! I could have really hurt someone!" Pree clung to me and cried on my shoulder. Will came over and sat on the bed next to me. She looked up through her dark, wet lashes. "I'm so sorry, Will."

"You have nothing to apologize for. You've already been forgiven." Will smiled at Pree and she returned the gesture.

Pree gave me another long hug and then wiped her tears in her sleeve. In true Pree fashion, she jumped to the next topic. "So, are you OK to talk about Justin yet?"

"Another time, Pree."

"Pleasssseee?" she begged.

I'd already lied to her so I would talk about Justin, regardless of how it hurt me to do so. "Fine." I gave her the cliff notes version. Before she could object to the lack of detail and the fact that I forgave Justin, I yawned dramatically and insisted that I needed my sleep.

"If it's OK with you Pree, I'll drive you home. Liddy does need her rest."

"No, it's OK. I'm going to walk home," Pree responded.

"Pree, it's freezing out. Please don't make me walk you halfway. Take Will's offer." I wanted to protest his departure, but it was a nice gesture. Plus, even though my parents were cool about Will being at my house, they would never let him stay over.

"And we can't have Liddy doing that after what she's been through," Will added.

"Ugh, you guys are so annoying." Pree rolled her eyes and I walked them downstairs.

"See ya, Liddy." Pree waved as she headed out the door.

Will hung back for a moment. "Night, Princess. Sweet dreams." He kissed my forehead, sending shock waves rolling through my body as he staggered backwards.

"See you tomorrow," I responded. Will smirked and jogged to his car.

Sleeping Curse

MICKEY HAD ALREADY CAUGHT THE BUS FOR SCHOOL by the time I made it to the family room and plopped on the couch.

"Are you hungry?" Mom called out to me from the kitchen.

"No, not yet. Thank you."

"You really should eat something," Dad said, peering over the top of his paper.

"Oh, I will. I just want to give my body a few moments to wake up."

As I watched my parents in the kitchen, I realized that, to anyone else, they would appear as an ordinary couple married for twenty-five years. Upon deeper inspection, their silent movements around the small kitchen were more like a dance they'd rehearsed over a thousand times. A dance of love. Dad would peek at Mom and smile or play with her hair as they sat next to each other, while he read the paper and Mom, her magazines. Mom would top off Dad's coffee to keep it warm and at times check to make sure his plate was full. I wanted to have that one day. Not the Hollywood version of a marriage, but one like this. A relationship where the couple was best friends, someone I could trust to see me as I am. A person I could be at peace with, and contribute to each other's happiness.

After taking his dishes to the sink, Dad kissed Mom goodbye.

"Bye, sweetie," he called to me.

"Love ya, Dad."

"Now Lydia, I will be volunteering at the Sparrow's Nest and then running errands. Mickey has a b-ball game tonight so we'll be home late. Unless you want me to stay with you, which I can absolutely do in a heartbeat."

Great! Alone time before Will gets here.

"I'm fine, Mom, promise. Will's gonna be here right after school."

"I figured, but won't you be bored?" Mom asked as she came to stand in front of me.

"No. In fact, I have that English assignment I have to finish up."

"OK, well, call me at Sparrow's if you need anything before two. After that, call Dad." She kissed me on the forehead and left.

I ran back upstairs. Propped at my desk, I grabbed my pencil to edit the paper.

Aurora was no ordinary princess. She grew up not knowing how special and important she was. Her natural beauty captured the hearts of anyone who laid eyes on her. She had long, flowing dark hair and blue-violet eyes that changed color depending on the emotions she felt. She was not slender and frail, rather, but lean and strong. Her coral colored cheeks complemented her flawless, bronzed skin. Her warm smile extended all the way to her eyes. The only thing more beautiful was her gracious heart. Aurora was the most generous and fair woman. She bettered everyone's life who met her, which caused her to become the target of a particularly evil sorceress. This sorceress was determined to destroy her and all the light she brought to the world.

Princess Aurora was independent, brilliant, and courageous. She did not need anyone to complete a task set before her. Or so she thought. Her isolation from the real world by the fairies skewed her interpretation of life, teaching Aurora to stay guarded at all costs. The fairies knew the dangers she faced.

Aurora's quest against evil would not be done alone, but Prince Philip was not just a mere companion. His real mission was to persuade Aurora to let him into her heart by convincing her of his love. Even though they were betrothed, he had known from the moment they met that she was his missing half. Prince Philip knew what many didn't; life was indeed designed to be shared with someone you love. The greatest challenge he would face would be to partner with Aurora and maintain his efforts to love and protect her, but also keeping enough distance to not distract her from being the heroine of her own story.

What we do know is that Princess Aurora would regain her rightful throne by ridding the lands of the evil sorceress, doing so with the help and love of her best friend, Prince Philip. What we don't know is whether or not she believed in her heart that he was hers and if she wanted to spend the rest of her days loving him beyond that barrier of friendship.

This was our story. I moved from my desk and plopped on my bed, eager to see how it ended. I turned to the final page.

How does the story end, Liddy?

From his own mouth, I already knew how Will felt about me, but it never truly sank in until my near-death experience. Was I willing to let my guard down and let him into my heart even if that meant a massive test of my patience while I waited for him? How long would I wait for him until he felt it safe to be with me? It would be totally unfair of me to remain nothing but his friend, knowing that I...I loved him. But, was I ready to trust a guy again in that way?

This was all so complicated and Nick was the main reason for it. I looked at the time. Only two hours until Will arrived. *How am I going to control myself around him?* Ever since I used the Christmas rose, everything I'd felt for Will only heightened, like we were physically bonded. One thing was for sure—we could no longer be alone together. I sat at my desk and got to work.

As predestined, Aurora was in fact placed under a sleeping curse. Only true love's kiss could break it, but Prince Philip wasn't sure if he had earned that honor. Not knowing how Aurora felt, but desperate to help her fulfill her destiny, he slipped past the dragon and reached her room in the tower. As he approached her, the Prince quivered, giving him pause. What if Aurora didn't love him? If she didn't wake, would he still slay the dragon for her? Find another way to break the curse? How long would that take? No! He would push his pride aside and take a chance. He would follow his heart. Prince Philip took the few steps that remained and knelt beside her bed. He leaned forward to kiss Aurora's rose red lips.

In her sleep, Aurora dreamed of her life. She dreamed of her time with her fairy godmothers and her heart longed for a relationship with her parents whom she'd only just met. She dreamed about how she would defeat Maleficent and to her surprise Prince Philip was by her side; an encourager as well as a force to be reckoned with. It was in that moment, fighting side by side, Phillip fearlessly risking his life, that the way for Aurora to reach her destiny became known. She opened the gates of her heart and finally understood what she had known from the moment she met him; that he was hers and she was his. After the battle was won together, she dreamed she boldly came to Philip, wrapped her arms around his neck and kissed him.

To both her and Philip's surprise, Aurora's eyes fluttered open. She saw him smiling down at her, his hand on her cheek; the dream turned to reality. Prince Philip not only broke the curse but he had also broken down the walls of her heart.

"We've got work to do," she said breathlessly to him.

"As you wish," he responded, a glint in his eye.

The Prince and Princess went on that evening to fight evil side by side and save the kingdom. And they lived happily ever after. The End.

I decided to take a nice, hot bath. I lit some candles, put on Enya, and turned on the water. I placed my forearm under the water and adjusted the knob until it was the perfect temperature. While the tub filled, I turned around and examined my body in the mirror. It should have been a broken, bruised mess. Instead, smooth skin and curves that developed impossibly fast over the summer stared back at me. *Am I really a freaking Princess? Will and I...glow? I'm a Watcher? What the heck is that anyway?* I leaned in to look more closely at how my face was healing when I saw the faint outline of Justin's hands on my neck.

A heaviness spread throughout my chest. I. Couldn't. Breathe. *Breathe, Liddy, just breathe.* I gasped, trying to take in air, but it wasn't enough. I could feel Justin's hands tightening around my neck. I tore at my throat, trying to loosen his grip, but my nails only scratched my skin. My thoughts crashed down on me like a poor jump off the high dive, water slamming my body on impact. I gripped the vanity hard when Justin's attack hit me again *BAM!* The empty look on his face. *BAM!* His eyes mixed with hers, a muddied orange full of hate. *BAM!* A punch in the face, the crunch of my nose too loud in my ears. *BAM! H*er wicked laugh as his cold hands enclosed around my neck. *BAM!* Saying goodbye to my parents in my final second.

With each pounding thought, I was drowning, seven feet, eight feet down... *I can't breathe.* The pain in my throat— excruciating. Nine feet, ten feet deep. *My. Chest. Is. Burning.* Eleven feet, twelve feet. Stars swam before my eyes. *I'm dying...*

And finally, I broke. I slunk to the ground. The tears rushed like a raging river and I let myself cry until I couldn't cry anymore.

I had no idea how long I laid there. At some point I had turned off the bathtub faucet and uncoiled from my crouched position. I picked myself up off the floor, part of my hair wet with my own tears. I felt a bit lighter, but very weak. I tested the water in the full tub—ice cold. I emptied some of it and turned the water all the way to hot. I caught a glimpse of my swollen eyes and blotchy face. I soaked a hand towel in cold water and pressed it to my skin. The cold delivered calm to my inner storm. I sighed and went to dip the towel in the water again when a glimmer caught my attention.

I looked up. My eyes! Brilliant violet shone back at me. "Don't freak out Liddy," I said aloud to myself. *Control it. Embrace it. Test it.* I thought about Will; what made his eyes ignite. *Here goes nothing.* I closed my eyes and imagined I was Princess Aurora and Will, Prince Philip. I imagined him leaning down to kiss me. My eyes sprang open right before his lips touched mine and they ignited. I understood why Will was so anxious about me seeing this in him. The changing of his eyes became even more exhilarating. I hoped when he'd see mine change, he would feel the same.

I slipped into the Epsom salt bath, sinking low enough so only my head was exposed. My body took its time, muscles lengthening and joints loosening, but it finally relaxed. It tensed again when interrupted by a knock at the front door. *Dang it! Who could that be?* Irritated at the disruption, I decided to wait and see if they'd go away. The knocking returned with increased raps.

"Fudgsicles," I hissed. I threw on my robe and peeked over the landing, a perfect view of the front door while I stayed hidden. The person's head was not visible, but I could tell they wore a United States Postal Service uniform. *Strange. Normally our mail doesn't come until after three.* I backed up and tiptoed down a few stairs to peer around the wall for a better view. A handsome young man around my age stood there. Or, he would be handsome if his skin wasn't so sallow, and his eyes so bruised. *A little young not to be in school.* His name tag read: *Jamie.*

I gasped. *It's him, from Mara's throne room.* The one who did her bidding. He carried a white embossed envelope that I'd recognize anywhere. He put his hand above his eyes and peered in the window, his green-orange eyes burning. I knew what that meant—danger. I turned and slinked back up the stairs to my room, locked my door, and hid under the covers. I trembled under that blanket for nearly thirty minutes, only relaxing when I sensed Will nearby.

An erratic knock came at the door as a muffled voice yelled, "Liddy! Are you alright?"

"Will!" I called out. Relief flooded me as I whipped off the covers and ran down the stairs two at a time. I opened the front door, Will spun away from me, fists clenched.

"Liddy, your, um, your robe..."

Oh geez! I hastily pulled the fabric tighter across my chest. "You can turn around now."

"Just...give me a second." Will strained.

"OK... I'm gonna get dressed. Stay here in the foyer. I'll be right back." I ran upstairs, opened the drain on the bath and blew out the candles. Slipping into some comfortable clothes, I grabbed my bags and hurried to the kitchen where I left Mom a note on the fridge:

At Will's
Xoxo, Liddy

"OK, I'm ready."

"Ready for what?"

"Well, we can't very well be alone together, can we? I figured we'd try the library."

"Considering I skipped school to get to you, faking a stomach bug, and getting chased out of the parking lot by the school's security van lady, I shouldn't be seen at the public library. How about my house? Nolan can check in on us."

"Fine with me."

"Another dream?" Will asked as he pulled out of the driveway.

"Come again?"

"You know, the thing that had you frightened that I raced out of school for?"

"No, not a dream. I had an unexpected visitor." Will looked perplexed. "I don't know who he was, but his eyes do our thing so I'm assuming he's a Watcher, but I don't think he was a good guy."

"*Our* thing? Liddy, do your eyes...glow now?"

"Darn it. I was hoping to surprise you with them. It happened today. In any case, his eyes were a bright mix of green and orange. We both had a bad experience with orange eyes recently. I just didn't have a good feeling."

"I could sense that." Will smirked.

"The thing is, he looked so familiar, but I couldn't place him...at first."

"Who was it?"

"A boy named Jamie, from my dreams. He tried to deliver a white envelope to me."

Will frowned. "I don't think you should be alone from here on out."

"Ugh, I hate that idea. Makes me feel like a prisoner."

"You're not! But you have to admit it's just not safe for you. I can be with you most of the days and evenings, but what are we going to do the rest of the time?"

"What if Pree helps with that?"

"Do you think that's such a good idea? I mean, we don't even know what's going on. Things are starting to get dangerous."

"I sort of feel bad that we gaslighted her last night. We may have to clue her in sooner than later," I suggested. "Plus, it would be nice to have another person to talk to. We may need her help."

"How much help could she be?"

"She could surprise you. She hasn't shown you her true colors yet. There's a reason Ms. Mullens adores her. She's extremely observant, great at researching, an excellent debater, and well, a good distraction for us."

"Give me a little time to think about it, please."

History Lesson

W E SETTLED IN THE FRONT LIBRARY AGAIN. Nolan was doing as promised, popping by often to offer more snacks or refill drinks.

"I know we said it was best to have Nolan check on us a lot, but we need to start looking at those books. He can't see us do that."

"OK, first I need to use the ladies' room." I needed a minute to calm and prepare myself. He was right that we needed to do this out of sight, but it was going to be hard controlling myself. When I returned, Will was reading the final page of our English paper, a huge smile on his face. My cheeks skipped pink and went straight to red.

"So, the Princess does love the Prince."

I paused with nervous anticipation. *It's now or never*

Liddy. "I love you, Will." I cast my gaze to the floor. "Sorry it took me so long to admit it." My nerves tethered me to the spot as he approached.

His voice turned low and husky. "You have made me the happiest guy in all the worlds."

"I have?"

"Are you kidding me? You've always known how I've felt about you and yet you have been a closed book. It's been torture not knowing how you feel here—" Will touched my temple— "*and* here." Ever so slowly he placed his palm over my heart. With his other hand, Will lifted my face and smiled at me. "Although, now it isn't quite as much of a mystery," he said as he gazed into my eyes which ignited beneath his touch.

"Torture is not being able to kiss you. Which is why you need to take a few steps back... Good. Now, please let Nolan know we are not to be disturbed for an hour."

"Yes, Your Highness," Will teased.

He left the library and I proceeded to the windows, closing the plantation shutters. Will returned and I knelt on a large pillow by the coffee table.

"I think it's best if you sit across from me." I gulped. Will locked the door and sat down without saying a word. We fought against the strong pull every single time our hands met.

"It's a little hot in here." I peeled off my red sweater and tugged down my white baby-doll tee. I swept my hair off my neck and twisted it into a messy bun.

"Maybe it would be a good idea to focus on Charlie, on protecting you and those other kids, before making we uh, make contact," Will suggested.

"That's a great idea." I grabbed the articles with the

victims' faces and spread them over the table. "To give us a visual reminder," I said, hoping that would quell any desires.

Will's suggestion did help, but not much because once contact was made, the flood of sensation was so overpowering we didn't last long.

"We need to try something else," I complained.

"Well, thanks to Nick's rose that he gave you, if you noticed we can let go and the words remain."

"Yeah, but only like for a minute."

"Let's do the best with what we've got."

We connected our hands across the table. As soon as the words swirled to life, we copied them down as fast as we could in a notebook. This allowed us the time to better inspect the information *unattached*. After an hour, Will and I were sweating and utterly exhausted.

"I need a break," I moaned, slumping into the couch.

"Me too. I'll let Nolan know we are ready for dinner." Will hustled out of the room and I closed my eyes.

So far, we had deciphered what appeared to be ancient family trees, genealogy tables, and censuses. There were also maps of lands called Mortalia, Beldam, and Cristes Adventus with sub-cities, though only one had a name—Eira. I got up and started pacing the room. Mortalia was the human realm where we currently resided. Cristes was where the Watchers lived and Eira was some prestigious island. Beldam was marked by a dead tree, signifying death. We couldn't find any more info on it.

Will returned. "Nolan said he'll be ready in about twenty with dinner. In the meantime, here's some ice water." Will handed me a glass, careful not to touch me.

"Will, neither of us know how to contact Nick, but we know where he lives. Maybe we should march up to his door and demand he help us, at least answer our questions." I stated, but Will looked uneasy. "What?" I asked after taking a long gulp of water.

"Liddy, the last time we went by there, you heard a voice and became possessed. A woman's voice," Will added when he noticed my blank stare. My knees wobbled and he helped me back to the couch.

"Mara's voice," I whispered.

Comprehension dawned on Will's face. "Now do you see why I don't trust him? She is probably in there...with him."

"It doesn't make sense. Why would Nick come to the hospital and heal me?"

"Because he is prepping you," Will said. "He is working with Mara. He probably gave Justin the poison and then healed you when that failed so Mara could have another go at you. He's nice to you so you trust him."

"Yeah, but he's been pretty insistent that we stay close to each other and..."

"Maybe so *she* can get to us both easily, kill you, and make me do her bidding. By trusting Nick, he can lead you right to Mara."

"So, what do you suggest?" I asked, not trusting my own thoughts and emotions anymore.

"Well, so far maybe some of what Nick has shared with us is true, to gain our trust. I think we should dive into these books and figure out who we are and what we are capable of. Then I seek him out while you remain nearby, my lookout."

"Will, what if something happens to you?"

"She won't harm me. You said it yourself. She wants me to fulfill her conquest."

"What's our timeline?"

"I don't know, but the sooner the better."

Nolan strode in and paused. He looked at the both of us, lingering for a moment longer than was comfortable. "Dinner is served in the kitchen tonight. A little change of scenery might be well received." He clicked his heels and strode swiftly across the atrium. He held the kitchen door open for Will and I, but Nolan did not come in after us.

Will and I barely spoke through dinner. We placed our dishes in the sink and walked back to the library. Nolan had started a fire and a large silver tea set sat on the table. A note was written next to it:

A little hot chocolate to give you energy to finish your project.
—Nolan

It was just after seven o'clock. "Maybe we should try again with a new book?" I suggested. "My parents should be home around eight. I'm beat but I don't want to go home yet. I don't want to be alone."

Will came over and hugged me. I should have pulled away, but I remained and melted into his arms. "We are strong, we can do this," he said.

We sank to the ground and Will reached for the nearest book. He settled behind me, his legs straddling my sides, and plopped the book down in front of me.

"Open it," he gruffed. I flipped it to the first page. Will slid his hands down my arms and entwined his fingers in mine.

Whirling into action, the inky black spiral turned gold and revealed:

History of Cristes Adventus
The Royal Family

"Great, more genealogy," I mumbled. Will squeezed my hand and I snuggled in a little closer before turning the page. Will tensed. There, in a hand drawn portrait, was a man who resembled Will; if Will had long blond hair and was at least thirty years older. Under the picture was written:

King William Lucas Jamison
Cristes Adventus—Eira
Noble Herald of Watchers

"So, I guess you really are a prince," I nudged Will, still in shock over the resemblance. We knew this, we were told this, but up until now, I don't think either of us truly believed it.

"I guess so," he responded, not taking his eyes off the King. On the page next to the King's portrait was a fair woman with blonde hair and ice blue eyes.

"Liddy, doesn't that kind of look like—"

"Nick? There does seem to be a strong resemblance."

Under her portrait read:

Queen Nicole Noel Klaus—Jamison
Cristes Adventus—Eira
Beloved Heralda of Watchers

The next few pages shared their history and images of their wedding ceremony.

"Interesting," I said.

"What is?"

"Look at their eyes," I flipped back a few pages.

"OK, what am I looking for?"

"Wait—" I flipped to the end of the wedding ceremony— "look here."

"They look the same."

"Now look," I directed as I flipped to the beginning of the wedding ceremony. Will leaned in a little closer.

"I see it," Will whispered.

"In their portraits and after the ceremony, their eyes are the same, an incandescent icy blue. But, at the beginning of the wedding, the king had green and the queen violet. Kind of like..."

"Us," Will finished my thought.

We dove into the remaining text on the page.

For the first time in Watcher history, the joining of King William and Queen Nicole offered near colorless-light, an untapped power. Studies are currently underway to determine what accounted for this transformation and the potential of its powers. The council is particularly curious about what transpired during the consummation ceremony.

I could sense that Will's face got as flushed as mine.

"There's a...a..." Will swallowed hard.

"Like royal families in the Middle Ages?" My stomach twisted.

Will slammed the book shut. "I think we've had about enough of that." He pulled away. "It's getting late. I should get you home."

My heart thudded a mile-a-minute as I considered that ceremony while Will drove me home.

"Same time tomorrow?" Will asked as we sat parked in my driveway.

"Yes, I'll make sure my mom stays home with me."

Will let out a sigh of relief. "Good, I would hate to ditch school."

"Oh no, you don't. Not on the last day before break. You need to turn in our English paper."

Will smirked. "It is pretty fantastic. We would not want it to receive a zero."

"Goodnight, Prince William."

"Sweet dreams, Princess Lydia."

School was officially out for Winter Break. I was proud of Will for not calling this morning, something I challenged him with. The night terrors were routine. Will had learned to give me some time, a chance to calm myself, though I knew it still made him nervous. Even though I was physically safe from Mara, my pallid skin and the dark circles under my eyes revealed the toll of the dreams.

Today's plans were more of the same—book time at Will's. I splashed cold water on my face before attempting to conceal the circles under my eyes and a few strokes of mascara to my lashes. I had just slipped into my jeans when my skin prickled and my heart pattered. *Will's close!*

I ran downstairs and through the kitchen. I swiped an apple, kissed Mom on the cheek, and slipped on my boots without tying them. Will pulled up and I was already at the end of the driveway slipping into my coat.

"Are you ever going to let me come to your door again or are you going to continue to use this new sensing device you've got going?" Will asked as he smiled and came around the car to open the door for me. He had an extra pep in his step and a sparkle in his eyes today.

"Are you ever going to quit using *your* sensing device on me?" I challenged, raising my brow.

"Touché, Princess."

I laughed as Will closed my door and ran to his side.

"Hey, we aren't even sure if I'm, ya know, royalty or not. We know you are according to the history book, but so far we only have Nick's word that I am."

"Well, whatever happens, you're still my princess."

"Whatever, dork."

"Did you really just call me a dork?"

"Sure did." A laugh erupted from me. It grew even more hysterical as the seconds ticked and Will eventually laughed along with me.

"I'm glad you find yourself so funny," Will quipped.

"Well, with everything that's going on, a little humor helps to cancel out some of the junk."

We got to Will's and went straight to the library. Nolan had it stocked with food and a roaring fire blazed.

"After yesterday, I figured we wouldn't want Nolan checking in on us so much."

"Shall we get started?" My voice broke, my nerves starting to take hold.

Will nodded. "Let's try the third book." He wiped his palms on his jeans before lifting the book out of his bag. "How do you want to approach this today?"

I grimaced.

"I take it you're excited for today's lesson?" he asked, wearing a smirk.

"HA, HA. I am, but...I've had a hard time accepting that you and I—"

"Can't be together? It's only temporary, Liddy."

"That's not it." *No matter how badly I may want that.* "I've had a hard time accepting that you and I are Watchers, according to Nick, who apparently can destroy an entire population. It bothers me that we don't know what being a Watcher means. Are we good? Bad? Nick hasn't exactly been forthcoming."

Will looked at me for a long moment. "I could never believe for one second that you are bad."

"Same. But this is taking for-ev-er. I'm ready to charge Nick's place."

"Whoa. Let's not be hasty. I've got an idea to speed things up. What if we browse chapter headings instead of trying to read page by page?"

My mood improved. "Yes, let's see if we can't find out what a Watcher is today."

"To the table?" Will asked. I nodded and followed his lead. "We've got this." Will gave me a reassuring smile and grabbed my hand.

I expected the overwhelming, magnetic pull that rushed

through every nerve of my body, but it was only faintly easier to deal with today. I pushed my mind to focus on our mission.

"Open it," I gasped.

Will flipped the cover to reveal an outline and connected hands with mine again. "We lucked out." He breathed.

The book was comprised of six parts:

1. *Cristes- The Guardians*
2. *Masters of Ceremonies*
3. *Hellebore Niger-Christmas Rose*
4. *The Fall*
5. *Cristes the New*
6. *The Second Fall*

I scanned them all. I let go of one of Will's hands, flipped to the third section, and began to read.

The Christmas rose, proper name Hellebore niger, has been of vast importance to Cristes and its Watchers since Emench Frosta first discovered it in Mortalia on one of his numerous expeditions for the Crown in 17 B.G.C.

We skipped the next few paragraphs detailing Botany101 on each part of the Christmas rose.

It was soon discovered that Hellebore species would not readily grow in Cristes, but their lifespan could be altered. As a result, trips to and from Mortalia each year became of great importance. The most abundant hauls were found near the end of the Mortals calendar year, in December. In exchange for harvesting the human's precious flowers, a gift of thanks was left near any home from which the flowers were obtained.

Legend began to grow in Mortalia that Watchers, Safeguards of the Realms, were mystical elves doing work for Saint Nicholas. Thus, their holiday 'Christmas' was born and we were safe from any speculations or assault.

Presently, every Christmas Eve we come in droves to fill our sleighs with Christmas roses leaving behind our gifts: oaths of our protection, food, sweets, oils, jewels, or gold all secured in a small sack.

Will and I separated. I patted my forehead with a napkin while Will wiggled out of his black sweater. The plain black t-shirt he wore underneath rode up with the sweater and his chiseled obliques were momentarily visible before we both collapsed onto the couch.

After a minute, Will looked at me. "So I guess we know where the idea of Santa and his elves come from."

I smiled. "Strange, right?"

"Totally." Will grabbed the book again and examined the covers, his hand sliding across the smooth leather on the inside cover.

My heart skipped and I remembered finding that white notebook inside one of the other book's covers. I ran to Will's bag and fished it out.

"I totally forgot!" I said excitedly and plopped down next to Will. He looked back at me expectantly. I opened to the back cover and peeled away the lining.

"Whoa," Will exhaled. "You knew that was there?"

"I forgot about it. It was the day I found you..." My ears went hot.

"Say no more," Will interrupted. "What is it?"

"I think it's a journal, though I never looked inside of it."

"Do you want to try to do this again so soon?"

"Yes," I replied in haste. I grabbed a mug from the snack table and filled it with apple cider. "I want to know what's in it." I chugged the warm drink down, grabbed Will's hand, and opened the journal.

The image on the front page came into view as if sketched in real-time by a speed artist. I gasped at the completed image and dropped Will's hand.

Nick's Place

"**W**HAT IS IT?" Will's eyes were round, alarm etched on his face.

Forcing myself to calm down, I closed my eyes and took a few centering breaths.

"Liddy, what did you see?"

"That picture. The young man was Nick and the young woman he was with was...Mara."

Will sprang up from the couch and paced the room. The heat radiating off of him weaved over my skin, and I knew without looking that his eyes would be ablaze.

"Are you going to say I told you so?" I asked him on his fifth pass across the room.

"I would never. He's done a pretty good job of trying to confuse us, especially you. He's come to you so many times, but never me."

So many thoughts jumbled up in my mind, but one word stuck out above the rest. *Deceiver.* How dare he! Nick made me trust him.

Will moved the coffee table and knelt down in front of me. He studied my face. "You're angry," he stated.

"Heck yeah I am. And why are you looking at me like that?"

"Because for the first time, I don't only get to feel what you are feeling, I get to see it in your eyes too." He brushed his thumb against my cheek.

His sea-green eyes shone, enrapturing me. I shook my head and forced myself to focus. "Will, Nick did this to us. What if we don't have any real magic at all? What if he poisoned us and the effects will just vanish? What if it's just a magic trick?"

Will put his hands on my shoulders, our connection igniting like a heated blanket. His eyes kindled and he grinned.

"What?" I asked, feeling his excitement ripple over me.

"How do you feel about hitting the sledding hill today?"

"Are you serious? We just discovered evidence that Nick may be working with Mara and you want to go sledding?"

Will looked confused for a moment and then laughed. "No, sorry. I don't mean *actually* go sledding, but a stakeout. Let's track Nick's movements and formulate a plan to get in the grate. I bet Charlie and the other children are locked in there somewhere."

"But what if he can track us? He'd know where we were and what we were doing."

"That's a risk we'll have to take." The strong set to Will's jaw let me know he meant it. "I'm going to grab some gear and food for the both of us. Any requests?"

"Hot chocolate and marshmallows, please."

He leaned in and kissed my cheek, lingering for a few heartbeats. He pulled away and his eyes were that bright, happy green.

"Cool. I like that shade of purple," Will said, smiling as he considered my eyes. He stood and headed towards the door. "Be back in five minutes. Mind packing the books for me?"

"Of course!"

Will returned and we started our new mission together: get into Nick's grate and save Charlie.

It was day three in our hideout just beyond the tree line, about thirty yards away from the entrance to Nick's place. Will picked me up a little after nine, and we stayed nestled against large rocks beneath the canopy of sweeping pines through dinner. Nolan took care of keeping us fed and hydrated. Will had purchased hand and feet warmers that worked wonders. The trees created a great barrier against the wind and my family's sleeping bags kept us extra toasty.

"Ugh, is he ever going to come out?" Will growled. "It's already been over four hours today and he hasn't shown his face in days."

"Maybe we should knock," I said, only half joking.

Will gave me an incredulous look. "I hope you're kidding," he huffed, placing the binoculars back on the tree stump. Will lay on his back, placing his hands under his head. "Want to take a short nap with me? It'll be warmer if we share a sleeping bag." He closed his eyes.

"One of us should be the lookout, right?" I wanted to, but one of us had to keep our wits about us. He looked a little deflated, so I added, "Raincheck?"

"As you wish." It was quiet for a few moments when Will asked, "Liddy, will you sing for me?"

I choked on the frigid air and coughed, not prepared for such a request. "I...I don't sing for people."

"It's a good thing I'm not people then." He chuckled.

I chucked a marshmallow at his head. "The answer is no."

"Please." Will popped up on his elbow, his beautiful eyes boring into mine. "It'll help me pass the time, distract me from wanting to go marching into Nick's and blow everything. Plus, I haven't been sleeping well and it will help me fall asleep."

My face grew hot and I could no longer blame the cold for my cheeks' rosy glow.

"Liddy, you have a talent and I appreciate it immensely. Your gift is safe with me. Let it out, it wants to shine." He lay back down. When he got comfortable again, he closed his eyes and waited, like he was sure I'd oblige him.

Five minutes must have passed, but he didn't say another word. I crept over to him and listened to his deep, slow breaths and watched his chest rise and fall. I grabbed the binoculars and looked out towards the grate. Still no sign of Nick. I looked back down at Will. He looked so peaceful. His lashes were dusted with snow and his cheeks and lips red from the cold.

Convinced he slept, I moved a few feet away and sat with my back up against a tree. "As you wish." Closing my eyes, I opened my mouth. Fleeting mist formed on the notes I sang, a lilting song created on the spot just for him:

Will, sweet you
For you, I'll sing
Our love goes on
'til the end of time

You are here
So good to me
And who you are
is a light to me

I'll sing for you
My sweet so true
Nothing seems to matter
As much as you.

I opened my eyes and there was Will, wide awake and propped up on his elbow, with the widest grin I'd seen him wear to date.

"Will! You tricked me! I thought you were sleeping." I kicked his foot.

"Someone once told me, 'you know what they say about people who assume'." I chucked another marshmallow at his head, hitting him square on the forehead. Will chuckled. "I'm the luckiest guy in the whole world, no, in all the realms. I think I'm going to need you to sing me to sleep every night."

I cocked an eyebrow. "But you didn't fall asleep."

"That's because your voice is so remarkable."

"Stop. That is *never* happening again."

Will pouted his lip out. "I'll *never* stop asking."

I rolled my eyes, turning away from Will to check the grate.

The binoculars dug into my chest as I dove to the ground. "Ouch!" I whispered as loudly as I dared.

Will army crawled over to me in a flash, rolling me off the binoculars and I clutched my left breast.

"Is he there?"

"Yes," I groaned.

"Are you hurt?" he asked, staring at my hand.

"Yes, and it's nowhere your healing touch can fix."

Will's ears matched his cheeks. He grabbed the binoculars and peeked out. "Finally! As soon as he's out of sight, I'm going in," he murmured.

"Will, I think we should wait. We don't know when he'll be back. We haven't spent enough time tracking his movements to know when he definitely leaves and how long it takes for him to return."

"Christmas Eve is tomorrow. You read in the books that there will be a whole bunch of Watchers here. Nick's place seems like a spot they will congregate since his garden of Christmas roses is huge."

"Will. This is dangerous."

"We cannot delay any longer." His eyes flashed and darkened.

"Let's sit for a minute and at least plan a distress call or signal or something," I pleaded.

"No time. You promised me you would stay here. If I'm not back in one hour, you go back home without me."

"I'm not going to leave you there."

"Liddy…"

"No. We're partners. You make it back here in an hour or I'm going in after you." This time, I saw the reflection of my eyes flash in his. I continued, "Would you leave me?" He grunted in defeat and turned away from me.

Hidden from behind the tree, I watched as Will trudged across the snow to the grate, quickly disappearing into it. I paced back and forth, my stomach tightening each time I scanned the entrance for his return. *Shouldn't he be back by now?* I checked my watch. *It's only been five minutes!* The sun set over the horizon and my stomach growled. I scarfed down a sandwich. Grabbing hot cider from the thermos, I leaned against a large stump. After taking a sip, I laid my head down. To pass the time, I started singing again so I wouldn't fret over Will. It was like I was in my own recording studio, the sound absorbed from all around me by the trees and snow.

"Hey, Liddy! Where'd you learn to sing like that?" Pree popped her head over mine.

I screamed. "Holy heck, Pree! You scared me half to death!" Lowering my voice, I continued, "What are you doing here?" I sat up, frantically scanning the area to make sure I hadn't called attention to us.

"You have been M.I.A. all break so far and I've been curious to find out what's going on with you and Will. So, I followed you here."

I cocked my brow at Pree "OK, OK. I called your mom to ask where you were. What are you doing here all alone?"

"Nothing really. Just hanging out." I checked my watch. *This has got to be the longest fifteen minutes ever.*

"Ch-ya right. You're the worst liar ever. What are you really doing here?"

An icy chill blew in. Mara's voice was a breath of a whisper riding the wind as she called out to Will. My skin prickled, my body sending me an alert. Will was in trouble.

"Will needs me," I muttered more to myself than to Pree.

"What, Liddy? Speak up, chica."

Now that Pree's here, she can be the lookout! "Pree, I've got to go for a minute. Can you stay and be the lookout?" I asked as I started walking in Will's direction, not waiting for her response. I didn't want to alarm her, but my heart raced a mile a minute.

"The lookout? Ohhhh, this sounds fun! What am I looking out for?"

"Shhhh!" I walked a few steps back towards her. "Lower your voice and stay right there! Look for someone with silver hair. You'll hear chimes when he walks."

"Like Santa?" Pree asked, confused.

"Um, sort of. If Santa were younger and thinner."

"What signal do I give if I see him?"

"Just scream and run, but don't come after me!" I instructed her before I ran off.

I approached the grate, wrapped my fingers around the bars, and yanked. It wouldn't open. "Will!" I yelled into the dark tunnel. "Will, are you OK?" *Dang it!* I wish I had paid more attention to how he had gotten in.

Squealing laughter echoed within the cave. Even though Will didn't answer, I could sense his rapid heart rate. How did he open this darn grate? I saw the Christmas roses on the ground and bent low to ruffle through them, inhaling their warm scent, hoping something would happen. Ordinarily, I could sense only Will's location, but this time it was me who could feel he was in trouble and the situation grew more dire. I again tried to open the grate, but to no avail.

"Darn it! Why won't you open?" I yelled. As soon as I said it, the gate unlatched and swung open. *How did I do that?* I stepped through the entrance and was about to turn back to close it when Pree rammed into me, slamming the grate shut behind her.

"Pree, you're supposed to be the lookout!"

"I know, but you left me without a flashlight."

"The moon is pretty bright."

"Let me finish." She brushed her hair out of her eyes and added, "And I was bored."

"It wasn't even a minute."

"Do you want to find Will or not?" Pree walked ahead of me.

"How did you know I was looking for Will?"

"Let's see, the fact that you two haven't left each other's side since the incident and he was nowhere to be seen at your little camp out back there? Or when you were screaming his name through the bars just now?"

"Whatever, please stay behind me."

"William," the voice taunted again.

"Liddy, if that's you it's not funny," Pree squeaked from behind me, her voice hitched in her throat.

"You hear it?"

"Yeah!"

"That's not me, Pree."

It was too dark in the tunnel to move any faster. "Stop stepping on my heels," I hissed.

"Oops, sorry. I can't see."

It wasn't long before the dark, narrow tunnel broadened. With every step, the darkness faded allowing us to pick up speed until light poured into the tunnel. After a few minutes, we reached a large, dome-shaped room. *It's so majestic; like a log cabin and what I imagine the inside of a fairy or hobbit's home looks like mixed together, only bigger.* The ceiling spiraled with hardwood clad in between each piece of roundwood timber. At the narrowest part of the ceiling, it opened up again into a vast night sky that mimicked space; something you'd see at one of those shows at the planetarium.

"Umm, you didn't tell me we were meeting Bilbo Baggins," Pree belly laughed, distracted by her surroundings.

"Shhh, Pree." I continued to look around. There were short hallways and a kitchen off of this main room, all distinctive with their rounded entrances. *Which one is Will in?*

"Seriously, Liddy, where the heck are we?" Pree asked.

"Liddy, get out of here! Now!" I heard Will yell. He was close, yet I couldn't pinpoint where. Fear gripped me tight around the gut and my skin turned hot. More uncontrollable, sinister laughter erupted.

"She has him."

"Who has him?" Pree stammered.

"Mara."

Pree's face turned ashen. "Liddy, I think I'm going to go back outside and be the lookout."

"Oh no, you don't! You forced your way in and now you are going to help me find Will. We should split up."

"Haven't you ever seen a movie? It's never a good idea to split up. Someone always dies!"

"Pree, no one is dying on my watch and we are running out of time! I'll go right and you go left."

Pree scowled at me. "Fine! If I die it's your fault."

We both ran and on the count of three we opened our doors.

"No-no-nothing in he-here, but a-a-a bedroom and b-ba-athroom," Pree called and skidded back over to me, her teeth chattering faster than a woodpecker pecking a tree.

The door I opened appeared to be a workroom. Broken objects, gold trinkets, and dusty vases littered every surface and parts of the floor. Potted Christmas roses grew in black soil under lights at random intervals. The room, circular in shape with wood cladding over the entire ceiling and floor, had earthen walls almost fully covered by a strange map. The map displayed four different lands. Many red strings connected the pinned faces of what I assumed were missing children to the land of Beldam. Cristes, the place Will and I had read a little bit about, was cut off except for one string stopping at an X. I slammed the door closed.

"This one's an office," I said to Pree who tried to peek over my shoulder. "Looks like we are going into room three together."

"Or I can stay back here by the fireplace," Pree said.

"Put on your big girl panties and let's go!" My hand reached for the iron handle when I noticed green and amber colored lights shining from under the bottom of the door.

"Liddy, leave now! Plea—" Will's pleading voice faded with the light.

"Will!" I screamed as I burst through the door. The thick, hot air hit me first. An incandescent tree lit the otherwise dark space. I took a few steps toward it, surprised by the slight sinking feeling under my feet and the effort it took to move them. I glanced down. *Pink sand?* I looked back at the tree.

Unlike anything I'd seen before, its massive trunk was smooth like peanut butter, not rough like most tree bark. Bright colors of red, orange, and blue painted its length in sporadic intervals. The tree's thick roots curled and weaved around the base before plunging into the sandy earth below. A tight canopy of fat branches made it impossible to tell how far the room stretched. Instead of leaves, countless familiar white envelopes glowed from each branch. I trudged closer to the tree and stopped short. The envelopes weren't attached to the branches, rather they floated mere millimeters away.

"Lydiaaa," the woman's voice echoed and the light emanating from the envelopes transformed from warm white to vivid green. They quivered and all the envelopes repeated the greeting, "Lydia—Lydia" in the same voice. My hair stood on end and a boost of adrenaline pumped through my veins, like a hit of nitrous oxide urging me to flee. I wanted to run away, but not without Will. *Where is he?*

"Pree, do you see Will?" I yelled over the voices still chattering my name, but she was frozen stiff in the doorway, eyes so round they might fall out of their sockets at any moment. I ran over to her and shook her hard. "Pree! Will...do you see him?" Pree flinched from me. She lifted her arm and pointed to the bottom right of the tree. I squinted, following her aim.

The flickering glow that emanated from the envelopes like burning candles caressed Will's face, the rest of his body hidden within the shadows of the roots.

I moved closer. *Why didn't I feel him?* And then my heart sank when I took in Will's face, his eyes closed, his body lifeless.

Shrill laughter blared from the envelopes and I clutched my ears. "Here to save your little princey-poo?" the echoing voices all asked in unison. "It's too bad he refused to come with me."

I knew that voice. *Mara.* I wanted to scream, to make her pay, but I ignored her. "Pree, help me drag Will out of here," I yelled over the chorus of voices still cackling with laughter. We dashed over to Will, pink sand kicking up behind us. Pree grabbed his feet while I hooked my arms under his shoulders and lifted. Will was dead weight.

"Liddy, it's no use. I can barely hold his legs let alone carry him," Pree cried over the echoing laughter, tears gushing down her face.

I closed my eyes and tried to recall the tingling power that overtook me when Justin attacked; the energy that allowed me to push him off.

"He's mine, Princess," the voice teased. "Say goodbye." A faint rust colored glow crept through Will's veins and a sickly-sweet scent filled the room. Will slipped further away, our bond threatening to rupture.

"Mara, you witch! Stop it! Leave him alone!" I screamed, anger and desperation bouncing in my core. I almost died because of her, but the thought of losing Will felt like a wrecking ball battering my heart. The bubbling fury that brewed erupted. Faster than a bolt of lightning and stronger than Wonder Woman, I dragged Will out of the room by myself, Pree trailing behind. We escaped and Pree slammed her body into the door, knocking it shut. I pulled Will towards the center of the main room. I felt his forehead and cheeks. He was ice cold.

I moved him in front of the fire with the little energy I had left, collapsing to my knees next to him. "Will! Will! Can you hear me?" I searched his face for signs of life. My lifeguard training took over. Positioning my knees near his ribs, I leaned down and placed my cheek by his mouth and fingers on his neck. Both his breath and pulse were faint, steady, as if he were...sleeping.

Pree paced back and forth on the other side of Will, stammering to herself. Tears streamed down her cheeks. "I should have never come here. What was I thinking? Why did I have to come? Why do I have to be so curious? Who am I kidding? I'm not cut out for adventure. I like to be pampered and taken care of!"

"Pree, enough! You're not helping! Grab me that pillow. Now, go look for a phone to call nine-one-one."

"Oh yeah, and where the heck do you suppose I tell them to find us, huh? If there is even a phone in here, I doubt there is, but if there is, do I say 'Oh hey, our friend is unconscious. Why? He was poisoned by a colorful, glowing tree. Oh, where are we? We are in the fancy hobbit house of an invisible, mad woman deep inside one of the park's many sledding hills. Oh, oh! And don't forget your magic. You'll need it to open the grate when you get here.'"

Pree spoke a mile a minute, her voice rising. She was right. I was depleted and still needed to get Will outside. But Nick could be here any minute; we needed to get out now. *That's it!* "Nick!" I screamed aloud causing Pree to jump.

Pree whipped around. "Liddy, you're losing it! No one else is here."

"He's not, but something Nick told me *not* to do gives me an idea. But I think it could help save Will. "

Pree charged towards me. "No. I think we are way past telling me later," Pree snapped but then stopped dead in her tracks. "What's going on? What's with your eyes?" I started leaning towards Will. "They're like Will's," Pree screeched. "Lid, what...what are you going to do?"

"This!" I leaned down and pressed my lips to Will's. His lips, warm and soft, only parted ever so slightly under the weight of mine. I pulled away in time to see his beautiful green eyes open and blaze a striking aqua. He sat up, never taking his eyes off of me, like a tiger hunting its prey. He struck, his mouth connecting to mine with an urgency that sent flames dancing across my skin. He grabbed my hips and pulled me into him. I let go of inhibition and all of my caged desires flooded to the surface.

"Finally," Pree muttered. A few seconds later, she cleared her throat, clutching a nearby wingback chair. "Ahem!"

But we didn't stop, couldn't stop, like we tasted our first sip of water after being stranded in the desert for forty days. Our kiss deepened and an invisible, but palpable pulse burst through the room—a tidal wave of pent-up tension broke free from within us, exploding through the floors and disappearing behind the walls.

A piercing squeal of delight came from behind the tree-room's door, followed by wickedly excited laughter. Just as quickly as it assaulted our ears, it went silent.

I pulled myself away from Will, our chests heaving as we gasped for breath. We both turned our heads to face Pree who cowered at the sight of us.

"You...you guys..." She tried again. "You guys are freaking glowing! And whatever you just did, you made that horrible chick in there happy!" Pree pointed back and forth between the two of us and the tree room falling backward on her butt.

Nick's deep, gruff voice filled the room. "What have you done?"

Sixty Watts

"WHAT HAVE YOU DONE?" Nick repeated, his voice severe. He didn't shout and yet his voice filled the room.

"What was necessary," I said, rising to my fullest height despite the fear that gripped me. "Pree's mom knows we are here and she'll be coming to pick us up soon."

Will stood and grabbed my hand. Pree, wide-eyed and open-mouthed, sat motionless where she had fallen.

"Well, look at you being all bricky. No, sweetheart. What you've done is put a big, fat target on William's back. And yours."

"We're not afraid of you. And we're not leaving without my brother," Will growled.

"Ah, I see. You think I have Charlie. Congratulations...on

being several nuts short of a full pouch. I didn't take Charlie and I'm not here to hurt either of you. For goodness sake, you two have entirely missed the mark and now our worlds could suffer as a result of your negligence. You gave her—" he motioned to the room with the enchanted tree— "a direct link to your whereabouts. All she needs is one of you to end it all."

I erupted in laughter with an edge of bitterness. "Always so vague, Nick. Let's say her name. Mara." Nick's eyes widened. "Yes, I know her name. She already knew where to find us. And how did we put a target on our backs if there already was one?"

"There are a lot of us who have put everything on the line to protect you two, hide your magic, dull it. Something that gets harder to do as you age and come more fully into your powers. Watcher magic can be augmented when combined with others, which is what you did."

"Enough!" I screamed. An indigo flash of light erupted in the room leveling Pree back to the ground. Nick and Will teetered, but maintained their footing. "And what the heck is with the blasts of light?"

"I've said it before, Your Highness. You are a princess of—"

"And how am I a princess? We think we've found Will's connection, but nothing about me. And I've never heard of a princess that glows."

"If you would kindly take it down a notch and cease with the interruptions, I could finish. You are a Princess of Cristes Adventus, well to some of us anyway. Cristes is not of this realm."

"We've figured that out already. Tell us something we don't know." Will scoffed.

"William, you and Lydia are Watchers. All Watchers are

blessed with innate magic. Our eyes indicate our subspecialties."

"Just tell us where Charlie is," Will yelled.

Nick's face twitched. "You are both misguided. I am not the enemy."

"If we have misunderstood who you are, and I'm not sure that we have considering what you have hidden behind your doors in this place, then that's your fault. You—" I pointed my finger at Nick— "have given us nothing, but tiny pieces of a puzzle that don't fit together. You expect us to just know everything. Will and I were good friends before you took us away from each other. Now that we're together again, I won't let you harm him any further. You said you know where Charlie is, and we won't leave without him."

Nick chortled. "The absurdity."

"She's being serious," Will growled.

"I know, I know, but you're so far off the mark and your poor friend Pree is about to have a heart attack. You should see the look on her face." He barely got his last words out as his laugh morphed from a chuckle into a deep belly laugh, and he swayed on his feet. Will and I exchanged an uneasy glance.

"You about finished?" Will asked, anger rippling from him.

When Nick composed himself, he wiped the tears from his eyes and walked over to Pree offering her his hand. She refused it with a *hell-no* shake of her head. He knelt down and smiled at her. Placing his hand on her shoulder, he whispered something to her. She snapped out of whatever level of shock she was in and took his hand as he helped her up. He sat her down on the worn, leather lounge chair placing a blanket over her legs.

"I'm heading to the kitchen. Anyone else care for some hot tea or cocoa and some cookies?"

"Are you for real?" Will asked.

"As real as it gets," he winked, gesturing for us to have a seat on the red velvet couch. "Seems like we have a lot to talk about and I'm famished."

"He seems nice," Pree said, watching Nick retreat into the kitchen. "Liddy, you also didn't tell me that he's a silver fox." She waggled her eyebrows at me, seeming unfazed by our current situation when moments ago her world turned upside down.

"Pree, don't be fooled by him. He kidnaps children. He took my brother," Will whispered.

"Nah, I don't get that vibe from him," she said with conviction.

"I didn't either at first, but the evidence is hard to ignore," I responded.

"What evidence? That room over there with all those pictures of those kids? That looks to me more like he is trying to solve something. Geesh! Haven't you guys ever watched Columbo? Hello! Those red strings connecting the pictures are always used to try and pinpoint similarities and locations—to find a connection."

"Pree, I've researched some of those disappearances and Nick can be found in most of the pictures of the crime scenes. Plus, it's like he's been spying on Will and I our entire lives. He climbed out the window the night Will's brother disappeared."

"Liddy, I admit that does seem a little suspect, maybe even creepy. But it seems no different than, let's say, Santa who uses magic and watches kids day and night."

"We found a journal with Nick all cozy with Mara."

Pree's golden skin lost its luster again. She turned to us

and whispered, "I didn't tell you guys last week, but I heard her voice in the closet at Joey's after party. She's the evil one. Nick genuinely seems to care about your wellbeing."

"I like this girl," Nick chimed in. "You should have clued her in sooner, seems afternoonified."

"Afternoon-a-what?" I asked.

"She's clever. And she's right, you know. I don't take kids. One of my duties as an Eira Watcher is to protect and serve them; like I saved you both when you were little and like I am trying to do now. William, what do you remember from the night Charlie disappeared?"

"I remember lots of things. Like you being in the room right when he vanished and fleeing out the window. And then, I learned eight years later that it was you who had taken away my memories of that awful night as well as most of my memories of Liddy...until recently."

"When I was *fleeing* out the window, did you see Charlie with me?"

"Well, no, but—"

"Interesting. Lydia, what do you remember from that night?"

"I was making snow angels outside and I remember seeing you. You smiled at me, but then you suddenly told me to get inside and ran off towards Will's house right before the lights flashed. And Mara's laugh echoed down the street."

"So, William, as you can see, I was with Lydia when your brother was abducted. I couldn't be sure who Mara would try and grab first, either you or her. Since I couldn't be in two places at once, I convened with our underground network and orchestrated your family's move to Illinois. I secured them a job and their home on Cherrywood Drive, though that did take a dash of charm.

"Lydia, I was with you because we thought Mara would come after you first. I never anticipated that she would try for William first, even though I now know why." He trailed off as he stroked his beard.

"Care to elaborate?" Will snarked.

"Taking William meant killing two birds with one stone. Not only would she prevent your union," Nick said, pointing to both me and Will, "but she aimed to produce an heir with him and train him to kill Lydia himself. Her way of driving home her revenge."

Pree and I gasped while Will paled.

"We figured out she wanted me to secure the throne in Cristes, but why is she torturing Liddy?" Will gulped and wrapped his arm around me.

"As I tried to share, you and Lydia are descendants of a place called Cristes Adventus, my home. No doubt you've read some about it. William is in a more direct lineage to the crown. Cristes has waited for this union for at least a century. The possibility of a white-light manifestation has not been seen since Eira's first King and Queen. If you both possess what some in the royal family believes you do, then you and only you can restore the pathways, power, and order in the realms; together you would watch over and protect Cristes Adventus. Many of us were displaced after the Second Fall."

"The who and the what now?" Pree interjected.

"I told you all it was complicated. Anyways, when I felt Mara at your house, William, I ran knowing that you were the one in danger. Mara was waiting for me, of course. I tried to stop her, reason with her, give her another chance to choose light instead of darkness, but she wouldn't listen."

"OK, so, like is anyone else confused on who this Mara chick is?" Pree butted in yet again.

"For goodness sake! We haven't even talked about Mara yet?" Nick said as he hit his forehead with the heel of his hand.

"We know enough. She was the one who attacked Liddy after the Formal," Will announced.

"Wait, but that was Justin..." Pree trailed off. A few moments of silence passed as we watched realization dawn on her face. "Ohhh, so we weren't drugged with like any human stuff?"

"More like you were her puppet." Nick frowned. He bowed his head and in a low voice said, "I think you had all better be getting home. It's getting late and I don't want your parents to worry, especially now that more and more disappearances are occurring. It's only just beginning. I have some work to do."

"But we haven't even cracked the surface!" Pree whined. "You guys are going to have to tell me about that glowing thing you all do, because quite frankly it is disturbing as sh—"

"Pree, manners my dear." Her face reddened at Nick's playful warning. "You seem to have warmed up pretty quickly to all this information and, as you put it, *creepy* traits Watchers have, although some might describe it as extraordinary. Are you up to joining us in our mission to save our world and yours in the process?"

"I mean, do I have a choice?"

"Yes. I can wipe your memories for the most part and send you on your merry way. Or, you can join us in what will probably be the adventure of a lifetime, though it will be dangerous. You may act like a wooden spoon, but who you are is a woman with a great purpose and your friends will need you. What say you?"

"My mom isn't going to like this one bit. Yes, I will take a ride on whatever crazy train this is. I'm all aboard—choo, choo!" Pree tooted an imaginary horn.

"Great!" Nick bellowed, clapping Pree on the shoulder. "I'll make you guys a deal. How about you all come and visit me tomorrow around noon; lunch is on me."

"Tomorrow's Christmas Eve," I blurted out.

Nick cocked an eyebrow. "And?"

"And isn't that a busy time for Watchers in Mortalia?"

Nick smiled. "I'm glad to see you have at least been doing some reading. I'll keep it as brief as possible. Believe me, I wish all I had to do was harvest Christmas roses with my friends.

Since the Second Fall, there are not nearly as many roses in Mortalia and though I have conjured a way to deliver some to Cristes, it is never enough. What's more, Watcher power is at its peak during this time, but so is Mara's. It is all very irksome, collecting flowers and trying to pass through the dangerous realm barrier whilst thwarting Mara from abducting more children."

"I need to know, before we leave..." Will sputtered. "If she was after me, then why did she take Charlie?"

Nick sighed long and hard. "I don't think we should get into that tonight."

"I don't care what you think."

"William, please."

"No! This is my brother we're talking about."

"I said, calm down," Nick thundered, his eyes flashing silver; a warning to Will.

Will sat back down and put his head in his hands. Nick plopped next to him.

"She thought he was you."

"What, how?"

"You left the envelope in his bedroom that night. I am sure you have figured out by now that those white envelopes bound to the Arbolias tree are laced with dark magic. They are Mara's way of ensnaring her prey. Do not fret. I've enchanted the ones in the Arbolias room. As long as they remain in my possession, she cannot travel through them, though it does not stop her magic from meddling with anyone near."

"Well, she got to Will earlier. Maybe your magic isn't—"

"My magic is just fine, dearie. You did not have to get all dramatic and kiss him. She did not get to him. What he experienced was my little fail-safe I set up in case anyone touched one. It puts you into a deep sleep for a few hours."

I blushed. Will grabbed my hand and gave it a gentle squeeze.

"To answer your question, William, I believe Charlie thought you left the envelope for him, or maybe was only curious about it, but he must have opened it. The child who opens the envelope is the one she must take with her to Beldam; it acts like a portal. She is quite ethereal, with fair features and gentle eyes, portraying an innocence children are naturally not afraid of. She lures them into an embrace and then disappears back into the envelope with them. But that time...that time she knew I was near. And so, she waited for me to get there, to see what I would do." Nick stared out into the main room as if he imagined himself back on that fateful night. "I remember bursting into the room and Charlie hugging her, his back to me. She laughed with pure delight, proud of herself for scoring the one thing that would fulfill her plan. I realized at the last moment that she had Charlie, not you. I tried to stop her, to reason with her that this was all for naught. Her only response was antagonistic laughter. At the last second, I whipped around and dashed toward Charlie, but she vanished just as my fingertips brushed the hem of his shirt. I couldn't save him, but I was able to save you."

"So, it..." Will's voice caught in his throat.

"It was not your fault. I went to great lengths to keep that envelope from you and take away the painful memory. You couldn't have known what that envelope had waiting for you inside."

"So, how did that envelope get to Charlie's room?" Pree asked, quite interested in all of this.

"I found it outside and brought it to his room," Will said as he hung his head.

"Yeah, but like how did it get outside your house?"

"We don't know how she delivered them at first. Now we know she uses those she kidnaps to deliver them."

"Like puppets?" Pree interjected.

"Exactly," Nick replied as he stood up, gesturing for us to do the same. He walked us all the way to Will's car, bowed his head to Will and I, and disappeared into the shadows of the night.

Will drove to Pree's house first, who was uncharacteristically quiet on the ride home.

"Pree, are you alright? We've been sitting in your driveway for a few minutes and you haven't moved."

"What? Oh, I'm home. Um, can you guys pick me up on

your way to Nick's tomorrow?"

"Sure thing," Will responded. He waited until she was indoors before driving off. We pulled into my driveway next, but I wasn't quite ready to say goodnight.

"Can you turn off your headlights?" Will did as I asked. "Will—" my voice came out small— "You touched the envelope in that Arbolias room. What were you planning on doing with it?"

Will avoided my gaze.

"You were going to leave me again, just like that." I choked down the pain in my throat.

"No! Not exactly. I'm desperate to get Charlie back, you know that. I thought if I could get on the inside, I could grab Charlie and get us both out of there."

"Did you stop to think what would happen if you couldn't get out?"

"No, I didn't. But she wouldn't hurt me."

"Maybe not physically, but she would have found a way. Like having you kill me."

We searched each other's faces, but neither of us spoke for a long moment.

I broke the silence. "Don't do anything like that again. Promise me." Tears welled up in my eyes and Will ducked his head in shame. "Promise me you won't disappear on me again. I don't think I could take it. Next time, we'll figure out a plan *together*."

Will kissed my hand. "As you wish."

I sighed. "Good. It seems like we are about to enter a very surreal, challenging season of life. I can tell you one thing. I promise I will be right by your side the entire way through." I blushed. "Why are you staring at me?"

"Most people would have had a nervous breakdown after all you've seen and been through, but not you. Here you are facing everything head on, all the while promising to help me at every turn. You're amazing and I was hoping, no, I've wanted to...never mind. It's selfish in light of everything."

"What? You can tell me anything," I implored as I took off my seatbelt and turned to face him. His eyes cast down to his lap.

"Liddy...I..." I gave his hand a reassuring squeeze; he looked up at me, his eyes a vibrant green. "Liddy, I have imagined our first kiss thousands of times and had to fight my desire to act upon those thoughts *at least* twice as many times. I wanted to be the one to initiate it, but under very different circumstances, and in a much different setting." His face flushed, and gaze returned to his lap. After what seemed like an eternity, he finally looked up at me again; his eyes ignited, drawing me in. "Do you think we will face any bigger demons than we already have if I kissed you right now?"

I couldn't respond. My heart fluttered a mile a minute. Earlier, when we kissed, it was out of necessity. I thought he was dying. I could literally feel him slipping away from me. Right now, at this very moment in his Wagoneer, it was a completely different scenario. He was very much full of life. I could sense him; a whisper of a fluttering heartbeat next to mine, a warmth bathing my muscles and encouraging them to move closer. And I think he could feel all of that and more from me.

I inclined my head towards him. "As you wish."

He closed the gap between us, bracing himself on the center console. "I love you Lydia—" he kissed my cheek sending chills down my back— "Andra—" he kissed my other cheek— "Erickson." And then his lips melted into mine. His passion only made me wish I could absorb all of him as I resisted the urge to crush my body against his, and I only parted from him for brief moments when drawing a quick breath was necessary to survival; that is until every physical part of us ignited in an array of colors.

"I guess this means we've taken things a little too far?" I asked.

"Are you kidding? This is, well, this feels freakin' amazing! And it's just the beginning."

He leaned in again, but I placed my hand on his chest, giving him pause. I searched his face for any hint of hesitancy. When I found none, I pressed my lips to his for one more kiss. He obliged and I allowed the weight of his mouth to part mine, pulling away before we reached sixty watts again.

"Goodnight, Will."

"Sweet dreams, Princess."

And sweet dreams they were indeed.

Christmas Presents

NOTHING WOULD DELAY MY VISIT WITH NICK TODAY. So, I scurried about the house, helping Mom with Christmas dinner preparations. With Mariah Carey on full blast, I belted out every word of her Christmas album. Knowing Will would be picking me up around noon to take me to Nick's, singing helped release the frenzied excitement that neared explosion.

As I carefully placed the delicate crystal glass in the top right corner of the place setting, I almost dropped it. I pressed my hand over my chest as a gentle sensation nudged my heart, and smiled. Will was on his way. I checked my watch, 11:10. *I better hurry.*

I placed the candles in their red tin holders and dashed upstairs. I searched the back of the linen closet for Mom's fancy guest towels and pulled out the cream and silver set. I shook them out and refolded them into neat rectangles. As I hung some on the towel bar, a surge of heat bloomed from my chest and into my neck and cheeks. I checked my watch again, 11:20. Will was almost here.

I leapt into my room and slammed the door. As I opened my closet, the red sweater I first wore to Will's caught my attention. I snatched it and threw it on with my dark jeans. As I checked my makeup in the mirror, my nerves thrummed with anticipation. Will was here and I didn't need the knock at the door to tell me that.

"Liddy! It's your boyyyyyyfriend!" Mickey yelled out the front door then slammed it shut.

"Not funny, Mickey!" I hollered. "It's none of your business!"

"You make it my business when you make out in our driveway!"

I ran down the stairs and out the door as fast as I could. I knew Mom and Dad were too distracted in the basement searching for the missing bin of Christmas place settings to have heard him, but still, I wanted to question Mickey about what and how much he had seen.

Will sauntered towards the house. I stopped dead in my tracks, slipping on ice, and nearly bit it on the porch step. Like his first day at Wheeling high when I fell out of my chair at the sight of him, I took Will in from head to toe. The sharp-angled buckles on his sweater emphasized his strong jawline. I needed to kiss that perfect face, right *now*. I charged at him and threw my arms around his neck.

"Woah...you look...and....you're early," I said breathlessly.

"I take it you are happy to see me?" His smile grew. "Mickey saw, huh?"

"I hope he didn't see too much." I whispered. Will didn't seem bothered by the possibility.

"So, am I?" Will asked, working his bottom lip and running his hand through his hair.

"Are you what?" I looked up at him through my lashes.

"Your boyfriend?"

"I don't know, I don't remember being properly asked," I teased as I led him back into the house.

"That's funny. I could have sworn that was implied *weeks* ago and most recently last night."

"Well you know what they say about people who assume things."

Mickey came running around the hall corner singing, "Liddy and Will, sitting in a tree, K-I-S-S-I-N-G." He had his back to us, his hands running up and down the sides of his back as he kissed the air.

"Mickey! Get out of here."

He bolted up the stairs and slammed his door.

"Hey, you want to come with me outside? I've got a surprise for you," Will asked as he pulled out a blindfold. "May I?"

"Umm, sure. Let me check with Mom if she's OK with me leaving." I returned with a bounce in my step. "We're good to go."

Will helped me into my coat. He placed the blindfold over my eyes and guided me out of the house.

"This first present is from Uncle Shai and Nolan. They received permission from your parents. We've all felt terrible that you haven't been able to work since...well, you know. In addition, I have selfishly been taking every last minute of free time you have. Anyway, my family wanted to get you something for Christmas. Nolan has loved having you around and my uncle is grateful that I've had excellent company while he's been so busy. And Liddy, I am grateful because I came alive again when you reentered my life. We hope you like it."

He took the blindfold off, but I hadn't opened my eyes yet. I hated opening presents in front of people. What if I didn't like it? I was terrible at hiding my feelings. My face always gave me away.

"Liddy, I took the blindfold off. You can open your eyes now."

"OK, but can you not watch me open them? You're making me nervous."

"But, that's the best part!"

"Please?" I insisted.

"Fine. I'm turned around."

I opened my eyes one at a time. A two-door Oldsmobile Cutlass Supreme in mint condition sat parked in front of me. My chin practically touched the ground.

"Liddy? You're killing me. Say something...anything. It's frustrating that I can't even *sense* what you might be feeling." Will tossed his hands up in surrender. "I can't take this. I'm turning around."

I walked around the car, my hand gliding against the glossy, cherry-red paint.Grateful tears stung my cheeks. Will's hands were stuffed in his pockets as he approached me slowly.

"You can tell me if you don't like it you know, but if you don't, your parents' sort of gave us limits on what we could get you."

I had no words to describe how blessed I felt in that moment, so I decided to let my actions speak for me. I grabbed him around the neck and brought his lips to mine for a quick kiss.

"I'm glad you like it," he breathed when I pulled away.

"Like it? I love it! Wait right here. I'll be right back!"

I ran inside, found Mom and Dad in the kitchen, and bear-hugged them both with a resounding, "Thank you!"

"I take it Will's family gave you your gift?" Dad asked, grinning like a kid in a candy store.

"Yes! Thank you for allowing them to do that!"

"I don't know anyone more deserving. We could scarcely hold the secret in any longer," Mom exclaimed.

"Can I drive it?"

"We paid for your first six months of insurance, so you are all set!" Dad proclaimed.

"Best Christmas ever!" I gave them both another squeeze and kiss on the cheek then ran out the door.

Will tossed me the keys and we were off to Pree's. When we arrived, she bounded down her front steps. The contents of her overstuffed backpack threatened to rip through the stressed seams.

"I couldn't sleep last night. I was so psyched. I had to keep pinching myself to make sure I wasn't dreaming. This is seriously only something you see in the movies. How are you guys hanging with it all? I'd be straight wiggin' if parts of me glowed like you two and I found out I was royalty."

"Pree, take a breath." *Why wasn't I freaking out more? Am I in shock? Have I always known this was a part of me?* "Have you always seen it in me, Pree? This, uh, glowing?"

"No. I mean, you physically changed a lot this summer, but I chalked it up to a crazy late growth spurt. But the glowing? That only happened at Nick's last night, when ya know, and then when you and Will kissed, *that* was a whole notha' level. How about you Will? Does it freak you out?"

"It did at first. Now I'm not sure what I think about this. My biggest concern is learning to control this magic or whatever the heck *this* is. Hopefully, Nick can help with that."

We parked and trekked to the grate where Nick greeted us like old friends. Scents of frankincense and myrrh with hints of cinnamon filled the air, setting me at ease, and leading us down the tunnel to Nick's cozy sitting room.

"Merry Christmas Eve," he said jovially to each of us as he crossed his arms, left over right, at his heart and bowed. We returned the gesture, uncertain as to what it meant. "I don't have as much time as I thought, but I still welcome the company. It's been a pretty lonely nine years. So, before we commence with the festivities I have planned, does anyone have any questions for me regarding what we know so far from yesterday?"

Pree wasted no time. She grabbed a notebook and gel pen from her bag. "OK, so first, I want to know how these envelopes get to their destination."

"I'm not familiar with the magic she uses to enchant the envelopes. But I do know, it's something dark. As I shared yesterday, humans aged approximately sixteen and older in this world that do her bidding. Some are Watcher descendants, but many are not.

I have been trying to deduce whether or not Mara enchanted these mailmen to do her bidding or if they do so willingly. So far, their delivery methods vary and are considerably inconsistent. No opportunity has presented itself to interrupt a delivery in progress. Many times victims find the envelope in their mailbox while others are strategically placed in areas the targeted child visits. I assume Mara's enchantments would do the rest.

"What about coming to your door to deliver it, wearing a certified postal uniform?" I asked.

Nick cocked an eyebrow in my direction. "I haven't seen that one yet," Nick responded. "Why do you ask?"

"Someone tried to deliver one of those envelopes to me the other day. He seemed...familiar."

"Interesting," Pree and Nick said at the same time. Nick raised his brow and smiled at Pree.

"Lydia, are you saying that someone tried to deliver an envelope to you—in broad daylight? Particulars, please," Nick said as he leaned back in his chair, folding his hands, his body tense. Pree was at the ready to take detailed notes.

"Yeah, sure, um... I was home alone after getting back from the hospital. I had drawn a bath when I heard a knock at the door. Answering it was out of the question because I was in my robe. Instead, I crept to the edge of the stairwell and peeked around the corner.

"He appeared to be around my age, but he lacked a youthful presence. Instead, he looked drained; the only pigmentation to his ashen complexion were rust-colored veins that feathered his hands and face. I couldn't tell if the purple and blue shadows under his eyes were from bruising or exhaustion. His dimly lit eyes glowed like Mara's, but weaker, fading from subtle green to a muddy orange. He looked so familiar. I wanted to open the door, but my body refused to move, like it remembered something I didn't. My memory tugged and pulled at me, urging me to remember. I *needed* to remember. Something was off about him, and this left me unsettled."

"Hmmm...she's more powerful than I thought." He muttered to himself, "What is she using as her power source there? What could give someone that much strength?" He returned his gaze to us. "I knew bringing you both back together would motivate her, but I never imagined she would be this far along. Now that you two have disobeyed orders and kissed, more than once may I add, things are looking more..." He trailed off tilting his chin up and looking into the distance as if in thought for a moment before continuing. "We are going to have to speed things along between you both much more quickly than I anticipated. Unless—" Nick sprang up from the couch.

"Unless what?" Pree asked.

"Unless I can figure out a way to get more help here. I may be able to convince more Watchers to try the channel if I can prove to them that Lydia is the princess we've been waiting for. They may trust me enough to help restore Cristes and go against Mara."

"What do you mean *speed things along* with these two lovebirds?" Pree asked, gesturing to Will and I.

"Certain things would need to occur in a ritual ceremony with William and Lydia to support them in unleashing their full powers. Ideally, they would be at least eighteen, but—never mind." Nick stalled and paced in front of the fireplace. "If I can find the missing pieces to the Rose Dome, which is a device Watchers use to travel between realms—" He pointed to what looked like a partially assembled snowglobe on the mantel—

"We won't have to bother these two with that pesky little ceremony," he said, wearing a mischievous grin.

I walked over to the fireplace. The large, clear marble displayed the cracks from where Nick pieced it back together. It was still missing a few chunks.

"We have some time, not much, but some before we need to concern ourselves with Mara returning. It is Christmas, after all. Let us enjoy it," Nick encouraged.

"Wait, I thought we were going to—"

"In time, dear Pree. In time." Nick smiled and patted her hand. "I brought you all here to let you know that I will be unavailable starting this evening. I don't know when I will be back, but rest assured I would not leave you in the dark again if it were not for a very critical undertaking."

"Where are you going?" I asked, unnerved by the sudden twist of my gut.

"I've received some intel from our underground network regarding some homes that may be a target of Mara's tonight. I will also attempt to deliver Christmas roses to Cristes, but it's a very dangerous journey since the Rose Dome was shattered in the Second Fall."

Nick sat beside me and placed his hand on top of mine. "Not to worry, Princess. I've figured out an easier way. I've done it before and I am still here." He pinched my cheek. "I will contact you all when I have returned, and we will commence with plans to save the world which will begin with your Watcher training." He winked. "You two will need to learn how to conceal and better wield your newly switched-on abilities. William and Lydia, be mindful with your displays of emotion. You don't want to light up the entire neighborhood. The less people know

THE WITCH IN THE ENVELOPE

about your giftings, the better. The average human can't see them as well as we do, but occasionally a certain type of person may take notice. So be careful. If you thought kissing was a little surreal, wait until you consummate—"

"Nick!" I screeched.

His contagious, deep belly laugh filled the home, melting my embarrassment.

"OK, OK!" He held his hands up in mock surrender. "You know what I am getting at. You have already made it increasingly difficult for us to keep you both safe and, furthermore your kiss has endangered our worlds by strengthening your powers. I do not blame you, though. A Watcher pairing is quite difficult to resist. Make absolutely certain nothing else happens beyond that."

"It's just kissing. What's the big deal? Geesh." Pree rolled her eyes.

"My dear, just kissing? I thought you were a little more afternoonified on the subject. I will have you know that where I come from, kissing is the first step in initiating a very powerful, practically unbreakable covenant. It also has the potential to unleash dormant abilities; something these two are starting to figure out. It is anything but just a kiss."

"Geesh, Liddy. I guess your prudishness did have a purpose," Pree acknowledged.

"Uh, thanks?"

"So, when can we start training and learning about these Falls? How about making a plan to defeat Mara? Rescuing Charlie?" Will asked.

"As soon as I get back within the next two weeks. In the meantime, you have books. They can help you research The

Falls."

"Nick, we saw a picture of you with Mara."

Nick's eyes turned dark, almost black. "Where did you find it?" he asked, his voice gravelly.

"Your white journal was hidden in one of the book's back covers. We didn't read it, promise."

"She and I used to be friends, best friends..." Nick's voice caught and trailed off.

"Would you like it back?" I asked. His shoulders sunk, bowing under an invisible weight.

"Not now. Keep it. If I don't return, you and William have my permission to read it." There was an awkward silence before Nick plastered a grin on his face. "Well, as I was saying before, it is Christmas Eve, one of the most special times of the year. Let's try to enjoy each other's company while we have this time together. Fancy a tour of my workshop?"

"Does a bear poop in the woods?" Pree blurted out.

We followed Nick to his office. Gifts of gold, oils and other trinkets were in neat piles near deep red colored sacks. "These are the gifts we plan to leave in exchange for the Christmas roses we harvest tonight," Nick informed us.

"Hmmm, this one smells heavenly," I said, noting the hints of orange and evergreen.

Nick looked at his leather cuff. "I must depart in an hour. You are all welcome to come and visit during my absence, as long as you promise to heed my warning and stay out of the tree room—Arbolias Sang. Care to join me in the sitting room for a treat?"

I sat next to Will on the plush sofa, Pree sat across from us in a tufted chair. Nick rolled in a gold serving cart. He lifted the silver plated kettle and filled our cups to the brim with creamy hot chocolate then cleared a space on the coffee table for the most elaborate display of Christmas cookies. We sipped our drinks and ate tons of cookies, some of the most delicious treats I'd ever had.

"So, Nick. What about your family?" Will asked.

"I am an only child. The King and Queen from the paintings in the books I gave you are my grandparents."

"Wait, don't you mean your great, great grandparents?" I asked.

Nick chuckled. "Nope. Watchers live a very long time. I am one hundred and twenty."

Pree spurted hot chocolate from her mouth in a perfect arc onto the table.

"I think that will do it for today." Nick laughed.

The time came for us to leave. Pree was particularly disgruntled as she'd hoped for more information and a chance to get some answers to her mountainous list of questions.

"Cheer up, Pree. We can't solve it all in one night. Believe me, I've tried. Something tells me that you are going to be an integral part of our entire operation. Help these two stay on track, will ya? Remember what we talked about."

"Yes, sir," Pree said, giving Nick an awkward salute.

"And Lydia, William, stay safe, be diligent, and whatever you do, don't let anyone know who you really are; *no one*. Keep yourselves in check, and all of you watch out for Mara's envelopes and whoever might be delivering it. If you come across any, bring it here to release into Arbolias Sang by sliding it under the door. The tree will know what to do with it."

"Are you sure we can't come with you?" I asked him as he

walked us to the gated entrance.

"Not yet.' Nick again crossed his arms over his heart and bowed. "Have a Merry Christmas."

We attempted to repeat the gesture and wished him a Merry Christmas as well. Nick smiled in approval and headed back inside as we walked back to my car.

I pulled into my driveway after dropping Pree off at her house, and turned the car off.

"I still can't believe this car is mine. I mean, I don't even have the words to express my gratitude. It was such a grand gesture and what I got you doesn't even compare."

"The car was not my gift to you, it was my family's. Besides, you can't compare gifts. They are a blessing, not a ruler meant to measure someone's love. Your gift to me is you and that is the greatest gift you could ever give me," he said as he kissed my hand.

"I forgot to tell you. My mom also invited Nolan and Uncle Shai to Christmas Eve dinner tonight."

"I'll ask Nolan, but my uncle has already left for business. Do you mind stopping by tomorrow? Nolan's preparing a special brunch for us."

"It sounds perfect. I can't wait to thank him in person for my gift."

Will came around and opened my door for me, entwining his fingers with mine. I reached to open the front door, but Will tugged on my hand, pulling me back towards him. "What's up?"

"Liddy, I've never asked you properly." He got down on one knee. "I have one more gift for you." I yanked my hand away from him and backed into the far corner of the front porch.

"Will, I'm only seventeen. I...I'm not..."

Will chuckled. "I accidentally dropped the box." He stood and walked over to me. "Liddy, when I ask for your hand in marriage, you will know." Will opened the navy blue box. "In the meantime, do you think you can wear this ring as a symbol of a promise to be my best friend forever and guardian of my heart?"

I took a step out of the corner. *It's gorgeous!* A hex-shaped opal stone lay centered on a white gold band. I took the ring from its velvet box. Small, brilliant diamonds surrounded the opal. The band twisted into an infinity knot on each side of the opal.

"Yes." I slid it on the ring finger of my right hand and countered with, "As long as you wear what I got you and promise the same." Before he could kiss me, I grabbed his hand and rushed up the stairs, tugging him along.

"Now, I know it is nothing compared to a car and this ring, but I hope you like it."

"Do I get to ask you to close your eyes when I open it?" he asked.

"Yes, that's only fair." I turned and closed my eyes.

I preferred it this way. I wasn't sure if he'd like what I'd made him. I had started a scrapbook for him from a box of pictures I'd found in the attic after Winter Formal. In honor of our childhood, I titled the album: "L&W's CLUB KEEP OUT." On the first page was my very favorite picture of Will and me as kids; I can't remember who took the aerial view photograph of us making snow angels. Each page contained carefully selected pictures captioned with what I loved best about him in that moment. I'd hand drawn or pasted images from magazines of moments I'd imagined we'd have shared had he not been erased from my life. I'd included all the journal entries I'd written about him during those two weeks.

Will came up behind me wrapping one arm around my waist. With his other arm he reached over my shoulder, then held out and read aloud the note I'd tacked in the first blank page of many.

"My best friend. My Prince Phillip. My soulmate. I can't wait to see what the rest of our adventures together hold. I love you, William Lucas Jamison."

He led me to the bed and sat me on his lap and grabbed the small satchel that contained his last gift—a small, brown leather cuff I purchased to complement the one he always wore. The cuff contained three personalized charms fastened to the cuff. On a handwritten tag I explained their meaning.

The Compass: So we always find our way back to each other.
The Christmas rose: So we always remember its magic
The C: For Charlie who will be with us again soon.

He'd been quiet for quite a while and I hesitated. When I'd finally looked at him, he already wore the cuff. His eyes misted over as he studied the scrapbook. Tiny explosions of joy, his joy, sang through me. And, a sudden hollowness in my chest, one that wasn't mine, sunk in. I wanted to comfort him, help him to look back on this night with pure delight. I tiptoed to my door, using my foot to maneuver my accent rug in front of the bottom before locking it, and walked up to Will.

"I wish there was more I could have put in it," I murmured. He stood and placed his warm, smooth hand on my cheek.

"The good news is, we have the rest of our lives to remedy that." He smiled as he closed my blinds. "Starting now."

And then we kissed; a kiss that would make any Christmas tree pale in comparison to the light we created as it fractured and bounced off the mirrors in my bedroom. A kiss that we would surely record in our scrapbook, a kiss for the ages. Soon a dark force would need to be reckoned with, but for tonight, in this moment, I embraced the light.

A BROKEN HEART,
FUSED BACK TOGETHER IN SCORN,
CANNOT BE BROKEN AGAIN.

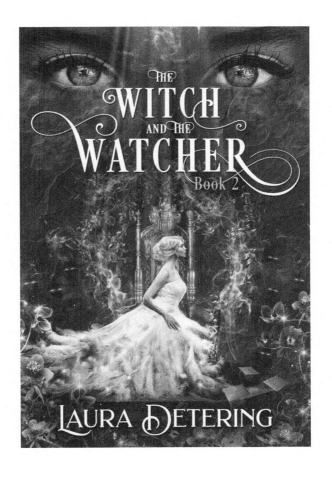

Acknowledgments

It truly does take a village and I have one of the best ones ever!

For the Waymaker, Miracle worker, Promise keeper, Light in the Darkness - the road has been long and trying, but GOD! Thank you for this gift. Thank you for your ultimate sacrifice of love. I have learned so much from you, but I will never forget to always choose love.

To my girls, Maya and Zoey - Thank you for sharing me with my characters. I hope I have taught you that it's okay to be a mom who loves her kids so much it hurts, but that it's also okay and necessary to pursue your passions. We are better moms when our cups are filled. I love you times infinity.

To my family both in blood and in Christ - This wouldn't have been a reality without you! Your support, tough love, and enthusiasm are things I will treasure forever. These were some of the hardest years for me and I thank you for sticking around, hearing, and believing me. Those with chronic illness often feel alone and hopeless and you all never let me stay in that place.

To all of my CPs and Beta readers - Andrea, Andy, Eric, Jared, Luke, Megan, Nicole, and Sarah- who read this *multiple times*. Your lovingly honest input and critiques helped to make this story shine brighter than Will and Liddy. Your occasional fangirling moments, enthusiasm, and encouragement when I wanted to quit kept me going!

To Ines, Julia, and Kim - friends I've met via the writing and chronic illness communities on Instagram- Thank you for being a wealth of knowledge and for your generosity in sharing it! You've been some of my best cheerleaders who have been amazing at helping me. I cannot wait to meet you in person someday and give you the biggest hug!

To Shawneen - Thank you to my friend turned editor! *SQUIRREL* Thank you for giving this little story a chance to contend with the big dogs. Holly-freakin-leujah we did it! You are truly a wonderful person. Your generosity is such a humbling gift. *SQUIRREL* Thank you so very much for sharing your spoons with me. I can't wait to work with you again and again and help you achieve your book dreams.

YOU... yes YOU. Thank you for reading The Witch in the Envelope. I know that there are thousands of books you could have chosen to read so the fact that you chose Liddy's story means so very much to me. Thank you in advance for leaving your review and recommending my book to others. I'd love to connect with you on lauradetering.com

Thank you to these generous souls for their donations without which I may not have been able to publish *The Witch in the Envelope*. You helped to make my dream come true.

Nick Deignan

Sara Jensen

Kim Chance

Toro Family

Cynthia & Evan
Hand

Susan Knodle

Ken Seybold

Ginger Steele

Maureen Gannon

Ines Kembel

Karen Belmonte

Jennifer Kaplan

Linsie Gilman

The Hyatt Family

Juan and Mago
Alvarez

About the Author

I grew up in Wheeling, IL. but now reside in sunny Florida. The change in weather took some getting used to, but my town has become my little paradise. My love of storytelling began at an early age when I would walk my little brother to the library. Getting immersed in a good book that can inspire, offer hope, help the reader get lost in a new world, and expand  the imagination is what I cherish most in stories. I mean, who couldn't use a little escape from 2020? I hope my novels can offer you the happy escape and adventure you desire.

I graduated from the University of Illinois at Urbana-Champaign with degrees in history and secondary education. I've always loved learning about people and the process around the choices they make.

A former high school teacher and echocardiographer, I have always been driven, but one of my many passions is the arts, especially singing and dancing.

In December 2017, I was struck with an invisible illness. MDDS and chronic vestibular migraines have left me disabled. At times I've wanted to give up. However, my faith, coupled with the extraordinary people God has placed in my life, has given me the strength to keep going—to be a lamp for others who may find themselves alone in the dark.

I am happily married and enjoy staying at home with my two daughters while pursuing my passions and investing quality time with my family and friends.

Visit me on the Web: lauradetering.com